PUSHKIN

VERTIGO

ORIGINALS

PUSHKIN VERTIGO

MARTIN HOLMÉN

CLINCH

A HARRY KVIST THRILLER

Pushkin Vertigo
71–75 Shelton Street
London, WC2H 9JQ

First published as *Clinch* by Albert
Bonniers Förlag, Stockholm, Sweden

Published in the English language by arrangement
with Bonnier Rights, Stockholm, Sweden
First published in English by Echo Publishing in 2015
First published by Pushkin Vertigo in 2016

1 3 5 7 9 8 6 4 2

ISBN 978 1 782271 92 5

Cover image © Todd Keith/Getty Images

Text designed and typeset by Tetragon, London
Printed and bound by CPI Group
(UK) Ltd, Croydon CR0 4YY

www.pushkinpress.com

For my daughter

PART ONE

PART ONE

There is nothing here but hatred.

When I check my pocket watch, it's already gone twenty past seven. I'm standing in the rain outside Zetterberg's house, where the city's most fashionable street confronts the back lanes. Here, in the blocks around St Clara's church, the moneychangers, petty thieves, pimps and whores rule the night. Swindlers lie in wait among the hostels, betting shops and drinking dens for country folk arriving at Central Station, water-combed and in their Sunday best. Within an hour or two they've been plucked clean as dead geese.

The rain doesn't freshen up the air, a stew of latrines, petrol and coal. Where streetlight falls on water, the tram tracks gleam like long knives in the middle of Kungsgatan. A few degrees colder and it would be snowing instead. Hoar frost has lain heavy on the telephone wires for some weeks already. I'm wearing my summer shoes with perforated uppers. My feet are already wet.

'You can always tell a poor man by his shoes,' I hear myself muttering, my voice hoarse from cigars and tots of schnapps in my afternoon coffee. Gently I stamp my feet on the paving stones to get some life into my toes. If Zetterberg is at home and my evening assignment goes to plan, I'll buy myself a pair of proper winter boots. No hobnail boots of box calf leather or any other crap from the shoe co-op. I'll have nothing less than first-class kid.

The caretaker has not yet locked the front entrance of Zetterberg's building. Inside, the foyer has a clean-scrubbed white marble floor. A red carpet flows down the stairs like a nosebleed. I get out the letter from the inside pocket of my overcoat and angle it to catch some of the light in the street. My job this evening is about a default on a payment for a second-hand motor. This Zetterberg fellow has swindled a certain Elofsson in Ovanåker out of the full payment for his old Opel. If I can collect the outstanding two thousand one hundred kronor and send off the money within five days, I get to keep fifteen per cent. My advertisement in *Landsbygdens Folk* has paid for itself again. More often than not, the jobs that come in from the country are about some runaway farmer's daughter or other. Usually I sniff the girls out in one of the cheap hotels, renting rooms by the hour in Norra Smedjegatan or a brothel in Old Town, and then I put them on a train back home. Other forms of debt settlement are almost as common. From time to time a person wants someone beaten up, and I have no qualms about that if the payment is right. A country girl is worth more than a bicycle, but less than a car or a thrashing.

I check the nameplate in the gloom. Zetterberg is at the top. I go back out and peer up at the grey-painted façade. Unless I'm mistaken, the bird has flown. Either that, or the damned bird is sleeping.

I go back in again. The elevator grille rattles forlornly. Someone has crushed a cigarette against the sixth-floor button.

The red carpet doesn't go all the way up. I take off my fat, boldly patterned tie and carefully fold it, then put it in my overcoat pocket. Zetterberg has a double-fronted door. I bang one side of it until the frosted glass rattles. No answer. After inspecting the lock I know it wouldn't present me with much of a problem, but if I'm waiting inside when Zetterberg comes back he'll have a natural escape route. I thump the door again, this time much harder.

There's a squeal of hinges behind me, then a whiff of root mash and pork sausages. I turn round. A small, thin bloke is examining me through a monocle. A few beads of sweat gleam below his receding hairline. He clears his throat.

'May I help you?' His voice is even whinier than the door.

'I have a delivery for this Zetterberg here. I don't suppose you know when he's coming home, do you?'

'Not so easy to say. Sometimes he's late. Some evenings he doesn't come at all. Usually you hear him.'

The little man taps his ear, as if to indicate that his hearing is still in good order. I stifle a groan. More than likely I'm looking at another late night in the rain.

'Is he noisy?'

'I never suggested that!'

'But it's not unheard of?'

'Sometimes he has company. There's a bit of running round. And I hear his gramophone.'

'Maybe I can get hold of him where he works?'

'He's a driver.'

'A cab driver?'

'I never saw him in a uniform.'

The man scrutinises me and opens the door a little wider. He's obviously the well-intentioned sort, eager for company. Concerned that he might offer to let me wait in his flat, I cut the conversation short. On the way down in the elevator I put my tie back on.

The portico opposite Zetterberg's building is a perfect vantage point. Finely dressed people under the cover of umbrellas are beginning to assemble on the other side of Vasagatan outside the Oscar theatre and the Palladium cinema for the early evening shows. Some of the men hold their top hats in place with a hand on the brim. A slim blonde in a full-length fur scolds an errand boy. Maybe he made a hash of it when he queued for her tickets.

A drain at the junction is blocked. Horse manure is dissolving in the puddle, and gusts of wind disperse the sweetish smell of shit between the buildings. Somewhere, a weathervane or shop sign is creaking. The streetlight outside Zetterberg's place is out of order, and the merchants on Kungsgatan haven't managed to get their Christmas lights up as yet. The vertical neon sign running up the façade of the Carlton Hotel in the near distance only partly makes up for the gloom.

I get out a six-öre Meteor from my pocket and bite off the end. I shake my box of matches. They used to hold fifty matchsticks, but the number has been considerably reduced in the last few years. Shares once held by Kreuger, the Match King, are being flogged in bulk in the classifieds. I open the matchbox.

'Not enough phosphorus for an abortion, but it'll do for Kvisten,' I mutter and puff some life into the cigar.

Opposite the Vetekatten café, a short distance into Klara, a stray dog howls as a man in a fur-trimmed overcoat and spats gives it a going over with his walking stick. The cur is a long-haired, brown-spotted sort, with legs that seem too short for its body. The man's got it hemmed in against the wall.

'Sit, you devil! Sit, I said!'

The man lashes out again, bringing the stick down over its back. The despairing yells of the dog bounce between the walls.

'Hey, you fucker!' I roar through the rain and take a few steps onto Kungsgatan.

The decorous gentlemen stops for a moment, his walking stick held over his head, and gives me a good stare. The mutt slips off across the junction with its tail between its legs and avoids by a hair's breadth being run over by an old A-model Ford. The man with the stick hurries off along Klara Norra.

I go back to my doorway. There's really no reason to beat a dog half to death like that. It's this damned autumn. The cold and the dark get under people's skin, cause them inner damage.

With my Meteor in my mouth, I do a bit of half-hearted shadowboxing to work up some body heat. I should have put on an extra jumper; I should have brought a crossword. I wonder what sort of bloke Zetterberg is, if he'll put up any resistance.

A black two-seater Mercedes-Benz, a sports model, glides past slowly, almost soundlessly, with the hood down. The wet street reflects the headlights, enveloping the black car in a glowing cocoon. The youth at the wheel is only just old enough to have a driving licence. Our eyes meet and he gives me a smile of recognition, as if we're involved in some sort of conspiracy.

I stop my ineffectual efforts to keep warm and keep my eyes on the car for a long time. The engine growls as it turns and disappears towards Norra Bantorget. I don't notice the woman slinking into the doorway behind me until she speaks in a ringing Dalecarlian accent.

'Lovely Lucia weather we're having!'

There's a heavy smell of perfume and Madeira about her. I turn around. She's probably not even twenty. Drops of water are clinging to her woolly, bell-shaped hat, like the transparent seedcase of a thistle. The grainy, dark liner around her slanted brown eyes is close to dissolving. Her coat of black serge has been worn to shining here and there. Beneath, one senses, is a more or less full-figured woman with a well-developed bust. Exactly my type. I'm not interested. Women have always thrown themselves at me, a scarred old boxer. Somehow I think they can sense who I am, and the woman who can resist a challenge hasn't yet been born.

She smiles and goes on: 'What are you doing out in the rain?'

'Waiting for a friend.'

A loud group of boys, gang types, cross Kungsgatan. Their high-pitched voices are already coarsened by tobacco and loud curses. A couple of them slow their steps when they catch sight of me. I flick my cigar butt towards them and stick out my chest.

'Bloody nob!' One of the smaller boys among them has drummed up some courage. An uneven oat-blond fringe sticks out from beneath his cap. He's wearing shorts and long woollen socks. One of his boot soles is secured with a dirty shoelace.

When I leave Sibirien, it's not unknown for some cheeky brat like this to call me names. Full-grown men don't dare, nor do women. They get out of my way. They respect me as one respects a dog that bites. In my home haunts on Roslagsgatan it's a different kettle of fish, of course. Lots of people say hello, some even smile. Last month I was invited to the street harvest party in number 41. I didn't have time to go.

''Cos Harry Kvist was a hell of a bloke,' sings one of the other boys, who's obviously recognised me. Involuntarily I clench my fist, and the vein on my forehead starts throbbing against my hat.

Yelling curses and empty threats, the boys are jostled away by their friends towards easier pickings in the adjoining lanes. Spoilt kids. At their age, I was lugging hundred-kilo sacks of salt or sugar in unknown harbours, or shovelling tonnes of coal through the night shift. I light a fresh Meteor.

'What are you up to, then, you and your friend?' The girl, again. 'I suppose you're off to some do for Lucia?'

'No.'

An elderly man with a grey goatee and a bowler hat, clutching onto both an umbrella and a walking stick, stops outside the entrance to Zetterberg's building. He opens the door and goes inside. Could that be him?

'My name's Sonja,' says the girl and holds out her hand. Her nails are dirty.

'Kvist.' Hastily I shake her hand.

An Ardennes mare with a cart of empty beer crates passes by, its iron-clad, shaggy hooves clattering against the paving stones. Its body heat radiates like mist. The driver sits stiff as a statue, a dying cigarette in his mouth and the reins in one hand. His other hand is tucked into his coat, like Napoleon.

The light in Zetterberg's apartment doesn't come on. The rainwater splashes in the gutter ahead of us. Sonja is wearing snakeskin heels, about as practical in this weather as my perforated uppers. I take a deep drag and blow out a plume of smoke from the corner of my mouth.

'I work as a dishwasher in a café on Drottninggatan. Or, actually, on Teknologgatan, you could say.'

'Looks like it's stopping,' I say, holding out my hand from the doorway.

'And I rent a room at Pension Comforte, it's not far from here. At first I was sharing with a girlfriend but now I have it all to myself.'

I nod without interest. Sonja rummages in her handbag and finds a butt she's saved, a filter-tip Bridge. While she's rooting about she starts talking about some blockhead who's stolen from her and tricked her. I'm not listening. On the other side of the street, a figure walks with agile steps towards the door of Zetterberg's building. This bloke is early middle-aged, wearing an elegant three-piece suit, an overcoat with broad lapels and a Borsalino. He's an athletic type but a few classes lighter than me: welter, or possibly middleweight. During the summer months I can usually guess a man's weight to the exact kilo, but in autumn and winter it's more difficult. The man goes inside and, before long, the top-floor light comes on.

Zetterberg has come home.

'Match?'

I'm startled. 'Excuse me?'

'I was asking for a match.'

I nod and give her my matchbox while keeping my eyes on Zetterberg's place. Something about this whole job feels out of kilter, but I shake off the feeling. The stump of my cigar takes off in the gutter like a bark boat. I loosen up my neck with a few side movements, and unbutton both my overcoat and jacket to create more freedom of movement.

Without saying goodbye to Sonja, I adjust my leather gloves and cross the street. The joyrider in the black sports car glides past again. A sopping-wet man driving an open jig reins in his horse and calls out to me in the rain. I ignore him. I'm looking forward to my little meeting with Zetterberg. If I'm lucky he may even put up a bit of resistance.

I could do with that.

The elevator is on its way down. As I'd prefer not to run into anyone, I take the stairs. By the time I've huffed and puffed my way up to the fourth floor, my cough has caught up with me. It tugs and rips at the inside of my chest. I lean forwards, my hands on my knees, and spit a viscous ball of phlegm at the red carpet. I stay there until my breathing has calmed itself. I remove and

16

fold my tie again, tucking it into my overcoat pocket, and resume my climb to Zetterberg's flat.

This time I use the doorbell.

I hear footsteps. The frosted glass in the door rattles when the lock jams before the door opens. The man standing there has one brown eye and one green. His hair is slicked back, compressed by the Borsalino, which is now sitting on the hat shelf to his right. Judging by his scent, he uses the same pomade as me, Fandango – 'The hair that stays put all day'. His braces are trailing below his thighs and his shirt's unbuttoned. He smiles. The first upper molar on the right has been replaced with gold.

'Yes?'

I peer over his shoulder. An elongated, dimly lit hall leads into the apartment. There doesn't seem to be anyone else there.

'I have a message for a Zetterberg.'

'That would be me.'

I give him such a hard shove that he topples over backwards. He pulls a chair with him as he goes down.

I step inside and lock the door behind us, but quickly turn round to minimise the possibility of a chair being smashed into the back of my head.

Zetterberg has no such plans. He crawls backwards on his elbows a couple of metres, past a little table, a wall-mounted telephone and a tall, gilded hall mirror with an elaborate frame. He likes gold, this bloke.

When I follow him he stands up, and is just about to dart off into the flat when I catch hold of his shirt collar. It's the detachable type, and for a moment I am left standing there with the collar in my hand before I grab his shirt tails and quickly haul him in.

The mirror beside us rattles when I catapult him into the wall. He opens his mouth. I quickly put my right hand just above his larynx. He makes a croaking sound and tightens his lips moronically. I press. He goes onto his tiptoes. The flank of his body is stretched and exposed. Just the way I want it.

'In August this year you bought a second-hand car from a farmer named Elofsson in Ovanåker. You put down three hundred kronor when you picked it up and you were supposed to pay another two thousand one hundred a month later. You never did, and now Elofsson is getting browned off.'

Zetterberg gargles by way of an answer. Does he think this is some kind of negotiation? With both hands, he tries to prise away mine from his throat. A classic beginner's error. I can easily regulate the pressure on his throat as I choose.

For a moment I stare at his fingers. They're unnaturally thin; pale as Italian stucco. On his right hand is a glittering signet ring with a couple of red stones.

I direct my first left hook to his liver – it's always been one of my favourite punches. Only an amateur aims for the solar plexus; it's to the liver or the heart that a solid body blow can do a bit of good. The head says one punch but the body memory says two quick ones. I go along with the latter. You can put the gloves on the shelf but it takes a long time to wash their smell from your knuckles.

Zetterberg twitches uncontrollably. One part of him wants to fold himself double, another wants to get out of my strangulation grip. I lean in so close that I can smell his Aqua Vera cologne, his tobacco and his chest pastilles.

'There, there,' I whisper consolingly into his ear. 'I'll give you till tomorrow evening to get the bread together.'

My mouth is watering. I release the grip on his throat somewhat and let him catch his breath, only to hit him again as he's breathing out. The same hook meets the same surface, but this time I let Zetterberg crumple into a heap on the hall rug.

I step over him and smile at my scarred face in the mirror. I button my suit jacket and take a look at myself. The lapels of my jacket are so wide that they almost cover my whole chest. I should combine the dark beige shirt with the pinstriped chocolate-brown suit more often. I turn up the shirt collar and put on my tie with a double knot. I'm just about ready for another cigar.

Zetterberg is crying. He lies in a foetal position with his arms wrapped around his stomach, trying to catch his breath while at the same time sobbing and slobbering like a child. Not a pretty sight.

'Tomorrow evening,' I repeat, softening up my neck with a few side movements.

I look around the hall for something to smash, just to add a bit of urgency to the threat. My eyes come to rest on the wall-mounted telephone, but they move on to the vestibule, where a number of lovely overcoats are hanging in a row. What a pity we're not the same size. Underneath is an umbrella stand with several walking sticks in it. Too far away.

I grip the hall mirror and tear it down over him. The sound of shattering glass rebounds between the walls of the narrow hall. Zetterberg gives off a shrill little scream but doesn't move. He stays under the mirror, sobbing.

For a moment I think about fetching one of the sticks and giving him a proper working over, but I give it a miss – it's important to know when they've had enough. A dead bloke doesn't pay his debts, a badly injured one ends up in hospital. It's a fine line. In the early days I crossed it a few times, but it's been years since that happened. These days I know what I'm doing.

The mirror glass crunches under my shoes as I go back to the door. I stop for a moment and run my hand over the overcoats, pausing at an elegant camel hair model. The lock makes a subdued, dry click and then I'm back on the dimly lit landing.

The elevator is coming up, creaking as it goes, and I quickly go down the stairs. The white marble floor looks grey, almost like slate, in the gloom. I push the main door open and look at the black clouds. It's stopped raining. I dig in my pockets for a cigar. A young man with a pushcart hurries past, the wheels thundering against the paving stones.

I keep my eyes on the dark skies while I'm rooting around for matches. Tomorrow there'll be a return visit. With such a salubrious address and so many overcoats, there's nothing to suggest that Zetterberg would be prepared to leave town because of two thousand one hundred kronor. I chuckle, get out my aniline pen, spit on it and write down the figures in my notebook, with my fifteen per cent. Four hundred and fifty kronor for less than an hour's work. Not bad and very timely. Better paid than any other job this side of Midsummer.

I'm mulling over whether to celebrate a good day's work at one of the unlicensed dives you can find in more or less every other courtyard in Klara, when I notice that Sonja still hasn't found herself a punter.

She moves slowly towards me with a timid smile. As she draws closer I notice that she's a touch bowlegged. I stop her with a gesture, to indicate that I'm heading off in the opposite direction. For some reason she gives me an anxious glance, but she nods, turns round, and then walks back up Kungsgatan.

I whistle Ernst Rolf's 'I'm Getting Better Day by Day' and turn south to catch the number 3 tram back to Odenplan. We also have plenty of drinking dens with smuggled-in vodka back home in Sibirien. A tram tinkles by on Vasagatan and I look up.

I catch sight of the car right away.

The Mercedes is parked in the pool of light cast by the Carlton sign. The slim youth is smoothing out the creases in his plus fours and leaning against the coachwork. On his head is a big, drooping beret. He's also wearing a sports jacket, a knitted jumper and white socks. Without any doubt at all the kid has both money and style. He reminds me of someone I used to know. I get the idea he's been waiting for me. I slow down.

'Cigarette?' The boy speaks with a lisp. As he offers me a pack of Stamboul, I notice a gold ring on his little finger. I stop and take the pack out of his hand. With a hint of a smile, the boy sucks his bottom lip between his teeth. I fish out a cigarette, put it in my mouth and hand back the pack.

He offers me a light from a fully automatic gold lighter. I take his hands, hold them in mine and try to protect the flame from the gusting wind. Distractedly I caress the back of his soft, hairless hand. This boy has never done a day's work in his life. The youth trembles slightly at my touch. The lighter makes a repeated scraping sound.

Finally, with our joint efforts, we manage to get the cigarette going. Before he withdraws his hand, he caresses my cheek from top to bottom. Despite my shaving this morning, his touch makes a swishing sound against my face, like someone sweeping a porch. I know I'll remember how it feels for a long time.

Someone laughs from the hotel doors behind us. I hear the sound of high heels clattering against the street. The youth doesn't seem to pay it any mind. For some it's so easy.

'Isn't that car a few sizes too big for you?' I take two drags, one after the other, and quickly look around.

'Ah, you're just jealous.' He brushes the raindrops from the hood and flicks the water off his hand. He smiles broadly, showing me a wide gap between his front teeth.

'Can I have a look?'

I lean forwards to examine the fascia panel, made of some light-coloured wood, with chrome gauges.

'You can even take it for a spin if you like.'

I straighten up and look at the boy. For a few seconds, his chestnut eyes stare right into mine. He's exactly my taste in terms of age and build. Will I have to pay him something? He clearly has plenty of money, but what else does he want from me?

'Okay.'

The car responds at once when I give it some juice, and we rumble off at a terrific speed. We travel in silence. For a moment I think he may have that sort of brooding nature you sometimes find among boys of his age with too little to do, but I change my mind when I look at him. His eyes are expressionless. His mouth is half open. I concentrate on the driving. Maybe the kid does this every night. When you have dough everything is obvious and easy. Maybe I just happened to cross his path this evening.

A few moments later we're turning into my street. The familiar shop signs of Roslagsgatan swish by: Lind's widow's cigar shack, Nyström's barber shop, Ström's wholesalers, and Bruntell's general store. A couple of boys aged about ten yell as loud as they can and run after the car for twenty metres or so.

I flinch a little when the youth puts his hand on my gloved knuckles on the gear stick. As if to shake it off, I change down and narrowly manage to overtake one of the grey-painted Epidemic Hospital ambulances. The youth inhales audibly and makes a slight whimpering sound. I'm reminded of why I am sitting here in the car.

Just you wait, my little boy, I think. Kvist will teach you a thing or two.

We draw closer to the brick monstrosity at the top of Roslagsgatan, where the number 6 tram turns round. Rickardsson, one of Ploman's gangsters running the booze smuggling in Vasastan, gawks as we drive by. In my rear-view mirror I see him following us with his eyes.

'You can stay there till the birds start nesting in your gob.'

'What did you say?'

'Nothing.'

'Tell me!'

'It was nothing.'

The boy shakes a cigarette out of the blue pack. The sudden flame of the lighter illuminates his face. He puts one arm across his stomach and rests the other against it, holding the cigarette in front of his face without actually smoking it. Suddenly I feel uneasy. I don't know why.

We pass the rocky knoll with the Epidemic Hospital at the top. Lazily, the boy nods for me to keep going towards Bellevueparken. I slow down and turn into the long alley of bare lime trees that lead into the park. The gravel makes the car's tyres change tone. We pass a pregnant woman wrapped in a shawl, waddling as she goes up the hill, both hands under her belly. We are close to the mansion of Paschen, the liquor smuggler, which was recently taken over by the workhouse committee. The rolling, leafy terrain of the park with its many large bushes offers several good hiding places, but this shouldn't be anything to worry about, as no one moves around here after sunset. The workhouse inmates will most likely be staying indoors on a cold December night like this one.

The boy giggles. I stare at him again. I can't make head nor tail of the kid. I continue towards the highest point of the park.

To the south one can make out the silhouettes of the houses along the ridge of Brunkebergsåsen, as well as the dome of Vasa Church. To the north, through the bare trees, are the black waters of Brunnsviken, empty of sails. I turn off the road and park on a patch of grass.

As soon as I turn off the engine the boy is all over me. He gives me a couple of deep, intense kisses. He tastes of tobacco. Panting and out of step with one another, our wandering hands explore each other's crotches. The boy is a real man, it seems.

We extract ourselves from the embrace and get out of the car. I slip, drop onto one knee in the drenched ground, and get up again. Hurriedly we squelch through the grass and meet in a clinch in front of the bonnet. The car's headlamps are still on; he has the beam against his back.

I kneel, open-mouthed, as if to receive the Eucharist from August Gabrielsson, my old confirmation priest. My knees sink into the wet grass and the moisture quickly finds its way up my thighs. I get one of his trouser buttons open. He wears short underpants with an elasticated waist. I push my hat back onto my neck and, in a single movement, wrench his underpants and trousers to his ankles with trembling hands. The headlights of the car send a cascade of light between his legs.

He's a well-hung boy. We both make panting sounds as my lips envelop him. This is not the average, crappy sort of conscript I usually get to meet. I smack my lips. With my other hand I unbutton my trousers. The icy December night caresses me. I stick out my tongue and swallow him deep into my throat a few times. My eyes fill with tears, the boy pants and groans. He likes that.

I keep working methodically. My jaw muscles are starting to get numb, I'm out of practice, but then I feel a familiar vibration

24

against the top of my mouth. I pick up the tempo. Hard and wet and fast, that's how this should be done.

Our loud whimpering blends with the sound of two rats fighting in the nearby bushes, and the youth fills my mouth to overflowing. I resist my first impulse to swallow, spitting into my hand instead and rubbing it into my skin. I stand up, grab him by the scruff of his neck and get him to bend forwards over the bonnet.

'Now it's Kvisten's turn.'

Slowly but confidently I work my way into the boy. It's warm and cosy, like stepping into the boiler room after a stint of freezing watch duty on deck. He yowls with pain, sobs and slithers, but it's nothing to be concerned about. Soon enough it gets easier, and his protestations turns to lusty moans. I pick up speed. Young men of this type usually manage to come twice on the trot.

'That's right, my boy.'

I hammer him against the black bodywork. He keeps out of the way of the headlights. The radiator badge breaks off with a hollow snap. Our shadows hurtle back and forth across the grass. From Albano, a locomotive makes a shrill whistle. Deep inside I feel a lurking coughing fit.

A drop of his come hangs persistently from the corner of my mouth. I lick it up and press both my hands into the small of his back to make him arch properly, so I can get my whole length into him. The moon peers out from behind the clouds, and the light collides with the beam of the headlights. The boy's arse is a milky white colour, and for a moment I have the idea that I'm assaulting a Greek statue.

Back home in the wardrobe I have a Husqvarna pistol, which I kept after my conscription years. The few times I've fired it, it's had quite a kick. When I come at last, the recoil of my ejaculation reverberates in the same way. The youth heaves against me another three or four or five times before also coming himself. Out of breath, I lie with my nose against his neck for a few seconds, then glide out of him without meaning to. I stand up and back away a little.

'Oh damn,' I mumble, breathing hard.

The days when I could run ten kilometres in forty-five minutes are definitely over. The boy pulls up his trousers and turns towards me. I stand there coughing, my hands on my knees and my trousers down to my ankles. The youth puts his hand on my shoulder and titters a little. I look up. What a stupid little dandy. Some people get everything served on a silver platter and sail through life without a care in the world, while others have to slave for every inch of happiness.

The vein in my forehead starts pounding. My mouth waters. Maybe it's because of his damned lisping. He must be retarded. By his age, he should have learned to talk properly. But that damned arrogant grin of his is the worst of all.

Again he sucks his bottom lip in between his teeth in that seductive way, while grinning idiotically. I stare for a moment at his fur-lined lace-up boots. They're polished, proper, and expensive. I inhale deeply and blow it out of my nose at the same time as I plant a quick left-handed upper-cut on the tip of his chin. It puts his lights out. At least it wipes that grin off his face.

My footwork is not the best because of the trousers, which means that some of the power of the punch is lost, but he's still out cold by the time he hits the ground. I lean forwards, coughing, with my hands on my knees again. The boy lies on his back with his arms stretched out at right angles from his body. The headlights form a half-circle of light around him. The scene feels very familiar. The teeth of his lower jaw stick out of the wound below his lip.

'That won't exactly help your damned lisp.'

My back clicks as I straighten up. I take off my hat and mop the sweat from my forehead with the back of my hand, before pulling up my trousers. The boy makes a pitiful gargling sound from somewhere at the back of his throat. I get out a cigar from my pocket to get rid of the aftertaste in my mouth and rummage for matchsticks, but can't find any.

I walk over to the kid and take his gold lighter from his trouser pocket, then get the cigar going and watch him struggling with his breathing for a while. I hold up the lighter, angling it so I can read the name engraved diagonally across it. Leonard. I put it in my pocket and then check my watch. It's half past eight.

I've knocked lots of people unconscious, I've harmed people so they don't function properly afterwards, and I've put them in month-long comas, but I've never beaten anyone to death. Not as far as I know, anyway.

Before I set off on the short walk home I roll the boy onto his side, so the blood can run out of him.

Lundin feeds the meter on the wall with a couple of gas tokens before he lights the ring and then puts the water on for coffee. Almost every day for the past ten years we've had breakfast in his kitchen behind the undertaker's reception. The room is almost identical to my own, directly above us.

I sit at the table while Lundin waltzes about at the hob. Through the window I see an accordion player on Ingemarsgatan, churning out one heartrending tuppenny opera after another. The undertaker and I sing 'Lioness Bride' so heartily that the window panes are practically rattling. We have both taken swigs from the bottle to prepare the way for the tot in the coffee afterwards.

The sun reflects off the accordion, making a sun cat whizz across the kitchen's yellow floral wallpaper, finding the shining surfaces of the copper saucepans.

'A roaring sound as our Lord sighed, then the lion tore the stranger's bride.'

The reflections shoot off Lundin's gold fillings as he opens his mouth wide at the end of the verse, then slink round a washing-up basin of marinated herring, hound across a selection of white-enamelled tins, and momentarily lose themselves above a shelf that holds a soap dish and other paraphernalia. Finally, the accordion player leans back with the instrument splayed across his belly, sending the reflections up to the ceiling, by the drying slats for laundry.

'Bread we're having, as well. Sausage and cheese. And a saffron bun each, in honour of St Lucia. Or what do you say, brother?'

The drying slats are bare. Like me, Lundin takes his laundry to Sailor-Beda opposite. I don't know how many black suits he has. When not wearing his cylindrical top hat, he brushes his grey tendrils over his bald pate. His sunken cheeks are always well shaven. His bushy moustache usually seems slightly skew-whiff, because he wipes it with the back of his hand from left to right. People around here say he brings bad luck, because he smells like the dead. I don't know. Not like when they're decomposing, anyway: Lundin gives off a sweetish, but not foetid, smell, like fallen fruit. He's going on seventy years old, with a sparrow chest, and a terrible, hacking cough that's even worse than mine. Maybe he's on his way to the other side. On several occasions I've thought his time might be up. He suffers from dizzy spells, and sometimes he collapses in a disfiguring fit. For his own part, he claims to be up with the cockerel every day, doing his morning gymnastics from the radio program with Colonel Owl.

'And then another scoop for the top of your head, and another just because.'

He throws a couple more heaped spoons of coffee into the saucepan from a bag of ready ground. We both like it strong, with sugar cubes and a tot of something alcoholic. The accordion player changes to 'The King of the Thieves'. I tip the kitchen chair, sitting there in my trousers, braces and a singlet. I always go downstairs in my socks. Lundin catches his breath. The coffee boils and he takes it off the ring to let it brew for a while.

He puts bread on the table, also the saffron buns from the bakery on Ingemarsgatan. He's in an unusually good mood, most likely because we've agreed that the rent will be paid today. I'd

29

asked for a deferment until St Lucy's Day. The Zetterberg job came along in the nick of time. I open the window and toss a fifty-öre coin to the accordion player, who catches it expertly between two notes.

The cobwebs in the window disperse the weary daylight across the table. At one end of the windowsill lies a dry wasp. Lundin puts the food on the table and sits down opposite. The accordion player finishes his song, and Lundin pours coffee and a tot of schnapps into our cups, then slides over the sweet wheat bread he has baked himself.

'The bread of knowledge he eats, the water of wisdom he drinks.'

Lundin inserts a sugar cube between his teeth and takes his coffee cup. I follow suit, and we enjoy a few bracing gulps. There's a soreness in my throat from my adventure last night in Bellevueparken. I pull out a drawer at the short end of the table and clatter with the cutlery. Lundin gets out his accounts book and slaps it on the table. He finds the page marked 'K' and slowly moves his snuff-brown finger down the lines.

'Let's see now…'

'It should be the same as last month.'

'It's the rent with two weeks of respite, plus…' He picks up a pencil and a little penknife to sharpen it.

'It should be about the same as last month.' I get my wallet out from the back pocket of my trousers and put it on the table. Lundin scrawls his squiggles in the book.

'Three litres, six each.' He runs the back of his hand across his moustache. I chew a piece of bread. The number 6 tram rings its bell as it goes by on Roslagsgatan. 'Eggs on five occasions, sausage on seven, ham on three.'

'We never had ham…'

Lundin holds up his brown forefinger. 'Ham on three. You can check it against my accounts with "B-b-bruntell with the Kodak",' he says, imitating the grocer's stutter.

'No need for that.'

I have a pull at the bottle. Lundin taps his pen shaft against it twice and makes another annotation.

'One hundred and twenty-seven kronor and fifty. Neither more nor less. Exactly on the öre.'

'That's three kronor less than last month.'

'Three twenty-five less.'

'Much obliged to you.' I pull the strap off my wallet and open it.

'Even the poor man shall find grazing in my pastures.'

Lundin sucks his moustache. I wet my thumb and count out the money on the table. The pipes surge whenever someone uses the toilet in the corridor. A bell tinkles: the door of the undertaker's is being opened. Lundin scrabbles the money together and puts it in his inside pocket.

'See you tomorrow morning, then,' he says. He puts on his top hat, adjusts the fit of his coat and runs his finger over his moustache again. I nod. He lowers his head as he goes through the door. I take a sip of the coffee and open the snuff-thumbed accounts book. I stay there for a long while, trying to get a grip on the figures.

A few hours later I'm standing by the window of my corner flat with my notebook in my hand. Dusk is falling over Sibirien. An old bat wrapped in a shawl is thrashing a boy on Roslagsgatan, holding him by his collar and striking at him with her fist. The brick building opposite, where Sailor-Beda has her laundry, catches the dull sounds of the thumps and accompanying oaths, hurling them all back at me. I push my hat away from my face.

'Thieving son of a whore!'

She lets go of the boy. Sobbing, he drops onto the pavement with a bloodied nose. The old nag gathers up her skirts and apron and resolutely marches south, past Bruntell's grocery store and Ström's junk shop.

I fish a Meteor out of the breast pocket of my unbuttoned shirt and bite off the end. Up in Vanadislunden, St Stefan's church tolls three times and, to the south, Johannes answers in baritone. Outside, the kid gets up on unsteady legs, rubs his nose and makes off towards Roslagstull. A fat rat darts across the street.

'That old girl had a decent punch,' I mumble, lighting the cigar and blowing a plume of blue-grey smoke at the window-pane. Outside, the day is dying in a welter of fire. The last few rays of the sinking sun are caught by the golden pretzel over the entrance to Ingemarsgatan's bakery, from where it reflects against the façade on the other side of the street. In a few hours it'll be time for me to go to work.

I go around the big oak desk that faces the hall. The green Oriental rug absorbs the sound of my steps. My wide trouser legs swish against one another. I pass the full-length mirror and hit the light switch next to the kitchen door. The electric chandelier has six tasselled yellow lampshades. Most of them have singed patches. Only four of the bulbs are working.

I cough drily and go and sit in the armchair by the desk. I take a puff and put the cigar in an ashtray decorated on the base with a hula-dancing figure. Smoke is already hanging heavy in the flat. My very own Battle of Lützen. Grey wreaths are sweeping across the brown wallpaper, trying to brush off the dust on top of the swine leather sandbag that dangles in a corner, and then seeking the hall, where the ceramic wood burner reaches up to the ceiling. The smoke attaches itself to the arms of the chandelier like ash-coloured streamers in a Christmas tree, and caresses the bindings of the books in the little bookcase to my left, where Strindberg rubs shoulders with Dahlin – a working-class author – and Piraten. I've read them all, and more still, at the city library a few blocks to the south. Not only tramps spend time at the library.

I turn on the green-shaded desk lamp and the flat now shows itself off to much better effect. The place is cluttered with souvenirs from my years at sea. Ships in bottles, a short-bladed paper knife of ivory from Kaolack, and a porcelain mermaid sitting on a flat rock from Kirkwall. The walls are bare. Above the wardrobe next to the sleeping alcove is a crooked nail. Behind the wardrobe is a photograph of Branting, which fell down years ago.

The one-room flat with a separate kitchen has both gas- and wood-burning stoves. On the landing is a room with a toilet, which I share with the neighbours. As far as I know, Lundin is also arranging to put a bathtub in the cellar for general use. I can't complain. Usually, husband, wife and a pile of children share the same space. Whole families live in what are little more than huts around Stadshagen or Vita Bergen; if you turned over one of the boats pulled up around Årstaviken, there would be a decent chance of running into the man of the house, telling you to close the door as there was a draught.

The number 6 tram rattles by. I open the top drawer of the desk and, as usual, it gets stuck halfway. I rummage among letters, old newspaper cuttings from *Boxing Monthly!*, a green scrap of fabric and a lot of other crap that I ought to clear out. I roll out a half-litre bottle of Kron and fill the schnapps glass, which is always ready on the desk.

'Good evening to you, Kvisten!'

The room-temperature schnapps sends a shudder down my spine as I open my notebook to plan out the route of my jobs. I almost always have plenty to get on with. People are desperate and impoverished and more or less at that point is when I turn up with my ugly mug and nail them. I've had a fruitful working arrangement with Wernersson's Velocipedes on Odengatan for a number of years. When people stop making their monthly payments, I turn up to reclaim the bicycles, and Wernersson pays me off with their deposits. This yields between ten and thirty-five kronor per object.

This evening's jobs include three bicycles: a black Monark lady's, a Pilen gentleman's and an Adler three-wheeler with a back-loading flatbed. All the addresses are conveniently located in Vasastan. From there I can easily pedal them to Wernersson before I go back to Kungsgatan to pick up the dough from Zetterberg, as agreed. I wonder if he's swept up the glass from the shattered mirror since last night.

Outside, the tram rattles past on its way back. I make a note in my book of the bicycle models, the registration numbers and the addresses, put the cigar down in the ashtray and push back my hat. I check my pocket watch. There's no hurry.

I sit back and put my feet up on the desk. A coin falls out of my trouser pocket and rolls like a torn-off uniform button across the floor of an officer's cabin. I close my eyes and smile.

With sixty-five kronor in my pocket and slightly aching knuckles, I close the door of Wernersson Velocipedes and stroll up Odengatan. It's raining again, and, on the corner of Standards, a voluptuous redhead stands smoking under a parasol. She follows me with her eyes.

I hurry my steps past the National Library. A coughing fit is tickling in my chest. As I reach the crest of the slope I can already sense the mighty dome of Vasa Church through the skeletal lime trees. I ignore the cough and jog the remaining distance.

A vendor on the platform between the tram tracks and the lanes of traffic makes a gesture over his spruce twigs and corn sheaves. He's had the good sense to dress himself in a thick imitation astrakhan hat and big clogs filled with straw. I shake my head.

My run sets my heart bouncing in my chest. I post off the completed crossword for the weekly *Social-Demokraten* competition. I send it because they promise a prize for a correctly solved crossword, but I've never got the slightest whiff of cash.

The bells of Vasa Church chime six times. Just a few years ago there was a dairy farm up here on the ridge, and one could hear the cows lowing at evening milking time. Now there's only the persistent sound of engines, the growling horns of trucks, shrieking factory whistles and the ringing of trams.

More and more people on their way home from work are crowding the shelter, and soon it's about as packed as the Söder baths on Saturdays. A lady in a grey coat that almost reaches her feet shakes the water off her umbrella.

'Oh, what dreadful weather!'

'It's even worse than snow.' A bloke in a cap and a long blue shirt under his jacket squints at the rain-heavy skies. There's soot around his eyes.

The lady looks him up and down for a few moments. 'That'll come along as well, soon enough.'

Like yesterday I take the number 3 tram to Norra Bantorget and walk the short distance to Kungsgatan. I've stopped by Lennartsson's renowned shoe shop on Vasagatan, and I'm standing there gawking at the window displays when I get an unpleasant

35

sensation in the pit of my stomach. I don't know why. Something feels wrong, and it's not just my wet feet.

Two stints in Långholmen Prison for assault and years of harassment mean that I can smell goons at a good distance. All of my adult life I've been hounded by goons. Just wearing a blue collar is reason enough for them to tail you in the park, at public baths, even in urinals.

I put my newly lit cigar in my mouth, shove my hands in my coat pockets and hurry towards the Kungsgatan junction. I peer round the corner.

'Damn it!'

I take my Meteor out of my mouth while I'm swearing. The area by Zetterberg's front entrance is being guarded by two goons in uniform. In the street, a vehicle from the fire department is parked alongside a car with stretchers. In the doorway opposite stands a mixed group of gossips: men, women and little boys. I turn up the collar of my overcoat and stroll forwards.

'Someone died in a fire in the night,' says a lady in a skirt, jacket and blue cape, apparently a secretary on her way home from work, when I speak to her. 'Someone called Zettergren.'

I clench my fist in my pocket.

'Zetterberg,' corrects a delivery man, clearly in no hurry to get anywhere.

'He lit the gas himself,' says a grey-haired bloke with a goatee and an elegant walking stick. I think I've seen him before but my memory isn't quite what it used to be. Several people in the group back him up.

I've heard enough. It wouldn't be the first time that some indebted wretch chose that way out. Quite the opposite. Nowadays, hardly a minute goes by without scores of executives and high-ranking public officials jumping off the edge.

36

'They haven't brought him out yet,' says the lady in the skirt and jacket. Her eyes shine as eyes often do when humans sense blood.

'Why not?'

'They said they were waiting for the county medical officer.'

I have a sudden headache. I take the cigar out of my mouth and massage the top of my nose. I shouldn't have gone in so hard. 'Should have given the mirror a miss.'

'What was that?' The old man stares at me.

'You what?'

'You said something about a mirror.'

'I'll be damned if I did.'

One of the goons shakes his sabre at a couple of curious kids. A half-full tram passes by, a boy in a Vega cap cadging a ride on the carriage's back coupler.

'Here they come!' the lady next to me cries in falsetto. First out, carrying one end of a stretcher, comes a corpulent young man whose tight-fitting trousers stick around his wide thighs. Zetterberg has been covered with a clean sheet. The other bearer is small of stature, grimacing with the exertion, and his face is quite red. I remember the taxing stairs to Zetterberg on the top floor.

Halfway to the mortuary car, Zetterberg's arm drops away from the body, falling out and dangling like a pendulum. The signet ring drops off the corpse's thin fingers and hits the street. It bounces a few times before it stops in the gutter.

A sigh goes through the spectators. The small bearer seems to swear silently to himself. He bends his legs, rests one of the stretcher's handles on his knee and reaches for the ring. For a moment the stretcher is on the verge of overturning, but in the nick of time the bloke picks up the ring and manages to get

Zetterberg back into balance. The lady next to me is panting with agitation.

I've seen enough. I leave the little crowd. The cold, razing December wind finds its way under my collar and into my sleeves, leaving the skin goose pimpled. My feet are colder than ever.

The bell on the door tinkles welcomingly when half an hour later I arrive at Lundin's Undertakers, bending my head as I go in. The premises seem to strain under the weight of the house's five floors, like a delivery boy under a piano. The office consists of a little tobacco-smelling reception, a desk, a couple of visitors chairs, a telephone and a potted palm tree with brown fronds.

A woman is sitting with her back towards me. Under her black hat is a grey knot of hair. Her head is bowed and her shoulders shake from time to time, although she doesn't make a sound. Her long skirt has dragged through the gutter on the way here.

'We can arrange for a more elegant hearse from Frey's rentals agency if you wish,' says Lundin in his timid salesman's manner. He looks her over and nods at the wall-mounted telephone. I shake my head. Out in the street a car honks its horn and a couple of agitated voices are swearing. A gang of excitable boys are causing a racket. I move an invisible bottle to my lips, as if having a drink. Lundin nods again, and the old woman blows her nose sonorously. I start pacing about on the spot.

'And what do we do about flowers?'

I run my hand across my chin several times and make a dry, smacking sound with my lips. One after the other, the clocks of St Stefan and St Johannes, and Lundin's American timepiece inside the flat behind him, toll, seven times each.

Weddings and funerals entitle one to extra rations of schnapps, and Lundin often takes a part-payment for his services in spirits, which he then sells on at high prices or dilutes with embalming fluid and flogs on the cheap. The rationing system, he likes to say, is the best thing to happen to the country apart from the Spanish Flu. He keeps the bottles in the safest place in the funeral home: a child's coffin in the cool room. I take a deep breath and button up my overcoat.

The room hardly measures twenty metres square and has no windows. The walls are tiled in white porcelain. The cold is sudden and harsh, and smells of forgotten, foetid flowers. A set of black tails lies on one of the long benches, but on the other are two small, white coffins of the simplest model. Under the benches are spacious basins in which Lundin, in the summer, keeps large blocks of ice under a layer of wood shavings. Beneath each of the basins is a drain.

The desolate echo of my steps rings out as I cross the rust-red clinker floor. I slide my fingers under the lid of one of the child's coffins. The sweat breaks out of my pores. My hands are trembling, my nails scrabble intensely at the edge. It sounds as if I'm with a Marconi operator on a ship in distress.

'For Christ's sake, Kvisten.'

I don't recognise my own voice. The lid opens. Inside the coffin, the bottles lie in neat rows, wrapped in flimsy brown or green paper. I don't check the manufacturers' brands.

A half-litre, I mime at Lundin on my way out and hold up the bottle. He nods. Over the door hangs a white tapestry with the words *Order in All Things* embroidered in red thread.

Moments later I'm sitting in my kitchen. On the windowsill lies a dusty, brown-speckled conch shell with six spikes. Flames crackle in the fireplace. Next to the fireplace is a basket of wood and a short axe. A couple of rag rugs from Ström cover the floor. A cigar goes out in the ashtray.

I sit at the table hectoring myself to get through the half-litre of aquavit. My shirt is unbuttoned and my hair stands on end. The newspaper lies untouched in front of me. I share *Social-Demokraten* with three of my neighbours. I get to read it last on the condition that the crossword has been left unsolved. The front page announces that the Swedish Match Company is under new management, diphtheria is raging up in Katarina parish, and Hitler and his regiment of scouts are on the rampage in Berlin.

A jazz trumpet wails from the radio of the spiritualist who lives on the other side of the wall. The aquavit sizzles through my system, making the vein on my forehead throb violently. My hands rest on the table between the bottle and my schnapps glass. My trainer always said they were too small in relation to their strength. The scars run higgledy-piggledy across them, my fingers crooked from all the little fractures. My left-hand little finger ends abruptly in a knot of red-streaked skin. Sometimes I still feel a smarting pain where the topmost joint should have been. I still feel iron eating its way through flesh and bone.

I lift my hand and gaze at the crackled photograph I have hidden underneath it. I close one of my eyes. She had pigtails and a cornflower-blue dress. I know that, I bought her the dress on the same day that I bore her on my shoulders to the photographer. She's mainly her mother's daughter: the eyes are hers, also the mouth.

I fire new life into the cigar with the gold lighter. I read the name engraved on it and remember Leonard's hand touching my cheek. The empty schnapps glass jumps when I thump my fist on the table. I refill the glass, raise it in a toast, and mumble,

'Zetterberg! Cheers to you, you damned self-slaughterer! You've swindled me out of four hundred and fifty kronor!'

I throw my head back and chuck down the contents. A dog barks from somewhere up in Vanadislunden. I peer out of the kitchen window. The top of the hill is crowned by the water tower that holds tens of thousands of litres. I imagine the brick building breaking apart, and the water pouring down the hill and washing away the whole district.

I fill the glass a final time, then pick up the letter from Elofsson, which has been lying on the kitchen table, and read it again. The chair topples over backwards when I stand up. I laugh emptily, regain my balance, and go over to the fireplace. I open the hatch with the fire poker. Heat radiates over my hands. I toss the letter inside and go back to the table. I toast the empty air, and the warmth of the schnapps washes through my chest and stomach.

Drunk as I am, at first I mistake the hammering, believing it to be Lundin nailing down the lid of yet another poor man's coffin. But soon enough I realise that someone is thumping at the door.

Goon knocking.

Two men in black suits and sturdy overcoats are standing outside the door. The younger of them is a pale sod, with ginger tufts of hair sticking out from beneath his bowler hat, and a downy, sparse moustache. The older of them has tired brown eyes and a receding chin. A thickset type, he stands slightly behind his colleague. These are no normal goons, but they are still goons. I can smell it.

'Harry Kvist?' The elder of them holds up his silver badge. Number 26, Criminal Division.

I stagger backwards into the cramped, dark hall. Narrow spaces are good if you get too many of them coming for you at the same time. They close in fast. I narrow one eye. My right punch flies through the gloom. I don't know if it's the drink or the older man's lack of a chin, but I miss by a couple of millimetres. His stubble rasps against the top of my hand.

The other goon hits me hard across the left knee with a wooden baton. The blow sends me reeling.

'Too low!' I drawl. 'Too low, damn it!'

The older one jabs at me with his right, but I duck and reappear on his starboard side. The baton comes flying from port. I hide my chin behind my shoulder and press my fist against my temple and ear. My hand shrieks as if it's broken. It isn't, it's just full of old bits of bone.

I fall backwards to the floor with both the goons on top of me. The younger of them straddles me at once. He lands his right fist on my eye and immediately follows this up with a baton blow across the top of my head. A lovely, pure flash of pain cuts through my intoxication. I shake my head to see if I'm bleeding. I try to resist but my muscles won't do as they're told. I think I'm smiling. I can't feel my legs.

'The swine is drunk and all.'

They heave me onto my side and clap my hands in irons behind my back before dragging me out of the flat and down the stairs, each goon firmly gripping one of my upper arms. They've hung my jacket over my shoulders and pressed down my hat on my head. My feet, thumping on every step, seem to wake some life into my legs again.

The cracked leather seat in the back of the squad car is cold against my hands. The motor splutters and starts; we steer into Roslagsgatan. I am also spluttering.

Outside, the dark city flickers by rapidly. I close one of my eyes. The dairy company's new automated illuminations have been switched on. A man has loaded several long planks across the saddle and handlebars of his bicycle, and is sitting on these, pedalling with his knees pointing out. Droves of unemployed blokes are hanging about by Vasaparken.

My breathing feels heavy. I make a wheezing sound and cough again. A group of dockers are hanging about outside Restaurant NORMA, close to the Atlas wall, the scene of a notorious murder of a whore in March. They gesticulate wildly, as if in dispute about something.

I look at the two short-cropped necks in front of me. Something in the car smells of old sweat. In the middle of St Eriksplan, a cluster of street missionaries stand together, immersed in prayer and holding hands. The blue neon of the tobacconist's shines like phosphorescence. Its glow envelops the members of the congregation, their eyes closed, and transforms them into a sickly little bunch.

The vehicle lurches all over the place, and I have difficulty staying upright in the bends. These goons are not the normal, beat-patrolling drunks with sabres, and they don't take me to the Ninth District station house, which would have been the closest. The car banks hard to the left towards Kungsholmen, and I tumble into the door on the right. My hat falls off. The leather seat creaks as I fly around. There's a thumping pain under my left eye, and I wonder if they've opened the fracture in my zygomatic bone that 'The Mallet' Sundström gave me in 1922.

'You think I'm afraid of goons, you bastards?'

It doesn't sound convincing. My mouth is well oiled with schnapps and the words come slithering out in any old way they like. The younger policeman in the passenger seat turns round quickly. The first baton blow comes in from the side. I pull my face back. The second attempt is also directed at my head. From above, this time. The baton thumps against the ceiling. The shoulder is the only possibility. I throw my head and body to the left, let the blow roll down towards my elbow. The jacket they've hung over my shoulders glides off. The pain is bracing, sharpening the senses.

'Take it easy!' the policeman at the wheel yells at his colleague. He purses his mouth under the moustache.

I laugh, cough, and laugh again. 'I could drink twice as much and still be quicker than you, you bloody swine!'

It's true. With my hands free I could go fifteen rounds against him without taking a single punch. The greenhorn's baton moves a little, but he manages to control himself.

We go across the bridge to Kungsholmen and turn abruptly to the left. A girl is watching her reflection in a window, the hem of her skirt under her coat stiffened with the dirt of Fleminggatan. The Strand is showing a film starring Harold Lloyd.

What the hell do the goons want? I turned the kid onto his side in Bellevue, surely he can't have choked on his own blood? Or frozen to death? And I didn't go in so bloody hard when I was collecting the bicycles. In the end, whatever it's about, it's bad news for Kvisten.

I watch the greenhorn relaxing his jaw slightly in the passenger seat. The other goon, the one without a chin, who's driving, starts whistling 'A Sailor's Grave'. I snort. I'll eat my hat if we're not heading for Kronoberg, where the goons have their headquarters.

By a wood pile along one of Fleminggatan's walls, a boy is holding a run-over rat by the tail, swinging it menacingly at his friends. The grey-black rat sways slowly back and forth like a sooty, rain-soaked flag. When the boy notices me looking, his eyes flash devilishly, and the dead rat is flung against my side window.

'Damned whelps!' hisses the ginger-haired goon as the boys make a run for it.

A thick string of blood crawls across the window like a red caterpillar.

They leave me sitting barefoot in the piss-stinking cell for a good while before they come to get me. Two different constables put me in handcuffs, this time in front of my body. I have to walk with my arms hooked into theirs, and my hands on my waistband to hold them up, because they took my braces as soon as I got here. I limp along without making any trouble.

My body, my head and my knee are all aching from the earlier rough treatment. A decent-sized swelling simmers below my left eye. My head is throbbing. The sharp scents of the cell seem to have impregnated my shirt and trousers. Several times I am almost overwhelmed by the impulse to vomit, and I tighten my sore muscles when the policemen's grip on my arms grows more insistent.

We go sideways through the doorway into the tobacco-reeking interrogation room. Without removing my handcuffs, they put me on a little wooden chair in front of a table. The room is not much bigger than the corner of a boxing ring. It has no windows. I have a feeling I've been here before. The constables walk out.

I need a cigar. My thoughts gnaw at me despite my thumping head. It has to be the boy. Surely he couldn't have frozen to death in the park? Anyway, I didn't leave any fingerprints in the sports car, and the rain should have taken care of footprints.

The door opens behind my back. An elderly man with a moustache the colour of a certain kind of driftwood pinches the front creases of his trousers and takes a seat on the other side of the table. The waxed tips of his moustache point upwards, in the style of Kaiser Wilhelm or the King. His well-tailored suit almost exactly matches the colour of his moustache. His necktie is slightly droopy. He removes his gold-rimmed spectacles and gets out a white handkerchief. In silence, he polishes every millimetre of the lenses. His handkerchief is embroidered with a red monogram but I can't see what it says.

Someone yells on the other side of the wall and a few muted thuds can be heard. Quick footsteps sound up and down the corridor outside. A bloke starts groaning.

The man makes eye contact and nods, with a smile. For an instant, the tips of his moustache seem to point directly up. I smile back and grunt.

'My name is Alvar Berglund, I'm a detective chief inspector. We have a few questions for you.'

Berglund puts on his spectacles. I wheeze. Berglund produces a fountain pen and a notebook from a briefcase and arranges these items in front of himself. First he puts the pen on top of the book, then he changes his mind and puts it to the right of it, before excusing himself and swiftly leaving the room.

My chair scrapes across the floor as I push it against the wall to my left. I lean my head on the yellow-painted surface, closing my eyes and trying to cross my arms over my chest. The handcuffs cut into my skin. I breathe heavily with my mouth open.

Suddenly my heart leaps. I open my eyes.

The damned gold lighter. Engraved and everything. It's still in my trouser pocket at home.

'So,' says Berglund after coming back and sitting down and making himself and his spectacles comfortable. 'We're wondering about your whereabouts last night, between eight and a quarter past nine?'

He smiles and twists the left side of his moustache. His shirt-sleeve is ornamented with a cufflink of gold with two crossed fasces over three crowns. I lift my handcuffed hands and massage the base of my nose with my forefinger and thumb. The pain darts around my head when I accidentally brush against my swollen eye.

'Between eight and a quarter past nine?'

'Exactly. In the evening.'

'I must have been at home. I came home before eight.'

Berglund nods and makes a first note on the white sheet of paper before he goes on: 'I see. Did you meet anyone after nine?'

I stretch my neck first to the left, then the right.

'No, I was alone. I did the crossword in *Social-Demokraten*.'

'Me too,' says Berglund and adds: 'It got the better of me.'

'Not me.'

'Did you know that one about the loser at Breitenfeldt?'

47

'Tilly? Everyone knows that, don't they?'

'Oh yes, that's right. I'll remember that. Tilly.' Berglund's pen rasps across the paper. 'How many years of schooling did you have?'

'Two.'

The dust lies thickly on the glass lampshade dangling over the table. Up in a corner of the room the ceiling has cracked. My headache has changed; it's grown duller and more persistent. Soon we'll be there. With Leonard. I know how these bastards work.

'What were you doing before you came home that evening?'

'Working. I had a job down on Kungsgatan.'

'And what do you do?' His spectacles slide down a bit when he quizzically raises his eyebrows. Does he take me for an idiot?

'You know,' I answer quickly.

Berglund chuckles tersely and leans back. 'Certainly. So you met Zetterberg?'

He notes that I flinch slightly.

'The suicide,' I mutter.

'How's that?' Berglund scrutinises me.

Is all this about the suicide who diddled me out of my four hundred and fifty?

'Yes, I met him.'

I smack my lips to get some saliva flowing. It feels as if someone put cotton wadding against the roof of my mouth. The nausea comes over me again. I cough drily. The boy is probably alive. At least that's something.

'Why did you go to see Zetterberg?'

'To collect a debt. It was a job.'

'And who hired you?'

I could have predicted that one. Berglund smiles again. What was that backwater called again? I fumble with my recall of the name. Sometimes I forget the simplest things. I've seen the same in many retired boxers, punch-drunk types with more stitches in them than a football, who can hardly tell right from left any more.

I close my eyes and again press thumb and forefinger against the top of my nose. Slowly the letter reappears in my mind. The paper is lined, the letter is written in ink without splodges, and the handwriting is forwards leaning…

'It was about a payment for a car… A certain farmer, Elofsson, in… Ovanåker parish.'

The relief spreads a warmth inside, like a slug of booze in my stomach.

'I see.'

Berglund makes another annotation. I lean back in my chair and cough. The handcuffs rattle as I clench my hands in my lap.

'Did he kill himself? Zetterberg?'

'Possibly.' Berglund glances up before he goes on with his notes.

I shake my head. On two occasions I've seen it happen. Both times it was prisoners throwing themselves off the top-floor walkway at Långholmen. Like icicles of prison grey, they fell through the air and were shattered against the stone floor.

'Just for the sake of accuracy,' Berglund goes on, smiling and leaning forwards. 'Did this Elofsson telephone you or did he write?'

'He wrote a letter.'

'Do you still have it?'

'I burned it when I heard of Zetterberg's death.'

'But you're certain of the name and the address?'

'The name I am absolutely sure of; the address, almost sure.'

'Do you own a light brown overcoat?'

'No, if your boys had let me dress myself properly, you would have seen that my overcoat is black.'

'I see.' Berglund writes. 'Would you object to my sending a courier for the coat, to verify this?'

'No, do as you wish,' I say, thinking about my reserve capital, seventy-five kronor folded between the octagonal plates in the kitchen cupboard, my best china. The pistol in the wardrobe and the notebook would probably be even worse.

'One moment.'

Berglund stands up, brushes down his trousers and walks out of the room. I hold up my hands. Is it the hangover or tension that makes them tremble? I stand up and pace back and forth across the tiny space. Zetterberg: why do they care about Zetterberg?

'The bloke puts his head in the oven, the goons go in full strength, and I lose out on a new pair of shoes,' I mutter hoarsely. A lump of phlegm blocks my throat, and I clear it with some coughing.

I lift my hands again. They're shaking even worse now.

I bend down and squeeze my knee. It's badly swollen. Berglund comes back in, but he stops in the doorway when he sees that I'm standing up, and eventually has to squeeze past me. We find ourselves face to face, he averts his eyes. Just like Zetterberg, he uses Aqua Vera. At the tip of one eyebrow, a slight scar spreads the wrinkles vertically. We sit down. The sound of the chairs scraping against the floor cuts through my cranium, as when my schoolmates used to pull their nails across their slates.

'What was your impression of Zetterberg? So you would have been there…' Berglund moves his finger over his notes. '… At around eight o'clock?'

'More like half past six, or maybe seven.'

'How did Zetterberg seem to you?'

'Accommodating.'

'In what sense do you mean?'

'The whole thing was a misunderstanding about the payment date. We arranged it. He said he'd go to the bank the next day.'

'I see.' Berglund smiles. 'Did you see anyone after your little rendezvous?'

'Sorry?'

'After your meeting. Did you see anyone after your visit?'

'I went straight home.'

'You didn't buy anything? A newspaper? Some groceries for dinner?'

'No. But I saw that bowlegged whore. Vanja.'

Berglund makes a note. 'Vanja. Where and when exactly?'

'We had spoken earlier while I was waiting for Zetterberg, and we bumped into one another when I left the house. She was walking between Klara Norra and Målaregatan. It must have been around seven. She said she was a dishwasher on Drottninggatan.'

'How do you know she was a tart?'

'A girl on her own who approaches a bloke she doesn't know? What would you say, chief inspector? And if she wasn't, then she was the first dishwasher I ever met who had dirty fingernails.'

Berglund nods, makes a note and then rings a bell attached under the table. The high-pitched tone of it makes me jump. The door opens at once and a uniformed constable comes into the room.

'Ask Linder to run a check on a prostitute by name of Vanja. Check the ledgers for assumed identities and run her through the register for nicknames too.'

The door closes behind me, and Berglund goes on: 'This Vanja, can you say with absolute confidence that she saw you?'

'It was dark but she saw me. I believe she even greeted me when I was on my way out.'

'Appearance?'

'Blonde, slanted dark eyes, almost like a Chinese, seventeen or eighteen years old, with a black coat. A bit bowlegged.'

'How do you mean?'

'Like someone in the cavalry. Too many men, perhaps? Or scurvy?'

'Anything else?' Berglund makes notes.

'Dales accent. Liked Madeira wine.'

Berglund nods and makes more notes. 'The chances of finding her in our records are good. We keep the street ladies under close scrutiny.'

The door behind me opens. I do not turn around.

'Could the chief inspector come out for a moment?'

Berglund nods, closes his notebook and takes it with him when he leaves the room.

I go back to massaging my swollen knee. Even though the girls change names more frequently than their underwear, there shouldn't be a problem finding her. Even if they haven't nabbed her yet she's bound to have a couple of cautions. I lean back and sigh with relief.

'And I managed to keep the kid out of all this!' I chortle. 'Not bad going for a one-legged horse, Kvisten!'

The goons most likely didn't leave me fifteen öre for the tram when they went through the wallet. It'll be a long, cold walk home to Sibirien.

The door opens, two uniformed goons come barging in and I feel a heavy hand on my shoulder. The physical touch sends an electric flash through my head, and I breathe in abruptly.

'Harry Kvist,' Berglund says ceremoniously behind my back.

'You are hereby formally under arrest for the murder of Gunnar Zetterberg, and attempted arson. You will be transferred at once to the remand prison.'

One of the goons grabs my arm and the other takes me by the shirt collar. They get me up on my feet and turn me around, so that I'm standing eye to eye with Berglund.

'The only Vanja to be found in our registers found the Lord and became a Salvation Army soldier several years ago,' he continues, monotonously.

My mouth opens, I snatch my arm away. Berglund raises his hand.

'I don't read *Social-Demokraten*, but I find it hard to believe that there was a clue about Breitenfeldt in the crossword the day before yesterday.'

'For Christ's sake! I can't keep tags of all the crossword clues!'

'We've also telephoned both the district police superintendent in Bollnäs and the parish constable in Ovanåker to check on your statement,' Berglund goes on and adjusts his bow-tie. 'It's strange,' he says with a sudden smile, 'but there isn't and never has been a farmer by name of Elofsson in that part of the country.'

I'm shivering under the blanket. All I can hear is the continuous pacing in the corridor outside, and the wheezing of my bronchial tubes. Every time the guards get close to my sturdy cell door of green-painted wood, I raise my head and listen. The bunk is bolted to the wall. A chain hangs from an overhead eyelet and runs down the brick wall.

Apart from the table without chairs under the little window, my bunk is the only furniture in the room. The bucket by the door fills the whole cell with its stench. The sound of footsteps grows and diminishes by turns. The rules do not allow singing, whistling, or any other form of noise. Those steps are all that I have. The screws here don't use the same silent moccasins as at Långholmen.

I fumble at the back of my neck and scratch myself. The wall lice have given me a proper pummelling in the night. It's still dark outside the bars. I need a cigar. I stand up and pace about in the cell to warm myself up.

'One thing's for sure, Kvisten knows how to wait. I've never done anything else. I've waited for orders in prison and instructions at sea. For the bloke in the bunk overhead to be done with himself. Or outside the damned schnapps company with the ration book in my hand.'

My voice echoes desolately between the walls. I lie back down on the mattress stuffed with pressed sawdust. For the hundredth time I read in the gloom what's been carved into the cell door: *What one knows, no one knows. What two know, the goons know.*

A purposeful stride in the corridor stands out from the usual shuffling, coming closer and then stopping. I raise my head. There's a click when someone hits the light switch outside. I cover my eyes with the palm of my hand. The swelling under my left eye burns. The slot in the door slides open, then closes again. The substantial lock is opened with a hollow snap, like when you break some poor bastard's finger. I squint at the light, heave myself up into a sitting position with the help of the chain and slide my feet off the edge. The screw is a young lad with a sparse blond moustache. In that big hat of his, he looks like a country bumpkin, holding a plate of smooth porridge with a spoon in it.

'What's the time?'

I'm still squinting. The screw looks at me with empty eyes. I sigh and take the plate.

'Surely I have a right to half an hour of exercise in the yard? You even get that at Långholmen.'

The porridge kid checks that the door is locked behind him by tugging at the handle. I shovel down a spoonful of the lukewarm porridge. It tastes every bit as bad as I remember it. I eat with ravenous appetite.

I stand up, put the plate beside the door and go over to the dirty little window. I push the table out of the way, grab the bars on the inside of the window and pull myself onto my tiptoes. It's still dark but I can make out a hint of light on the wall out there. At Långholmen they served rye porridge made with milk at half past five. This must be later.

The remand prison is at the bottom of the police station. From here, an underground passage leads to the town court. The alley of sighs. I've walked it before. Maybe I'll be the first man facing the bar today. I scratch my back: damned lice!

The eighteenth paragraph. The homophile paragraph. They've taken me for it twice before. If I name the boy as my alibi I'll go to Långholmen either way. He would deny it to the hilt. All I have to show for our adventure in Bellevueparken is the kid's gold lighter. Hardly top-notch evidence.

And Sonja then, the tart? Sonja? Vanja? I stand up and rub my back against the wall.

'For Christ's sake, Kvist! It was Sonja.' I gave them the wrong name yesterday. I smile. No wonder they couldn't find her in the register.

I could do with a decent bath with hot water and soap. A shave is also called for. I let rip with a couple of upper cuts into the air. Kvisten won't go down so easily. Never had to take a count. A pale strip of daylight comes in through the window.

In the end, when they finally come to fetch me, they don't take me to the town court. Instead they lead me up the stairs and place me in yet another cramped interrogation room. It's furnished exactly as the last one was, and it stinks just as much of tobacco, but there are more cracks in the ceiling, and I'm fairly sure that I'm in an entirely different part of the building. My shirt sleeves are rolled up and my jacket hangs over my shoulders. The handcuffs are so tight around my wrists that my hands are throbbing. The man who makes his entrance soon after is also a new acquaintance. He's a large-hewn bloke, his face marked with smallpox scars. His black trousers finish above his ankles and his stomach oozes over his waistband. More than half of his white cuffs stick out of his jacket sleeves.

I know him from the newspapers. His name is Oskar Olsson and he's the head of the Criminal Division.

Olsson hangs his overcoat on the back of the chair and puts his bowler hat and stick on the table. I've read about that stick in a biographical portrait in *Fäderneslandet* or maybe one of the other gossip rags. Apparently it once belonged to Dahlman, the city's – and the nation's – last executioner.

The inspector runs his hand over his short, grey-speckled hair. He looks like a captain I served under, to and from La Boca. A wicked bastard whose trousers once fell down in front of the men while he was going hard at one of the young midshipmen with his belt. I wonder what it will take to make Olsson lose his trousers.

Without looking at me, he stuffs a straight-stemmed pipe with tobacco from a pack of Farmer's Blend, lights a match and gets it going.

'Your name is Harry Kvist and you're hardly an angel, are you?' The smoke dribbles from his mouth, and he points at me with the pipe stem. 'You were cautioned for an indecent and immoral act after an incident in the third-class section at the Svea Baths in 1924, and you were detained for the same crime the year after. On this occasion it concerned an incident at the old urinal near Sturegatan in Humlegården and you were ordered to pay a fine of seventy-five kronor. You have faced charges for assault on five occasions but you have only been found guilty of two of them. The first conviction was for a brawl with an abattoir worker and the second was about an intermezzo with a toilet porter at some public conveniences in Nybroplan.'

'A damned blackmailer.' I try to inhale a wreath of pipe smoke through my nose without him noticing.

'For these two episodes you served two sentences at Långholmen,' Olsson goes on, as if he hasn't heard me. 'It could have been a good deal more, because your name has turned up

57

in many more reports and investigations, mainly into assaults and intimidation, but you have been lucky. Until now.'

Olsson puts the pipe between his lips, hauls out my notebook from his inside pocket and slaps it on the table. I rub my beard stubble. Olsson removes the pipe from his mouth.

'One assumes the people in this book would have a thing or two to say about you.'

'On the second to last page you'll find the details of Zetterberg's debt. My fifteen per cent.'

'The only thing written here are the figures. All they prove is that you can't count.'

What the hell does he mean? My fists start pulsating under the table. Olsson taps the notebook with the stem of his pipe.

'Zetterberg was convicted of drunk driving on the eighteenth.'

'What of it?'

'I think you two were seeing each other. Was that why you beat him to death? Had he met someone else?'

'I never touched him. In any sense of the word.'

I force a smile. Olsson picks up his stick and strikes it hard at the table, like a schoolmaster smacking his pointer at the lectern. I try to laugh but something gets caught in my throat. A coughing fit rips at my lungs.

'Shut your mouth,' splutters Olsson. 'Do you own or have access to a short-handled axe? A so-called mason's axe?'

'Should I shut my mouth or answer the question?'

'Shut your mouth! Answer the question!'

'No, I don't even know what it is.'

'But sometimes you use weapons in your so-called work?'

'No, I believe in using my own two hands. I suppose I'm a little old-fashioned that way.' I hold up my scarred hands.

'So you don't own and have never owned a short-handled axe?'

'Absolutely I do, it's at home by my fireplace. I use it to split kindling.'

'I heard that you're limping, what's happened?'

'You should keep your boys on a shorter leash.'

'Why did you lie about Elofsson?'

'I didn't, I obviously made a mistake.'

'And the tart?'

'Got that wrong as well. Her name was Sonja, not Vanja.'

'You're changing your mind?'

'Hardly a crime, is it.'

'Do you own a brown overcoat?'

'I've already answered that. Don't you talk to each other in this construction site?'

Olsson knocks over his chair as he rises abruptly, throwing a big shadow over the table as he grabs the edge of it and shoves it against my ribs. I push my chair back and get to my feet in the nick of time. The metal cuts into my wrists as I grab the edge of the table. The jacket slips off my shoulders. Somehow I regain my balance. A sense of calm envelops me, my heart slows and transports the feeling throughout my body. I grin at him.

Olsson stares at me, keeping the extinguished pipe between his bared teeth. At any moment now he'll bite off the stem. His face is a deep scarlet. There's an absolute silence and for a moment I fancy I hear the second hand of Olsson's watch whipping along. The table vibrates with our exertions. My hands pulsate with every beat of my heart. The veins on my lower arms are swelling under my skin. The table doesn't move one way or the other.

Finally Olsson lets go and sinks down on his chair again. I do the same. The inspector is breathing heavily and his hand trembles as he tries to relight his pipe. I cough loudly. In the end he puts away both the pipe and his matches and rings the bell under the table. A constable comes in at once.

'Take the swine back to his cell,' orders Olsson and meets my eyes for the first time since our tug of war. 'Considering you're a bloody homophile you're certainly damned tough.'

A couple of hours later, evening has set in. Two uniformed goons are driving me the short distance to the crime scene. A deluge is hammering at the roof of the car and the raindrops run down the windows.

'The hell I have to go there for, and to do what, I don't know.'

'Shut it back there!'

'I never said anything.'

'Idiot.'

I have been given back my shoes, braces and overcoat, but neither wallet nor cigars. The handcuffs chafe my skin. The leather-upholstered seats creak complainingly as my lice-bitten back rubs against them.

'Hildur wants me to go with her to visit the family farm in Östergötland.'

The younger of the goons in the passenger seat is doing the talking. His thin, pointed features do not match his deep voice. Bony, well-tended hands; I noticed them when he was putting me in the cuffs.

'Don't bloody do it. It'll make it official, you know! You haven't knocked her up, have you?' The older of the two goons glances at his colleague as we drive onto Kungsbron. He has a sharp profile, a strong jaw and hooked nose.

'No bloody way! I make her drink a glass of warm stout every time.'

'And remember what I said about the squirter? They're devious, they forget. That's how they snare you. That's what my old bird did, I'd bet my right arm on it.'

Below, a fast-moving cargo train pounds out of Central Station. The locomotive sounds its whistle. We pass the covered market.

'You really believe that?'

'Mark my words. And now I'm stuck with Lilly, Anna on the side, and five snotty kids. On a police salary! No, you watch out. Watch out bloody carefully.'

The younger colleague nods as we drive past the Palladium. Between the goons' heads I see the yellow sign of the Carlton and I'm reminded of Leonard and Bellevueparken. The constable at the wheel glances at me in his rear-view mirror and raises his eyebrows at my pious smile. I lift up my hands, rub my bristles and close my eyes. The boy's touch has burned into me, in the same way that the city seal used to be branded into the foreheads of repeat offenders.

Berglund and Olsson meet us on the stairs. Both are wearing decent overcoats. Berglund's Ulster has a fur-trimmed collar and his newly polished kid-leather boots show themselves at their best against the white marble floor. He smiles and offers his hand; Olsson only raises Dahlman's stick to the brim of his bowler hat. I flinch. Olsson smiles.

'Should we free the prisoner from his handcuffs?' The older constable straightens up as he's talking.

'I think we'll leave them on for the time being,' says Olsson, stuffing his pipe. He keeps smiling. 'And you'd better come up with us as well.'

We follow the smell of smoke as we go up the stairs in silence. Berglund is polishing his glasses again.

The whole sixth floor is still sealed off. Just by the stairs, our company has to take a long step over a sizeable pool of congealed blood. From this a wide trail of blood leads to Zetterberg's door in an almost unbroken line. We stand on the other side of it, shoulder to shoulder, like a group of farmers inspecting their land.

'What do you think?'

Berglund turns round and looks at me over the rims of his glasses. Olsson looks at me over Berglund's head. Does he think I can't see him? I shrug.

'A hell of a lot of blood. Someone hit him hard on the head or cut him open with something sharp.'

'Yes.' Berglund caresses his moustache.

'He moved very slowly,' I go on. 'He crept or dragged himself to the stairs where he bled dry. Unless someone dragged him.'

'Why would someone drag him?'

'Why are you asking me?'

The two goons exchange a glance. Olsson nods towards the corridor while he strikes a match and gets his pipe going. I tighten my fists until my nails cut into my palms.

Berglund makes a gesture towards Zetterberg's flat. He and one of the older goons follow me while the other constable and Olsson stay behind. We reach the double doors. Berglund throws out his hand.

'As you can see, Kvist, there's no damage here. Possibly, Zetterberg let the perpetrator in voluntarily.'

'Possibly.' I remember how I pushed Zetterberg into the flat. The sound when he fell and dragged a chair with him.

Berglund presses down the door handle and invites me to go in first. We step into the smell of smoke. Berglund turns on the ceiling light in the hall. I feel his eyes on my back.

The floor is covered in crushed mirror glass and blood. The chair and the mirror are still lying there, overturned in the hall, but the mirror lies the other way around, with its back against the floor. Zetterberg must have crawled out from beneath it at some point. There are still some pointed shards of glass in the frame. Along one wall, large bloodstains have been ringed with chalk and, just above floor level, there's a rust-brown handprint. I point at it.

'It's Zetterberg's.' Berglund doesn't take his eyes off me.

'The blood?'

'Two different blood groups. We're working on the hypothesis that Zetterberg tried to defend himself and that the mirror was broken during the fight. The murderer cut himself on the glass, or Zetterberg caused him some kind of injury.'

'Which would rule me out, wouldn't it?'

'Yes. Unless it was a question of a nose bleed or similar?'

'You'll have to tap me for some, quite simply.'

'And if it matches the evidence?'

'I still didn't kill him.' I wonder if I dare ask Berglund for a cigarette. After all, we're supposed to be on good terms.

'Go inside,' he says. 'No need to tiptoe around. All the evidence has been secured.'

'Fingerprints?'

'A whole lot of various ones, but none on the murder weapon.'

'What did he use?'

'What makes you think it's a man?'

'That's what you said.'

Berglund doesn't answer. He gestures into the spacious apartment. I walk through the hall towards the kitchen. They asked me about an axe. What was it they called it? A mason's axe? I feel like asking if I can have a look at it.

The decent-sized kitchen lacks both a table and chairs. Most likely there's a dining area through the closed doors on our right.

The stainless steel draining board has a double sink with a splash guard of glass. The taps suggest the sod had it piped in both hot and cold. On the draining board are a couple of big cognac balloons. On an enamelled shelf there's a washing-up brush and a yellow dishcloth. There is also a pair of horn-rimmed spectacles. When I met Zetterberg he wasn't wearing them. Maybe the murderer rinsed himself off here and then forgot them?

'Did Zetterberg wear glasses?'

'We haven't any confirmation about that as yet.'

The kitchen wall around the gas cooker has been scorched by the fire. The flames have consumed a good part of the cork mat and also licked at the wall on the other side, apparently without really taking hold.

'Here the murderer makes a mistake,' says Berglund and holds up an empty, unmarked, glass bottle. 'Do you know what this is?'

'Paraffin oil?'

'That is probably exactly what the murderer thought when he started the fire to get rid of the evidence.' Berglund smiles and peruses me over his spectacles. 'In actual fact it is carbolineum, not a very flammable liquid. It burns, but not very well.'

I shrug again. Outside the kitchen window the rain is belting down. Increasingly it's looking like a proper autumn storm.

I hope I'll be allowed to see the other rooms in the apartment, but the two goons turn back into the hall and head for the door. On the way, Berglund stops and turns to me.

'We found a twenty-five öre coin here on the telephone. Possibly the murderer's excuse could have been that he wanted to use it to make a call.'

He scrutinises me again. Lord knows what he's after.

'But the bloodstains are much closer to the front door,' I object. 'It doesn't look as if they got this far.'

'Maybe Zetterberg stayed here during the phone call, and was then beaten to death?'

I look around the hall for a moment before I stride up to the door. The frame of the door has a deep gash in it at the top. I point at it.

'The inspector is mistaken,' I say. 'The murderer had hardly come into the hall before he raised his axe.' I look around the vestibule, and slide my hand across the overcoats. 'Did you find any clothes hangers in the hall?'

Without waiting for an answer I open the door and go into the corridor. Berglund quickly tails me. I crack my finger joints.

'Yes, it's being checked for fingerprints at the Central Agency but we haven't had an answer yet. How did you know?'

'I'd swear on a huge pile of Bibles that there was a camel-hair overcoat hanging there when I came to visit,' I tell him as we're walking down the stairs.

Outside in the illuminated circle under the streetlight, Olsson is waiting in the pouring rain with the extinguished pipe in his mouth and my hat in his hand. I'll have to have it re-pressed.

I turn up my collar. The street is empty but for a bloke swaying back and forth as he stands there thoughtfully counting in his wallet. You know the weather's bad when Kungsgatan is deserted on the maids' Saturday off.

'Now for some gymnastics,' Olsson half yells to make himself heard over the wind. 'Put on your hat and run down to Vasagatan, then turn left and stop by the constable.'

'Hold up, now,' I say. 'What's the idea?'

The wind knocks down a couple of potted plants that someone has put out on the window ledge, and the pots slam into the street ten metres from us. The weathervane is spinning so fast that its screeching has turned to a constant wail.

'We need to reconstruct the getaway with you in the central role.'

'The conditions are hardly the same,' I call out and point at the streetlight outside Zetterberg's house. 'It was dark that evening, it was like looking up a chimney sweep's arse.'

'Something you must have done scores of times,' says Olsson.

He looks at the streetlight before he lifts his stick and crushes both the lampshade and the bulb with a well-directed blow. Fine shards of glass rain over us. Berglund gives Olsson a look and brushes himself off.

'Are you as careless as that with Dahlman's stick?' I venture.

'Dahlman's stick? Like hell,' the large-hewn inspector calls out, before adding: 'I only use it on Sundays.' We stand in silence for a few moments.

'I need to smoke,' I holler through the bad weather and look around.

A few floors up in the house opposite, a bloke stands in a window looking up at the dark sky, but before long he turns back into his flat. Cold rainwater finds its way inside my collar and runs down my neck. The lice bites sting.

'Your position,' Berglund snorts with irritation, 'is hardly one in which you can start making demands. Surely it's in your own interest to clear your name?'

'I also want to wash myself down and shave.'

'We can take care of it,' Olsson interjects. 'That's not too much to ask, is it, Alvar?'

Berglund removes his steamed-up spectacles, squints, and then puts the spectacles back on again.

'As long as you run, so we can leave this place,' he cries, getting out a pack of Carat from his inside coat pocket and handing it over.

I shake out a cigarette. Olsson offers me a light. I shudder as I smoke slowly, the cigarette held between my thumb and forefinger so that the glowing ember is shielded from the rain while I'm looking around. The drunk is still rifling through his wallet in the middle of the street. An open invitation to be robbed if I ever saw one.

The shards of glass from the streetlight crunch under my feet. They make me run four times before they're satisfied. When I limp back panting after the last pass, I can finally see what I've been trying to understand since we came out of the front door: in the house opposite Zetterberg's, a curtain moves in a dimly lit window.

'So that's where you are, you bastard.'

'What the hell are you on about, Kvist?'

'Nothing.'

Someone has seen the murderer leaving the crime scene. There's a witness.

When I was pushed back against the ropes for the first time, my old trainer yelled at me that closing your eyes didn't make it hurt less. I was a newcomer in the ring, but already sparring with heavier and tougher lads, and sometimes I tried to dig myself in by putting up my guard.

I only wake when the key is inserted into the lock. It's a cold morning in the cell. I've draped my jacket over the blanket but I'm so cold that I'm shivering. The same screw as yesterday brings me similarly smooth porridge. I don't look up but I take the bowl. I shiver so violently that it's difficult to eat.

I think about the trainer's words while I'm eating. He was right. In actual fact, it hurts even more when you close your eyes. That's when the memories ambush you, run riot while you lie sleeping. Some things cannot be gotten rid of; they stay with you as stubbornly as ash in the pores of a stoker.

I swallow down the last spoonful of cold porridge. I am already missing Långholmen, missing the company and the work. There's not such a difference between life at sea and life in prison: both places harbour a gang of blokes in similar clothes who do as they're told. From time to time you find someone whose warmth you can bask in, and no one raises an eyebrow about it. As long as I managed to keep out of the metal cages of the isolation cells in the cellars, life was much better on the island than here.

'Better tuck, lovely lads.'

I stretch and yawn. The key is re-inserted into the lock. The goon, roaring at me to follow him, doesn't require me to put on handcuffs.

'By no means have you been ruled out of the investigation,' Olsson informs me without looking up as I enter the little interrogation chamber. He has three thick piles of paper in front of him. At the top of one is a photograph. It's impossible to see what it features. Olsson looks up and follows the direction of my gaze.

'Sometimes I'm still surprised when I see how much blood there is inside a bloke.'

I remember the first time I was made aware of it myself. It was in the port of Cherbourg, just a few months before I was paid off for the last time. There was a strike and we couldn't unload the cargo. I was hanging about on the ship's railing. A fresh, salt-spattered breeze was making the flags flutter. Much further down on the quay, a couple of stevedores had got hold of a scab. They were working him over hard with their loading hooks. They stood in a ring around him, someone rolled a cigarette, and the scab bled dry. A couple of sturdy blokes hooked him in the back and dragged him off towards a crane. Behind him ran a wide rivulet of blood. Soon he was swinging by his feet under the crane.

I flinch when Olsson clears his throat. He slides a card across the table.

'Speaking of blood, we have to take some of yours, but then you're free to go. Currently we're working on the hypothesis that you were the last person, apart from the murderer, to meet Zetterberg. Call me if something occurs to you about your meeting.'

I take the card and pocket it. 'So the witness freed me?'

'If you mean the street girl, we never found her, not a Vanja and not a Sonja either.'

'You know who I mean.'

'Don't call me unless it's for a good reason. I don't like you.'

I walk through the monotonous corridors of the police station to the Anti-Smuggling Section at the other end. This temporary specialised task force is expected to track down home-distilled wares from the northern parts of the country and smuggled spirit from the east. At the same time, the section manages now and then to close down the odd drinking dive, preferably the sort of place frequented by nonces, communists and artists. With all its points of entry, harbours and long quays, Stockholm is in fact quite impossible to keep under control. The Anti-Smuggling Section always makes its raids when the big syndicates are getting some competition from a lesser newcomer. Anyone with any insight into the business knows this.

In the heart of the section is a table several metres long. On either side of it are five chairs. Three desk goons, all with their ties undone, sit there pushing papers.

My old friend Johan Hessler isn't at all happy to see me. The constable in charge of the Anti-Smuggling Section is the sort of bloke that most women would describe as handsome. His thick, dark hair is carefully tended, with a centre parting. He has one of those small, ridiculous moustaches like Ronald Colman. Certain members of the police corps must find his facial hair too daring, but every button of his blue uniform is well polished, as are his shoes. I think his main task is to pose with what they've seized for the newspapers.

When I come in, Hessler stops what he's doing and stands up abruptly. Without greeting me, he grabs me by the arm and bundles me into an adjoining cubbyhole. The room is filled with bookshelves and dusty boxes. It smells like a dry sauna at a gentlemen's Turkish bath. The door closes heavily behind us.

'What the hell are you doing here?' Hessler's voice is an octave higher than usual. 'I heard they put you up for Kungsgatan? And look at the state of you!'

'I was in the house. Visiting an old friend.'

'When did they release you?'

'Just now. A witness wouldn't cooperate.'

'You seem to get out of trouble that way at regular intervals.'

'It happens.'

Hessler lowers his voice. 'So there's a witness?'

'There are more. Among others a tart, Sonja, but they can't find her.'

'Shouldn't be so hard.'

'Precisely.' I stroke my beard stubble. 'Make a note of it! I have to know if they find her.'

'But that's on the first floor.'

'Don't you have a notebook?'

'I don't know what's going on up there.'

'A goon without a notebook. Listen carefully: her name was Sonja, you got it? In case they find her. A bit of public insight into the investigation wouldn't do any harm.'

Hessler looks around the minimal space and shifts his weight from one leg to another. 'I do have a notebook.'

'Well, then! Sleuth around a bit and call me at Lundin's in a couple of days.'

Hessler goes on walking on the spot as if he needs a pee. Most likely he doesn't. I take a step towards the door, but he clutches my elbow.

'Harry,' he whispers. 'It's been so long since I could stay the night with you.'

I prise his fingers off. It's not so difficult. 'Sleuth around. Call me when you've come up with something.'

I leave the door open when I walk out. 'By no means have you been ruled out of the investigation.' I laugh to myself. I'll show the bastards. I'm not only going to clear my name, I'll make it clear to them who's the best snooper. I've tracked down whores many times before.

I'll present Sonja to them before evening has fallen. The easiest way of catching a moth is in daylight, when it lies sleeping.

The water in the big saucepan on the wood-burning stove is slowly coming to the boil. I close my right eye. A half-extinguished cigar is wedged in the corner of my mouth. I slap banknotes onto the table. Count them a second time. The money is still here, as well as the Husqvarna pistol – etched with the navy's K.Fl. stamp – in its hiding place in the wardrobe. The long arm of the law has kept its inept paws away for a change. The poor man sleeps more soundly.

The AGA radio is switched on, at high volume. In a lifeless voice, the radio announcer reads out the names of all those who have contributed to the Christmas collection for the city's poor. I drag the saucepan off the stove and slosh most of its contents into the big bathing tub. It is already half filled with cold water. My clothes are left in a lousy little pile on the kitchen floor as I step in, a brush in one hand. St Stefan's church bells strike once, and before the reverberations have completely ebbed away, St Johannes answers in its deep timbre, like the last punch in a perfect left-right combination.

I soap myself, work over the tattoo of the full-rigger on my chest and continue scrubbing under the water. My skin smarts wherever the brush works its way. The lice bites burn. I massage my scalp with liquid soap and rinse my hair with the help of the saucepan. I forget that I have a Meteor in my mouth. I put down the saucepan and spit the cigar onto the draining board.

Cooking fumes with several different and competing smells find their way into the flat. I fancy I can distinguish mashed turnips and fried herring, pork sausage and meatballs. I smack my lips. There's a firm knock on the door. It opens with a click, then closes.

Lundin comes into the kitchen. Not only does he come and go as he pleases, he also lets in potential clients if I'm not at home. Doesn't want me to lose out on the dough, he says.

I stand up, the water dripping off me, and snatch up a towel by the draining board. Lundin takes a few big strides and sits at the kitchen table. He removes his top hat, puts it on the chair beside him, brushes off the crown of his head and folds his hands in his lap. I take the cold, hard lice comb and bend over the draining board. My scalp is smarting from the soaping it got earlier. One by one, the lice drop audibly onto the metal.

'Your eye looks like a tram headlight.'

'I feel as if I ran into one.'

'You always said they started calling you Kvisten – twig – because you were tall and lanky.'

'For a boxer, yes. That's ten years and ten kilos ago.'

'I had breakfast ready this morning.'

'I was in the clink.'

The water spills over the edge when I pull the tub towards the table. I take the paddle strop, the cut-throat razor with the mother-of-pearl hilt, and the mirror, and sit opposite Lundin. A few brown grains of lip-snuff stand out against his white collar. The seat of the wooden chair feels rough under my buttocks, but the badger hairs are soft against my cheeks.

73

I put the mirror in front of me. Droplets of water in my chest hair make the full-rigger sparkle. My eye is red; the swelling beneath has a colour scheme of yellows and purples.

'Also yesterday.'

Lundin runs his finger over his moustache. The wad of banknotes on the table flexes under his hand when he gently presses it. I put the strop against my knee and sharpen the blade. The whispering changes tone as I roll the knife onto its back at the end of every movement.

'I was inside.'

'Stockholm – Motala,' crackles the radio voice.

'Eggs on both occasions. And sausage the day before yesterday.'

Lundin puts on his hat again. Carefully I test the edge of the knife against my thumb. It'll do for shaving. Also for castrating piglets, in case the need arises. The blade rasps against cheeks, upper lip and throat. At the end of every pass I flick the stubble and shaving soap into the bathing tub, which I have placed at my feet.

'I hope you ate mine as well.'

I remove the razor from my throat so I can cough. The radio voice is giving ski-wax tips for the winter holiday in the mountains.

'I'll have to make a note of it.' Lundin stands up.

'Obviously.'

I bend over the bathing tub and rinse my face. I snort and blow my nose into my fingers.

'It'll have to be noted down. What else is there to do?'

'Please do note it down.'

I dig out a good scoop of Fandango from the jar and pull my fingers through my hair. The pomade smells of sandalwood.

Lundin nods at me as he disappears out the door. He lowers his head as he crosses the threshold, to avoid knocking his hat against the top of the door frame.

I go into the wardrobe and get out my best suit. It's a black, three-piece number. Herzog himself, the tailor on Biblioteksgatan, sewed it for me a couple of years ago. I keep it for funerals and other cheery occasions. So far I have only used it once. I put on a white shirt and make a knot in a gleaming tie of deep red silk. I put the Viking timepiece with the gold chain in my waistcoat. I fold up yesterday's copy of *Social-Demokraten* and put it in my overcoat pocket.

I go into the kitchen, count out ten five-kronor bills and put them in my wallet. I wrap the cell clothes in newspaper and tuck the package under my arm. Whistling Ernst Rolf's 'I'm Out Whenever My Old Girl's In', I leave the flat. On my keyring is the key to my left-hand-drive Buick, which broke down this summer.

At this time of year, the heat and steam from the Roslag laundry on the other side of the street collide with the colder air and wrap our part of the block in a fine mist. The three-point mark of vagrants, scratched with a needle into the brass plate on the door, announces that there are no coins to be had here, but certainly the odd sandwich for someone in need. A little bell on the door tinkles. I'm enveloped by the harsh stench of ammonia.

'Well, if it isn't Kvisten!' Beda slaps her wrinkly hands together and sways from side to side behind the counter of dark wood that divides the premises in two. 'Pay attention, Petrus, hold the door open for our customer!' She wipes her hands on her apron and gesticulates wildly.

Petrus, her son, is posted with a broom in a corner, as usual. He's the sort of unfortunate that everyone addresses by his first name, a large bloke of about my own age, with a sheepish smile under his blond fringe. As deaf as an artilleryman. He puts down his broom and makes a few slow movements towards me, but then stops halfway, blushing and staring down at the floor. Beda rushes into action, opens a hatch in the counter and frees me of the clothes I've brought.

'Don't pay any attention to Petrus! He arrived with his back end first but he's a good soul and he usually does as he's told. He can sweep and put sheets through the mangle as well.'

She puts the laundry on the counter and starts arranging it.

'It doesn't matter.' I fish a cigar out of my pocket and light it. Soon the laundry has been separated into three piles. I toss the gold lighter into the air and catch it. She turns to me.

'Oh, and you see, last night we had a visit from his grace the King himself, me and Petrus.'

'Again?'

'Yes, and you'd stand there with your hat off, wouldn't you? If you met his grace the King?'

'Kvisten doesn't take off his hat for anybody.'

I wink at Petrus. He can't possibly have heard me, but he blushes again. I think he likes blokes. Beda gets out a pen and a receipt book. She spits at the pen and closes one eye while she's writing.

'Yes, and you see, His Majesty praised me so much about my graceful feet and then he took Petrus out for a spin in his impressive car!'

'Sounds like quite something.' I take the receipt she gives me, putting it in my wallet and tapping my cigar ash into my hand.

'Yes, and I had nothing to offer him when they came back.' Her hands, chapped after all the years of working with the laundry vats, make a dry, rustling sound when she rubs them together.

'Oh well,' I say, with a hand on the door handle. 'There'll probably be other opportunities.' I start to whistle again and the bell rings.

'When he whistles, Old Nick shakes his behind,' Beda calls out after me as I go outside, onto the pavement.

The cold spell keeps the city in its silent, deadly embrace. A few flimsy brown leaves sweep across the big playground outside the grammar school. They look as if they've been cut from the crepe paper Lundin uses to wrap his contraband. Heavy trams whine across the sidings by Norra Bantorget. I try to stamp some life into my feet.

The slightly famous hotdog man at the south-eastern end of the grammar school playground is wearing a hat with earmuffs and straw-stuffed clogs. Even so, his dentures rattle in his mouth as he counts out the change from a little unica box. He was run down in this very spot by no less than Prince Adolf Fredrik himself, when the heir to the throne skidded in his sports car a couple of winters ago.

The sausage tastes like any other. I eat it while I push my Rambler towards Kungsgatan. I forgot my gloves. The wooden handles are cold and the air stings the back of my hands. It's about to start snowing, I can smell it.

I park the bicycle outside Zetterberg's house, then pick up my notebook and write down the address of the house opposite. There's no elevator and I have to walk all the way up to the top floor. I start with the neighbour. That is how things should be done – in roundabout ways. In the olden days I liked pedalling about, watching my adversaries from a distance. Sooner or later they opened themselves up, in pure frustration. *Boxing Monthly!* described my style as 'elegant' but that was not why I danced around like that. Anyone can knock out an opponent, but only a technician can take a bloke's heart away from him.

I hear the sound of high heels. The draught of air when the door is opened is loaded with sweet perfume.

'Yes?' The lady in the doorway has a cropped hairstyle, an even shorter skirt and the shortest imaginable tone of voice. A string of pearls is wrapped around her neck.

'Police.' I push Olsson's card under her nose. She doesn't look at it. Her hand rests on the door frame. Her nails are clean, with no black edges. 'As you may know there was an accident in the house opposite last Tuesday.'

My stomach is growling. The sausage didn't do much good.

'Yes?'

Does she think I'm a beggar? Can't she see my suit for herself? I pocket the card and take out my notebook.

'Did you see anything out of the ordinary on Tuesday night?'

'I don't understand why you have to come here all the time, asking the same questions.'

'Please be good enough to answer.'

'My husband invited me to the cinema and dinner and we came home quite late. The kitchen maid was at home but her window faces the inside yard. So, no, apart from Marlene Dietrich, I didn't see anything out of the ordinary. And to be honest, I can't see what's so extraordinary about Dietrich either.'

'So nothing to report, then?'

'Have a word with Olivia next door. She's a widow, always sits in the window.'

'Thank you, I will.'

She shuts the door right in my face. Her fragrance hovers in the corridor. I turn to the next door. It says 'Trysell' on the brass placard. I knock and wait. Always at home? I hammer until the door's fixtures are rattling. The letterbox squeaks, I listen: nothing. She's not opening. I make a note in my notebook and leave the building.

It's time to track down bowlegged Sonja. Locating a whore is not as simple as people seem to think. The girls are careful: they change names and addresses more often than their drawers and use a legion of code words. Some turn around the number badges of their telephones to stop the Johns working out who they are when they come visiting. Others stuff their doorbells with paper so neighbours don't complain to the assistant landlords about all the movement at night. But they don't fool me. I know all their tricks.

As we're dealing with a street whore here, I may as well give the brothels of Old Town a miss. I'll start on Kungsgatan and gradually widen my circuits like a bloodhound. Every place in Klara with a telephone is worth a visit. If I don't get a bite there, I'll have to take on the hostels and salesmen's hotels on Norra Smedjegatan. The five-kronor bills in my wallet should come in handy. Most people in Klara are willing to sell out a tart for a fiver.

The cold immediately bites my skin when I walk out of the door. The shops and restaurants along Kungsgatan are all lit up. I know as of old which of these establishments have telephones and which of them I can skip.

I start with Restaurant Dussinet a bit further up the street and re-enter the warmth. Inside the door is a little room with a few clothes rails, watched over by a smart cloakroom girl. Above an arch in red granite leading into the dining room hangs a large painting depicting a bareheaded Charles XII. The warrior king stands straight-backed before his army. Behind him are officers, standard bearers and soldiers.

A muted hum of voices is streaming out of the dining room. I glimpse the end of an American-style bar in the gloomy, smoky room. A bloke with thinning hair sits on a stool, his elbows resting on the counter. A waitress dressed in matt black silk and a white apron stands on duty under the arch. She curtsies and sniffs.

I turn to the girl in the cloakroom. She's a pale-faced lass in her late teens with plenty of padding around her rump and bust. The sound of clinking glasses penetrates the buzz of voices inside the restaurant. One or two of them are celebrating Friday night in advance. I hold out my card.

'A police matter. Do you have a telephone?'

'Further inside, in the booth on the right.'

'No, dearie, I was only wondering. Tell me, I'm looking for a girl by name of Sonja. Not a guest, necessarily, but possibly someone who comes in now and then to use the telephone. A beautiful, ample girl like you, just under twenty.'

'The telephone is only for paying guests.'

The cloakroom girl looks down at her shoes. The frail cough of the waitress rings out against the background noise. She tries to keep it in check and her shoulders jerk. My stomach growls again.

'Maybe a little slovenly in her dress?'

'We're not allowed to let people use the telephone, not even if they offer to pay. The director has put his foot down.'

'Thank you, then.'

I make a gesture towards the brim of my hat and look into the dining room again. I rub my chin. I could allow myself a tot to warm up before I carry on.

Slightly warmed up, I go back into the streets with Olsson's card at the ready. I limp between restaurants, betting shops, workshops, tobacconists and telegram offices. All premises with a telephone are paid a visit. I talk to morose waitresses, bar managers with soiled white aprons, and suspicious workers. The temperature quickly drops even lower. The bells of St Clara keep a check of each quarter-hour.

By the time the trams are filling up with workers it's no longer a good idea to use the card; the streets of Klara change character once the day shift knocks off and the night shift begins. The smuggling syndicates have control of the city's suburbs but there's still open war in Klara. Anyone with a bit of hair on his chest can try to take over the entry of home-distilled and Estonian vodka. Many have tried but so far none have succeeded. Sooner or later they are found carelessly buried in Lill-Jansskogen or with chains wrapped round their feet in Barnhusviken, where they have been dumped out of sight behind the railways embankment opposite the old lunatic asylum. It's not as bad as it was five or ten years ago, but it still happens from time to time.

I continue through the beer cafés with their stale smell of spilled pilsner and large-bodied, seasoned waitresses who like to give customers a thump on the back with each order. I throw my lot in with the artists, communists and temporary workers. No one has heard of Sonja. Finally I pay a visit to the shacks that house Klara's unlicensed drinking dens. I pull aside thick leather drapes that protect against the December wind and speak with whores and beggars. Their intoxication is already like a thick veil over their eyes. I envy them, but my work won't allow me to follow their example. When talking to a tart or a waitress I rely on my natural charm, my best suit, and a sob story about a missing sister. With bookies or beggars, I have to sacrifice a five-kronor note; with promises of more of the same to come and Lundin's telephone number, I leave them shaking their heads. I tick off the addresses in my contacts book.

I have just come out from a newspaper vendor's place at the far end of Gamla Brogatan when I catch sight of a full-figured woman walking with a graceless gait along the pavement. She is only about ten metres from me. The coat is different, it's longer, but her motion is that of Sonja.

I kill the cigar under my heel. My steps hammer against the pavement. My frozen-stiff feet start thawing out.

When I have almost caught up with her, she turns. Her eyes, two white buoys with a bottle-green top, are about to pop from their sockets. The wrinkles around them are stretched out. She hunches up and raises her handbag with both hands. Her light-brown leather gloves are clutching it hard. She makes a panting sound.

I stop abruptly.

'I'm so sorry, I thought you were someone else,' I tell her.

The middle-aged woman backs away a couple of steps without taking her eyes off me, then crosses the street and hurries off. I watch her for a long time before I raise my eyes towards the sky. Not a star in sight. I sigh.

'You know what, Kvisten, it's time for some chow. You've earned it, you ugly sod.'

My stomach answers. It dins like a ship's boiler.

It's half past seven. I'm sitting in the third-class section of the Restaurant Pilen, opposite the Savoy Hotel. On the plate in front of me are the remains of a potato and anchovy bake. I am eating pureed pears with cream, and drinking coffee. The white tablecloth is pierced by cigarette burns in a couple of places. The premises offers some thirty similar tables with four chairs around each. There's a small number of diners and the sound level is still low. Up in the cross vaults hang simple, round lamps that spread a warm light over the tile floor.

The newspaper lies open on the table. I brush some cigar ash from the foreign news section. General von Schleicher seems about to be made Chancellor in Berlin; Göring will become the

Parliamentary Speaker. The annual emigration quota for America of 3314 Swedes is far from filled, even though we're in December.

I look out of the window. Just imagine leaving this cold, dark land behind. That had been my intention. More or less everything but my signature was ready on the professional contract when I took a wrong step. But it's too late. My last ship has long since slipped its moorings.

A white cat has taken cover from the bad weather under a parked Ford, also from the catapults of gangland boys. I think about Sonja. I wonder if that's her real name. Probably not.

'Strange that no one's seen the lass anyway.' My voice disappears into the empty air.

Ten years earlier I could quite simply have gone down to the whore agency in Old Town and bribed the registrar with a half-litre bottle of schnapps to get every imaginable bit of information about her. Now more footwork is needed, and more five-kronor notes. And I have painful feet and a painful lack of five-kronor notes.

A cycle courier pedals past on a Monark with a box on the front. It's a two-year-old model. The white cat sticks out its nose from under the car outside and carefully sniffs the air. I roll up a piece of anchovy in a page of the notebook, put it in my pocket and go to the cashier to pay before fetching my overcoat.

'I don't know her but I know someone who does.' The shabby cloakroom attendant stares at the folded-up five-kronor note I hold up between my thumb and finger. He's a big bloke with a grubby collar and gold-coloured buttons on his coat. His hair is slicked back, and his eyes are hungover slits under his bushy eyebrows. His tongue flicks quickly over his thick lips. He glances into the restaurant.

'Well?'

'The night porter next door here. At the Boden Hotel,' he whispers.

'Name?'

'Petersén. Like the hockey player.'

'What does he look like?'

'Short, skinny sort, thinning hair. Sometimes he comes here to eat before his shift starts at eight.'

'And you're sure he knows Sonja?'

'She's been here many times. Bandy-legged girl from the Dales.' He leans towards me and lowers his voice. 'He lets her stay over if it's not fully booked.'

'At a price?' I offer him the fiver and he snatches it.

'Nothing's free.' He smiles.

I haul out my timepiece and make a couple of quick decisions. 'I'll go around the corner and wait. If he comes here first, maybe you can come and get me?' I hold up the wallet. He nods so eagerly that his oiled hair rises from his bald pate and stands on end.

The cold hits me as I open the door. I bend down, unfold the bit of paper and throw the piece of fish under the Ford. There's a click at the base of my spine when I straighten up. Just as I turn into Klara Norra the first snow of the year starts falling with large, downy flakes. I cross the cobblestones and take up a position outside the pawnbroker's place next to Café Leoparden. From here I have a view into the hotel vestibule on the other side. There's a hollow thump as a porter throws chunks of wood into the firewood hatch of the house on my left. Overhead, someone is quickly winching in slips and torn sheets on a washing line hanging across the poorly lit street. A shaggy tramp looks up at the sky with concern and hurries his limping steps.

I turn around and see my reflection in the barred window of the pawnshop. The shiner under my eye is illuminated when I light my cigar. In the window, wedding rings, typewriters, necklaces, pocket watches and other heirlooms are lined up on a white cloth. I straighten my tie knot, take a couple of quick drags and mumble at my reflection: 'You can bloody wait. You hardly ever did much else.'

The porter hurries off with his wheelbarrow. An ash-grey light from the hotel vestibule falls across the pavement. Big snowflakes fill the narrow, dark gap between the houses. I haven't bothered asking in the many hotels around Central Station. The staff are usually good at identifying the girls, and don't even let them in if they are dragging along a big suitcase. Sonja is smart, keeps a low profile. When all this is over, maybe I'll invite her for a glass of Madeira.

A man in white spats, a dark overcoat and light grey scarf hurries up to me. He has the same ridiculous moustache as Senior Constable Hessler. The snowflakes are hitting his black top hat, where they dissolve into velvety, gleaming patches. He takes a big stride onto the pavement and tugs at the door handle of the pawnbroker, then sighs and stamps at the ground. The brim of his hat is worn. There's a red-brown stain on his scarf.

'Excuse me, sir,' he says. He speaks in some southern accent. I blow a plume of smoke into the night. The man shakes his head with a doleful look. 'What bloody rotten luck.'

'That's often how it goes.'

'You see, my wallet got stolen. Just as the hotel bill was going to be paid.'

'Get lost.'

'But look here, my wedding ring, it's worth at least five hundred, you can keep it as surety.'

'Get lost.'

Oldest trick in the book. The man paces about for a while, before he crosses the street and stands in a door on the other side. He glares at me. I pick up my newspaper and leaf through it.

I've smoked about half of my cigar and I'm standing there stamping some life into my frozen-stiff feet when I see a little bloke in a sports cap come jogging along. Apart from the trickster opposite, the street is deserted. I peer up at St Clara's new copper roof. It's five to. It's got to be Petersén. A lightweight. I can definitely save myself five kronor by going in hard. When it comes to unpaid debts there are advantages in holding back, but not with information. As long as you keep them conscious and alive, everything is allowed. I open my overcoat, my best suit underneath.

I go towards him. Once we've passed each other I quickly cross the street and come up behind him. He's a head shorter than me. The sound of my finger joints cracking as I straighten them is so loud that he stops and turns around. I flick his cap off his head. He's almost completely bald. The crown of his head is soft as baby soap. I toss the cap under a car as if I'm skimming a stone. The bloke gawks, opens his eyes wide and curls his upper lip. He has a weak mouth, a girl's mouth. I take a drag on my cigar and blow the smoke into his eyes. He blinks.

'Didn't your mummy teach you about going bareheaded when it's snowing?' I hiss.

He looks stupefied. I have a hard time stopping myself from bursting out laughing. With my left hand I grab him by the chin and whack him into the wall. I puff a few times on my cigar and move the glowing tip so close to his eyes that his eyelashes start curling up.

'Sonja?'

He yells and makes a proper racket. I'm glad there aren't a lot of people about. I move my hand down. The yell turns to a croak.

'Sonja?'

I puff gently at the glow and gently brush his ear with it. He wriggles about.

'The next time I'll take out your whole eye.'

The stench of his burnt eyelashes is more or less like the slaughterman singeing a pig. I give Petersén such a slap that the sparks fly all around us. His nose springs a leak. An old bat overhead opens a window and threatens to call the police if we don't keep the noise down. The man, who's almost wilting in my grip, pees himself. I feel I'm about to lose my temper. I blow on the cigar again. The glow lights up his face – it's scarlet like the mug of the uniformed goon who patrols the third-class section at the Sture baths.

I release my grip.

'Yes,' says the porter, tears hanging discordantly in his voice. 'I know her. I know Sonja.'

'Sonja,' I say for the third time. 'Where is she?'

The little hotel room is stained yellow with tobacco tar. The furniture consists of a bed, a secretaire with a matching chair, and an armchair next to a little side table. A lighter square on the dark floorboards indicates that there was once a rug. The walls are hung with everyday pictures, city motifs. I sit in the armchair. In the ashtray the cigar smoulders like a discharged weapon. Petersén sits on the bed with one hand on his wet knee. The handkerchief he presses to his nose is red with blood. He's pale as a deckhand during his first proper storm. The type that has to be lashed down a few times before he learns to cope.

'That I don't know.' He blinks unceasingly. 'Is she…? Does she owe you money?'

I sigh. 'I just want to talk to her.'

'Everyone wants to talk to her, but she doesn't want to talk to anyone.'

'When did you see her last?'

'That must have been…' The porter pauses briefly. 'Three or four days ago. She came by in the evening. She needed money.'

'What day was that?'

'It must have been Monday. I'd been to the barber's in the afternoon. She thought my hair looked nice.'

Petersén caresses his bald head. I leaf through my notebook. That was the day I visited Zetterberg. The gold lighter clicks, I fire some life into the cigar. The night porter straightens up.

'That suits you better.'

'She was in a right state. She needed money. For Doctor Jensen up in Katarina.'

I chuckle.

The porter looks down at the rug, mumbling, 'She said it was mine.'

'Obviously.'

'She's very careful about that. With the others. Guaranteed rubbers, you know? Royals? We're a bit special, the two of us. More like a couple.' He clears his throat and spits out a reddish lump into the handkerchief.

'She's a beautiful lass. Must pull in quite a penny.'

'It was very urgent.'

'What happened?'

'I borrowed money from the till and went to the bank the next day.'

'And?'

'She was staying at the Pension Comforte but she's not there any more. I've telephoned.'

'Might she have gone back to the Dales?'

For a moment the porter looks bewildered. 'No… she's as much of a native here as myself. Her mother and father moved down from Rättvik twenty years ago. The dialect is just something she does. She's very cautious by nature.'

I push back my hat with my forefinger. The stench of urine is slowly filling the little room.

'Are they alive?'

'I think so. Her father is a carpenter on Bondegatan.'

I pick up my indelible pencil, spit on it, and make a note.

'Bondegatan is a long street.'

'Sorry, that's all I know, unfortunately.' The bloke gives me a guarded look through one eye. 'Were you… were you involved?'

'Nothing like that.'

'No, she said I was special.'

'Bloody right you're special. My daughter was potty-trained at two. You look like you're forty but you still need diapers.'

'I have problems with my nerves. I'm worried about how she's feeling. Do you think she's resting up somewhere? Or might something have gone wrong?'

'How do you mean?'

'With Jensen.'

It takes a while before I understand what he's talking about. I nod listlessly, take a last pull on the cigar and mash it in the ashtray. The porter crumples slightly. I turn the pages of my notebook. Suddenly it dawns on me. My heart does a somersault and for a moment I think I'm ready for one of Lundin's coffins. I fly to my feet. The man in front of me makes a panting sound and protects his head with his hands.

'When exactly did she come by the last time? Think – it's important!'

The porter exhales at length. Slowly he lowers his guard. 'It was just after the other staff had gone home, because I was on my own here. They finish at nine.'

The time. What did Berglund say during the interrogation? So that was why she was keeping out of the way. Surely it had been about eight or nine?

'She was in a state, you say?'

'She had every reason to be.'

The porter sticks to his story, but I feel even more certain: Sonja saw something that made her need money immediately. I was probably not the only person she ran into that night. Either she has left the city, or she's holed up somewhere. Everyone wants to talk to Sonja.

'I'm an old-school, stubborn type,' I say as I write down Lundin's number in the notebook. 'People aren't made now like they used to be. Take Johnsson, who had the Oden-Bazaar on the corner of Roslagsgatan. You know about him? Old man Johnsson, I mean, not his dish-rag boys, they're not worth much. In all I think I had to visit him three times about a debt, and I made a mess of him every time.'

The porter jumps when I tear out the page.

'The third time he paid but he never really came back after that. We run into each other all the time. He limps and he's got a stutter. The bloke is cock-eyed, put it like that.' I give him the telephone number. 'Call me if you see her. You don't want to run into me again.'

The little man nods, then shakes his head.

I point my forefinger at him and repeat: 'You don't want to run into me again.'

'Tell her I'm waiting here if you find her,' he calls out after me as I go towards the door. 'Tell her she can count on me!'

I shake my head. On the way out I take a couple of quick foxtrot steps. The gong has sounded. The match has started. No one is cheering.

The wet snow is not yet settling on Klara Norra Kyrkogata. The clotheslines are empty. I fold up my collar and shove my hands deep in my coat pockets. Outside the pawnshop stands the man with the top hat. A fool of a peasant with his trousers tucked into his high boots is scrutinising the ring he holds out. I walk the short distance to Kungsgatan at a brisk pace.

The tower window of Olivia Trysell, the widow, is lit up, but the assistant landlord has locked the doors for the evening. At a loss, I stand with my bicycle in front of the house where Zetterberg died. For a few moments I stare at the spot where his signet ring hit the pavement when they almost dropped the corpse.

The air is saturated with the smell of lignite and burning birch wood. Probably all of Stockholm has got its wood-burners and ceramic stoves going at the same time. For several months, the sooty black emissions of industry will mix with the yellowish smoke of coal and the ash-grey fumes of wood smoke. Chimney heat will collide with the cold and Stockholm will be wrapped up in a permanent fog.

The snowfall intensifies in the yellow light of the Carlton. The flakes hurtle through the light like flocks of storm petrels. I hear that screeching weathervane again. It's at least three kilometres to Bondegatan and with the rebuilding work going on at Slussen and the damned metro construction site, I probably can't cycle the whole way. But there's no alternative, and if I stay out in this cold for much longer I'll be short of my toes as well as my little finger.

A mare harnessed to an empty cart trots by, the reins hanging limply across its back. When the horse tosses its head I notice it only has one eye. The driver, who's wearing leggings, smokes with his free hand, and then makes his presence known with a slight tug on the reins. If this weather goes on, every bloke with a horse will put on the blade tonight so he can make a killing on snow clearance in the morning.

A tall, lanky sort limps into the Carlton, his bowler hat covered in snow. Behind him come two laughing ladies with Garbo haircuts, their arms locked together. An engine roars somewhere towards Målaregatan. I look up and scan the area. A white Cadillac passes Kungsgatan. I root about for a cigar.

A young man whistling 'La Paloma' passes with brisk steps. He's an imposing lad with brown eyes and bony fingers. He carries a typewriter in one hand, while in the other he holds a whisk of chewing tobacco, swinging it like a stick. On impulse, my eyes wander over his crotch. For a second or two I remember Leonard. Fleetingly I touch my cheek.

From the other side of the street a bearded, scruffy bloke waves at me. He wears a stained Guernsey jumper under his jacket. There's no sign of an overcoat. I look around and hold out my hands. He gets out of the way for a putt-putting Volvo and comes striding towards me. I take a deep breath.

As he comes closer I recognise the smell of ingrained sweat and poverty. A passing stray dog sniffs the air and turns around. I raise my arms again, quizzically. The man is bareheaded, and his eyes are too close together. The lapels of his jacket are worn to a shine.

'Are you the gentleman looking for a whore?' His voice is unnaturally gravelly.

'Not just any whore.'

'A certain Sonja?' He smiles. The gaps between his teeth are black with snuff.

'I might be.'

'Yeah, the bowlegged one. The one from the Dales?' The down-and-out with the gravelly voice points his knees out and makes an odd, swirling little jig.

'Do you know where she is?'

'I don't, no.' Now he starts thrashing his arms about as if he's semaphoring as well. If it goes on like this I may give him a penny for the dance number.

'So you don't know where she is?'

'I know where her brother is. Do you know your way around the Mire, sir?'

'Like the inside of my pocket.' The slum area lies a stone's throw from home, exactly where Birger Jarlsgatan meets Karlavägen. I've tracked down one or two missing country molls there over the years. One of them bit me so hard on the hand that I still carry the scar. She only had three teeth in her upper jaw but she bit quite well in spite of it. When I was done with her she'd lost one more.

The tramp abruptly stops dancing, breathing heavily. 'He lives there.'

'Give me a name?' I get out my wallet. If he wants more than one krona I'll leave it.

'The gentleman is mistaken.' The folds of his hands are lined with dirt. 'I don't want any charity.'

'You don't?'

'I have an honest job and I was paid today.'

Judging by the stench, he's emptying latrines. I put away my wallet. Free information is difficult to evaluate: either it's the most reliable of all, or there's something shady in the offering.

Maybe he just wants to lure me away from the lit-up street into some dark alley.

'I'm cycling. You don't have to come with me.'

'I'd be quite happy to do that but unfortunately I don't have time.'

I nod at him. 'So,' I say. 'What did you say his name was?'

About a half-hour later I am almost back in Sibirien. I hop off the bicycle on the corner of Tulegatan and Rehnsgatan. To my left, Norra Real rests its head between the mighty paws of its gable buildings.

I park outside the bookshop, Nationen. A pair of enamelled cufflinks with black swastikas cost one krona and thirty öre. The cold feels like a flame against my skin. I walk around the grammar school, slapping myself to get my circulation going, and knocking snow off my shoulders as I do so.

'Damned cold. Worse than the North Sea.'

The coffee has run right through me – I need to piss. The clock on the façade has gone eight. At the edge of the slum on the other side of the street the digging machines have already helped themselves to some land, and new houses have sprouted, but there's still a host of people living and working among a welter of planks and corrugated iron. The shacks proliferate in any old way, as if tossed from a bucket of swill.

Where the mud that constitutes the main thoroughfare of the slum starts, the Salvation Army has two mobile kitchens. Two slum sisters in blue uniforms with gleaming buttons serve up soup to a colourful line of ragamuffins. A stooped woman wearing a shawl holds hands with a little girl, who hangs her head. A bloke in a floppy hat is staggering about and falling out of the line, only to barge his way back in with oaths and curses. The distinctive smell of fusel oil indicates that the Salvation folk are not the only ones to keep a pot on the boil.

I limp across Roslagsgatan, convinced that I am on my way into an ambush. First the man with the signet ring, and now this. It might be because I'm wearing my best suit and pocket watch, or it could be down to the afternoon trail of scattered five-kronor notes. I'm bait for all kinds of sharks in this swampy water.

'Do they think Kvisten was born yesterday?'

But apart from Sonja's parents, this is, after all, the only lead I have. I take off my tie and fold it up in my coat pocket. I look around. The line of sick, silent faces shines palely like a pearl necklace dropped in the gutter.

At the front of the line, a young woman raises the soup bowl to her mouth with bony fingers. She slurps. Shaking with cold or ague, she wipes her pointed chin with her sleeve. The underskirt that sticks out from her coat once had a blue border. Her eyes, shiny with fever or schnapps, are oddly vacant. She is bareheaded, her thin blonde hair hanging down dead straight, as if someone had emptied a saucepan of melted butter over her head. I tip my hat slightly and let a couple of coins jingle in my other hand. She looks around.

'Sir will have to come with me, then.' Her voice is husky, marked by sickness and misery. She nods at me to follow her to the unpainted wooden shacks.

We squelch into a corner between two grey fences, a short distance away from the Salvation Army soldiers. The liquefied mud almost goes over the edge of my shoes. She gives me a brown-toothed smile. Before I know it, she's unbuttoned her coat. She wears a shapeless, beige jumper underneath. Her slip is held up by a safety pin. She lifts the fabric and moves my hand up her naked thighs. Her skin is chapped with malnutrition and cold.

It's icy between her legs. She wears no knickers. I feel the edges of her pubic bone through her skin. Her pubic hair frazzles against my hand when she rubs hard, up and down. The smell of dried-in urine is released from the rough bush, mixed with the reeking alcohol fumes from her mouth.

'Now give it a good squeeze, sir.'

I've been given my orders, and I obey. The fingers of my left hand dig about in her most sensitive parts and tighten. Her eyes change; she starts whimpering. I let the coins rattle in my trouser pocket and fish out one krona. She grabs my wrist with both hands, skewered between my thumb and forefinger. I pinch even harder. She whines and doubles over. I support her with my shoulder. I hold the one-krona coin in front of her eyes.

'Lill-Johan?'

She closes her feverish eyes and nods quickly.

'Where?'

'Almost at the far end. By Götgatan.'

I know where it is. I let go of her and jump out of the way when she falls sobbing into the mud, her legs beneath her. I sigh. The mud has spattered all the way up to her hair. I bend down, take her by the elbow and pull her to her feet.

'There.' I press the coin into her hand. She curtsies, by way of thanks.

I limp along one of the plank walkways that form bridges across the mire. The planks are stained with old mortar. They're so narrow that I have to balance on them not to fall off. If I meet someone coming from the other direction, it certainly won't be me who gives way.

The snow falls more and more heavily. A light wind brings a

fragrance from a tobacco-drying place further up the street. An open fire on a metal plate throws out long, tremulous shadows from the people surrounding it. A few of them are squatting, their palms held out towards the flames. They watch me in silence. I jump to the third plank. It sinks into the mud and I shiver when my low shoes fill up in the quagmire. One of the tramps works up the courage to laugh hoarsely.

By the time the Engelbrekt church on the hill announces that it's gone a quarter past eight, I've managed to work my way half into the labyrinthine slum. My feet are numb with wet and cold.

The wall of the shack in front of me has been constructed from a big piece of hoarding. *The Metro Construction Project*, it says in large black letters. A map shows the three stations of Slussen, Södra Bantorget and Ringvägen, and underneath is a caption: *For the benefit of Götgatan's merchants*. The hoardings have been temporarily erected all over the city and are easy to unscrew and take down.

I can hear a screeching, hacking cough inside.

I bang on the door.

The bloke who opens it is holding a rusty tin can in one hand. His eyes are deep-set and close together. A flap of skin on his throat hangs down like a washed-out blue collar. His tongue flicks across the snuff-daubed whiskers around his mouth. He wears a Horse Guards uniform, an older style; it looks as if it got in the way of a cluster of hungry rats. He hasn't got long to go but at least he has a plank floor, a fire and a bed. On the hearth is a trivet, and there's a smell of coffee granules.

'Lill-Johan?'

He shakes his head, coughs and spits sooty phlegm into his tin. 'Three houses down,' he wheezes and points with his tin towards a cul-de-sac.

'How little is he?'

'Not little at all.'

I nod. As I approach Lill-Johan's door I think about my limp. If he's armed and in a bad mood, I could have problems. It's not knives that gleam in the dark that I worry about. Glittering, sharp blades leave clean, fine cuts that any tailor's apprentice can stitch up without the slightest problem. The knives I fear are the ones that do not gleam; dull Mora knives full of dirt. Even a small cut from one of those can be fatal. The poorer one's enemy, the more dangerous.

The hinges of Lill-Johan's plank door groan when he opens it. Straightaway, a big, filthy mitt gives me a shove in the chest. I slip and reel backwards while fighting to regain my balance. Lill-Johan follows, his belly oozing under his dirty blue shirt. His curly black hair is long and oily. At the top of his head, a large, pale bump erupts from his locks. The whites of his staring eyes shine in his dirty face. With a grunt, he pulls his knife at once. The blade is short and brown with rust. Slowly he moves towards me.

'Now you listen…'

I retreat until I can't go any further, cornered in a cul-de-sac with my back against a wooden fence. The mire reaches over my ankles, my toes are aching.

Lill-Johan approaches gingerly, holding his knife in his right hand, in front of his huge belly. Quickly I take off my overcoat and wrap it around my lower left arm. Maybe it would be easier to get away by smashing my way through one of the walls of the surrounding shacks.

'Watch, wallet,' he says monotonously and slightly laboriously, as if the words are strange to him.

There's a squelch as he takes one more step. Less than two metres separate us. He changes his grip so that the knife points down at the mud, ready to hack rather than stab. My misgivings yield to that strange sense of calm that always precedes violence. I feel as if I'm back in a corner of the ring. I look up and, for a moment, let the snowflakes fall over my face. I stretch out my arms as if inviting him to embrace.

I fought my first bout with my hands wrapped in sailcloth, against a mess dogsbody inside a ring of drunk, roaring sailors. I remember the fear in my opponent's face when they pushed him towards me. I remember the way the sea breeze came wafting through a wall of bodies that had washed in salt water for too long. How they bellowed my name.

On that day I won and I've won ever since. I've never taken a count. I'm not about to start now. Knife or not: I'll knock the swine over the ropes.

Lill-Johan raises the knife above his head. Bellowing, he takes two squelching steps forwards, but he's absurdly slow. My shoe is left behind when I move. I block the blade of the knife with my wrapped-up arm above my head. The edge shreds the thick fabric. Shielding myself behind my arm, I release a straight right at his midriff. In its quest to find the sensitive internal organs embedded somewhere in the blubber, my whole fist sinks into the distended gut.

Lill-Johan's eyes threaten to pop out of their sockets when he finds that I am confronting him. A stale waft of pilsner left standing overnight hits me right in the face. Like the smelling salts my trainer forced on me between rounds, the stench makes me even more alert. I load my left fist, but when I twist my foot outwards to send it off, I slip in the mud and lose my balance. I roll my upper body to avoid any blows and retire a metre or so until once again I am against the fence.

Again the knife comes hurtling down at me. Like last time, I meet the blade with my coat. My hat falls off. There's a prick in my lower arm but it's not much more than a scratch. Sometimes one has to take a few blows and bleed a few drops to learn how one's opponent works and make him reckless.

If I am not wearing gloves in a fight I can only use my left fist two or three times, or it'll turn to smithereens. I hold back, but the hook connects as it should. His jaw, not my fist, shatters with a sharp, distinctive sound. A couple of teeth lose themselves in the snow.

The dog collar, August Gabrielsson, once consolingly said to me that there are all sorts of people in the world and they all react to things in different ways. I've always liked observing how people behave when their lights go out. Some lose their sinews and crumble into a shapeless heap, like 'The Mallet' Sundström in the last round of our much-analysed match in 1922, while others stiffen their limbs and fall like overturned statues.

Lill-Johan belongs to the first category. First one, then the other leg wilts under his massive weight. His eyes are open but there's no one at home. He falls forwards. My mouth waters. If he had the ropes of the boxing ring behind him I'd keep him on his feet with a couple more punches just for the sake of it, but now I step aside.

There's a squelch when his bulk hits the ground. The mud spatters a long way up my leg.

'I'll be damned. Bloody hooligans, always making a mess, and never anyone to send the bill to.'

I look down at my best suit and wonder if Sailor-Beda can save it. My right fist is hurting. I unravel the overcoat from my arm and put it on. It has a couple of serious rents in it.

I bend over Lill-Johan and move the flame of the gold lighter close to his face. He's fallen on his stomach with his face to the side, partially covered in streaks of that long, oily hair. His mouth is open and half filled with mud and blood. I begin to worry that he has fallen on his own knife. I heave him onto his back. He coughs. A pulse of black-brown mess rises in his mouth and goes back down again.

My knees crack when I straighten. I stand with my legs on either side of his massive chest. He coughs again. It seems to be contagious. I cough as well and stand there doubled over for a minute or so before I catch my breath.

I put my lighter in my pocket and unbutton my fly. It's abominably cold.

'Unfortunately I left my smelling salts at home in Sibirien.'

I piss Lill-Johan clean of mud and blood. The dirt comes off in little chunks wherever the jet hits him, leaving cracks of pale white skin in his mask of grime.

'Not bad, a hot drink for you, and a top-up too.'

The warm, wet sensation makes him slowly come to life. His eyelids tremble, he's making some fairly odd sounds and shaking his head. His jawbone seems to have completely broken off.

I get rid of the last few drops and button up my fly. I take my necktie from my pocket and put it back on. Lill-Johan blinks maniacally. I step over him and locate my shoe by the plank a short distance away. Lill-Johan tries to crawl away from me on all fours. He whimpers like a tethered dog outside a government schnapps shop. I pick up his rusty knife from the deep mud. It has a home-carved hilt.

'Stop!'

Lill-Johan freezes. With the shoe in one hand and the knife in the other, I squelch after him. I squat down in front of him. His chin hangs lopsidedly from its broken hinge.

'Give me your paw!'

Lill-Johan's eyes are still swimming after his knockout. He doesn't understand what I mean. There's no point being subtle about it. Hard people need hard measures. I give him a belt on the jaw with the shoe. There's a slap. His chin flies sideways and then snaps back. He bellows, bends down and buries his face in his hands.

'Come on! Give me your paw!'

Without raising his eyes, he holds up his big, dirty hand. It's trembling. I let go of the shoe, take a hold of his mitt and position the knife blade diagonally across his palm. Then I let rip. The warm blood swells over my muddy fist. Lill-Johan roars again, his voice echoing between the wooden walls. I throw the knife over the rooftops. It clatters against something made of metal.

'My name is Harry Kvist. Remember that. Remember it every time you look at your hand. The man who tailored my suit is called Herzog. One of the best tailors in town. I had to dig deep in my pocket to pay for it. Sit up!'

I grab his chin. He whimpers with pain and can't do anything but obey me. I empty my shoe, stand on one leg and put it on. Lill-Johan kneels in front of me. He holds his injured hand in the other. A lone snowflake finds its way into his bleeding gob. He sways slightly.

'Listen: do you have a sister called Sonja who's on the game?'

The sounds flowing out of Lill-Johan are transformed into gargles when he tries to speak.

'Quiet! Shake your head or nod! Sonja?'

He doesn't stay quiet but he shakes his head.

'Do you know anyone called Sonja at all?'

Again he shakes his head. I nod and turn around. After a beating of that order there's no reason not to believe him. It's completely stopped snowing now. I examine my right hand and give it a squeeze. It seems to have survived.

The gravel scrapes in my shoes as I balance along the planks. Lill-Johan whines hoarsely like a kid with a hacking cough. Every inhabitant in the Mire seems to have locked himself in his hovel. The fire on the metal plate by the entrance illuminates the cold December night like a lighthouse, but the down-and-outs have gone.

The sun is as high as it can manage in December. The sallow light makes Roslagsgatan glitter. Everything has frozen over in the night. People step along carefully like the transvestites one sees in the parks I sometimes visit in the summer months. Motorcar drivers avoid the tram tracks in the middle of the road. Horses place their hooves hesitantly.

I'm standing outside the laundry, smoking and waiting for Sailor-Beda to mend the tear in my overcoat. The hat is still lying in the mud among the shacks of the Mire. I am wearing a black jacket with non-matching trousers. The combination does not have my usual dignity. It's cold, but when the rays of the sun get through there's a little warmth. I hope the good weather keeps. A gaunt cat comes and rubs itself against me. Two hundred and fifty kronor of my emergency capital burns a hole in my wallet.

The gang of wiry boys from around the block are trying to climb the streetlight outside my house. They usually hang about on my corner, smoking, passing around torn-out photos of Josephine Baker and identifying the makes of passing cars. I can hear them from my window. If it's a Ford or a Chevrolet they content themselves with simple statements of fact. Volvo, the home-grown challenger, raises their voices a little, and a Dodge makes them yell. What's really bad is when an old Thulin or a Scherling comes spluttering by. First someone makes a piercing cry, then a wild discussion erupts before someone gets a punch on the nose. Usually they don't calm down until someone opens a window and throws a shoe – or the contents of a chamber pot – at them. I have no shoes I can get rid of, and not a potty either. If I need to get up in the night I use the sink.

I squat down and scratch the cat behind the ear. The grease in its pelt glimmers. My knee feels better but I have a slight stiffness in my back, stomach and shoulders. There's a little scratch on my lower arm, but it was no match for Sister Ella's Salve for Cuts and Grazes. This morning I loosened up my body with Danilo's dance course, as seen in *Stockholms-Tidningen.* Lundin tears out the page of instructions every Saturday breakfast. Tomorrow it's time for another one.

The cat darts off when the door tinkles as it's opened. I straighten. Beda waddles towards me with the overcoat.

'I did what I could. It was a nasty rip.'

'I'm sure it'll be fine. I'm only off to PUB to buy a new one.'

'Your suit from Herzog's. With all those stains.' Her voice is filled with sorrow, marvelling at all the world's evil.

'I understand. Do what you can.'

Beda puts her hands together and starts swaying back and forth. I look around. Further down the street, Bruntell has rigged up his Kodak to photograph the kids. He chooses the oddest motifs. In the background, Ström is up on a ladder, screwing down his factory-painted sign with the elaborate text: ALL BOTTLES BOUGHT, ALL KINDS OF METALLIC JUNK, RAGS, RUBBER AND VARIOUS OTHER ITEMS AT THE BEST POSSIBLE PRICE.

'A new chemical laundry has opened on Observatoriegatan.' Beda rubs one eye with the knuckle of her forefinger. It's tearing up. Must be the cold.

'I'm sure it'll be fine. You've taken care of my laundry for ten years.'

Beda stops swaying and smiles fondly. On the other side of the street a rye-blond boy manages the feat of climbing all the way to the top of the streetlight, and the kids are yelling as if deranged. He's wearing long trousers, a cap on his head.

The owner of the general store folds up his camera tripod and carries it inside. Old man Ljung comes up from Frejgatsbacken, leading Lundin's rented black horses.

A young woman without either a hat or a handbag comes out of the doorway of number 41. The blokes around the block call her the Jewel. The gossiping old bats at the General Store call her the Fashion Doll. Lundin firmly maintains that the shape of her head signifies an abnormally highly developed sense of 'amour'.

Her heels clatter against the paving stones when she marches up to the junction. The Jewel stops and shouts at the kids, telling them to shut up. They screech back at her and laugh. Her hips swing hard when she turns around again. Her buttocks bounce from side to side like a pear-shaped ball.

It's been years since I last had a woman. Maybe, in spite of all, I've missed it. I take a deep drag on my cigar.

'Surely you're not going bareheaded? In this weather?' Beda gives me a concerned look, and rubs her running eye again.

'It should be all right.'

'Out of the question! You'll catch cold! I'll have a look among the unclaimed hats!'

'It's not necessary.'

'Now just you wait here!'

The bell on the door tinkles and Beda disappears in a puff of bleach. I look in my notebook. The first stop will be Oscaria's shoe shop, then PUB Department Store before I go on to Söder and Bondegatan, in the hope of visiting Sonja's parents. If they still have the sweetmeats with peas at the Corso wine bar, I may stop off there first. I may also allow myself a couple of snifters. I borrowed a bit of dough from Lundin this morning.

The doorbell rings again. Beda comes out. To the north one can hear a march playing – the Johannes Folk School orchestra is beginning its usual Friday practice session.

'Look here,' she says, proffering a checked cap with earmuffs. She stands on her tiptoes and puts it on my head, then pats my cheek with her chapped hand.

'Damn!'

Beda raises a gnarled finger. 'He who swears gets worms in his teeth.'

'Ever since my twin brother and I tore my mother in two while she was giving birth to us, worms are all we've had to eat.'

Beda laughs, swaying and opening her mouth wide. Judging by the state of her teeth, she's sworn once or twice as well.

She goes back into her laundry and I cross the street. I daren't take off the cap yet, in case she's standing in the window watching me. I head off towards Lundin's Undertakers. A coal delivery man has parked his cart against the wall and is unloading a couple of sacks. He takes a sack on each shoulder and goes around the corner into Ingemarsgatan.

'Kvisten!'

The blond urchin with the Vega cap has crept up without my noticing. His eyes are rebellious but he has a childish, round face. He stretches out his little mitt and smiles, his mouth full of topsy-turvy teeth. Clearly he's the tough of the gang. The others stand a bit further off. They twist and turn, pushing each other and tittering.

'Yes?'

'My dad says Kvisten was an ace boxer?'

'My name is Kvist, as far as you're concerned.'

The boy nods, the gang behind him titters even more. 'My dad says Kvist was the best boxer we ever had. Better than Harry Persson, even.'

'That's not the only thing your old man says, I imagine.'

'Why didn't you turn pro like HP?'

'Clear off!'

'What do you mean, mister?'

Behind him, the street urchins have lined up like a little choir. One of them at the edge, a little shit with a bruise under his eye, starts swinging his elbow and the whole gang give it all they've got, as they roar out: 'Harry Kvist was a hell of a bloke!'

I flick the stump of my cigar towards them and grab the nearest boy by his ear.

'Clear the hell out of here!'

My growl comes from the very bottom of my throat. The boy opens his mouth as if he's about to answer back. I slap him so hard that it stings the palm of my hand. The boy hits the paving stones on his face.

The other boys screech and scatter like a flock of seagulls. I bend down and pick up the wriggling boy by the scruff of his neck. There's a scarlet mark on his cheek. I brush him down.

'Go home to your father. Tell him not to talk behind honest people's backs. If this continues I'll have to teach him a lesson as well.'

The boy wriggles free. I let him run. I take off my hat and find a Meteor in my pocket. The gold lighter is on strike. I sigh and open the door of the undertaker's.

'The kids are making a lot of damned noise,' says Lundin as I lower my head to come through the doorway. He's sitting in his black suit, noting something down on a paper at his desk.

'Shouldn't they be at their school desks? It isn't even lunch-time. No discipline.'

'*Until tribute comes to Judea, and the obedience of the peoples.*'

'Give your piety a rest, you old hypocrite!'

'I take it my brother has been to Bondegatan?'

'First I was going to get a litre for her father. Kron if you've got it.'

'You know where it is.'

'I'd rather you get it if you don't mind.'

Lundin stands up and closes every other button in his jacket. If I know him, he's trying to avoid wear and tear on the button-holes.

'People are desperate for a life beyond earthly existence. That's why the old girls stand in line to see the spiritualist up the street. They live in hope. But the bad news, I have to announce, is that there are no ghosts. I should know, if anyone.' He caresses his grey moustache.

Lundin disappears and soon comes back with a bottle wrapped in light green crepe paper. I take it and nod by way of thanks.

'You want it put on the tab?'

'And a pack of matches.'

Lundin sits down and pulls out a desk drawer. He finds a box and tosses it over. It rattles when I catch it with one hand.

'So I hope my brother gets hold of her old man, then. And then let's see if he's as bowlegged as his daughter.'

'And has something to tell,' I reply, with my hand on the door handle. 'It's the only lead I have.'

'Good luck!'

The clock chimes and I am back on Roslagsgatan. With the bottle under my armpit, I strike a match. There's almost no wind. I light the cigar and look around.

The kids haven't dared come back. The widow Lind from the tobacconist's further down the street nods as she passes with a box of food from the NORMA restaurant under her arm. She has draped a dirty grey shawl over her head and shoulders. In the corner of her mouth is a short, fat cigar.

'My only lead,' I mutter to myself.

I button my overcoat all the way up and shove my hands into my coat pockets. I hear Lundin's hacking cough inside the door. The coal delivery man's cart is still there, its shafts pointing up into the air like the arms of someone drowning.

A couple of hours later I'm standing at the crossroads towards Folkungagatan, watching the pavers at work. They tore up Götgatan for the sake of the Metro and now they're at it again, putting it back together. The workers are in teams of five, with one foreman. Their hammers ring out into the sunset. Stone splinters fly through the air like grey sparks. On my right the paving stones are already in place, but to the left the gravel road continues all the way to Skanstull. A worker sits on a steam excavator, watching the others. That special smell of iron imposing itself on stone mixes with the smoke of the trucks. The blokes are on their knees, their shredded fingertips wrapped in rags. The foreman's voice, gravelled by the road dust, cuts through the rhythmical hammering: 'Keep it up! No one goes home until we've filled the quota!'

I have new light boots made of sports leather and a long black overcoat with heavy lapels. I also found myself a bargain at PUB's hat department, a black thing with a low crown, a narrow brim and a broad grey band, for eighteen fifty. In the bag between my new boots is the old overcoat and the bottle of schnapps. My other shoes had to go straight in the bin. I get out a Diplomat,

110

bite off the end and light it. If I'm to get through Christmas I have to urgently contact Wernersson to see if he has any more bicycles for me.

'Damn it, Larsson. Were you one of them what built the Tower of Pisa? Can't you see, it's bloody out of shape?' the foreman shouts at an old man, who sits up on his knees and throws out his arms.

A boy approaches, pushing a pram filled with coal, which he has most likely nicked from the barges by Söder Mälarstrand. God have mercy on any kid from Söder who comes home without something flammable at this time of year.

I look around. Outside NORMA, on the other side of the street, a couple of dockers are milling about, trying to pick up some lunch company by three o'clock, when the restaurant is on full ration. Further off, a lanky bloke in a bowler hat is checking prices in the window of a gentlemen's outfitters. Overhead, a single-engine aircraft is writing an advertising message across the sky, but there's too much wind to be able to read what it says.

I have a puff. Although the cigar is twice as expensive as a Meteor, it tastes sour.

A coarse-limbed draught horse, its two-wheeled cart loaded with paving stone, weaves its way through the workers. Steam shoots out of its distended nostrils, as if from a locomotive. I'd never get into an underground train. The mere idea of it is utter lunacy.

I toss away my half-smoked Diplomat. As I turn off towards Stora Teatern, I notice a street kid snapping up the cigar and blowing on the glowing tip.

The matinee is *Tonight or Never*, the same show as at home in the Lyran. The newspaper boy outside the cinema tries to make himself heard above the hammer blows. Somewhere from under the ground, a whole team of blokes start singing a work song. The boy raises his voice even more.

'Murder on Götgatan,' he roars. 'The son the perpetrator!'

I slow my steps and stop.

'Read all about it in *Svenska Dagbladet*! Everything about a murder, just a few streets away!'

'Is there a crossword?'

'Yeah, but it's the trickiest one in the whole country, if you know what I mean.' The boy smiles.

I take out a one-krona piece and give it to him. He puts it in his pocket and folds the newspaper over his arm while he's counting out the change. I raise my hand.

'Keep it.'

'Right you are.' He hands me the newspaper.

'A carpenter on Bondegatan. The daughter has flown, if you know what *I* mean.'

'Well that'll be old Ljungström on Bondegatan, just a few blocks down.' A high-pitched signal in short pulses interrupts him. 'Hold on, the moles are letting off dynamite again,' he cries.

'You know the street number?'

'No, but check around. The old gossip girls will know all about it.'

I write down the information in my notebook before I open the newspaper. The international competition for amateurs against Poland ended 8-8. Vangis Eriksson won the heavyweight title with a knockout.

The detonation rolls like thunder across the open sea. The vibrations run through me, sending ripples to a corner of my newspaper.

I wander down Götgatan until I come to a small gathering of people on the corner of Bondegatan. There used to be a cinema here, but nowadays the bottom floor seems to be some sort of warehouse. A dark woman wearing a soiled stripy pinafore and a man's jacket stands pointing at some cement medallions on the façade.

I stop. Slightly to one side stands an elegant, greying gentleman with a goatee and spats. He sticks out among these Söder locals. I have a sense that I have seen him before, but I can't place him. It's odd how certain memories take off and fly away right away, while others have to be lugged about like heavy putting shots.

The smell of malt from St Erik's brewery further up the street hangs over the area. I give an urchin a poke with my elbow. He's a pale-faced kid of about ten, with a big bandage around his throat and two water-filled buckets at his feet. Copper for the drinking water and zinc for the rest.

'What's happened here?'

'Signe spilled a lick of coffee over herself,' says the pinafore woman in a shrill voice. She has a foreign accent. When she turns around I can see that her eyes are swollen red with tears under her joined eyebrows. 'Even during the war we had enough to go round!'

'What do you mean?'

'Well, back then we used chicory, of course! Not real coffee! But still!'

The boy fidgets. Maybe the old nag is his mother.

'We roasted acorns too, they fetched five öre for a half-kilo. Me and the kid next door picked them like mad.' A worker of more or less my own age has involved himself in our conversation. Sweat has painted clean stripes on his dirty face at some point today. Friday pay-day's half-litre bottle sticks out of the pocket of his tatty coat. He's got a unica box in his hand.

'Acorns? Pffft! And now she's offering coffee to our Lord the Father.' The woman puts up two fingers and makes the sign of the cross across her bust.

'Gas,' says the wage slave, swilling his saliva and gobbing between his dirty boots. Both of his upper front teeth are missing.

'Damn if I believe that.'

'Straight up, sir. The son put it on.'

'Acorns,' mutters the bag. 'Not Signe. Never.'

I get out another Diplomat, bite off the end and light it with a match.

'I'm looking for a carpenter here on Bondegatan. Ljungström.'

'Bloody rubbish.' The worker snorts. 'Excuse me, mister! You mean old Ljungström? The builder. Dalecarlian?'

'Precisely.'

The flame goes out in a thick cloud of smoke, and the singed matchstick ends up on the pavement.

'Avoid that one. Ljungström needs fifteen hammer strokes on a two-inch nail and still the sod ends up all crooked. The best carpenter in Söder is Jakobi, on Nytorget.'

'Still, it's Ljungström I'm after.'

'I don't know his street number but the district is called Timmermannen.'

I nod and get a Diplomat from my coat pocket. The wage slave inclines his head slightly as he takes it. His hand is rough and callused as it touches mine, and for a moment we measure each other up. He raises his eyebrows and nods affirmatively.

People move out of the way as I make my way through the little crowd. On the other side of the lane, two street urchins sit tightly pressed together in a doorway: a boy and a girl. The girl has wrapped a blue scarf around her head. Her dirty brown curls hang down over one eye. The boy holds a piece of string in his shaking hand. On his forehead, a set of red, clawed flea bites are fighting for space. The string leads to a forked twig, holding up a wooden fruit box, under which the December wind stirs among some breadcrumbs. The city pigeons of Söder are hard currency in these times.

I find the name almost at once while searching the doorway of a yellow building with badly applied pointing further up the street. I look around a few times. Over the course of the day I've had a vague feeling that I'm being watched, and I wonder if the goons have put a tail on me. They wouldn't need much of a reason. I shake off my unease and push the door open.

It's two floors from the top. My new boots are chafing a bit. On the way up I have a coughing fit, and I spit on the stairs. In front of the door marked 'Ljungström' lies a folded-up jute sack on which to wipe one's feet. I give the door a decent tap with the joint of my forefinger.

The apartment smells of liquid soap. The wife of the house has the same slanted eyes as her daughter, and she could be anything between forty and sixty years old. She has a scarf wrapped around her head, and she wipes herself on her apron before she shakes hands, with a little curtsey. From inside the flat there's a loud sound, like a window being slammed.

I peer over her shoulder. In the hall, some rag rugs have been rolled up and left on a firewood bin. A big bed is folded up against the wall. Most likely they rent out the hall. There's a scrubbing brush on the floor. They're normal, subservient people; poor and hardworking. For a moment I think of the lady on Kungsgatan yesterday. This one couldn't possibly be anywhere near as angry.

'I'm looking for your husband.'

'He's down in the workshop. In the yard.'

Her Dales dialect doesn't sound quite right. I nod, touching the brim of my hat in acknowledgement, and I'm just about to leave when she grips my arm with surprising strength. I look down at her wrinkled hand.

'Tell him to come in and eat. I can heat it up for him.' Her voice breaks and her grip tightens.

At least they have a wall-mounted clock; I can hear the seconds ticking by in there.

Her eyes seem in danger of welling over. I nod, alarmed, then free myself of her grip, back out into the stairwell and quickly close the door on her and her weeping.

The courtyard isn't paved. The weather has hollowed it out and created small hills and valleys in the gravel. If it rained, one would have to jump the pools on the way to the shithouse in one corner. Between a couple of cowering, knotty trees runs a tangle of empty washing lines.

Two filthy little girls disappear into the house dragging a basket of firewood. One industrial worker in four is unemployed. There's certainly no shortage of waitresses or seamstresses sewing pockets or buttonholes at a piece rate. In a few years, they may find positions as maids in Östermalm, with a weekly wage corresponding to what Sonja pulls in from one half-impoverished bloke. That is, if they're prepared to work from daybreak to late at night.

I need a snifter. I take out my half-litre and look around.

At the far end of the yard, under a bare apple tree, is a small peeling shed with a roof of tar paper and a lopsided, rectangular window.

I walk up to it and knock on the door. It glides open. The lock is broken. I step into the gloom.

The little workshop smells of timber and resin. The earth floor is covered in wood shavings. A variety of tools lie scattered across the workbench, including chisels with handles of black string and a handsaw. On the far wall are two pictures. One of the King, smiling. The other of Christ on the cross, not smiling. Under the pictures is a wooden chair with a broken back, a spade without a handle, and an old dowry chest. A small, unpainted chest, about a metre in length, rests on two sawhorses. A wood-cutter's axe has been left on the lid to stop the rats getting in.

On another broken chair sits a man, his chin slumped against his chest. He's wearing clogs without socks, rough-spun trousers and a workman's shirt, yet he doesn't seem cold. His dirty, callused hands are curled up in his lap. A mottled light seeps in through the window, illuminating his legs.

I take off my hat and find myself an overturned three-legged stool by the door. I pinch my front creases and sit next to the carpenter, who doesn't notice me. We remain silent for a while. I rest my lower arms against my thighs, my hat balancing on one knee. My boots squeeze my feet even though I'm not moving, my overcoat is tight across my shoulders. I send Sonja a thought, then straighten my back, clear my throat and glance at him. There's a clicking sound when I break open the screw-top lid. A mouthful of schnapps tumbles through my body. I have another. A crack runs diagonally across the dirty pane of glass. It holds together, but only just. I tap his shoulder with the neck of the schnapps bottle.

'Just bought schnapps.'

He takes it and, after putting away a decent gulp, sends it back. I wave my hand dismissively, and he helps himself to another. I feel the heat of his fist when I get the bottle back.

'My condolences.'

He glances quickly at me. I keep looking straight ahead. It's best that way. He looks back down at his clogs.

'She's gone, now I have no one to follow me,' he mumbles.

I pick up some of the wood shavings from the floor and crumble them between my fingers. They smell good. I have another sip. My stomach has grown accustomed now. The schnapps is warming. Looking at him once more, I realise I can't ask about Sonja.

'Your wife is waiting upstairs with the food.'

I stand up. He remains seated, shaking his head. I dust my hat.

'No one to follow me,' he repeats.

I take a deep breath: there's no air in here. The carpenter shakes his head. With a nod, I put the bottle on the small chest in front of him. The bag rustles when I get out my old overcoat. I drape it over his shoulders and pat him on the shoulder a couple of times. I don't want to see him cry.

One of the girls is still out there in the yard. Quickly she pulls her finger out of her nostril when I leave the shed. It's growing dark now. The afternoon smells as if it's going to snow again. The wind sighs softly, like a paraffin flame under a tin lampshade.

I hop across the yard and reach the door. The rusty handle feels rough through my thin Nappa leather gloves.

My new hat is pushed back when, momentarily, I rest my forehead against the door. The coldness of the handle is a comfort to my trembling hand.

'There's a policeman waiting up there,' says Lundin when I look in, for the usual reason, about an hour later. He offers me a bottle of Skåne Akvavit and I take it.

'Who?'

'Nervy type. At least you're properly dressed, my brother.'

I nod. So it's neither Olsson nor Berglund. Lundin makes another entry in his ledger.

'Did anyone call?'

'Wernersson. Did you find her?'

'I found her father. You got anything other than aquavit?'

'Did he know her whereabouts, then?'

'It wasn't the right moment to ask.'

Lundin nods and pockets his accounts book. 'Sneaky little whore.'

'Mind your language.'

'She did it, and you know it.' He caresses his moustache.

'Who?'

'She killed him. That's why she's keeping her head down. *Cherchez la femme.*'

'I beg your pardon?'

'Let us go down and create confusion in their language, so that the one does not understand what the other is saying.'

'What are you going on about?'

'It's from the scriptures.'

'The other bit.'

'French.'

'I heard that much. What does it mean? And have you got anything else? OP at least, if it's got to be aquavit.'

'It means she killed him.'

'Do you have anything else?'

'Don't keep the lawman waiting.'

Lundin points upwards with his chin. I sigh and drop the bottle into my inside pocket. Lundin pulls at his lapels and puts his hand on the door to the ice room. I nod goodbye to him and walk out.

The soles of my new boots dampen the sound they make on the stairs. *Social-Demokraten* is lying outside the door. At the top of the front page someone has scrawled four digits in blue ink. It looks like a telephone number. For a short moment I'm left standing with my hand on the door handle before I take a deep breath and go inside.

Senior Constable Hessler sits with his legs crossed in one of the visitors' chairs in front of the desk. He's in uniform, smoking a cigarette between his slim fingers. He turns his head and smiles as I come into the hall, but remains seated. His hair is perfectly coiffured as usual.

I hang up my coat and go into the room. The ashtray with the hula dancer is full of cigarette butts. Either he's nervous or he's been waiting a very long time.

I grunt at him by way of a greeting, loosen my tie, then put the bottle on the desk and turn the label towards him. Hessler shakes his head.

'I don't partake any more. You know that.'

A dark finger of smoke arrows between us like a Cape dove when he stubs out his cigarette in the ashtray. On my way into the kitchen, I run my hand through his hair to rough it up a bit. By the time I come back with a schnapps glass, he's tidied it and lit himself another cigarette.

I sit in the armchair and fish out a Diplomat from my breast pocket, then change my mind and open the desk drawer. It catches halfway but a Meteor rolls into view. I light it. Hessler coughs.

'Nice.' He nods at the ship in the bottle on the windowsill behind me, then his earlobes flush.

I take a deep puff. 'We had a donkey man who was a master at making those.'

Hessler crosses his legs the other way. 'It's nice and warm here, Harry. Lovely to have a warm apartment in the winter.'

'For Christ's sake, Hessler!'

He goes silent for a few moments before he exclaims: 'I'm here about the Zetterberg case.' His ears are completely red now.

'Didn't I tell you to telephone me?'

'Yeah, well… it's better this way. You never know if some operator is sitting there, listening.'

'Right. What are they saying about me on Kungsholmen?'

'Olsson thinks someone else killed Zetterberg, but Berglund… well, he thinks it was you.'

I snort and fill my glass with schnapps. 'And what do you think?'

'Blast it, Harry!' Hessler crumples his cigarette in the ashtray so violently that the air is filled with little flakes of ash. 'It can't have been you! It wasn't you, was it?'

'It wasn't me.'

'Did you know,' Hessler goes on, lowering his voice, 'he's been convicted under the eighteenth paragraph?'

For an instant I see Zetterberg's signet ring in front of me. The thin hand dangling from the stretcher.

'Haven't we all?'

'Not me.'

'Speaking of which, how's the wife? And the children?'

'Damn it, Harry!'

'Just wondering.' I raise my hands defensively.

Hessler snaps his mouth shut and caresses his ludicrous moustache with his thumb and forefinger. We sit in silence.

'The blokes are busy with that axe. There's an owner's mark engraved into the handle. Half the force is going around the building sites asking about it.'

'And the bowlegged girl? Sonja?'

'Do you remember when we met the first time, Harry?'

'What's that got to do with it?'

'You didn't muck about, you just took me in your arms!'

'Sonja?'

Hessler gives off a little sigh. 'Am I too old for you now, Harry?'

121

'That's got nothing to do with it!'

'Every day.' Hessler purses his lips. His silly moustache arches over them. 'Every day I train with chest expanders and weights in the police station cellar.'

It's my turn to sigh. I look up at the ceiling. 'Sonja?'

'Gone with the wind. All the usual sources are keeping their mouths shut.' Hessler twists and unbuttons his uniform jacket. He gets out a pile of papers and waves it in front of me.

'What have you got there?'

'Documents about Zetterberg and the murder scene.' He remains seated, the notes in his lap. 'They have to be returned by this evening.'

The neighbour is playing jazz again, at high volume. Out in the yard, the door of the potato cellar slams. Someone whistles 'A Cross for Ida's Grave'. My chest feels heavy.

Hessler drops his voice again. 'I'm taking a hell of a risk for you, Harry.'

I nod, then stand up and throw my jacket over the back of the armchair. I pick up the cigar from the ashtray and re-light it.

'Can I see?'

Hessler hands over the documents. Quickly I leaf through them; there's a crime scene investigation and a pathologist's report. I read a bit and then look up.

'So the murder weapon is a thirty-centimetre axe, a so-called bricklayer's axe, which was found in Vasagatan. They haven't managed to get any fingerprints from the birch handle, but the hairs on the edge matched Zetterberg's after being examined under a microscope?'

'Most likely the murderer wore gloves.'

In the street, the number 6 tram rattles by. I open the post-mortem protocol from the Karolinska Institute and read: *The deceased died of significant wounds to his scalp and skull as a result of traumatic violence. Nothing in the nature of the wounds contradicts the supposition that they were caused by the axe mentioned in the police report.'*

'Someone really wanted to kill him.'

'I understand that some people think I did it. The blood in the hall was type B.'

'The same as yours, Harry?'

'I think so.'

'I have to get back to the station shortly. Before someone misses the documents.' Hessler crosses his legs and clears his throat quietly.

'One moment.' I take a puff on the cigar and go back to the crime scene investigation.

I whistle. This is no simple robbery. 'Almost ten thousand kronor found in the apartment?'

'I'm taking a hell of a risk with this for you, Harry…'

'Ten thousand. A lot of bread.'

I unhitch my braces and chuck down my drink.

Hessler inhales and leans forwards on the chair, whispering: 'There's more about that in the personal investigation. Every month someone paid five thousand kronor into Zetterberg's account.'

'Who?'

'We don't know.'

'The neighbour said he was a taxi driver or something like that.'

'He hasn't declared any income in years.'

I nod and give the senior constable an appreciative smile as a reward, then pour myself another schnapps.

'Hessler, my friend, you're not completely bloody useless.'

I toss down the contents of the glass. Hessler smiles ingratiatingly.

I keep thinking about the money. Five thousand per month. That's more than a bishop makes. There's really only one murky business that turns over sums of that size. Zetterberg must have been involved at a relatively high level in organised liquor-running. And I mean definitely, as definitely as 'amen' in church. He was a gangster. I nod at Hessler.

There's a thump when the senior constable throws himself down on the floor in front of me. He puts his hands on my hips. I can feel him trembling as I pop my fly open.

Questions are teeming in my head now. Luckily enough I know someone who ought to be able to come up with some answers: Belzén in Birka. The smuggling king of Kungsholmen.

Kungsholmen, Gloomholmen, Povertyholmen: a backwater with winding, soot-stained streets bordered by workshops, small factories, military barracks and heavy industry. Here, dilapidated apartment buildings coexist with low-slung wooden houses and shacks. In the day there's a cacophony of slamming and noise, but it's absolutely silent at night.

I'm wearing a grey woollen suit with wide lapels and a matching waistcoat. The weight of the little bolt cutter in the inside pocket of my coat causes the latter to have a certain lopsidedness. In the grainy evening light further down Hantverkargatan, a cattleman leads a black-spotted cow towards Rålambshovsparken. From a workshop behind me comes the sound of whining lathes, spluttering machines and regular hammer beats. It feels as if it might start raining at any moment. Two pensioners carefully prod the ground ahead of them with their walking sticks as they cross the street arm in arm. Everything smells of horse manure, kidney beans and poverty.

A little lass in a teddy coat and wool gloves slips out of a doorway on my right. She has turned down her socks over her boots and her hair is held by a blue bow on her head. A window upstairs opens and someone whistles shrilly.

'Your sandwiches!'

The girl stops, looks up and catches a package wrapped in newspaper. She heads off, running towards Kartagos Hill. A detachment of ice-clearers come along the road. They carry long saws and large icicles on their shoulders.

Between two houses in the quarter known as Kulsprutan is a red-painted fence with three rows of barbed wire and spy mirrors at the top. There's a black garage door in the fence. Behind the barbed wire, the head of a bloke wearing a fox-fur hat bobs up and down, like a bright yellow buoy. Nothing in the street evades his notice. For instance, he seems very interested in the cigar I take from my inside pocket. I identify strongly with him, as if I've met him somewhere before, but I can't remember where.

On every corner of the block some school-age urchin has been posted to warn the lookout about approaching goons or other enemies. With their sharp wolf whistles they could prob-ably even wake the dead in the morgue further down the street.

The fuel in the gold lighter has run out. I sigh, put it in my pocket and meet the guard's eye. Neither of us smile.

A Norwegian pony comes trotting along. The guard and I follow the two-wheeled cart with our eyes. Broom handles and shovels stick out like swaying masts.

'Make way for the whore taxi!' the man holding the reins yells at me, revealing a line of broken teeth, and sticks out his chest. The dustmen often give the street girls a lift home at dawn if they can have a little squeeze in return.

Set into the façade beside the garage door is a modest door with sun-bleached curtains in the window and two signs. One of them says, JESUS IS COMING – ARE YOU READY? and the other says, LINDWALLS TRANSPORTATION AND CARRIAGE RENTAL. Somewhere inside sits Belzén from Birka. It's been seven years since we last saw each other. That was when, for the first and last time in my career, I agreed to take a dive.

Everything had gone to hell for me. Quite simply, I needed the money. I used to drink a fair amount in those days. When Räpan picked me up, I was standing cap in hand at the Salvation Army or Filadelfia, exchanging psalm singing for soup. Räpan represented the Söder villains who, in those times, controlled the quays of both Söder and Norr Mälarstrand. The match would be held on neutral ground in Klara.

It was the usual arrangement: two blokes with bare torsos were supposed to pummel each other until one of them could no longer get up. No gloves. I had gone about fifty such fights without defeat, and for a few months I'd no longer been of any interest, I was too good. According to the agreement with Räpan, I had to stay on my legs for ten minutes, go easy on my right, and then collapse. On that one occasion I had no problems with it. I was getting a hundred and fifty kronor for a couple of shiners.

Most likely someone spilled the beans. Three days before the match, everyone was suddenly betting against me, and then, one day before the fight, I had another proposition: from Belzén in Birka. Belzén wasn't much cop in those days, just a short, semi-deaf, small-time gangster running a couple of illegal drinking dens and gambling dives up in Birkastan. He was willing to advance me a fair sum of money if I didn't take a dive, and just did what I always do instead. The odds against me were pretty high. Long after, I found out that Belzén himself had put ten thousand on me in various betting shops. Räpan and the Söder villains would give me a hiding, of course, but I was getting a hiding anyway. I thought it sounded like a good idea.

The match didn't take much longer than a pissing break. That same night I was able to get my hands on two thousand cold. A day later, Räpan and a couple of underlings got hold of me. They worked me over with a pickaxe handle and a chain, before Räpan took to my little finger with a blunt pair of pincers and a sledge-hammer. I clearly remember his flushed face as he leaned over me and promised that the next time he'd take my whole hand.

There was no next time. Some fifteen minutes later, Räpan and his Söder gangsters were liquidated. This was the opening shot in a long series of confrontations. When the smoke finally settled about a year later, thirty people had lost their lives.

I press down the door handle of Lindwalls and step into a minimal office. The walls are bare except for a four-year-old calendar and a faded map of the inner city. A young woman in a plaid dress and nicely fixed blonde hair is sitting on a little desk, painting her nails red. She looks like a voluptuous version of Tutta Rolf. On the desk is a floral-patterned cup and saucer. Behind her is a solid metal door. There's a smell of good coffee and nail varnish.

'Sorry,' says the woman without looking up. 'Everything's fully booked.' She puts her little brush back in the bottle on the desk. She flaps her hands in front of her and smiles with satisfaction.

'Belzén. Give him Kvisten's regards.'

She stops flapping her hands. 'Blow,' she says, and holds them out. She has one of the most dangerous jobs in town, but she keeps her style. I can't help but admire her.

I do as I'm told.

'You got a match?'

She flaps her hands in the air one last time, then leans back across the desk and opens the drawer. The fabric of her dress tightens around her body and swells over her breasts like the leather stretched across a couple of boxing gloves. She gets out a box of matches and gives it a shake. I catch it as it comes flying.

'One moment.' The fabric makes a scarcely noticeable sound against the top of the desk as she slides off. She presses a bell beside the door behind the desk. It takes a while before the lock clicks and she goes inside.

The first drag of the cigar sends a pleasurable shiver through my body. The fragile porcelain of the cup rattles slightly against the saucer as the heavy door open and shuts again. I straighten up.

'Wait by the door to the side,' says the secretary. She goes round the desk and sits on the chair, scrutinising her nails again and curling her upper lip. I put the cigar in the corner of my mouth and squint with one eye. She pulls out the drawer, gets out a nail file and pulls the bottle of nail varnish a little closer. She looks at her nails and says: 'By the garage door. Don't keep him waiting.'

I doff my hat just slightly and put my paw on the door handle. Damned women, always making themselves so difficult.

A silver-haired man with a cap on his head and a shotgun on his shoulder receives me inside the garage door. He's wearing rubber Wellingtons. His face is wrinkled as an old apple. Most of them don't live this long. Up on the ramp the man in the fox-skin hat stares at me. He has a heavy-calibre rifle in his arms. He's about the same age as myself, with a cleft palate. Several trucks are parked in the yard. Everything stinks of alcohol. There's been a leak somewhere. The trawlers go out and meet the Estonian and German booze ships just outside territorial waters. In the archipelago, ten-litre cans of pure alcohol are reloaded into fast Italian motor boats, which take them into town. A significant part of it ends up here, where it is diluted to the proper strength and decanted into beer bottles.

The old man nods at me. I hold out my arms. I get the feeling that the harelip is staring at my cut-off little finger.

'I've got bolt cutters in my inside pocket.'

'You need that for?' The old man's voice is not much more than a wheezing.

'I'm picking up a couple of bicycles later. Could come in handy.'

'Leave them here.'

I haul out the bolt cutters and put them at my feet before I stretch out my arms again. The old man gives me a pat down with his liver-spotted hands and gestures towards the trucks.

We go to a blue-painted door at the far end of the courtyard. The cigar is killed under the heel of my boot. The old man nods at me to walk on ahead. The cold double barrel seeks its way through my layers of clothes and finds a point in the middle of my spine. If you took a swarm of shot there, your heart would jump clean out of your chest.

There are no windows inside the high-ceilinged premises. Up above, naked lightbulbs hang in rows. Wooden crates piled one on top of another form a narrow corridor through the warehouse. They are printed with words in languages I do not understand. Our steps echo between them in waves.

At the far end of the gloomy corridor is another door leading into a large, bare office. At the other end of the room, at a desk made of some light-coloured wood, sits Belzén of Birka. The girl sits on the desk, smiling, with another cup of coffee in her hand. Behind the boss is a massive man, standing more than two metres tall in his socks. I've seen his lumpy boxer's nose somewhere before, but can't remember where.

The giant comes to meet us with a wooden chair in one hand. He puts down the chair a good distance from the desk. I'll have to yell for Belzén to be able to hear me. I sit down. The girl comes forward and gives me the cup of coffee. The double barrels find their way between my shoulder blades. The man behind me cocks both barrels. The coffee tastes as good as it smelled in her office.

Since the last time I saw him, the thin man behind the desk has got himself a pair of spectacles. He's wearing a blue waistcoat and a bow-tie. A long, thin scar runs from his stiff jet-black hair, past a bushy eyebrow, down into his dark beard. His enemies say that he has a good deal of gypsy blood in him. Whether that's true or not I don't know.

'Kvist,' says Belzén. 'It wasn't exactly yesterday.' He folds his hairy hands together on the desk. He smiles and looks really quite docile.

'Any chance of a tot of booze in the coffee?' I raise my cup. 'If you have any going spare, I mean.'

Belzén laughs and throws out his hands. 'You have to promise, Kvist, not to shoot your mouth off about it.'

'Promises are a habit of the gentleman, and a necessity for the poor man.'

The girl's heels echo between the walls when Belzén sends her over with a bottle.

'Well?'

'Zetterberg.'

'What? You have to talk louder! I had scarlet fever when I was a kid, and I'm a bit hard of hearing.'

'Zetterberg!'

'Who?'

'The Kungsgatan murder. I need to know if he was mixed up in anything.'

'Kungsgatan?'

'That's it.'

'We don't have any Zetterberg in our little organisation. Do we, Hiccup?'

Hiccup. Something clicks into place. Ten years ago the giant behind Belzén shot three blokes in an argument about two litres

131

of OP Anderson. As far as I've heard, there have been many others since then.

'No.' Hiccup gets out a metal box from his pocket and crumbles some tobacco into a paper. I can't see that he has any reason to lie.

'I need to find out if he was working for one of the others.'

Belzén shakes his head. 'That would be hard for me to find out.'

'I know that you make about thirty kronor for each litre. There must be thousands of litres brought into the quays here every week. Since you took control of Norran a couple of years ago it must have been full steam ahead, I imagine?'

'There are a lot of costs, and Ma has ten per cent on everything.'

'But still?'

Hiccup laughs and licks his cigarette paper.

'Listen,' Belzén goes on, 'Ma and her sons have Östermalm and ten per cent on Kungsholmen, Ploman Vasastan and Piggen Söder. The boundaries haven't changed in years.'

'I know who's got what.'

'And certainly there can be… differences of opinion in the border areas but I can't risk – I think you know, Kvisten, the way it used to be?'

'I remember. And I could swear that somehow I became a pawn in the game when you took control of Kungsholmen.' I hold up the stump of my little finger. Both Belzén and Hiccup grin. They exchange a glance.

'With Ma, I could just ask her. With the other two it'll be more difficult.'

'But not impossible?'

The contents of my coffee cup are almost spilled when the old man behind me pokes the double-barrelled shotgun even harder into my back. Hiccup laughs again and lights the cigarette with a phosphor stick.

'If against all expectations we get hold of any of them, we can't let them run home afterwards and spill the beans,' says Belzén.

'That's your business.'

'What did you say?'

'Of course!'

Belzén waves the hairy back of his hand. The gun disappears from my back, and the muted steps of the Wellington boots fade away. The woman slides off the desk and goes around it. She bends down and whispers something in Belzén's ear, before disappearing through a side door. Belzén smiles again before he meets my eyes. I wonder if he heard what she said.

'Is Kvist still living in Sibirien?'

'It could be worse.'

'I'll give it one night. I'll put one of my best lads on it. Meet them at the water castle in Vanadislunden at midnight, and then we'll see.'

I nod.

'So, Zettergren on Kungsgatan, is that right?'

'Zetterberg.'

'Zetterberg, Zetterberg, Zetterberg,' mumbles Belzén and nods at Hiccup.

I touch the brim of my hat by way of thanks and stand up. Hiccup takes hold of my elbow with his massive hand. Belzén puts his hands together over his chin.

'It's a pity what happened to your finger, but business is business and Räpan got what he deserved, if I'm not mistaken.'

I stand up and put my coffee cup on the chair. Belzén looks through a few papers.

With one mitt on my shoulder, Hiccup escorts me through the warehouse and towards the door at the other end of the premises.

My hand leaves a damp mark on the handle when I push the door open and walk out.

As the factory whistles announce the end of the working day, a heavy squall of rain comes down. I pick up my notepad, my hand still shaking, and check some addresses that are only a few blocks apart. The afternoon's bicycles include a three-wheeler Monark and a Hermes gentlemen's model.

I'm on the corner of Fleminggatan and St Eriksgatan. The shop owners are rolling down their metal awnings over the shop windows. From Separator, Karlsvik and Ekmans, a large group of workers come welling like a retreating army: first a vanguard of cyclists with empty lunch boxes on their racks, followed by wide columns of infantry. Some of them are holding newspapers over their heads like white parliamentary flags. One or two shirts sport gleaming oil stains. Cupped hands protect the glow of the evening's first cigarette from the rain. From the dairy, woman run for home with cream and baskets of bread, which they try to keep out of the rain. A woman shielding her undulating blonde swell of hair with her handbag looks around hastily a few times before she blows a kiss at a tram speeding off towards Vasastan. A young man in a compartment window waves back. The streetlights buzz and turn themselves on. The din of hobnail boots and wooden soles drowns out the sound of the rain. Greetings criss-cross to the right and left, but no one stops to talk.

I wonder if Belzén's blokes can give me the information I need tonight. For the first time since my release I feel I'm getting close to something.

I fight my way against the torrent moving down Fleminggatan. Petrol fumes and cooking smells blend with the tangy scent of wet harnesses and sweaty men. I pass the butcher's on the corner. Outside, a bunch of dirty kids are waiting to beg for dog food at closing time. I suspect that far from all of them have dogs.

The crowd starts thinning out. With wet feet I jog along the street. The bolt cutters thump against my chest at every step. I pass the square lamp of Kungsholmen Fire Brigade, and then the children's home. Not much longer now. I cough and spit.

On the other side of the street is a woodpile as high as a man, running along the entire façade. Some kids are playing awkwardly on top of it. I remember we passed the same woodpile on the way to the police station some four or five days ago. I wonder if the goons are aware of Zetterberg's possible gangster connections. I smile under the brim of my hat; clearly I'm one step ahead of them. With so much money in the bank it could hardly be anything else. Five thousand kronor a month on the nail. Again my thoughts go back to the dangling hand of the corpse, the thin fingers and the expensive signet ring.

The courtyard on Fleminggatan 23 smells of printer's ink and latrines. In one corner is a shack with a heavy leather drape behind the ajar door. Probably a drinking den. Behind the water pump in the yard is a three-wheeler with a box on the back. Just to be on the safe side, I take my notebook and check that the four-digit registration number under the saddle matches my information. The sturdy length of chain around the back wheel is heavy and mottled in my hand. It rattles when I let go of it.

The scratched mirrored door of the main house has rusty hinges, but it glides open without a sound. I remove my hat, shake the water off it and put it back. The stairwell is gloomy and smells of fried liver. I have to go all the way to the top again, and this time, unlike at Zetterberg's place, there's no elevator.

I find the door and bang on it. As soon as it opens I thunder into the flat with my arm raised.

It's the very worst kind of attic. A border of black mould runs around the whole flat. The ceiling is insulated with curled, water-damaged cardboard. The roses risk being frozen off the wallpaper when the winter comes. As for the furniture, it consists of a discarded drop-leaf table, a commode with a dirty washbasin, and a pull-out sofa with a lumpy rag-stuffed mattress, lined with cut-open sugar sacks. In the middle of the ceramic stove are two black-painted rings, like weary eyes. It mourns the absence of its hatches, which, presumably, the old bloke has sold.

The hallway lacks any light. A white pallor gleams like hoar frost on his throat and chin. He has a sunken chest, a grubby linen shirt lacking a collar, worn-out braces, and brown traces of lip snuff in the corners of his mouth. A pair of moist eyes flicker unsteadily at me. What was he ever going to do with a three-wheeler?

'The Monark,' I say.

He gives me a glance filled with anxiety, like the nervous eyes of a farmer's wife when her husband gets out the liquor. I sometimes have that effect on people. But he summons a bit of courage.

'That one down in the yard is mine.'

I glare at him. He presses himself against the wall. I clear my throat and fire off a decent gob over his shoulder, five centimetres from his face. He flinches and opens and closes his mouth a couple of times. He must have been one of those who were left out in the cold when they closed the General Care Home on Fleminggatan a couple of years ago.

'The chain is my own,' he mumbles at last.

I nod sharply. He takes the bunch of keys from a rusty nail inside the door and walks ahead of me into the stairwell. His hand is knotty and gouty.

A word and a gob. That's all it takes.

I cycle down to the end of Fleminggatan, past the tall chimney stack of Separator, down towards Kungsbron. Dark has fallen completely now and the rain has cleared the street of people.

I find the address a few streets away, but there's no sign of the bicycle anywhere and I don't get an answer when I knock on the door. I stand in the doorway. There's a lingering smell of evening coffee. I put my last Meteor in my mouth and manage to get it alight with a match. My feet have started going numb.

'One cigar, no longer than that.'

To my right I see the long, electrically lit King's Bridge reaching across Klara Sound and joining the slope known as Drunkard's Hill. I hear the water sloshing against the bridge pillar. A thick-limbed horse pulls an open cart across it. The driver sits immobile in the seat. On the other side of the water, the flags of the boat masts poke holes in the darkness. A steam train whistles on its way into the station.

If I stick my head out I can see the wall-mounted billboards of the Central Market Hall over the huge windows of the brick building, but I can't read what they say. It stops raining. A barge glides quietly under the bridge. In the distance, the barge pilot is ticking someone off.

Just as I've thrown away my cigar stub to pedal homewards, a young man arrives, cycling on a Hermes gentlemen's bicycle. I pick up my notebook. He's changed the registration plate but the colour, manufacturer and address are all correct. A boy of about twenty, he brakes just in front of me and gives me a nod. I nod back. He removes his cap and wipes the sweat from his brow with the sleeve of his jacket before getting off. The thighs of his trousers are dark with water, also his back and shoulders.

A locomotive howls again from the embankment. I take a step forwards but stop there. We have the bicycle between us. He looks at me with large, blue eyes. He has a thin mouth, his chin, a pit in the middle. He puts his cap on the frame and runs his hand through his thick mop of hair. He's a fine young man. I let my eyes wander over him. A part of me wants to beat him to a pulp.

I put my hand on the bolt cutters in my inside pocket. Sometimes they try to cycle away, and it's good to have something to hand to insert into the back tyre.

'It's about this,' I say, and put my other hand on the handlebars.

The boy stiffens. I feel the entire weight of the bicycle in my hand when he lets go of it. He backs away a few steps into the street. I nod. Quite right.

'I was going to pay…'

I shrug with my right shoulder. Everyone is always going to pay.

'We're on strike,' he goes on. 'I haven't worked for months.' He puts his hand on the bicycle. I give him a look. He lets go of it again. 'Please…'

'Get lost!'

'Please, sir…'

I make a movement towards him with my upper body and growl. He bounces up and quickly darts around both me and the bicycle. The door closes behind him.

Easy jobs tonight. I fetch the three-wheeler and lead it back to the other bicycle. The cap hangs at the bottom of the frame, like a dropped flag. I hang it on the door handle.

My pocket watch reveals that I still have many hours before my meeting with Belzén's boys in Vanadislunden. I'll have time to take both bicycles to Wernersson, have dinner and a nap.

My knee clicks as I swing my leg over the frame of the black bicycle. I put my hand on the handlebar of the three-wheeler and start pedalling down Fleminggatan. One of the tyres screeches against a fork. A couple of seagulls are making a din, although it is now entirely dark. In a house at the bottom of the street, despite the rain, fire has taken hold in a sooty chimney. A cone of embers is flung up into the blackness, looking like fireflies.

Usually by this time I'm asleep. I yawn, a couple of raindrops and maybe a snowflake land on my tongue. The clouds hide the moon, and the park lies steeped in darkness. My lungs are smarting.

The pedestrian path curls off up the slope. It's almost midnight and there's not a person in sight. A coughing fit is lurking in my chest. Up on the ridge lies the large brick building like a medieval fort, four towers at the corners and thick walls sitting on a base of granite. In the summers, the kids often lie in wait up there and pepper passing people with their pea-shooters. The sleet forms a transparent, jellified layer over the lawns. The deciduous trees stand naked, frozen stiff in the December night.

The bells of Stefan's church strike twelve times. It doesn't take long before I hear the sound of a car approaching from below, past the workhouse buildings. With its headlights turned off, it passes the white, octagonal music pavilion a short distance below.

I light a cigar and hold the lit match in the air. The dark green paintwork of the vehicle almost merges with the night. It stops next to me. Hiccup is wearing a black raincoat, a stiff hat and rubber boots. He snivels with his broad nose. I can't make out the driver.

Hiccup nods at me and opens the back door. He leans inside and grunts as he drags out a bloke with his hands bound at his back.

'This is the heavyweight.'

He's a large man in a green hunter's coat. The jute sack over his head is red daubed. Around his neck is a neatly tied noose of hemp rope. Hiccup drops him on his stomach in the wet grass. He writhes in the snow gunk, sobbing. Another comes splashing into the slush behind him. He's smaller, wearing a dark suit. He doesn't move at all.

Hiccup gets hold of the shirt collar of the first one and pulls him to his knees. He grabs the other, who falls forwards again. Hiccup mutters something that can't be heard. After another attempt he leaves him lying there. The rain splatters against the grass, against the roof of the car, and against Hiccup's raincoat. For an instant, a match illuminates the face of the driver as he lights a cigarette. He has a straight, pointed nose and a big gold ring on his finger. His eyes are hidden by the brim of his hat. I stifle a yawn and pull down my neck between my shoulders.

Hiccup places himself behind the bound men. He's holding a black, stub-nosed revolver. It looks like a little toy in his enormous hand. His little finger doesn't even have space on the hilt; it sticks out as if he's holding an elegant tea cup at a society gathering.

'If it freezes over in the night it won't be much fun getting in to work tomorrow.' Hiccup looks up at the dark sky. He shakes his head. Then he nods at me.

I put my cigar in my mouth and walk over to the kneeling bloke. I pull at one of the rope ends and remove the sack. His face is a mess of compression wounds, swellings and blood.

I grab him by the shoulders and give him a shake. His body is utterly limp. I've seen it before among small-time gangsters who know they've done wrong and are going to be punished for it, or timorous women who have taken a beating too often from their men: they just want to get it over with. With one hand on

140

his collar and the other in his hair, I lift him up so that his knees are off the ground.

'Zetterberg?'

He whimpers and shakes his head. His knees squelch back down into the grass. I take a few rapid puffs on my cigar as I turn my attention to the other one. I pull off his sack and grab his blond hair. I force his face up into the rain. He's already out cold. There's not a whole tooth left between his lacerated, gaping lips. A large part of his ear is missing. He wheezes with irregular breaths. He's dying. I nod at Hiccup and gesture at the man in my grip.

'Zetterberg?'

'He's never even heard the name,' answers Hiccup.

I drop the man's face back into the grass.

'What sort of types are these?'

'This one's from Söder,' says Hiccup and points limply with the revolver at the kneeling man. 'The other one's on his home turf. They're not high up, but they're not at the bottom either. They'd know.'

'And Ma?'

'Not involved.'

'Is there anything here that could be traced back to us?'

'No, damn it, nothing. You don't want the Reaper on your heels, do you?'

He's referring to Ploman's weasel of a bodyguard. I nod, turn up my collar, and step aside. The man on his knees raises his face to the sky. The rain cuts pale grooves through his blood. The first four shots follow so closely that they almost sound like two. As if the Söder gangster has already figured out what's about to happen, he tries to turn around and get back on his feet. Hiccup puts a few slugs in his body and he falls with his face looking up at the rain. The other one hardly moves as he takes two shots in his back. The report sounds even louder in the rain. My ears start ringing almost straightaway.

With his revolver smoking, Hiccup goes between the two bodies. He leans over the first one and squeezes another shot into his face at close range. I take another step back. He turns round, leans down and shoots the other one in the back of his head. The bullet makes a hole in his skull, and the rain makes holes in the gunpowder smoke that hangs motionless in the December night. Hiccup empties the chamber of the revolver and puts the empty cartridges in the pocket of his raincoat.

'Both have wives and small children,' he says, as he reloads. 'I suggest we leave them here, so they'll be found.' I nod. 'And even though it's a hell of a day I reckon you should get rid of your boots.'

I nod again. He reaches across Ploman's bloke and we shake hands. He looks as if he's about to leave, when suddenly he stops.

'Damn, that's right, I was going to ask you: can you breathe through that nose of yours?'

'Just about. You?'

'Hello, no. I can't even smell my own shit any more.'

He grunts at his own joke, nods and gets into the motor. It splutters a few times before it starts. The driver backs into the grass, turns, and drives off. The bound men lie not far from the walls of the fort. I smoke, and I watch them for a while. The rain washes them clean of blood, pieces of bone and brain matter. Soon, only two small black holes can be seen in their skulls, no bigger than two-öre coins. They stare back at me. I think a bit about death and my almost-new boots. The corpse closest to me has a wedding ring on his finger. It gleams through the water running over it.

By the time the nausea catches up with me I've made my way to the bottom of the park. It comes over me like in the dressing room after a match, when your stomach suddenly becomes aware of just how much sweat and blood you've swallowed. I put my hand against the black metal railing of the stone stairs leading down to Ingemarsgatan and bend over it. My jaw is buzzing.

I hold back from vomiting. I hiss and spit and dry my mouth with the back of my hand. I'm trembling. I straighten up again. On the façade of the old whorehouse to my right, a single word has been set in yellow brick above the door: SALVE.

Tottering down the steps, I think again about Zetterberg. I was wrong about the bloke's mob connections and two families lost their providers because of it.

'So where the hell was he getting the dough from?'

The questions keep buzzing in my head while I stumble down to Ingemarsgatan.

Lundin almost gives me a heart attack when he opens the front door of the undertaker's. He's wearing a faded dressing gown with red embroidery along the collar. His grey locks of hair stand out around his head. It's the first time I've ever seen him wearing anything but a black suit. He's half a second away from getting his nose slammed, just on impulse.

'Where the hell have you been, brother?'

The nausea almost overwhelms me again. 'Damn, you scared me!' I lean forwards with my hands on my knees.

'I spent half the night banging the ceiling with the broom for you!'

'I just went out for a bit of air. Couldn't sleep.'

'You can't have people calling you in the middle of the night!'

I straighten up again. 'Who was it?'

'It doesn't matter if it's a Saturday. Decent people are abed, sleeping!'

'Who called?'

'You have to make sure it doesn't happen again!'

'Damn it! What was it about?'

'It was from the Toad. They'd seen her there. The one-legged one.'

'The bowlegged?'

'That's what I bloody mean, the bowlegged one.'

I'm the only customer the following morning when I walk into the betting shop known as the Toad. It's situated among the stables on Karduansmakaregatan, in a quarter known very decorously as the Tortoise. Behind the counter sits an elderly man with black armbands and spectacles on the tip of his nose. He's counting betting stubs. Standing on a stool, a youth is writing playable matches and odds on a blackboard that covers almost the length of the room. He's wearing plus fours with Argyle socks. His hair is copper coloured.

'Someone called about a bowlegged prostitute?'

The boy turns around. He's freckly. I feel I recognise him. He looks first at the old man and then he nods at me to come outside. With the boy in tow, I walk out into the slippery-as-glass yard. Even though it's late on a Sunday afternoon, the whole area smells of printer's ink. The boy wraps his arms around himself and pulls up his shoulders.

'Kvisten?'

'Yes?'

'I used to work as the soap boy at Nyström's.'

The barber's at home on Roslagsgatan. I vaguely remember a freckled whippersnapper always strutting about with the soap cup when I was there. He's grown. A lot. There's an itch in my crotch. It's been itching since last night. Ever since I enlisted under an Irish flag running coal to Stettin, I've had a soft spot for ginger lads. Last time I thought a boy was pretty I went with him to Bellevueparken. Apparently I got crabs at the same time. I have to remember to pass by a pharmacy and buy grey salve.

The boy looks around, assuring himself that no one's listening.

'Was it you who called?'

'Maybe.' He smiles mischievously.

I sigh. 'What have you got?'

'She was here last night to use the telephone.'

'Yesterday isn't a great deal of good to me.'

'She was babbling on. Talking about how she needs help to move. And then she said a number… I mean a telephone number.'

'Yes?'

'And I was standing there with the chalk in my hand and so I wrote it down. The number.'

'How much?'

'Twenty.'

He's pretty but not that pretty. I don't even have twenty kronor on me.

'A five-kronor note.'

'What do you say, double or nothing?'

Before I've had time to agree to the wager, a one-krona coin is flipped into the cold December air. I snatch at it. It probably wouldn't be noticed in a hurry, but one edge has been filed down – I can feel it quite clearly although I'm wearing gloves. I'm unsure how the trick works in detail, but it's irrelevant. I grab his mop of hair with my free hand. An almost silent yell forms a cone of steam out of his mouth when I take the sharp side of the coin and rake it across his cheek, from his eye to the corner of his mouth. The red graze matches his hair. The boy throws in the towel without fuss.

'Twenty-three twelve.'

He's panting. I nod and go back into the warmth. For some reason he doesn't follow me. I walk up to the wall-mounted telephone, pick up the receiver and ask for the number.

'The Hostel Prince,' croaks a woman at the other end.

I spin the lever to cut off the call. According to rumours, the proprietors of the whorehouse in Old Town strew a fine narcotic powder over Yxsmedsgränd at night to seduce unsuspecting country girls, who are then kept prisoner in the cellars. What is undeniably true, however, is that they rent out rooms to girls who, for a sizeable percentage of their takings, can receive their clients there. I feel my heart beating quicker. This is right. No doubt about it. Most likely Sonja moved to another part of town after she'd burned her bridges in Klara. A futile tactic when I'm on the hunt. When it comes to street girls, I'm a regular bloodhound.

I button up my coat and am just about to leave when the old man behind the desk rises to his feet. He opens a hatch and comes limping into the room with a smile on his damp lips. He folds up his glasses and puts them in his pocket.

'What did you do with my assistant?'

'He suddenly felt unwell and had to get some air.'

'Heads or tails?'

'He lost.'

'You have to forgive him, he's young and doesn't have the sense to choose his victims.'

'We've all been young.'

The old man nods gravely, as oldsters do when just for a change they remember something.

'When I found him he was running the job exchange up in Maria with a companion.'

'Is it still going?'

'Better than ever. People are desperate for jobs. Don't you read the classifieds? Every other person is paying a commission just to get an interview.'

I chuckle. 'Hope.'

'It's the last thing the human being gives up on, they say. A lack of jobs, but plenty of hope. In actual fact it makes people act beyond the pale of reason.'

I chuckle again and start coughing.

'I saw you, you know,' the old bloke goes on. 'Against "The Mallet" Sundström. Early twenties, I'd say.'

'That's right. Sture Sundström. Twenty-two.' I take half a step towards the door.

'The best fight I've seen to date. That spectacular recovery. The knockout in the last round.'

'Thanks. I was four kilos overweight a week before.'

'I heard it was six.'

'I don't remember so well.'

'How's your form now?' He taps his forefinger lightly under one of his eyes and peers at my fading shiner.

'Dwindling.'

'It can only get so low, I think. Come by if you want another fight. I mean the conditions are a bit different now. Well, you know how it works.'

'Thanks.'

'Well, let's leave it at that, then.' He hauls out a cigar and puts it in my breast pocket, then pats me on the shoulder. 'Whatever people say about you, you were a damned fine boxer, one of the best we ever had. Don't let anyone take that away from you.'

'For the conversation,' I say, and toss over the rigged one-krona coin.

The old man catches it, slaps it down on the back of his hand and mutters something I can't hear.

'If you see him, throw him back inside for me,' he calls as I head for the door.

I wave with the back of my hand over my shoulder. The cold hits me. I think the temperature has gone up a few degrees. I shove my fists in my coat pockets, walk past the parliament and into the Old Town. Svensk Filmindustri's talkie film bus is parked by the castle. A couple of kids with Sunday time on their hands are hanging about the bus, shivering in the cold wind from Strömmen.

At the corner of Stora Nygatan and Yxsmedsgränd I see piled up in the street two landscape paintings, an old mirrored chest and a rag-stuffed mattress. A couple of removal blokes have already loaded a lot of tatty furniture on a truck. A group of people have gathered around them, calling out loudly. Oaths and curses fly through the air. A porky goon is there to keep them all in order. On the pavement sits a woman under a blanket of patched horse cloth, weeping into her apron. A parish district visitor is ushering a bunch of children in front of her down the cobbled street. Most likely they'll be taken to the children's home.

'Aren't you going to hock the clothes off her back as well, you swine?' A red-nosed bloke in a rock-blaster's vest aims a blow at the constable, who ducks, but slips. His peaked cap with the gleaming metal emblem hits the ground. People laugh. I light a Meteor. The goon draws his sabre and chases his assailant. His sabre glitters in the dying light. He gives up after only ten metres or so.

'Now the sod's coming back as well.' A boy in the crowd picks up the goon's cap. Before he runs off he spins it as far as he can down the street. The goon comes running after him.

The boy loses his footing on the slippery cobblestones right in front of me and ends up on his back-end. The goon's apple-red face splits wide open in a smile. I step into the street and brace myself. The goon hurtles into me. He struggles to keep his balance, then loses it and hacks his sabre into the cobbles. The kid darts in behind my back, grabbing my coat arm.

'What the hell's the matter with you?' The goon spits saliva in all directions.

'Excuse me, I didn't see you.'

For a few seconds his grey eyes stare into mine. I drill my gaze into him. Soon enough, the anger dissipates from that mound of pork. He looks around hurriedly and shambles back to the truck. The boy darts off through the lanes.

I take a last puff on my Meteor. One of the removals blokes drops his end of a double bed, which slams into the street. I step on my cigar butt and turn off down Yxsmedsgränd as the truck ploughs its way through the crowd. An old man, in a gesture of futile despair, cracks his stick against the paintwork. There's permanent shadow in the alley, which is scarcely two metres wide. The ice is like translucent mortar between the paving stones. The ochre-coloured façades are streaked with soot.

At the corner of Lilla Nygatan I stand watching the men making circuits around the Pensionat Prinsen. A seaman wearing a shipmaster's winter coat walks up and down the lane three times before summoning his courage and disappearing into the foyer. He comes out soon enough. Maybe the cost was a little steeper than he'd had in mind, or his requirements were too specific. The establishment's sign sways slowly on its hinges above the black door. The agitations on Stora Nygatan have abated. My hopes of finding Sonja in there set my heart aglow.

A tall, lanky bloke in a bowler hat and unusual heeled military boots remains outside for a long time before he disappears in the direction of Stora Nygatan. I have a sense of having seen him before quite recently, but I can't remember where.

A rat scurries across the lane and follows the gutter around the corner. There, a man and a school-age boy pass by. The man is dressed in a black three-piece suit. He's holding his cap in his hand. The boy is wearing a sailor's hat.

I stroll up to the door.

The foyer, with its worn red carpet, smells of coffee and cheap mulled wine. The little crystal chandelier hanging from the ceiling is turned off, and the foliage of the large pot plant on the floor looks as if it's been burned through by cigarettes. A large-busted elderly woman in a black velvet dress sits under a key cabinet. She's knitting. In the gloom, one can make out a few grey whiskers on her chin. A cigarette smoulders in an ashtray beside her. I assume she's had the occasional odd request before.

'I'm looking for a girl with a Dales accent.'

She raises a finger and finishes counting her stitches before she replies. I feel my heart beating.

'Oh, but then you're a bit late, sir. We had a girl here from the Dales but she moved out last night. We do have a blonde jewel from Östersund, though. A bit short but very popular. Kept company for a while with the motorcycle ace Vicke Gustavsson.'

Disappointment falls heavy as a plumbing weight into my chest. No bowlegged Sonja, no witness, no alibi for this damned murder and no comeuppance for the goons.

'Where did she move to?'

The woman scratches herself between her eyebrows – pulled into a deep furrow of concern – with the tip of one of her knitting needles. 'She was in a hurry and didn't say anything about it. Rushed out like a shot. But she was off anyway, she didn't even put on all that colourful stuff they usually wear.' The woman laughs so hard that her breasts look about to jump out of her dress. 'We have a girl from Medelpad. Slightly lame but not even twenty.'

I shake my head and write down Lundin's number on a page of my notebook, tear it out and hand it over with a five-kronor note.

'Call me if she turns up.'

The woman nods, snatches up the five-kronor note and quickly tucks it into her sleeve, although she leaves the telephone number where it is.

'Of course.'

'Have you cleaned her room?'

'No, haven't had time yet. There's been a blasted high turnover.'

'Clearly. Can I have a look at the room?'

Unconcerned, she keeps knitting. 'We don't usually do that. A question of discretion, you see.'

'Can I pay for an hour?'

'We only rent out rooms at a daily rate.' She nods down at the table.

I mutter and get out another five-kronor note.

'One floor up. Number three.' Without looking, she reaches for a key behind her in the key cabinet, and puts it on the table.

The key catches a little, but after some fiddling the door opens. From the room next door comes the sound of a bed thumping against the wall. On the shelf in the hall lies a lady's hat in black plush. The door of the wardrobe has been left open. It's empty, and three of the clothes hangers are on the floor.

I step inside. The room has green wallpaper. Maybe I can still pick up the scent of her fragrance. The furnishings consist of an unmade bed, a low table and two sunken armchairs with tassels. On a table covered in a lace tablecloth is a full ashtray, an empty vase and two glasses, still with a red residue inside. I move one of the glasses to my nose. Port wine.

The room gives me bad memories, and suddenly the itching starts again. I straighten my back and put my hand inside my waistband, to give myself a bit of a scratch. 'Damned creepy-crawlies.'

Next to the ashtray lies a promotional card for a boutique on Kungsgatan offering fancy goods, and a couple of hat pins with big glass marbles at one end. A man bellows in the room next door. I pull the elastic off my wallet and tuck the card into it.

On the windowsill are a couple of women's magazines, *Allers* and *Allt för Alla*. I pick them up and give them a shake but nothing falls out from between their pages.

In the wastepaper bin lies a piece of discarded chewing gum and a couple of packs of cigarettes of various brands, Bridge and Negresco. My knees click as I go down on all fours. There's an open condom packet under the bed. I stand up, holding it in my hand. Royal. To this extent at least the lovesick porter from Boden was right. In the middle of the dirty sheet is a small, rusty-red bloodstain.

The bathroom is hardly more than a square metre in size. There's a zinc tub on the floor. The hand basin is of porcelain. A few long hairs cling to the edge. I've seen enough.

'She had a visitor,' I say to the velvet-wearing woman in the foyer. The note with Lundin's telephone number is still on the table.

'At night. In that case, I never saw anyone.'

'Any other friends?'

'Not as far as I've seen.'

'Ring me if she comes back.'

The alley still lies steeped in shadow. I'm hungry but don't have much money left in my wallet. I go and stand in the doorway next to the hostel. As the girls come out I'll grab each one for a chat. I'm calmer now. I've picked up her scent. Sonja is up and moving. I'm looking forward to seeing Berglund's face when I stroll in with Sonja on my arm. I smile.

'Kvisten's going to show them. Trying to pin a murder on a bloke when he's as innocent as a bride!'

From the castle a hundred or so metres away comes the sound of a band playing a march. It's the changing of the guards. The lane is empty apart from a messenger boy hurtling round the corner to Lilla Nygatan. Once I've spoken to a few of the girls I might make my way up to Tjärhovsplan so I can rule out Doctor Jensen from this story. On the way I could stop off to see my old confirmation priest August Gabrielsson in Katarina and have myself a cup of church coffee, unless he's busy with the service. He used to be a seaman's chaplain, and he's the only one of the black coats you can actually talk to. Sometimes I read about him in the newspapers, because he's outspoken about the Nazi threat, but it's been a good while since I saw him in person. On the way home I might also look into the boutique on Kungsgatan to ask if Sonja is a regular customer. What was the name of it again? I get out my wallet from my pocket.

An emaciated mutt comes up and carefully sniffs at me. I squat down, let him feel the warmth of my hand and scratch him behind his ear.

From Stora Nygatan, the tall man in the bowler hat appears. Maybe he's drummed up a bit of courage in one of the licensed premises further down among the lanes. His iron-shod boots clatter against the cobblestones. The dog pricks up its ears and turns about.

I look around and put my wallet in my pocket. I don't know what it is that makes me stop. Maybe it's the lanky man's determined gait. Maybe it's the slight but clear limp on his left leg. A good boxer knows to duck well before the punch comes in.

We're less than ten metres from each other when our eyes meet. He smiles as if he's caught sight of an old friend. His coat-tails flap like a burial shroud when he parts them. The pistol has a long, black barrel. The hilt is made of a light-coloured wood. He gives a full-throated bellow as he picks up speed, raising his pistol without closing his eye.

I throw myself into the doorway at the same time as a shot hits the wall next to me. A cloud of ochre-coloured cement flies around me like a swarm of angry wasps. The bullet removes a piece of the façade.

I'm running. Far ahead of me I see the dark waves of Riddarfjärden splashing against the abutments of the train line out in the water. Another two shots ring out. The echo chases me down the narrow lane.

I go around the book printer's on the corner and turn into Lilla Nygatan, slip and hit my knee hard against the pavement, swear loudly and get back up on my feet. I just have time to skip across the path of an oncoming truck and gain a moment's respite. Its signal blares out, hoarse as a fog horn in my ears. My heart jumps between the walls of my chest. My pumping lungs are freezing themselves solid in the cold December air.

Behind me, the steps thump irregularly but too fast for my liking. I turn off down Kåkbrinken. The sound of our racing steps echoes between the houses. A sharp, smacking noise, as when the old women work over the laundry with clubs down by the jetties in spring.

The man is starting to gain on me. I give in to the cough, it tears and tugs at me, makes me stoop with pain at the same time as I keep stumbling on. Viscous strings of slime are rising from my chest.

The steps behind me halt. This means he's taking aim. I throw myself around the corner into Munkbrogatan at the same time as the fourth shot is fired.

Twenty or so metres on, the cobbled lane opens into Mälaretorget. Here, the market stalls stand side by side, enveloped in a light fog rising up from the water. The more elaborate ones have grey canvas roofs, whereas the cheaper ones are nothing but a couple of planks resting on a pair of up-ended apple crates. The market madams sit on split herring barrels filled with straw. The stalls offer semi-soft winter potatoes and turnips packed in sod, big jugs of country cream and piles of round crispbreads. Old blokes from the archipelago, their hands shimmering with fish scales, stand behind mounds of perch, zander and pike, and eels slithering in zinc-plated buckets. On the edges the down-and-outs are loitering: the ones who have spread blankets with boot straps and ribbons, the dextrous shoeshines, the knife sharpeners with portable whetstones, and along with them, the pick-pockets blowing on their hands to keep their fingers warm.

'Out of the way!' I shove past a butcher's apprentice, who has half a pig on his shoulders, and dive headlong into the busy square, one hand on my hat. An express train passes, whistling shrilly, towards Central Station, on the connecting track a distance out over the water.

My pursuer doesn't give up. I slip just as another shot goes off. The bullet smacks through the ribs of a wooden cage, takes the head off a cockerel and hits a young girl wearing an apron and a knitted orange hat like an upside-down flower pot. With a surprised look, the girl wraps her arms around her stomach, curtsies, and collapses. She gives a heavy sigh.

'What was that?' someone screams.

I jump over the girl just as her green eyes are going out. I turn a corner into the old Meat Market. Here everything stops.

It's Advent. Between the block known as Icarus and the southernmost of the market halls, the merchants have framed the square with booths decked with spruce cuttings. Ladies with mittens are braiding goats out of straw, there's a wealth of tapestries with embroidered quotes from the Bible, also dip-candles and carved Santa Clauses. A cul-de-sac. I curse the Redeemer.

I back up against the house wall and try to stop panting and get my lungs into order. I look up at the gravel pit of planks and reinforcement rods known as Slussen. Up on the Katarina lift, through the haze, I can make out the neon sign with the Stomatol tube. I close my eyes, inhale what feels like an ice block, and listen. I've had to trust in my hearing many times when I was on the ropes, when the swelling around my eyes was such that I couldn't even orient myself, or when I was blinded by blood or sweat.

At first I only hear the screams from the market square and the cries for the police and the sound of my bolting heart. A high-pitched whining is ringing in my ears. I exhale and hold my breath again. I hear the swishing sound of yet another train approaching, and a lot of footsteps.

'Look alive, Kvisten.' My whisper is hoarse but it calms me. The noise of the train is just starting to build as I think I can make out the sound of a pair of boots moving with an irregular rhythm, just like the sound of the pistons of the locomotive.

I lunge from behind the corner, exhale through my nose and throw out my fist. The man in the bowler hat runs right into it.

There's no bodily sensation that can measure up to a straight right, the sort of punch that connects with your opponent when your arm is almost completely straightened, your hip turned in the same direction, and the heel facing almost directly away from the body.

The pain vibrates and shoots back into my shoulder. The distinctive sound of bone and gristle giving way is even louder than the express train, rushing past no more than thirty or so metres away from us.

The man drops his bowler and sits on his arse with his upper body leaning forwards and his military boots far apart, showing the gleaming metal fittings on his heels. It looks as if someone threw a sticky clump of red kelp in his face. Thick strings of blood dangle over his hands, which are fumbling over his thighs towards the Mauser pistol that has ended up between his legs.

Flummoxed, I back away with my hand on my aching shoulder. No one's actually meant to be conscious after a punch of that quality. He looks up at me. There's something wrong with one eye. His face looks like something you might find hanging at a butcher's stall behind us in the market hall, and as for his nose, there's really no sign of it.

Through the blood, with a strangled, gurgling sound, he hisses: '*Scheisse.*'

Because the German bastard finds his pistol between his legs at the same time, I don't stop to hear if he has something to add. I turn and run across the empty market square. A couple of the stalls have been overturned, a jug of milk has been spilled. I see the girl. She is lying where she fell, her blood forming a pattern between the cobblestones.

I peer over my shoulder before going any further into the little lanes of Old Town. The German swine is tottering about on unsteady legs, with the pistol in his right hand. A police whistle pierces the air.

By the time I'm a few more blocks away, a couple of sharp cracks of gunfire roll through the narrow passages.

Only after dusk has completely fallen do I make my way home via detours and back streets. It's snowing. The snowflakes are collecting in small, neat drifts on window ledges and the brims of men's hats. The city is buzzing with gossip. At newsstands, spontaneous groups of curious people gather around newspaper vendors and police booths. Where one person says that the desperado was mowed down by the police, another claims that he hijacked a car and managed to get away. Another rumour maintains that the perpetrator swam away under the connecting railway line. Most people agreed that he must be a Jew or possibly a gypsy. One boy who says he was on the scene has given an opinion that the perpetrator's appearance precisely matches the description of the Carriage Man, who caused mayhem in the city a few years back.

It's almost six by the time I walk into Ström's miscellaneous goods store. The junkshop owner appears behind a pile of rolled-up rag rugs. He's a sizeable old bloke, near on sixty, with a tangled blond beard shot through with quite a few grey hairs. Today he's got a pair of rough trousers on, and a collarless linen shirt. In one hand he's holding a little globe and, in the other, a pair of skiing boots. Loose talk on Roslagsgatan has postulated that although there's never been a seaman in Sailor-Beda's life, it was in fact Ström who fathered the simpleton, Petrus. The old man puts the ski boots on a shelf of empty jam jars.

'I've closed.'

'I'll be quick.'

'Have you heard what's happened?'

'In the market?'

'No, at the laundry!'

'Is the King visiting?' I massage my aching shoulder.

'No, Count Hamilton!'

'At the marketplace, then?'

'Terrible story. Fourteen years old.'

'I heard she was sixteen.'

'How can I help you?'

'A naval-issue leather holster. For a Husqvarna.'

'I have one of those somewhere.'

'I sold it to you.'

Old man Ström runs his hand over his beard and mutters something before he disappears among his treasures. I stand looking out over Roslagsgatan, scratching my crotch and thinking about the vermin nesting in there.

It's snowing plentifully. The number 6 tram ploughs through the darkness in a glittering cloud of snow crystals. Not far from the junction between Ingemarsgatan and Roslagsgatan, a shining white two-door Cadillac is parked. The Good Templar, Wetterström, who lives two flights of stairs above me, has stopped for a moment to peer in through the side window of the car. He cups his hands around his face to get a better view. A woman with a shawl over her head and shoulders hurries from the general store, carrying a basket of carrots, rolled-up newspapers and milk bottles with screw-top lids.

I would bet good money on Sonja being able to place the German swine on Kungsgatan at the time of the murder.

'I think the bastard followed me to Old Town to find Sonja. What a prize swine.'

When I look back on the last few days he makes the odd appearance here and there in my memory.

'What luck that she had time to move from the hostel. Who knows what might have happened otherwise?'

'What are you standing here muttering about?'

I jump at the sound of Ström's voice. 'Nothing.'

'Two seventy I want for that.'

'You only gave me ninety öre for it.'

The holster has the national coat of arms pressed into the leather. I count out the money. I have one krona forty öre left in the kitty, and thirty kronor between my best china plates at home in the kitchen, and not a cent in the bank. I have to talk to Wernersson to see whether he has any more bicycles that need picking up.

I look about and hurry across the road. If the police haven't already arrested the pistol-wielding lunatic in the bowler hat I want to get out my own shooting iron as quick as possible from my wardrobe.

Cheap Bengt, the itinerant knife sharpener, cycles past on an old Nordstjerna with a pack of sandwiches tied to his handlebars. He's wearing a brimmed hat and a pair of thick woollen socks in his clogs. He waves cheerfully, I nod back tiredly.

As I reach the other side I almost drop to my knees in a furious coughing fit. I don't know if I caught silicosis in the boiler rooms of the various ships on which I served for some years, or if it's caused by my consumption of a hundred cigars a week. Every winter I cough myself half to death. My throat feels slimed up, as if I've been guzzling fat country milk. Toto's throat lozenges don't help, nor camphor drops.

I put one hand on the façade, lean over and spit. My breast is burning. The Good Templar, Wetterström, slows his steps but I wave dismissively at him and straighten up.

'Nothing to be concerned about. From youthful speed, old men go to seed.'

My throat rattles like a coal chute during unloading.

'Did you get hold of her?' Lundin stands in the doorway, kneading himself a venerable quid of snuff.

'She slipped away this time as well.'

'Your last clue?'

'Well.'

'So maybe we can talk about something else at breakfast tomorrow?' Lundin stuffs the wad in.

I sigh and put a cigar in my mouth. 'Tomorrow is tomorrow's concern.'

'Did you hear about the murder in Old Town?'

'Ström mentioned something about it.'

'Twelve years old.'

'They'll catch him.'

'And this morning there were tonnes of police up in the park.'

'Oh?'

'You have a visitor again, my brother.'

'Who?'

'Well, not a one-legged whore.'

'Bowlegged, I told you.'

'Not a bowlegged whore. This one should even stir the interest of someone like you.'

I remove the cigar from my mouth and stare at him.

With the long, yellow nail of his forefinger he scratches off a flake of creamy white paint from the door frame, and then goes on: 'Did you see the car parked outside? It's hers. I think you can earn yourself a decent bit of cash.'

I nod before I turn my back on him. I open and close the fingers of my right hand a few times before I go up the stairs.

It's swollen but nothing seems to be broken. Before I press down the door handle, I take a short breather. The warmth of the flat hits me.

'I usually like to talk business over a glass of red,' says a woman's voice when I step into the hall, 'but you seem to lack wine glasses.'

The lamp on the desk is the only source of light. It's directed into the hall, at my face, and I hold up my hand to get a better look at the woman sitting in my armchair with her feet on my desk. Beside her lies a pair of green leather gloves, a similarly green silk scarf and a wide-brimmed hat. She angles down the desk lamp.

'You have to excuse me but I have a new pair of shoes and they're *absolutely deadly* for my feet.'

By her voice I'd say she's a big-time smoker. She lets me admire her long legs before decoratively sweeping them off the table. Her silk stockings are so thin that, in the lamplight, you can see her red toenails through them and a couple of bruises on top of her feet. She fires off a smile with her crimson-red lips, then bends down and straps on her shoes.

There's a wide gap between her front teeth. Although she's probably a good deal older than me, a thick layer of powder makes it more or less impossible to be precise about her age. Her eyes are chestnut brown, and she keeps her eyebrows severely plucked under the permed waves of her shoulder-length ash-blonde hair. Something about her features reminds me of someone I've seen before.

Remembering that I have a hole in one of my socks, I keep my shoes on. I lean my shoulder against the ceramic stove, cross my legs, light a cigar and watch the performance. She's dropped her brown fur coat on the floor in front of the desk. It lies on the cork mat like a run-over pedigree dog in the gutter. As she fluffs up her hair with her hands, showing me the pink pearls in her ears that match both her necklace and the brooch on her modestly swelling bust, I note that she's too bony for my taste, while undeniably giving off a strong scent of class, style and oodles of dough.

'Certainly I have wine glasses. You can't have had a very good look in the cupboard.'

I give a thought to my money, hidden between the plates. There's not a lot left, and though my total assets are obviously just small beer for this lady, you can never be sure. Some people steal because they need to, and some do it out of sheer boredom.

'Then you must fetch some at once! You see, I had lunch at Cecil where my husband's a regular at table three, even though he never goes out, and I had a glass of St Emilion and I told Hugo I absolutely *must* take home a bottle of it.'

The Oriental carpet absorbs the sound of her heels when she circles the table and parks her backend on the desk. She takes a cigarette from a case and inserts it into a long black cigarette holder embossed with narrow streaks of gold.

'Hugo?' I let her wait, the cigarette unlit in front of her.

'The waiter at Cecil. Haven't you been to Cecil?'

'It's been a while.' I'm familiar with the restaurant on Biblioteksgatan, but my current financial situation probably wouldn't even allow for a visit to their bathroom.

'Then you should go there again soon.'

She waves her cigarette as if trying to point me in the right direction. I nod at a box of matches beside her on the desk. She purses her mouth. Outside, two of the alley cats are slugging it out.

'I'll absolutely do that.' I point at the kitchen. 'I wouldn't mind having a glass, I've had a tough day at work.'

When I come back with glasses and a corkscrew, she's capitulated and fired up her cigarette under her own steam. I take the bottle she offers me and I open it. A waft of her perfume finds its way into my ruined nose when I lean forwards and fill the glasses on the desk. The fragrances of each are soft, full-bodied and warm.

I put the bottle on the table and step back. I haven't bathed for three days. Anyway, it's probably safest to keep her at arm's length. She hands me the wine.

'You've dropped something.' I gesture with the glass at the fur coat on the floor.

'Your good health!' She sweeps down half the glass in one go. She doesn't quite seem the connoisseur she purports to be. I have a sip. It's good, as far as wine goes.

'And so?'

'It's about a theft.'

'A theft?'

'My name is Doris. Doris Steiner. Does that mean anything to you?'

I keep the glass hovering somewhere in the region of my mouth, before I take a big mouthful.

'As in the Steiner Group? As in Doris…' I search my mind for her name. 'Doris Lugn?'

So that's why she feels familiar. I haven't seen her since the days of the silent movies, not since Stiller and Sjöman. Her hair is fairer and she's lost some of the intensity in her eyes, but it's her all right. She's slimmed down a fair amount but on the other hand this is the fashion of the moment, and every woman in photographs from the red-carpet premieres on Kungsgatan seems to have starved herself. I saw her in a couple of films after I signed off the navy payroll, but eventually she married someone filthy rich and disappeared from the silver screen.

The wedding ring is in place, on the very same hand that so eagerly empties wine down her gullet. Since Ivar Kreuger bowed out of the race, Steiner must be in a good second place behind Wallenberg. I have an idea that he made his fortune in the building business. The former movie star pours herself yet another glass of the exclusive wine and knocks it back. The rest of the land may be on its knees, but clearly not the Steiner family. Now, Kvisten, you have to play your cards right.

Doris buffs up her hair again. 'At least I made a bit of an impression.'

I go over to the desk. I pour myself another glass of wine.

'How can I be of service?'

My facial muscles are resistant when I smile. Doris presses her cigarette into the ashtray with a quick movement and immediately inserts another into her cigarette holder. I put down my glass and strike a match. She has a beauty spot just under her left eye. I light her cigarette. Lundin bangs the floor three times with the broom. Apparently there's a telephone call for me, but right now nothing's more important than this. Doris holds out her cigarette case.

'They're flavoured with rum.'

I raise my cigarette, roll it gently between my thumb and forefinger.

'What can I do for you?'

She looks around the flat, takes a few drags, and smiles. 'You don't have any photographs?'

'No.'

'None at all?'

I think about old Branting, who fell behind the cupboard. 'None.'

She closes her cigarette case with a metallic click, stands up and puts it on the desk in front of her. Her nails are as carefully manicured as those of the secretary, yesterday, at Belzén in Birka.

'It's really quite silly.'

'It may feel that way to you.'

'It's our housekeeper, she's been stealing, but I can't prove it, and my husband won't believe me. Really it's a triviality, just a few things from my jewellery box. But I want to teach her a lesson.'

'Teaching people lessons is my speciality.'

'Can we discuss it over dinner? I'm hungry and the wine will be finished in a minute. We can take my car.'

I shake my head. 'Thanks, but I've eaten.' I have a couple of eggs and a piece of bread in my kitchen cupboard. I'd rather have a police vagrancy caution than get stuck with the bill at Grand or Cecil. Not a chance.

She reaches for the bottle. Her hand trembles when she pours the last of the precious liquid. The vibrations travel up her body and reach her lower lip. My stomach goes into knots, as I suddenly remember the carpenter's wife, Sonja's mother – how she wept quite uncontrollably in the doorway. This time I can't get out of it. There's no possibility of preventing what is about to take place.

'Really, just a triviality,' whispers Doris.

A tear works itself free from the corner of her eye, ploughs a thin furrow through the powder of her cheek, takes the beauty spot with it and makes way for more tears. Suddenly she's standing with her face in her hands, heaving with sobs. I have to say something consoling, anything, but can't think of anything. How does one console a desperate millionaire? I take hold of her upper arms. She gasps. I press myself against her and kiss her deeply.

PART TWO

Both Lundin and I hold our breath as he carefully rolls up his newspaper. The winter fly stops polishing itself when the shadow darts across the table top, but it's too late. The dry smack of the newspaper resounds through the little kitchen, which smells, deliciously, of fresh-baked bread. The coffee cups rattle against their saucers.

'Rest in peace.' Lundin nods thoughtfully and wipes the rolled-up newspaper against a corner of the table, as a butcher cleans his knife on his apron. He opens the paper and puts it on the table. Over the photograph of Olsson and Berglund is a gleaming bloodstain and a crisp fly wing. In the photograph, the two detectives are standing on Mälaretorget. Olsson is pointing away towards Slussen and Berglund is following his gaze. They look grim. That was the escape route taken by the German creep after shooting a wholesaler named Hildebrandt in the face and hijacking his car to get away from the chaos in the market square. The headline announces, *No Trace of the Market Murderer*.

'Where was I?'

The chair legs scrape against the floor when Lundin leans back and pops his thumbs into his waistcoat pockets. He drums his chest lightly with his fingers. I dilute the morning cup with some schnapps from the bottle on the table, even though my head hurts after yesterday's excesses of champagne and wine.

'You just said I didn't have a nose for business. That I should stay damned clear of it.'

'Exactly. Stay damned clear of it. There's nothing for you to gain there. Unless the wholesaler's family are offering a reward.' Lundin takes his thumbs out of his waistcoat and tips forwards. He taps the newspaper article and flicks away the fly wing with his snuff-stained nail. I have a sip of coffee. It's almost cold but the schnapps is bracing.

'That German creep is the solution to this whole case.'

'This case is no longer your concern. The German is a snag for the police to deal with. They have two telephone lines for witnesses and *Aftonbladet* has hired a clairvoyant. Most likely he has already left the country, but if he's still here they'll nab him soon enough. Forget the whole thing: forget Zetterberg and Sonja, the only thing you should put your abilities and energy into, my brother, is the director's wife. There, my friend, you will find a surfeit of coin to collect.'

'The case is totally overblown. Her bloke found out about the jewellery theft and he immediately fired his entire household staff.'

'Is it really so hard to understand? Let's go through it again.'

'No need.'

'Ludvig Steiner's wife comes into your office and more or less throws herself in your arms.'

'They haven't shared a bed for years. She says their bedrooms are in separate parts of the house.'

'He must be more or less the same age as myself. At which point there's little to think about except your infirmities. And they already have an heir?'

'A son.'

'See. She comes to you about a jewellery theft, but when you meet again the old man has pre-empted you and fired every sod in a fit of rage. None-the-damned-less she wants to see you. And not only that, she invites you out to the Grand.'

'Yesterday. Tonight we're going to the Continental.'

'Three evenings in a row? You've got her in your pocket? No young woman has time for an old man, for God's sake.'

Outside, in a sparsely lit expanse of Ingemarsgatan, a rat gives off a high-pitched scream. I look out of the window, and see it has been cornered among the shadows by an emaciated black cat. The cat inches forwards, moving laterally to cut off any escape route. I take another mouthful of coffee.

'It smells of trouble.'

'You've lost your salt, old boy. She's good for millions.'

'She's old.'

'In her right hand she holds long life, in her left, wealth and renown.'

'What the hell is that supposed to mean?'

'Surely you must bloody know, you who have done the rounds of all seven seas?'

Lundin's excitation whips up a bout of coughing. I put down my coffee cup and watch the starving cat ripping the rat to pieces in the street. Little tufts of fur hover above the cobblestones for a moment. Lundin gets out a grubby handkerchief from his trouser pocket and spits into it before he opens the newspaper. I draw my hand across the night's production of beard stubble.

The newspaper rustles as Lundin spreads it across the table. He turns it halfway around and taps on the classifieds. 'Looks like HP has been out on a binge.'

I lean forwards and read: WHERE ARE: *A silver sports trophy, 3 boxers holding a bowl, on the latter a shield of gold, also a gentleman's fur coat with an astrakhan collar? Finders contact Harry Persson. Tel. Haga 15 93.*

Gold trophies and an astrakhan collar. That could have been me, if everything hadn't gone to hell. I grunt and turn my thoughts again to Doris Steiner's millions. I reach over and firmly grip the schnapps bottle. I'm taking the day off.

Dixie, Doris's fat black dwarf schnauzer, jumps up and down my leg, barking. Her long silly eyebrows sway as she slants her head and looks at me with her coal-black eyes. I stand in front of the hall mirror, buttoning up the rust-red shirt Doris bought for me. It fits me perfectly, as if made to measure. I have never felt softer cotton. Doris claps her hands excitedly next to me.

'The tie as well! And the black jacket!'

Her voice is hoarse with cigarettes and cognac left out in the night. She presents a broad silk tie. I do as I'm told and make a double knot. Doris slips her arm under mine. She's wearing a straight black evening dress with a fishtail hem, and a stole of red mink that reaches her elbows.

'Now we match each other! You look really quite sweet!'

She squeezes my arm, goes up on her tiptoes, kisses my cheek and quickly rubs off the lipstick with a wetted thumb. I comb through my hair with Fandango and smile sheepishly at my broken physiognomy in the mirror. Not much can be done about the nose and the scars, but the rest just about passes muster.

There's a tentative tap on the door. Probably just one of the kids who's worked up the courage to ask for Christmas news-papers. They've already come running here once or twice to collect them.

I take my boots, the shoe polish and an old newspaper and walk into the kitchen. These days I shine them better than the pretty shoeshine boy outside the big library on Sveavägen. The secret is to use silk cloth. Dixie follows me and lies down on the rag rug with her head between her paws. Lundin thumps the broom once on the ceiling. It means Doris should take off her heels. She ashes her cigarette in the sink. He's just jealous.

'Could you be *an angel* and take Dixie for a walk before we go out? As you see I have a few things to take care of.' Doris makes a sweeping gesture over her face.

I nod, check my boots, go over them a few more times and lace them on. I stand up and go to the sink. Dixie yawns excitedly when I find the leash and fix it to her collar of fake rubies. At least I think they're fake.

With the lead dragging behind her, Dixie posts herself with her front paws against the door. I take off my jacket and clip on the shoulder holster. I made the straps myself, using a pair of discarded braces. I open the door and Dixie runs off ahead, down the stairs. Doris doesn't like my wearing the Husqvarna when we are together, and as yet I haven't been able to bring myself to explain why I need it. If we're off to eat, I leave it at home, because then we rarely go much further than from the car door to the restaurant. In other situations, the weight of the pistol against my ribs is a necessity.

I'm going to take Lundin's advice and stop chasing both the German creep and Sonja. In time, once the worst turmoil has settled down, the lanky figure in the bowler hat will come looking for me, and then I'll be ready for him.

Even though Dixie's a bitch, she nonetheless lifts her hind leg when she wees against the big bank of snow that divides the pavement from the street. It has been snowing more or less without interruption for two days and nights. A couple of kids from number 41 are strolling back home with their skates slung around their necks by laces. Maybe the Christmas orchestra has

175

started rehearsing its repertoire up by Albano's rink. On the other side of the street, Wallin is tottering towards number 54. He walks with his arms stretched out from his body, as if he's preparing to lunge at his own shadow. On weekdays he's an auxiliary at Konradsberg's hospital for the mentally ill, at weekends he has a good crack at the bottle.

'Has Kvist got himself a dog? What a sweet little rascal.' The widow Lind, who owns the tobacconist's further down the street, stops and runs her hand through Dixie's coat before putting the short cigar back into her mouth and hurrying on. Dixie tugs at the lead. Maybe it's too cold. On the way back we pass Doris's car.

There's only one model of its kind in the whole country. It's a sixteen-cylinder white Cadillac from 1930 with blue-sprayed wheel arches. Steiner purchased it for his wife at Osterman's Marble Hall during a publicity tour a couple of years ago. I'm mad about it.

Doris lets me drive.

'To Hotel Continental,' she calls out when I turn onto the Roslagsgatan, which is slippery as glass. The rear-end swings round and I struggle to straighten the car up. We both yell with excitement as if drunk. We aren't. Not yet. But it's probably just a question of time.

We drive down Sveavägen at speed, past the Metropol restaurant and the Stockholm School of Economics. Doris spins the wide gold bracelet over the edge of her Nappa leather glove.

'Four days to Christmas and Ludvig fires our entire service staff.'

'Could have been a bit of an overreaction.'

We pass the NORMA where the gangsters hang out on the corner of Kungsgatan. I change down into second where the street narrows by Ateneum girls' school and the statue of Karl Staff. A couple of girls in teddy capes are standing outside the school. One of them has tightened a strap around a pile of books, which she carries in one hand, even though school must have finished hours ago.

'And just at the one time we're not heading south for Christmas.'

Adolf Fredrik's church, newly renovated, shines white in the evening. Along the outside of the iron railings, a bent-over old woman in a large knitted scarf and an apron of sack weave walks back and forth by a stall selling decorative spruce twigs for Christmas. She's slapping herself, trying to work up some warmth.

'Times are hard. We all have to make sacrifices.'

'I suppose that's right. And anyway I met you.' She puts her hand on my thigh. I keep my eyes on the road, fully aware that she's smiling.

I slow down and turn right by the Concert Hall into Kungsgatan.

'Who will you be celebrating with?'

'With Lundin, one supposes.'

'So you have no one else?'

A couple of quick memories flash before me, but I discard them. 'No one.'

I pick up speed as we approach Zetterberg's house. There it lies, grey and immobile in the darkness, with crystallised ice emerging like static eruptions from the drain pipes.

I turn into Vasagatan and park outside the Continental. A tramp with a bottle of cheap plonk in one hand runs up to hold the car door open and maybe earn himself a five-öre piece, but the doorman rushes forwards and kicks snow at him. The doorman's an elderly bloke with slanted, tired eyes and white gloves. All the gold in his coat makes him look like an admiral. For a moment

I am reminded of the sleazy cloakroom man at the Restaurant Pilen's third-class dining room.

'I'm terribly sorry, Mrs Steiner! How very nice to see you again.' The doorman bows slightly and hurries off to hold the double glass doors open for us. Doris wriggles out of her fur coat and he folds it over his arm.

'Sir?'

With a nod, I give him my overcoat and hat. Doris's soft arm steals under mine. I adjust my tie, get out a comb and pull it through my hair. The thick rug yields under our feet as we walk into the music café. The cigarette boy and the toilet attendant stiffen attentively. A couple of electric chandeliers spread a muted, pleasant light over the tables. In a corner, a morose-looking pianist with protruding ears and a strong chin tinkles a low-key, droning melody on a white grand piano. He's so short that they should really have put a telephone directory on his seat.

I briefly remember going to Kompaniet to choose a doll's house for my daughter's second birthday. It must have been about ten years ago. The most beautiful of them, a great monstrosity crafted in the Jugend style, reminds me of the large music café in which I'm now standing. The walls are in white and red, and the room is furnished with heavy mahogany chairs and tables and enormous potted palms. I couldn't afford the pretty doll's house and not any of the simpler models either, so in the end I had to make one myself from off-cuts I got from the wood yard on Tavastgatan.

Doris breaks free from me. I follow her.

The big windows towards Vasagatan are spotless. A young, blonde waitress in a white pinafore and bonnet quickly changes our vase of drooping red roses for another one a few tables along, and gives the little rack of HP and Worcestershire sauce a poke, to adjust its position by a fraction. We sink into the plush armchairs. Outside, another filthy tramp is playing the comb or a harmonica, his cap in the snow in front of him. My reflection flickers over him in the window, our faces merge. I know that he could be me tomorrow, or I could be him.

Next to the grand piano sits a young man in a black wool suit, his hair slicked severely back without a parting. His tie shines a deep yellow against his white shirt. He holds a glass of wine in his hand and taps his foot lightly at the floor. He has white socks and he can't stay in beat.

At a little table next to the young man sits a couple. The man is about ten years older than the woman. She's wearing an evening dress buttoned asymmetrically, with a fur-lined collar and a beret, even though she's indoors. Gazing demonstratively over the man's shoulder and out of the window, she looks utterly bored. Meanwhile, he's reading a newspaper.

Doris waves at a slim, slightly hunchbacked waitress who's probably taller than I am. Her spectacles are hitched onto her pinafore sash. At first she gives us a friendly smile, but it quickly fades. I stare out of the window while Doris conveys her wishes.

'It's so beautiful here! I want to eat *in here*! I don't want to eat in the dining room! I want to eat *in here*!'

'Yes, miss.' The waitress's eyes flicker, she curtsies and soon returns with a couple of menus.

Behind our table, half-obscured behind a palm, sit two young women without male company. Both of them have their hair in a bob, also false eyelashes and evening dresses cut low across their backs. They titter and whisper among themselves. I glance through the menu. Some of it is in French. The liveried cigarette boy walks around with jaunty strides.

'Don't worry about them,' says Doris.

179

'Who do you mean?'

'Oh nothing.' She slides her finger across the menu. 'I'm *absolutely* having the sole gratin. What are you having?'

'Medallion of venison.'

'Oysters as a starter? Have you had oysters?'

'I've spent a quarter of my life at sea. What do you think?'

I wave over the same waitress. She holds her spectacles in both hands as I'm ordering. Doris picks up her handbag. She has already calculated what the feast is going to cost. Just like yesterday, she hands me a wad of banknotes under the table. I transfer the money to my wallet. Sonja's card from the boutique on Kungsgatan falls out and lands on the soft carpet. I pick it up, then drop the wallet into my inside pocket.

The pianist changes to something more upbeat, the girls are still tittering. A waitress pours a smidgeon of red in my crystal glass for tasting. I knock it back with a nod and she fills the glass.

'*No one* has an elasticated wallet any more,' Doris whispers while the waitress produces another bottle. But Doris doesn't taste her white wine, just gets right to it and fills her glass. 'You look like a horse dealer at market. I'm going to buy you a proper wallet.' She lights a cigarette without using the cigarette holder.

'I like it.'

'You want to look like a horse dealer?' She laughs squeakily at her own joke.

'I like it the way it is.'

Doris knocks off the ash with her forefinger. Most of it ends up on the white tablecloth.

'Sorry,' she whispers. 'Now I was horrible again. Old habits, you know how it is. Let's forget about it.'

The oysters are brought in with lemon and special knives. I watch Doris and then try to follow her example. After a few

180

botched attempts I finally manage to munch down the mess. I like the taste. I like the consistency as well, the way the pulp grows in your mouth. Pieces of shell crunch between my teeth, sort of like when you've bitten off someone's ear.

Doris has four of them. I eat the rest of the dozen. I'm kept pretty busy with the oysters and the knife. We don't talk much. Once we're done, a waitress comes swanning in to clear the table.

'Harry Persson sauce,' says Doris and clinks the HP bottle with her gold lighter, before lighting another cigarette.

'You said you didn't know anything about boxing?'

'Well surely everyone knows about HP?'

'I suppose.'

'I met him several times. He made a few films after he retired from professional boxing.'

'I know.'

'And Ernst Rolf sings about him in that funny song!'

'"The Kid with Chocolate Inside".' I pat my jacket. I've left my cigars in the overcoat.

'That's right!' Doris offers me a cigarette and gives me a light before going on: 'Did you ever meet in the ring?'

'No, he boxed ten or fifteen kilos above my weight, but the newspapers liked making comparisons. I'm hungry. Those blasted oysters didn't help. Won't that food come soon?'

'It'll be here soon enough. Why did they compare you? If you weren't going to fight anyway.'

'Same first name, same year of birth, the most promising boxers of our generation and all that. It was all set up.'

'If you'd put in a bit more elbow grease you might have become a pro as well.'

The main courses come in on trays, to be put in our laps. Doris changes the position of her cutlery. I do the same. For an instant, the angled blade of her silver knife reflects her beauty spot.

'Did it annoy you, what I said about your wallet?'

'What are you talking about?'

I get started on the meat. It's so tender that it hardly needs chewing. Maybe it could do with a bit more salt and pepper. Doris lights another cigarette and spills ash all over the table again. She doesn't touch her food.

'Would they go back into the dining room and fetch us some salt and pepper?' I look around for a waitress.

Outside the window, an old Ford applies its brakes, the rear-end slides across the street and gets stuck in a snow drift. The girls at the table next door draw a collective sigh, raise their voices, and point.

'Yes of course, just ask.'

Doris crushes her cigarette in the ashtray, tastes her food and pours more wine.

'My *son* is spoilt.' Slowly she shakes her head. 'First he was *expelled* from Lundsberg and then he rode my favourite mare so hard that she skewered herself on a fence at the cross-country club. Before he even got his driving licence he stole my Packard and sold it. Did you know I grew up with four siblings in a one-room flat on St Paulsgatan and had to take care of my simpleton brother? Every morning my father got up at six to go out to Ropsten. He was a paraffin delivery man. I'm not concerned about what sort of wallet you have. Forget it.'

'It's nothing to be ashamed of.'

'What do you mean?'

'That you've come up in the world. Your story. You've nothing to be ashamed of.'

'Sometimes you're pretty funny, Harry! A bit enigmatic.'

The driver of the Ford gets out, takes off his cap and scratches his hair with the same hand. A waitress appears, tops up my glass and brushes the cigarette ash from the table into her palm. She disappears before I have time to tell her what I want. Doris smiles.

'Yes! You're *exactly* like the masked man in *Dans la nuit*.'

I don't know what she's going on about. I nod listlessly and try to make eye contact with another waitress on her way towards us. Doris puts down her cutlery on the edge of her plate. She lights yet another cigarette.

'Could I just ask you…' I start with my fork in the air, but the waitress has already moved on to the next table.

'And God how I slaved at stage school,' Doris continues. 'I spent my nights sewing, then went to school on weekdays and at the weekends I worked as a catwalk model at Marga Fashion Salon.' The waitress passes our table on the way back. 'Salt and pepper!' says Doris.

The waitress curtsies and rushes off. Outside the window a couple of blokes are trying to push the Ford out of the snow drift.

'And then you started making films?'

'Yes, Stig Göthe gave me a couple of leading roles. The best-known of them is probably *After Midnight*, which was a bit scandalous and very successful.'

A memory glimmers somewhere in the depths of my mind: 'Well hello, girls, this is all very lively!'

'Exactly.'

'Was that when you met Mauritz Stiller and Sjöman?'

The owner of the car, after finally managing to dislodge it, drives off. The tramp is still standing there with his cap in the snow. The tram pulls into its stop in a cloud of fine powder snow. A group of people, all warmly dressed, come welling out, several of them also dragging large suitcases, or holding piles of parcels.

'Victor Sjöström. You've done your homework, haven't you?'

'And then Steiner.' I'm mopping up the sauce with a bit of bread when the waitress finally brings the seasoning rack. Doris holds out her hand and stops her.

'We'll have the bill instead. Put a Lafite on it. And your finest cognac, and a couple of bottles of soda.' She consumes half of her cigarette in a single drag and releases a large cloud of smoke over the table. I peer greedily at her sole, left untouched on her plate.

'Excuse me, miss, but I don't think…'

'I'm sure it can be arranged. Talk to the head waiter, tell him Mrs Steiner sends her regards.'

The waitress curtsies and leaves without a sound. I put my fork into the sole and swiftly transfer it to my plate. Doris places her hand on my thigh.

'So you see, Harry, we're the same sort, you and me. I don't care what kind of wallet you have.'

I don't want to be reminded of the whole Zetterberg mess, so I take another route home and take aim for the spinning NK clock up on the telephone tower by Brunkeberg Square. Doris sits there looking out of the side window. The snow is coming down heavily. The compartment is filled with the rhythmic sound of the double windscreen wipers, and the glass is misting up on the inside. I'm behind a police pursuit motorbike with a sidecar on Malmskillnadsgatan, so I take it easy, keeping one hand on the white knob of the gear stick and another on top of the steering wheel, a Meteor between my fingers.

We pass Oxtorget. In the summertime, the carriage drivers often sit here playing cards in the evenings. Now it's utterly deserted. In front of us, the illuminated skyscrapers rear up on both sides of the bridge.

'My husband lost out on his bid for those, you know.' Doris nods at the buildings, but I don't know what she's talking about.

We cross the bridge over Kungsgatan and drive up towards Johannes's chapel. As we approach its green-scarred sugar-loaf dome, a bloke on the pavement outside the fire station waves cheerfully with his walking stick. Doris buries her face in her hands. I turn left and go round the churchyard.

The same sort. Sure.

I drop Doris outside my house and drive off to find a parking space. The banks of snow between the road and the pavements are as tall and wide as the foaming wake of a steamer going full speed ahead through a choppy sea. The odd caretaker here and there is already busy with a shovel. At five o'clock tomorrow morning, hopeful casual labourers will gather outside the job exchange for the chance to hack at the snow and shovel it away after the snow ploughs have done their rounds. I make a couple of loops by Roslagsplan and finally park in the playground of the elementary school a little further up the street. I shove my hands deep in my pockets and hurry home.

There are crackling sounds in both the ceramic burner and the fireplace as I'm hanging up my overcoat in the hall. Dixie jumps at my legs, yapping in welcome. She'll have to wait. Just like on that first evening, Doris sits with her legs up on my desk. The only difference is that this time she's kept her shoes on.

'You took your sweet time. I've already had a couple of glasses.'

When she smiles, the gap in her front teeth is briefly visible between her deep red lips. Her clothes lie in a pile by the desk.

Little pools of water gleam on the cork mat where she walked. On the table are two wine glasses and a half-empty bottle. Her black slip has slid up her legs, so that I can see her pale, spindly thighs where the stockings end.

Taking a mouthful, I nod at her. She pulls up the silk fabric a little further. She is naked underneath. A couple of grey hairs gleam like silver thread in the black bush where her thighs meet. Only a couple of nights ago she was utterly unknown to me. I have not possessed a woman for years, but before that, the ones I saw wore big cotton nightshifts to look their best between the sheets. I've already got used to her. Anyway, her body is a bit like a boy's.

I put my glass down, push back my hat and pull her into my arms. Gently I kiss her and slide my hand into the warmth between her legs. She lifts her arms as she pulls off her slip. Only now do I notice that she somehow removes the hair in her armpits.

'Do you shave under your arms?'

She takes my cheeks between her hands and tries to kiss me, but I move my head away.

'Everyone does, nowadays.'

I respond to her kiss. She breathes hard. I toss away my hat, loosen my tie and wriggle out of my jacket. I run my tongue along her throat. Her red nails claw into my neck. I fumble with her girdle and stockings but she stops me.

'You want to keep them on tonight as well?'

'Quiet!'

The buttons of my new shirt scatter in all directions when she tears it open. One of them tinkles against the wine bottle on the desk. I grab her upper arms, pick her up and toss her at the bed. Her bottom bounces against the mattress and then she falls flat on her face. There's a smacking sound when her kneecaps hit the

186

floor. For a moment she stays, immobile, on all fours. Her hair hangs down over her face. She whimpers.

I pull her up on her feet. Her arms wrap themselves around my neck. She kisses me greedily. The springs groan when we fall down into the bed with me underneath. The sheets are as cold as burial shrouds.

Her mouth and lips work their way down the ship tattoos on my chest and make a detour to the bruise that the weight of the pistol has caused against my ribs, before she follows the dark string of hair that bifurcates my stomach. Her fingers shake as she unbuttons my fly.

With one hand between her own legs and another round my shaft, she starts sucking me. If Steiner hasn't been touching her for years she's certainly been practising elsewhere. She feasts on me and makes a show of it. I put my arm behind my head so I can get a good look.

Pink rouge runs between her breasts. My cock vibrates like the needle of a tachometer. When she moves her mouth away, a thin string of saliva hangs like spider's web between the glans and her lips. Around the shaft runs a deep red ring from her lipstick. Her chestnut brown eyes meet my gaze as her hand moves up and down. She's left-handed – it occurs to me that she always switches her cutlery around when we eat out.

She straddles me. This is quite another sort of wetness than I am used to, hot and slithering. Slowly she starts forming circles with her hips. Her fingers taste of a woman's sex. She pants with increasing urgency and a few droplets of sweat emerge, gleaming, on her neck. Her eyes look up at the ceiling and her nostrils widen like a mare going uphill. When I look at her body, flexing in a backward arc that tightens her ribs against her skin, it doesn't strike me as that of a woman who's ever been pregnant.

Her fingers clutch the skin above my knees. I think she's close. For a few moments it feels as if I'm about to soften.

'What time do you have to be back with your husband?'

The neat breasts stop swaying for a moment. She bends forwards. 'You bastard,' she hisses.

The sweat sprays as she hammers her fist into my chest. I grab her hips and thrust hard in and out of her. She keeps hammering at the full-rigger tattoo and swearing at me. For a few seconds we find exactly the same rhythm and very briefly it feels as if we have melted together.

'Yes,' she cries. 'Yes, yes, yes!'

I take hold of her buttocks, part them and soften up her boy's opening with a wetted finger. Lundin bangs his broom at the ceiling.

'If he could see you now, eh? Old man Steiner?'

Her brown eyes spark up. She raises her fist again. Pain fills my head like a white light when she thumps the bridge of my nose. My eyes fill with tears, blood spatters around us as I try to control it. I heave her onto the floor. She lands on her back with a thump. One of the eyelets holding up her stocking snaps. She loses a shoe.

'The same sort,' I hear myself wheeze as I step out of my trousers.

She nods while she slides a half-metre backwards on her elbows. 'The same sort!'

She lies flat on her back, parts her legs and starts rubbing herself between her white thighs. I kneel before her, put my hands behind her knees and push her thighs up. I spit on my cock and guide it into her anus. She squeezes her eyes shut and turns her head away. I feel her cramping up around me. Her jaw grinds under her skin. I hold her arms above her head. Our upper bodies are sticking together. Her pointed hip-bones jab into me. She's making sounds as if she's crying.

Thick, viscous strings of blood from my face tremble over her and hook into her hair and eyelashes. We're drenched in sweat.

It tastes and sounds and smells like home.

The city has braced itself for Christmas. Across the shopping thoroughfares, strings of decorations have been put up with big stars and shining Christmas trees. In the dairy hall, all the cheeses suddenly have red wrappings, and the tobacconists change their usual sheets of bookmarks for bigger ones with angels. The Santa Bus drives around collecting food for the poor. Vending machines spit out stamps with Christmas motifs. Even the booze smugglers keep the peace. Over the holiday period the demand for strong beverages is so immeasurable that there is space for everyone, whether big fish or small. Anyway, the frost has gone too deep into the ground and the inlets have frozen, so corpses become a problem.

It's mine and Doris's last day together for a while. I'm swollen around my nose and a little red scab runs across it. Every time I see it I am reminded of the boy in Bellevueparken. I wonder if he has a scar from our last meeting.

It's snowing. Odenplan has been transformed into a small forest of Christmas trees. A black-dressed youth league fascist is rattling his collection box at the edge of the square. The sounds of blokes chopping at the trees with their axes to make them stand straight on their wooden feet mixes with the deep-throated voices of the chanting stallholders, their breath rising above them like smoke from the fuselages of Atlantic liners. Fires crackle in oil drums. The air smells of fire, pine resin and exhaust.

'Ekerö trees! Come here for your Ekerö trees!'

Brunkarna, the skiving gang boys from Observatorielunden, follow every potential customer with their sledges, ready to offer home delivery for fifty öre. This is their patch and damn any kid from Vasa Park who dares come down here.

The Christmas tree is Doris's idea. Arm in arm, we weave our way through the vendors. Dixie would rather stop and sniff every tree. The young fascist's collection box rattles desolately. Doris wears a double-breasted coat with padded shoulders, full-length trousers and a hat that might look better on a bloke. The bargains don't interest her; she's after the most expensive tree she can find. I'm not bothered about the Christmas trees, I'm constantly scanning the crowd. Luckily the German creep is a head taller than average. If he's also wearing the bowler hat I should be able to catch sight of him before he finds me.

In the end she decides on an Ekerö tree. A Salvation Army soldier with a guitar sings 'I Know a Door That Is Open' in the distance.

'I want a krona.' The boy we've hired wipes his nose with the back of his woollen mitten.

'A half-krona seems to be the standard rate.'

'All the way to Sibirien? Never, sir! A krona, not more nor less.'

'Okay. When we get there.'

The boy struggles to get the tree on his sledge. Doris, standing opposite me, takes my hands. In the middle of the triangular plaza she goes up on her tiptoes and kisses me full on the mouth. Our hats collide and mine ends up on the floor after scattering snow over my shoulders. Her mouth tastes slightly of cognac. She squeezes my hands hard.

'I love your smell,' she whispers into my ear. 'When I come home I go directly into my bedroom. My dresses smell of you, smell of Fandango and cigars, and I hang them up in a special

191

wardrobe. I'm going to bottle the smell of you until Christmas is over. And I like the way you take me; God, it's been years since anyone took me like that.'

The stallholder winks at me over Doris's shoulder. The Salvation Army soldier changes to 'Far from God You've Wandered Long'. Quickly Doris caresses my cheek and kisses me again before she turns to the boy.

'Are we ready to go?'

We wander homeward through falling snow. Her arm rests on mine. The boy struggles with the tree in front of us. The display window of the toy shop on the corner of Norrtullsgatan has almost misted up completely. Outside, the kids stand in line, their eyes sparkling with Christmas present dreams, and their snotty noses pressed to the glass. Doris holds onto me when I lose my footing on a patch of ice under the snow. A mare with a snow bell works her way towards Odenplan with yet another batch of trees on the wagon.

'Where do you want to eat tonight?' Doris squeezes my arm and leans her head against my shoulder.

'I'll put my trust in you on that score.'

'Maybe we should go to the cinema?'

'If you like.'

'It would be nice. Lordy, it's been a while since I last went out!'

We slip and slide down the hill and are just passing a couple of little boys outside the old geriatric home next to Metropol Restaurant when there's a loud bang, without any prior warning, behind our backs. The German caught me off-guard, after all. I could do with a pair of eyes in the back of my head.

Doris squeals as I push her into the doorway on our left. I throw myself in after her. Dixie whines as I haul her in. Doris beats my chest, her eyes wide open with fear. I give her the leash. She opens her mouth but stays silent.

The distinctive smell of gunpowder is stinging my nose. I already have the Husqvarna in my right hand. With a racing heart, I click a bullet into the chamber, then carefully peer around the corner to see a group of boys behind us lighting a few more Russian bangers and rockets.

Our tree delivery boy has stopped some ten metres further ahead. He wipes his nose with his woollen mitten. Panting, I lean against the door. Doris stares at me. I make the pistol safe and look into her eyes, which have filled with tears. Dixie lies cowering in a corner of the doorway.

'It's time someone really explained what's going on!'

I nod and put the Husqvarna back in its holster. 'A damned mess, that's what's going on.'

She takes my arm and again we step out into the falling snow. I'm trembling. I pick up Dixie and try to shush her. Our boy goes back to pulling his sledge in front of us. Maybe he didn't see the pistol. I put Dixie down and light myself a Meteor.

'Tell me anyway!'

I sigh and choose my words well. I understand I have to calm her down.

'A couple of weeks ago I was helping a client, a certain Elofsson, collect a debt from a bloke known as Zetterberg. Nothing unusual about it.'

The smell from the tobacco roaster further down the street hangs heavy in the December air as we pass Sveavägen. Doris walks along stiffly, her eyes fixed on the ground.

'What happened?'

'I did what I was supposed to do. Three people can back up that I was on Kungsgatan – a widow, the neighbour and a prostitute saw me leaving the scene.'

We stroll down Odensgatan. A telegram delivery man athletically throws himself off the number 4 tram and dives into a house entrance. Dixie has cheered up. She lunges at snowflakes and snaps into the air.

'The prostitute, do you know what her name was?'

'What difference does it make?'

Doris lets go of my arm. 'I do think I have the right to know, don't you?'

'Her name is probably Sonja,' I tell her with a nod and a sigh. 'Unfortunately Zetterberg was beaten to death with a bricklayer's axe only some hours later, and the goons started taking an interest in me.'

I put my cigar in my mouth and my hands in my trouser pockets. The snow creaks under our steps.

'Thanks to the widow I was released, and that was the only luck I had. Even so, the goons seem to think I'm the one who killed Zetterberg. I've turned Klara inside out looking for Sonja, without success.'

Doris considers me. 'Are you in trouble?'

I shrug. 'Then a few days ago I had a bite. Sonja had borrowed a telephone over at the Toad, if you know where that is?'

Doris shakes her head. She bites her lower lip.

'A betting shop in Klara. I got hold of her telephone number from there.'

We pass the Oden Bazaar and our boy turns off into Roslagsvägen with the tree. I remove the cigar from my mouth. Not far from the junction, a run-over mutt lies in the gutter. I blink away a snowflake that's found its way in under my hat.

'What happened?'

'That was the day we met. The trail led to a hostel in Old Town. When I went there, a bloke with a pistol turned up and shot at me. I managed to get away on Mälaretorget.'

'The Market Murderer.'

'Exactly. The same man who killed Zetterberg. The same man Sonja and the widow saw when he was leaving the house on Kungsgatan.'

'Are you sure?'

'How else does all this make sense?'

'What does he want with you?'

'I must be getting close to something big, but I don't even know what it is.'

Outside widow Lind's cigar hut on the corner of Frejgatan stands a sooty snow-lantern with a burned-out paraffin candle. Our Christmas-tree boy checks the numbers above the door and keeps going.

'To begin with, I was combing the whole city to find this Sonja, but it doesn't seem as pressing any more. And the police should get their hands on the real murderer soon.'

Doris threads her arm under mine once again, and squeezes it hard. 'Where might she be?'

'Sonja?'

Doris nods.

'The police will find her soon enough.'

'But where is she?'

'No idea.'

'Was she beautiful?'

'Bowlegged.'

'But beautiful?'

'Not like you.'

We reach my house. The boy leans the tree up against the wall, then takes off his cap and stands there holding out his hand. It's sticky with resin and red-pricked with pine needles. When he gets his krona, he bows.

After the boy has gone, Doris works her way into my arms, standing on her tiptoes, kissing and hugging me. Her body is trembling.

'Are you cold?'

Dixie throws herself around, snapping at the air. The snow gets caught in her silly beard and bushy eyebrows.

'Let's not think about that any more now,' whispers Doris in my ear. 'Help me up the stairs with the tree instead. Let's go to the cinema tonight.'

She kisses me again. Dixie spins her lead around us. The metal of the pistol presses painfully into my ribs.

I've always liked the smell of weapon oil. I'm sitting at the kitchen table in my trousers and singlet, cleaning my Husqvarna. I've just worked out how to take it to pieces and now I'm sitting there with the various components spread across a newspaper next to an empty food box from NORMA. It's been years since I last did this.

The draining board is full of dirty coffee cups, wine glasses, a bottle of Hoffman's drops for bad nerves, a hot-water bottle for stomach aches, a small glass bottle with a brownish medicine for rheumatic pain and pots of fragrant creams for God knows what. Across the chair backs, soft silk slips have been slung, and no less than two fur coats. On the table is a pair of electric perming tongs, which can be plugged directly into the wall if you're brave enough. Doris goes home to change her clothes once or twice per day, and brings back more stuff every time.

I hold the Husqvarna's barrel up to the light. The groove looks good. This pistol has not been fired many times. Earlier that day I went to Wigfors's Weapons to purchase thirty new bullets. When I get the chance, I'll do some target-shooting at

Lill-Jansskogen. I'm an awful shot: my hand trembles too much, my eyesight's too poor.

Dixie bounces up from her place under the chair when the door handle moves. I quickly pick up the photograph of my daughter, which I've put on the table, and return it to my wallet. Dixie yaps happily and Doris makes a fuss of her in the hall.

'Good girl! Yes, you're such a good girl!' She's in a good mood. Often she hardly notices the dog at all. It bodes well.

Her heels dance across the cork mat when she comes into the kitchen. She's changed into an evening dress of black silk, which drags along the floor. A white fur reaches to her waist. The beauty spot is on the other cheekbone. She's holding a large paper bag in her arms, and a bouquet of flowers. I don't know what they are. I put away the revolver parts.

'Christmas tree decorations.' She kisses my cheek and puts the bag on the kitchen table. She smells of cognac and perfume. 'Do you have a vase?'

'Look in the cupboards.'

The cabinets open and close repeatedly. 'Up there! Can you reach it?'

I stand on my tiptoes and manage to grab the deep-green vase. I give it to Doris, who fills it with water and tries putting the flowers in.

'They're too long. You have a knife?'

'In the drawer.'

I call for Dixie, who comes trotting along straightaway. She slides to a halt on the rug, bunching it up as she does so.

'Watch this.'

'What?'

'Bang!' I point my forefinger at Dixie, who immediately throws herself onto her back with her legs in the air. Doris laughs, clapping her hands and tossing her head back, showing the gap between her teeth.

'That must have taken you a bit of time.'

'A bit.'

'I'll say. She's impossible to train. *Absolutely* impossible. I should never have started giving her paté for breakfast.' Doris laughs again and fluffs up her hair before she starts arranging the flowers in the vase. 'You really are funny, Harry. I don't think I've ever laughed as much with anyone as I do with you.'

Dixie and I repeat the trick. I go to the larder to cut her a thin slice of smoked sausage as a treat.

'That's not the latest, is it?' Doris points at the newspaper on which I've been oiling the weapon. I shake my head and nod at yesterday's copy of *Social-Demokraten* in the window. She leafs through it from the back page. 'We could make the eight o'clock show. What would you like to see?'

'It doesn't matter.'

'What's this?' She taps at a newspaper page, on which I have circled a classified in aniline pen.

'*AB Nordic Travel Agent*,' she reads. '*Gothenburg – New York. M/S* Kungsholm *departing on 22/12*. That's tomorrow.'

'We could be in America before New Year.'

I give Dixie the bit of sausage. Doris cackles.

'America?'

'I was thinking we could run away together.'

'You're mad! The cinema will do me just fine!'

'Calm down, Doris, I'm only horsing around. It's like my trick with Dixie. Watch this!'

I point at the dog again and shoot. She rolls around, legs in the air, but this time her tongue flops out of her mouth as well.

'You two!'

Doris slips into my arms, tittering. I calm my breathing and embrace her.

'Sweets, get your sweets here!' cries a uniformed boy with a pillbox hat on his head.

It's the end of one screening, with another soon to begin, and, in the half-light of the Palladium foyer, a thousand people are exchanging places. A porter gesticulates wildly with his torch, as if trying to direct the horde single-handedly. The weak beam of light flies through the dense tobacco haze hanging under the ceiling. A couple of young women in three-quarter-length evening dresses give us odd looks and whisper among themselves. One of them is wearing gloves reaching up to her elbows. Both wear green eye shadow. Behind one of the columns, a young man gets a loud slap in the face when he tries to kiss his girl.

I am standing there holding out Doris's fur coat for her, my hat between my teeth, when a spotty teenage boy with a grammar school badge in his hat approaches with a slight bow.

'Excuse me, could I trouble you for a moment?' He holds out a pad and a fountain pen.

'No trouble at all.' Doris scribbles in the pad, and adds with a laugh: 'Just a pleasure.'

I wait there with her fur coat until she puts it on. The boy bows again, then shakes her hand.

'He was hardly born when your films were around.'

'Ah, it happens all the time. Some movie fan remembers me. It's not so very strange. Or maybe you thought he was coming over to you?'

I grunt. Doris laughs again.

'You should never have stopped. If they still remember you.'

Doris doesn't answer, but I feel a poke of her elbow: 'Watch out, here comes Signe Rudin.' She fires off her most magnificent smile at an elegant lady in a fox-fur muff and a long fur coat, who's heading directly for us.

'Who?'

Doris leans in closer to me. 'Good God! Who wears a muff nowadays?' She rolls her eyes. I put on my hat and fumble around for a cigar.

'Wasn't she in *Uncle Frans*?'

Doris doesn't have time to answer. At last I find a cigar.

'Doris! How nice!'

'Well hello there, it's certainly been a while!'

The two ladies hug each other. Signe Rudin glances at me. I recognise her long, aristocratic nose and dark eyes.

'So you're out amusing yourself. Where are Ludvig and Leo, then?'

Doris laughs and puts her hand on her arm.

'Do you know, I decided to go out on my own tonight. Not very respectable, perhaps, but what's one supposed to do?'

I light my cigar.

'You should have called, my dear. You know how people talk when they see an unaccompanied lady.' Mrs Rudin throws me another glance. Her teeth are white and even when she smiles.

'My driver,' says Doris, nodding at me over her shoulder.

I blow out a heavy cloud of smoke.

'Driver?' The old bat coughs a little.

'I'll go and bring the car, then.'

I blow out another blue-grey cloud of smoke. Doris laughs sharply and shakes her head. I get out the car key and rattle it in front of the ladies before turning my back on them and walking out of the foyer. Doris's laugh rings out clearly even as I am walking through the front doors. I've started suspecting that she has a whole armoury of different laughs, but she usually only deploys this particular high-pitched variety when there's a bloke around. Not that it makes any difference; there isn't a jot of sincerity in any of them.

The middle of the five glass doors opens with a metallic sound. Outside it's freezing, the falling snow sweeping down. On the pavement, a shivering bloke in a grey sheep's-wool cap is holding a placard that says, TRY MUNKEN'S DELICACIES. A young man without an overcoat approaches. His coat sleeves are rolled up and he wears a straw hat even though it's midwinter. The skin on his face is flaming red in the cold air.

'Buy a song from an unemployed man.' He holds a little paper leaflet in his blue fingers. I shake my head and march off through the whirling snow, scratching my groin. Behind me I hear the monotonous sound of wheels clattering across the joints in the rails as a train lumbers into Central Station.

The car is parked on the other side of Vasagatan. I turn up my collar and hold it in place with one hand as I jog down Kungsgatan. A weather vane screeches in the cutting wind. One part of me would like to drive off and leave Doris here, just to see if she knows how to hail a taxi.

'Who was that?' I ask a little later as we're passing Zetterberg's house. Snow is coming down chaotically from all directions. I sit with my nose pressed close to the windscreen, trying to stay on the right side of the tram track. The snow ploughs will have plenty to get on with tomorrow.

Doris opens the glove compartment, gets out a green bottle and takes a pull at it. It smells like cognac. She passes the bottle over and I have a little sip myself.

'Signe Rudin, the actress. Slapstick movies and other rubbish.'

'Were you ever in a film with her?'

Doris laughs. 'No, that was after my time.'

'Why did you stop?'

'I met Ludvig, I got pregnant, and then I started suffering from rheumatic pains. I couldn't just bounce out of bed and pick up where I left off.'

'How did you meet?'

'Through girlfriends we had in common, at Feith's Patisserie.'

'No, I mean you and your dear husband.'

Doris takes another gulp and jams the bottle between her thighs. We turn into Sveavägen. The number 14 tram comes towards us, ploughing its way through the snow. She fishes out a cigarette from a pack of Camels.

'Why do you want to know?'

'He interests me.'

'It was a few years after the war. Spring 1923. I really needed a big part to get my career going again.'

The matchstick snaps when she's lighting the cigarette, and she gets out another. This time she has more success, and she blows a thin jet of smoke right at the windscreen.

'I was working with Mauritz Stiller. He'd more or less promised me the main role in *Gösta Berling's Saga*. He invited me and my brother for a dinner with Kreuger, on a ferry crossing. Ludvig was there. They knew each other from way back. Especially Ludvig and Mauritz.'

'So you knew Ivar Kreuger, then?'

'Of course!' Slowly the car fills with smoke.

'What was he like?'

'Polite, urbane, considerate. Generous.'

'I heard he was involved in a fair amount of shady dealings.'

'I doubt it.'

'How did your husband and Stiller know each other?'

Doris takes a deep drag and stares out into the night. 'Don't know.'

'What happened at that dinner?'

She sighs.

At the junction of Sveavägen and Odengatan the passengers have had to get off the 51 bus. A policeman in the characteristic fur hat of the Traffic Division is directing a group of blokes pushing it up the hill. On the back of the vehicle is a promotional poster for milk, featuring a big smiling mouth with evenly shaped, white teeth. The wheels spin round, spattering sooty, slushy snow over the volunteers.

'Mauritz and Ivar discussed the construction of yet one more picture house and other projects. My brother played at the edge of the water. Ludvig was mainly occupied with me. He was courting me.'

'Why did you fall for him?'

'Can we stop by a chemist?'

'It's gone ten o'clock. There are none open now!'

'You can always ring the bell.'

'We're almost home. Do you have a prescription?'

'It should be fine.'

'Not without a prescription. Then what happened?'

'What do you mean?'

'After the crossing.'

'Do you remember that accident, the big explosion in Ropsten?'

'Sure.' I don't have any idea what she's talking about.

'Ludvig kept calling on me in the following days. We got engaged. On the same day that Mauritz told me the main part had gone to Greta Garbo instead of me, my father was killed in that accident.' I hear Doris unscrewing the bottle top. 'Three days later Ludvig proposed.'

'Every cloud has a silver lining.'

I turn into Roslagsvägen. The back end of the car almost spins out of control. I accelerate out of the skid, and the car lurches. Doris puts her hand on the chrome-plated instrument panel.

'I had my mother and younger siblings to think about.'

'So you became pregnant almost straightaway, then?'

'I could really do with some more Veronal. And I've run out of cigarettes.'

'I can get you some cigarettes. Should I drop you off first?'

She nods. We pass the junk shop and Bruntell's. She takes a pull at the bottle and stares straight ahead.

'That fucking Greta Garbo.'

I glance at her. It's the first time I've heard her swear.

Cautiously I slow down outside my house and Doris gets out. She holds the long black train of her evening dress as she goes inside.

I let the sixteen-cylinder engine throb for a moment before I release the clutch and softly pull away. For a moment I think about turning round and going to the cigarette boy outside Restaurant Monopol, but I keep going.

By the folk school I drive past a man in an elegant overcoat and decent boots. He's holding onto the low crown of his hat, and he walks doubled up like an old miner in the stiff breeze. Just as I pass him he straightens his back. I stiffen. It's Rickardsson, one of Ploman's gangsters. There's really nothing untoward about it; he lives somewhere around here with his wife and daughters and he likes to take an evening walk, but the look he gives me makes me tighten my grip on the steering wheel. I think about the shootings up in Vanadislunden and I realise that I have now got myself a bunch of powerful enemies.

I turn into Vallhallavägen. I try to shake off my disquiet, and put a cigar in my mouth.

On the corner of Frejgatan stands a chestnut mare with an empty cart. The driver stands beside the horse. He's wearing a long coat and a scarf wrapped around his chest. His hands are buried in the horse's coat, to keep the warmth.

The late-opening tobacco kiosk by Östermalm Grammar School on Karlavägen has run out of Camel. The falling snow is intensifying, flying under my hat, lodging in my eyebrows and lashes. I blink.

'Something that's like Camel, then?'

'Carat? Almost sounds the same.' The man behind the glass window is wearing a hat with earmuffs and keeps his hands tucked into his armpits, even though on the floor behind him there's a little glowing metal radiator.

'What about the taste?'

Someone sighs loudly behind me. I turn around. It's an old bloke with a monocle hanging by a black silk ribbon across his chest. He's wearing a grey cylindrical hat and a black overcoat with a fur-trimmed collar, his stick hooked over his right arm, a pair of gloves in his hand. I smile at him. He doesn't like that; he seems to withdraw.

'Stamboul. But it's filterless. What about Arab? Arabs and camels?'

'Stamboul will be fine.'

'One?'

'Fifty.' I'm stamping my boots at the snow. I can no longer feel my toes.

'Fifty Stamboul. That'll be two seventy-five.'

I hurry back to the car with the cigarettes. The snow is blowing directly into my face and I'm cowering behind my hat like an amateur keeping up his guard.

When I look up for a moment to see where I've parked, I sense a familiar figure on the other side of the street. I stop. The wind almost sweeps off my hat.

It's Leonard, the kid from Bellevueparken. He's coming out of Gnistan Restaurant on the other side of the street and walking towards his black Mercedes. My heart skips a beat, then beats, then skips again.

'Hey! Leonard!'

The broad lanes of Karlavägen are separated by an alley of bare trees with a pedestrian path in the middle. The wind catches my voice and tosses it back towards Karlaplan. My back groans as I bend down and scoop up a handful of cold powder snow. It seeps between my fingers as I try to form a snowball. Leonard is keeping one hand on his hat. As he moves along he puts a cigarette in his mouth. He doesn't light it. He's swaying slightly.

'Wait, Leonard!' I'm roaring as loudly as I can. By the time he finally sees me he's reached his Mercedes. I take off my hat, and breathe a sigh of relief. He stares at me from the other side of the street. I break into a sweat.

He hops into his sports car, the engine rumbles to life and, before I know it, he's sped off in a roaring cloud of exhaust and snow crystals.

I'm already back at the Cadillac, but when I open the door, it rebounds with a dull thud against the snowbank along the verge and closes again. I punch the spare tyre hanging on the side of the car, then open the door again and squeeze through into the driver's seat.

The spinning wheels pack the snow down until the tyres gain some traction. The power of the engine presses me back into the seat. After a U-turn at the roundabout on Karlaplan some twenty metres away, I'll be on his tail.

I reach the roundabout at high speed. From the left comes a small, four-horse-power delivery van, but I squeeze ahead of it, spin the wheel to the right and apply the handbrake. The back wheels glide away from me, but then the brakes bite and send the entire vehicle into a spin. The headlights pass over the Christmas trees piled up under Karlavägen's own line of trees, then over the sign on the roof of the delivery van, which announces a MASSIVE SALE OF WHITE GOODS, and then finally reflect against the corrugated iron of the shacks around the Pit.

I release the handbrake and pump the clutch up and down. Snow sprays in all directions. The car keeps spinning, passing the pool construction in the middle of the roundabout and, for a moment, facing a truck from Karlavägen. My eyes meet the driver's. He has a potato nose and a big, bushy moustache. Before the beams of his headlights hit me square in the eye, I see him opening his mouth in a silent cry.

I lunge at the accelerator and turn the wheel. The engine roars like a wounded bear. For a moment the truck is up on two wheels, and while I am accelerating north in the right-hand lane, a deafening din erupts, when dozens of milk churns fall to the ground.

Quickly I work my way up the gears. Because there are many more vehicles in the left lane on Karlavägen, I keep to the right, where the number of oncoming cars are few. The grammar school whizzes by, a Ford veers ahead of me and hurtles into the snow drift that borders the road on both sides. I'm gaining on Leonard. If I put my nose against the windscreen, I can see the tail end of his black sports car far ahead.

The shop signs in the corner of my eye get ever hazier as my speed picks up. The Swedish-American Tailor's Firm, Karlavägen Art Materials, Lindgren's Lighting Oil & Home Furnishings Shop, the tobacconist, the piano tuner. I pass Siewertz's Patisserie and floor the accelerator. The engine growls in protest. The bare alley of trees along the pedestrian path in the middle seems to be on the move, the trees walking along with their arms joined. My fingers cramp around the steering wheel. The Pharmacy Elefanten flies past. From Humlegården a police car quickly approaches on my side of the road. It's time to change lanes. It should be possible to do it in two steps.

My heart is bouncing like a ball in my chest. Where Sturegatan crosses Karlavägen, I press down on the clutch and swerve to the left before I wedge the car onto the pedestrian path on my right by once again stamping on the accelerator.

Snow is spouting all around the car. The American speedometer quickly rises beyond the sixty mark again. The snow crystals clamber over the split windscreen but the speed of the oncoming wind forces them to the sides. The police car sounds its horn at length as it surges past. When I get to Floragatan I repeat the manoeuvre and end up in the appropriate lane.

Leonard is only about twenty metres ahead of me. The street lies empty between us.

'Now I'll show you!'

We pass Humlegården. He increases his speed but I stay with him. Far behind us I hear the police car in pursuit. I press the needle past seventy miles per hour.

On the roof of the Soviet Legation the red flag droops in the snowfall. Inside the welter of shacks and lean-tos in the Mire, a couple of weary campfires are gleaming. I gain a few more metres on Leonard. We draw close to the crossroads with Odensgatan. He doesn't slow down. I keep my hand on the horn.

A woman in a grey coat and shawl appears from behind one of the snowbanks, pushing a wicker pram. I step on the brake. Leonard speeds up.

The woman shoves the pram forwards and throws herself back into the snow. The black car misses her by a hair's breadth. I hold my breath. My heart is close to blowing up inside. Doris's car makes slow revolutions as it glides sideways along the street. I'm surrounded by white snow. The whole car is vibrating. I throw my arm over the seat and turn my head. The back-end misses the pram by a half-metre or so. The car lunges to a stop. There's a smell of singed brake pads. The gauges in the chrome instrument panel have gone back to zero. My breath shivers with agitation.

There's no sign of the black sports car. The police sirens cut through the woman's piercing scream. She can't stop. Her shawl is still on the snowbank like an old fishing net on a bone-white beach. Through the side window I see the red emergency lights approaching through the snowfall some hundred metres or so away. I turn the wheel, change down and press the accelerator. I want to go home.

Despite detours and extra circuits of the streets at home in Sibirien, I get home in five minutes. I sit for a while in the dark stairwell to catch my breath. I think about the woman with the pram. The elastic snaps when I open my wallet, get out the photograph and angle it to catch the faint light of the streetlight outside. The crackled picture is like a glittering grey mosaic. I push back my hat.

Lundin's sign is creaking in the wind.

'Little Ida,' I hear myself muttering. I slide my thumb across the photograph and put it back. I stand up and climb the stairs, massaging the bridge of my nose. I've got a hell of a headache.

I go inside. The hall is also dark. Dixie comes hurtling along. Her claws scrape against my knees. She whines and yaps. There's a smell of coffee and tobacco. I let my overcoat fall to the floor in a heap.

Doris is leaning against the draining board. She's changed into a white, toga-like evening dress, with white heels. As usual she's wearing false eyelashes, and her absinthe-green nail varnish matches her earrings. Behind her lie two of her fur coats. She's holding a coffee cup.

'I could only get Stamboul.'

I hand over the cigarettes and she gives me her empty coffee cup in return.

'Everyone has a telephone nowadays.'

'My social circle is not so very big.'

'Why don't you have one?'

'Lundin's telephone does me fine, I've told you a thousand times.'

I put the coffee cup on the draining board. The cigarette butts in the sink are sooty black at one end and crimson red at the other. In the yard, the door of the potato cellar slams again. I wriggle out of my jacket.

'Don't get undressed.' She picks up the fur coats and presses them into my arms. 'I'm in pain. I need my medicine.' She picks up a half-full bottle of cognac. Lundin bangs his broom against the ceiling as she walks out of the kitchen.

'Have you taken Dixie for her walk?'

The Husqvarna is still in pieces on the newspaper on the kitchen table.

'It's *urgent!*' She turns around and puts one hand on her hip. Lundin has another go with the broom. I swagger along behind her with the fur coats held like two overgrown cats – by the scruff of their necks. She throws the door open and walks on ahead down the stairs. I hang up the furs in the hall and get back into my overcoat. By the time I'm walking out into the falling snow, she's already sitting in the passenger seat of her Cadillac.

I walk round to the driver's side and open the door. Doris lights a cigarette as I'm getting in. The seat hasn't even had time to go cold. She's staring fixedly straight ahead.

'The furs.'

'Furs?'

'Yes, you idiot! The furs!'

I feel a sizzle of anger, but rather than clocking her one, I slam the car door. I go up and fetch the damned furs, walk back down again, throw them at her, then get in.

211

'And now?'

'The pawnshop on Storgatan.'

I check my watch. 'It's almost eleven.'

'I know the owners. They live in the flat above. They won't say no to Persian and seal musquash.'

'Doris. It's almost eleven.'

'Harry, if you had a telephone we wouldn't need to have this conversation.'

The engine spins to life and we drive off. Doris knocks back a mouthful straight from the bottle, lights a new cigarette from the old one and blows a smoke ring. It hovers between us like an empty speech bubble.

There's no point reasoning with a drunk. I remember what a balancing act it is from the years when I looked a little too deep into the bottle myself. It's all about finding the right balance between various beverages and staying on your feet for as long as possible, before collapsing on one or the other side of the tightrope. Maybe it's possible to have a couple of good hours per day. Whatever side you fall on, it's going to hurt. The problem is, there's no choice. You have to find your way back up that damned rope. Without exceptions.

It's snowing less now. I drive down Sveavägen with the windscreen wipers switched on. In front of me, a Central Garage tow truck is pulling a Volvo home. I have trouble finding any purchase in the curve as I turn into Hamngatan. The rear-end flexes with the soft suspension. Doris keeps one of her hands on the instrument panel and looks out of the side window. Maybe she's crying. I daren't look.

Nybroviken ice rink lies there gleaming, silent and deserted in the night. As we pass the National Theatre and drive into Strandvägen, I notice a police car in my rear-view mirror. We go

212

past Kreuger's old house and I pick up speed. Most likely the goons on Karlavägen have stopped and put out a call for our Cadillac, but it seems unlikely that it's gone out to the other cars yet, and probably they didn't get our registration plates. We follow the road for a while to the east.

'You can't build a city on islands and peninsulas.'

'What do you mean?' I peer into my mirror. Because the police car doesn't seem to want to veer off, I turn into Torstenssonsgatan.

'Sometimes I think it's sinking right into the water. So slowly that we don't even notice,' Doris whispers hoarsely.

'A rotten city,' I say.

Doris lights a new cigarette from the old. She looks down at her hands. She puts her cigarette in her mouth and spins her wedding ring on her finger. I can see her skin shining all white, like a scar, underneath. I drive past the post office and check that the police car is no longer following us.

The back wheels spin as the car lurches into Storgatan. As we pass by the Apothecary Stork, Doris looks up. By Schröder's bakery, twenty metres on, she touches my thigh. Gently I apply the brakes and park by the black, barred windows of the pawn shop. I get out my pocket watch. It's ten past eleven.

'Wait here.'

Her make-up is intact. A little light under the fascia panel comes on, and a cold wind sweeps into the car when she opens the door and gets out with the fur coats in her arms. I follow her in the rear-view mirror as she shuffles around the snowbank by the police station on the corner of Skeppargatan. I light a Meteor. The snow is piled so high that she can only been seen from the waist up. She rings the doorbell, then tugs at the door. She walks back out onto the pavement and looks up at the façade. I start the car.

Suddenly she slips and disappears behind the snow. She's wearing the wrong shoes, of course. Standing up again, she flings her furs on the ground, and stands there with a stooped back, covering her eyes. At long last she bends down, picks up her furs and comes back.

'Do *not* smoke cigars in my car!' She sits next to me with the furs in her lap. One of them gets caught in the door, so it can't be closed. She swears and tugs at her coats. I roll down my window a fraction and flick away my Meteor.

'Closed?'

She shrugs. 'Drive to the Italian Club.'

The Azzurra Cave: the nightclub on Grev Magnigatan only opens at midnight, if it's open at all in the middle of the week. I've been there a few times although it's actually a members-only club.

'It's not open for an hour yet.'

'Drive me to Kommendörsgatan, then!'

'I'd like to remind you I'm not your driver, whatever you may tell your girlfriends.'

I have a good mind to put her across my knee and spank her until she's covered in blue stripes, but instead I start the car. There's not much else to do. I peer at her. I suppose every ship must have its ballast, however fine she may look.

The engine spins to life. I release the clutch and the wheels spin a couple of turns before gaining some traction. We travel in silence. By Östermalm square we meet the grey snow-plough tram, chugging through a cloud of fine powder snow. Soon after I almost run over a warmly dressed bloke taking his fox terrier for a walk. It's impossible to see the yellow-striped pedestrian crossings in this weather.

When I turn into Kommendörsgatan we go into a heavy skid. The car thrashes along. I accelerate out of it. Doris doesn't react at all. She points at an anonymous iron door, hardly even visible behind all the snow.

'Here.'

I stop. She opens the car door. It gets stuck in the compacted bank of snow. With much effort she squeezes out of the opening. She puts her head inside again.

'Come with me.'

'I can't park here.'

'With this car you can.'

I shrug and do as I'm told. As soon as the car door closes behind me I have a cigar in my mouth. The cold nips at my skin. The house is a big brick thing. A row of balconies in cast iron, bunched one on the other, split the façade into two sections. Most of the windows are dark but a big crystal chandelier is lit on the first floor. Elegant streets, these.

Doris slips up to the modest door. It's half a stair down. She roots around in her handbag as she carefully goes down the steps. I puff some life into the cigar and look around. These are not my home haunts. Doris knocks on the door and immediately a little viewing slit opens in it. Doris holds up a card. At least two locks rattle, and then the door is opened.

A passage steeped in gloom leads into the cellar. The corridor is draped in heavy red fabrics, and the ceiling is painted in the same colour. The cement floor is covered with an elongated Oriental rug. Beside the door is a three-legged stool in some light-coloured wood. Jazz can be heard from the cellar.

A short man in a blue double-breasted suit receives us. His collar is perfectly fitted around his neck. A pistol bulges disquietingly under his pinstripes. His eyebrows join in the middle. If what I learned at sea is correct, this means he will die from drowning.

'Who's the thug?'

'He's with me. He's okay.' Doris removes her hat and pats her hair.

'I have to search him.'

I stretch out my arms and the little bloke pats me down through my layers of clothes. Doris looks utterly bored. She rests one of her heels against the wall and inserts a Stamboul in her gold cigarette holder, while her handbag sways from the crook of her arm. Her hat is wedged between her body and her other arm.

He's thorough. He smells of Triumf aftershave. I'm a head taller than him.

'Okay.' He nods for us to move on down the passage. I jog along behind Doris. Our steps are muted by the thick rug. Her heels make her bottom swing irritably from side to side. Her garters are visible under the thin white fabric of her dress, first on the right side, then on the left.

If this is an unlicensed drinking place, it's the most exclusive one I've ever been in. It has to be Ma's place. She and her sons are running things up here in Östermalm. It's been that way ever since the Reaper rigged up Old Man's car with a couple of Nobel's dynamite sticks.

The passage bends abruptly and yet another iron door with a spy hatch appears. Now I hear the high-pitched tones of a trumpet. Doris thumps the door hard. Music wells out of the hatch and the door opens just as the trumpet once again shreds the melody with its sharpness. I take a step back.

'Welcome!' The girl in front of us smiles, tilting her head. She has sequins on her dress. Doris pushes past her. The girl keeps smiling.

Variously coloured lights whirr about like chaff in a barn. Patches of red chase yellow, blue and green. They play catch over the thick rugs, speed around between the small, round tables, sparkle off the hostess's sequin dress, hit the mirror and the bottles behind the long bar counter and lose themselves across the little dance floor, where a few people seem to have lost track of each other in the confusion of lights and music. On the tables and along the bar, paraffin lights glimmer. In a corner of the large premises, an entire jazz quintet with a double bass is crowded onto a small stage.

Someone gives me a slap on my upper arm. On reflex, I shield my chin behind my shoulder, quickly duck and move forwards and resurface on Doris's left side. She moves her lips and gesticulates. I lower my hands and nod. The girl with the sequined dress tucks her arm into mine and pats my hand as if I were an old pauper from the workhouse.

Doris makes off towards some booths with sofas and tables. The hostess ushers me to the bar. The club is half filled. The quintet stops abruptly and there's scattered applause. Behind the bar is a battery of colourful, curvaceous bottles. Over the mirror is a row of portrait photographs of former heroes of the ring. I recognise the yanks, HP, and some others too. The drummer whisks up a new, slow, suggestive melody. A bartender entirely dressed in white, with cotton gloves on his hands, leans towards the hostess.

'Give him one on the house!' The hostess nods at me and disappears into the throng.

Soon there's a tall, slim glass on the bar counter. A little pink paper parasol is attached to a toothpick. Carefully I pick it up. By sliding a little paper cylinder up and down along the toothpick, one can open and close the parasol. I do so many times before I lift the glass to my mouth. Its yellow contents taste mainly of lemon.

I light the cigar, which has been left to go out and droop in my mouth. I turn my back to the bottles and rest my elbows on the counter for a while.

On one side of me is a bloke in a tailcoat and a crooked shirt-front. He's sitting on his tails. On the other side of me stands a youth in a large beret, a city suit, plus fours and plucked eyebrows. He looks like Leonard. Between his long fingers he holds a slim cigarette, which gives off a thin sliver of smoke that wraps itself around the rising dark grey from my cigar.

A few couples are slowly floating around on the dance floor. Despite the darkness, I can make out that some of the girls with red lips and mascara around their eyes are actually boys, dressed in spangled crinoline. One of them has a tiara in his hair. I lean over towards the youth at my side.

'Do you know a boy called Leonard?'

He shakes his head. I show him the little parasol and how one can open and close it. He gives me an uninterested glance.

I turn to the counter, and the bartender leans across.

'You want a job?'

I shake my head.

'A girl, then? Or maybe a boy?'

I shake my head again and drain what's left of the fruit squash. I'm just about to ask him about Zetterberg when Doris taps me on the shoulder. She tucks her arm under mine and drags me towards the exit. On our way we bump into a transvestite in evening dress, whose chest hair wells out of his cleavage. In the short summer nights of Humlegården he's known as Snuff-Josefin. He nods at me. Doris doesn't notice.

When we come out of the club the temperature has fallen to ten below. The car has survived without any bangs or scrapes, although it is parked almost in the middle of the lane. I don't make a note of the address but I try to remember the house and the cast-iron balconies. Doris hums the last song the jazz quintet was playing.

'My rheumatism always gets worse in the winter,' she says, as I drive along Karlavägen for the second time that evening.

'We live on the wrong side of the world.'

'We often go somewhere warm over the Christmas holiday, me and my family, but not this year. Ludvig has too much going on, he says.'

I grunt. The street lies deserted and I turn on the full beam by pressing a button above the horn. There's not a skid mark left from the crazy car chase on Karlavägen just a few hours ago.

I shouldn't have clocked Leonard in Bellevueparken. That must be why he cleared off as if he had a fire up his butt. I don't even know why I decked him.

We don't talk much on the way home to Sibirien. Only when we turn back into Roslagsgatan do I notice that Doris no longer has her furs.

Dixie has been walked. She lies contentedly at my feet. The flat is quiet, apart from a blazing wood fire in the hearth. We're sitting at the kitchen table. I've taken off my jacket and shirt. I blow at the Husqvarna's recoil spring and thread a page of rolled-up newspaper through it.

Doris is busy with her own things. She opens a little bottle of brown liquid and holds it under her nose. She lets a drop fall on her finger, and puts it in her mouth. She smiles. Her long fake eyelashes flutter.

Dixie spins around and lies on her other side, across my feet. Her body warmth feels good against my socks. Doris gets out a little case of dark wood from her handbag on the table. Inside is a cylinder and a plunger in glass and steel, as well as two needles embedded in purple silk. She gets it all out and goes to rinse it in water.

'Do you have any spirit?'

'In the cupboard. I'll have one myself.'

I nod her in the right direction. The cupboard doors slam. She opens the bottle and fills two schnapps glasses with Kron. I put the recoil spring down and pick up the silver-grey pistol muzzle. I tear another page out of yesterday's newspaper. There's a snap when I open the lid of the gun oil.

Doris gives me one of the glasses and sits back down opposite me.

I knock back the drink. Doris dips one of the needles in her glass of schnapps. She removes her shoes, stands up and unclips one of her stockings, then sits down to roll it off. Dixie gets up and shuffles out of the kitchen.

The top of Doris's foot is flecked with little purple scars.

'This is strong stuff.' She sits at the table and sucks some of the contents of the bottle into the syringe. 'I'll pass out for ten minutes but it's not dangerous.'

'As long as you know what you're doing.'

Doris holds the syringe up against the lamp and slowly presses the air out. The glass makes a deadened sound when she flicks it with her nail. She pushes back the chair and puts up her bruised foot, gives the pin-pricked skin on top of her foot a good rub, then taps it gently to get the blood going. After dipping her forefinger in the schnapps glass and rubbing it into a spot just below her ankle, she injects herself and the skin sags for a moment under the downward pressure of the needle before it goes in.

'Damn!'

She retracts the needle, again puts the tip of the needle against her skin and jabs it in. This time she hits it right. She tenses her lips and draws a few drops of blood into the cylinder before slowly injecting the contents into herself.

She rolls up her stocking halfway and puts her shoe back on. Her lips open. She exhales and straightens her back, still with the syringe in her hand. The stocking hangs like boot lining under her knee. For a moment she looks as if she wants to say something. Whatever it is, it remains unsaid.

She may as well have walked smack-dab into my right-handed punch. First her head falls hard backwards and then bounces against her breast. The empty syringe rolls away over the table. She takes a long breath.

Dixie's claws come rattling across the floor; she lies down under Doris's chair. Meanwhile, Doris's arms hang down limply. I hold my breath for as long as she does. When at last she exhales, I reach across the table, take her schnapps glass, knock back its contents, then stand up and walk round the table. Dixie is growling under the chair. I reach down and Dixie sniffs my hand and then licks it. I lift Doris's face up and give her a little shake. Her eyes are half closed, a thread of saliva hangs from her mouth. I wipe it off with my hand.

'The best china,' she slurs with a dark, dragging voice. I bend down and slide my arms under her knees and around her back. The white silk of her dress is soft against my hands. 'And my best little brother.' My back protests when I pick her up, despite the fact that she hardly weighs anything. Dixie follows as I carry her mistress over to the sleeping alcove.

'It's itching. It's itching so terribly. Can you scratch me, Father?' Her voice is still unnaturally deep. I start shivering.

I lay her on the bed and prop up her head with the down pillow. She's breathing calmly. Dixie jumps up and lies at the foot of the bed. I check my pocket watch. Ten minutes, she said.

I've just put the Husqvarna together and checked that it works by cocking it, when I hear Dixie's claws against the cork mat. Doris's heels give off an irregular sound as she staggers about in there. It reminds me of the endless nights spent tapping the walls between the cells at Långholmen. She kicks off her shoes. I hear them striking the wall with a couple of dull thuds.

Soon she comes slowly into the kitchen again. She's swaying alarmingly, and her eyes are glazed. I put my pistol down on the table and stand up in the nick of time. I catch her when she trips on the rag rug. Her body is limp and pliant. She laughs emptily. I heave her onto the chair and push it tight up against the table.

'Harry, you bastard.' Her voice is still as dark. Her head rolls languidly from side to side, like a boxer when the neck muscles have stopped working, just before he goes down. She grabs the big conch shell in the window. It smashes against the floor.

Her head stops. The fake eyelashes on the left side have come away and hang drunkenly. She's lost one of her absinthe-green earrings. Her pupils are as small as one of the needle pricks in her foot.

'You bastard. I think you've given me crabs.'

Before I have time to react I'm staring into the black barrel of the Husqvarna. It points all over the place but it's not the first time she's held a pistol. My fingers, gripping the edge of the table, turn white. I wish I hadn't sat down. She's slow. I'm quick, but I'm not as quick as I used to be.

'Doris, for Christ's sake! Let's calm things down. There's a bullet in the chamber.'

She makes a hollow laugh. 'You like your pistol, don't you!'

'Christ's sake, Doris!'

'Lucky for you… I don't… share a bed… with my husband.'

The sentence ends up too long and she makes a mess of it. The weight of the pistol makes her hand start shaking. I sigh and close my eyes, thinking about my daughter, Ida. I think about Lundin, Beda and the vicar, Gabrielsson. I think about Dixie. I think about my Ida.

There's a gentle click when Doris cocks the trigger. I still have my eyes closed. My fingers firmly clutch the edge of the table. Every little muscle in my body is tensed up. Thoughts are racing through my mind: I wonder if she has finally understood who I am. Maybe it dawned on her at the bar earlier that evening.

I wait. She doesn't squeeze the trigger. I drum up enough courage to start breathing again.

At long last I open my eyes when the Husqvarna slams onto the table. Her chin drops limply onto her breast, her hair gives a sudden shake, and her arms dangle from her shoulder sockets. I snatch up the pistol, release the cock with my thumb and flick the safety catch.

'It'll be such a long time till we see each other again. I don't want to leave you, Harry. Not tonight,' she slurs into the cleavage of her white evening dress.

I put the Husqvarna in my lap. Doris manages to lift her arm and put her hand in front of me on the table. I stare at her bony fingers and green nail varnish.

'You have to get on with your Christmas preparations at home. And what would your husband say?'

'Ludvig? He's nothing to be concerned about. Nothing at all.'

'Well you can't stay here. I also have things to do. I'll drive you home.'

I stand up and take a stiff pull of the schnapps bottle. Doris lays both her arms on the table and buries her face in them. Dixie fusses along behind me while I'm collecting Doris's clothes, which I leave by the door. I clip the leather leash to Dixie's collar, the one with the red stones. She stands on her hind legs and waits, her front paws on the door.

By the time I've come back into the kitchen with her shoes, Doris has straightened up. My knees click as I squat by her feet. Her silk stocking is soft in my hand as I slowly roll it up. I fumble with the eyelets before finally managing to fix the stockings over her thighs. Doris takes my hand and guides it up between her legs. I feel her pubic hairs through the flimsy fabric of her panties.

'Harry…?'

'Not now. We need to get you home.'

'I don't care about myself. We can do it the way you like it. Any way you like,' she drawls. I grunt and put the white, high-heeled shoes on her feet. She sobs and draws breath. 'My earring. I can't possibly go home without my earring.'

I look up. She's tugging at her earlobe. Her fake eyelash flutters.

'You've already got half your belongings here as it is. It'll be fine.'

'Out of the question. Ludvig would know something was up.'

I sigh and manage to do up the ankle straps with their tiny buckles. Doris's breathing rattles as she struggles for air again. I stand up and walk out of the room. The green earring is between the pillows in the bed. I put it in my pocket.

I go out into the hall and put on my overcoat and hat while Dixie is jumping around my legs. I bend down, throw Doris's coat over my shoulder and thread the loop of Dixie's leash over my wrist.

When I come into the kitchen again, Doris has almost fallen asleep over the table. I poke her and she slowly lifts her head. One of her fake eyelashes is still hanging loose.

'Hold still a second,' I say, and pull it off between my thumb and forefinger. She doesn't react.

I slide one arm under her knees and the other around her back. She puts her arms around my neck while I carry her out of the flat and down the stairs. Resting her face against my chest, she sighs with satisfaction, like a child.

'You're a headstrong bloke, Harry,' she whispers hoarsely once we're in the street. 'That's what made me give in to you at first. You didn't give up when I played hard to get; you kept chasing me.' She sighs again. She must have me confused with someone else.

I get the car door open. Dixie jumps in and curls up below the passenger seat. I heave Doris in and drape the coat over her. There's a cold draught. When I close the car door I notice a big patch of saliva and lipstick on my white shirt piece.

Doris sobs all the way to Karlaplan, but she starts coming out of it as we turn off Narvavägen on the roundabout. She gets out a cigarette. We've hardly met a soul on the way, but when we turn into Linnégatan by the garrison building, we pass a Norwegian pony harnessed to an unused cart. The creamy yellow animal stands immobile in the cold under a streetlamp as though it were sleeping. There's no sign of a driver. The scene fills me with disquiet.

'I hope Bengta makes a better job of the Christmas food this year.'

I'm startled by the sudden sound of Doris's slovenly voice. I stare at her, sitting there staring out of her window. Her reflection is bright when she lights her cigarette.

'Bengta?'

'The maid.'

'Didn't you say you always go away for Christmas?'

I turn into Strandvägen. We pass the red-brick monstrosity of the English Church, with the slanted gravestones scattered across its churchyard.

'I didn't go with them last year. I was ill, you see. Here it is.'

Doris points to a big dark villa rearing up behind a high white wall exactly where Nobelgatan and Strandvägen meet. I veer off towards the waters of Djurgårdsbrunnsviken, so we can come around at the front.

'You can park in the street.'

I slow down. The white wall looks as if it's just been re-painted. Quietly we glide past a pair of cast-iron gates. On each of the gates is a lit-up golden numeral: a two and a one. I peer through the bars. I remember walking past this house on the way to the World Exhibition a few years ago and wondering who lived here.

From the gates there's a path leading up to the front steps. It has not been properly cleared of snow, and it's bordered by lit lanterns, which make the surrounding crusted snow glitter at regular intervals. Four Greek columns around the main entrance hold up a terrace. The four-storey house is steeped in darkness. The small mullioned windows are entirely surrounded by Virginia creepers.

I stop behind an elegant company car, a Rolls Royce, some three or four metres to the left of the gates. When the sound of the powerful engine dies, the compartment is filled with silence. Doris crushes her cigarette in the ashtray but remains seated. Between the trees along the water's edge one can make out the snow-covered ice of Djurgårdsbrunnsviken. Cut spruce branches have been thrown down in the snow to define the edges of the ice rink, but it's been a few days since someone last cleared the snow.

I glance at Doris, who's staring at the coat in her lap. I get out, walk round the car, and open her door. Dixie jumps out onto the ice-covered pavement, twitching her cropped ears. I offer Doris my hand, and she gets out laboriously. She puts on her coat and I give her Dixie's leash. Doris straightens her back with a sigh, sooty black rings of mascara standing out around her eyes. She pats her hair.

'See you on Christmas Day, Harry. Take care of yourself till then.' She leans in towards me and misses my mouth.

I peer up at the dark house while fishing for a Meteor in my pocket. 'It's only a couple of days.'

Doris nods, turns around and heads for the gates, swaying slightly as she goes. Dixie whines and slides along behind her for a metre or so, before getting up on all fours. Doris's right heel abruptly folds inwards when she steps on a patch of ice. She mutters indistinctly and continues through the gate while scratching her shoulder.

I look around. The spiky auras of the stars are shredding the black December night. Across the ice, I see the radiant lights of Sirishov, where Wallenberg lives, in the darkness. The imposing house is even bigger than the Steiner's place. Wallenberg and Steiner could more or less call out to each other across the water if they wanted to. I don't read the business pages very attentively, but for some reason I don't think either of the finance magnates would want to do that.

I have probably a two-hour walk ahead of me through the dead city. I take a few steps and glance up at the house again. Then I recoil.

On the top floor, a dark figure is standing in a dimly lit room. He's a short, squat bloke, his outline hazily defined by the light behind him. His face is faintly illuminated when he draws on a cigar. He seems to be looking directly at me. I think he's smiling.

I put my Meteor in my mouth and look down at my shirt, while fumbling with the buttons of my jacket and overcoat. Doris's lipstick gleams over my chest like the bull's eye of a marksman's target.

It's about ten o'clock at night a few days later, and it's been some time since the snow was last brushed off the statue of Berzelius in the little park in front of Bern's Club. By Nybroplan, the pavilion with Aerotransport's travel agency has been closed. On the quays of Strandvägen, the bent silhouettes of the cranes lean over the ice. This is where the Roslag skiffs usually reverse in stern first to unload firewood. The snow has stopped falling for a while, and the sky is clear and starry.

It's the day before Christmas. In the famous song, this was the spot where the guardsman and the Stockholm maid first met, but that must have been in summer. Now the park lies deserted. When the bugle sounds in a few hours and the sentries stop the sailors from going back to Skeppsholmen and the garrisons have closed for the night, the whole place will be crawling with recruits looking for somewhere to spend the night. Not for nothing is the pontoon linking Berzelii Park with Skeppsholmen known as the Last Hope. Probably Zetterberg used to hang around here a good deal.

I sit on my bicycle between Mille's granite sculpture of playing bears by the east entrance to the park wearing an oversized beret, long johns, baggy trousers with an elastic waistband, a singlet, a shirt and a knitted tennis jumper under my sports blazer and overcoat. And still I'm cold.

A bloke in a top hat in a group heading towards Bern's stops and asks for a light. His cigar smells more expensive than my own. Although there's a lull now, it's been snowing heavily all day. I counted six snowmen as I cycled through the park earlier. Under Tornberg's clock, at the front of the Royal National Theatre, a well-dressed gentleman paces back and forth, rubbing his hands together. In the distance is a green urinal with a glass ceiling. It's of the French model, with walls that do not quite reach the ground. A couple of plain-clothes goons, public decency officers, have been circling the urinal since I arrived fifteen minutes ago. They walk up to it at regular intervals, get down on all fours and look under the wall. They almost always work in pairs: recruits from the Svea Life Guards, horse guardsmen from K1 and the boys from the Marine Corps are rarely cooperative.

But the goons don't seem willing to give up on this one. In Humlegården there are more pissoirs and they're warmer too. I throw my leg over the bike and start pedalling, still with the cigar in my mouth. The pistol jangles against my ribs with every push of the pedal. I think about Doris at home, just a few hundred metres away, busy with Christmas preparations. It's a relief to be rid of her for a few days. I'm doing a couple of jobs for Wernersson and, as usual, I'm having Christmas luncheon with Lundin. When we see each other again, she may be in better spirits and also willing to do without the syringe.

It doesn't take long. By the side of the telephone booth, a short distance in under the bare trees, I can make out the urinal on the corner between Humlegårdsgatan and Sturegatan. I smile to myself. I have many happy memories from here. The snow billows around me as I apply the brakes.

Really it's more of a rank-smelling wooden house than a urinal. The frozen, gold-glittering spike of water in the gutter has been perforated at various points by jets of body-warm urine. Bill posters have been put up on the ceiling, all slightly wonky. They're so old that it's no longer possible to read what's written on them. The messages on the walls, carved with knives, are easier to decipher. Here, swastikas sit alongside spiteful remarks and pick-up lines. One of them says, *I fornicate better with my thing than the King*.

I'm on my way out when I run into Göteborgs-Olga.

'Oh, Kvisten!'

Göteborgs-Olga is wearing an overcoat with a broad belt that's done up a touch too tight. His hair spills out from under his hat and almost reaches his collar. Like nearly all park queens, he uses a female nickname. He tells everyone that he works at the theatre, but as far as I know he's nothing more than an unpaid prompter.

'Wasn't exactly yesterday!' He pushes the flat of his hand into my chest.

'Olga!' I stop. 'You old bitch!'

'Bitch *yourself*!' Olga points his finger at me and throws back his head, laughing so hard that he drops his hat.

I bend down and pick it up. I've missed this place.

'Oh, Kvisten, always *such* a gentleman!' Olga smiles and opens his eyes wide while he puts the hat back on his head. 'Tell me now! Why are you loitering here in midwinter?'

'I'm looking for a bloke. By name of Zetterberg.'

'Oh it's *always* like that! Bloke looking for a bloke and the girl has to go home on her *own*!' Olga puts his fists on his hips and struts about a bit in the snow in front of the urinal. In the background, a man who seems in a hurry suddenly stops as he's making his way into the park, and turns around.

'Have you ever met someone called Zetterberg? One of his eyes is a different colour from the other. Elegant type, bit of a snob, between thirty and forty. A large signet ring of gold.'

'Elegant, you say? You *know what*? In that case I'd rather do without!'

'Well, I'll make a loop round the park and ask about.' I squeeze his arm.

'Oh but do let *me* come with!' Olga puts his arms around me. 'I can show you Humlan in her winter clothes.' He whispers into my ear: 'I know all her hiding places, every nook and cranny! *Come*, let me be your Virgil!'

He tugs at my arm and I push him away. I don't know who Virgil might be, but I assume that Olga prefers it in the Greek manner. I doff my cap by way of a farewell, and stroll off into the park.

I walk round Humlegården for about half an hour, seeking information. I wander between the Royal Library and the gentlemen's toilets, up around Linné's statue and down the sheer, icy slopes of Klara Hill where the kids have compacted the snow with their sledges. On spring evenings, bluebells and crocuses fill the slopes and there are considerably more friends about. But in spite of all, I do run into the odd acquaintance. The hoar frost lies thick on the branches of the trees. There's not a sod anywhere who's heard of someone called Zetterberg.

'I was here the day before yesterday. I got offered a job by the kid in the bar,' I say when the spy hatch in the door on Kommendörsgatan slides open.

The lock rattles and I am let into the warmth. The short gangster on the other side of the door has changed suit to a black thing with wide lapels.

'I have to search you.'

'I have a pistol.'

I open my blazer. The gangster nods. He puts on a pair of leather gloves before he pulls it out.

'Pretty holster.' He grins at my home-made effort with the braces. I hold out my arms and he starts patting me down. It's quite a drawn-out process, given the amount of clothes I'm wearing.

'Why don't you use that if you can't reach?' I point at the little three-legged stool behind the door. He doesn't seem to find it very amusing, but nonetheless he nods down the passage.

'I'll give you the shooter back when you're coming out.'

The smoky premises are darker than before, and there are considerably more people both on the dance floor and in the bar. I step inside just as the jazz orchestra finishes a number to a round of applause.

'What an entrance!' The same hostess is here as when Doris and I visited. She smiles.

I remove a couple of layers of clothes and hang them up on one of many hangers by the entrance, then draw a comb through my hair. The hostess tucks her arm into mine and leads me across the dance floor. A trumpet player has been added to the jazz quartet. He takes the microphone and says a few words in English. He speaks a little too fast for me to keep up.

The drummer counts them in and quickly starts whisking up the beat. One by one the instruments fall in, people on the dance floor start moving their hips. Finally the trumpet player breaks in with a long, plaintive note, and some of the dancers hold their hands in the air and start shaking them.

A bloke in a dinner jacket and spiked hair dances onto the floor. He's pretending to play the trumpet with an empty bottle of champagne. The hostess's smile intensifies, and she takes a few sharp Charleston steps back and forth. I hang in there as she dances.

At the bar is a gang of young men in dinner jackets and girls with red-painted lips and evening dresses in various colours and styles. They all have glittering paper hats on their heads. The trumpet player sings a few lines.

'And so we're here!' The hostess makes a little twirling pirouette under my arm, fires off a last smile and leaves me at the bar. I hop up on the high stool and put my boots on the foot rail. The lady next to me is wearing a pair of gentleman's tails and smoking through a long cigarette holder. Under her veiled hat is a blonde, short-cropped head of hair. In her earlobes are round green stones.

With his white cotton gloves, the short bartender looks like the cartoon mouse in *Stockholms Dagblad*. I make a sweeping gesture at the shelves of drinks, and he nods. I can smell perfume, sweat and dope, a treacherous smoking blend that I once tried in French Morocco.

A young, spindly man with his dark hair in an unimpeachable, slicked-back hairstyle stands at the bar looking lonely. I get my fruit squash. This time it's red and it costs ten kronor. I can't stay here for long.

'Hey, kid,' I say to the bartender. 'I didn't get a parasol.'

'We've run out.'

'Okay. Do you know someone called Zetterberg?'

'Sure, if you stay he'll be along later.' The kid smiles.

'Young man, well dressed, one eye a different colour from the other?'

'Exactly.'

'Gold tooth and a signet ring?'

'That I don't know.'

'Hasn't been here for a while?'

'Now you say it, yeah that's true, but sooner or later he'll turn up, you'll see.'

The bartender makes eye contact with someone and seems about to walk off. I grab his wrist.

'Does he socialise with anyone who's here tonight?'

'Don't you cause any trouble now.'

'There's not going to be any trouble.'

'We don't gossip about our guests and they don't gossip about us.'

I let go of him and follow him with my eyes. I wonder how much he knows. I can't afford to sit here all night, and if I'm going to beat the truth out of him I'll have to wait outside in the cold. The youth at the bar finally gives me the eye. I raise my glass and smile at him. The squash tastes a little less of squash than when I last sipped it.

This must have been Zetterberg's home pitch. For once my intuition seems to be right. I spin round on the bar stool. In a corner sits a young man with black mascara round his eyes, a white shirt, bow-tie, and a red silk smoking jacket over his clothes. Sure enough he's smoking, also biting his nails. On the dance floors, one of the stripling transvestites is hysterically waving his arms above his head while spinning round on his high heels.

Who did Zetterberg see socially? My eyes sweep across the room. What if he saw something or someone he should not have seen in a place like this, and demanded a lot of dough to keep his mouth shut? Maybe that was why he got an axe in the head? I spin towards the bar again and knock back my drink.

I'm halfway through my second glass when the boy with the slicked-back hair comes forwards. He moves languidly, a cigarette in his right hand and his other inserted into the left pocket of the buttoned-up jacket. I spin around. My legs are wide apart and my boots rest on the circular rail of the stool. One of my elbows is leaning against the bar. I smile. I can't afford another drink. Not for myself and even less for him.

'Hello.' He adjusts one of my dark locks with his forefinger. As he leans towards the bar, he brushes his crotch against my knee. I smile, spin back to the bar again, and run my hand down his lower back, over his muscular buttocks and the backs of his thighs.

'Are you here with anyone?' He smiles, showing his white teeth.

'I'm waiting for a good friend. Zetterberg. Do you know him?'

The boy shakes his head. He rattles one of the empty glasses on the bar. I look up at the price list. My lone five-kronor note is burning the inside of my pocket. He follows my eyes.

'Broke, right?' He smiles and takes a sip of my drink before putting his hand on mine.

I shrug. The orchestra kicks in again. 'I'm a good friend of the Steiner family.'

The boy chuckles. 'That could have bought you the whole bar a couple of years ago. But now? Hardly!'

With another smile, he empties what's left in my glass. Again he presses his crotch against my leg as he manoeuvres himself past.

'Merry Christmas, anyway,' he whispers in my ear, kissing my neck.

I close my eyes, and for a very short moment everything disappears: the sound of the music, laughter, clinking glasses. It's rather like when you take a really hard blow on the jaw. The world around you slows down, reduces itself to a tiny, silent, black point, and then quickly expands, all while you're falling back onto the ropes.

The best thing to do in a situation like that is to take your opponent in a clinch, but when I open my eyes, the boy has already disappeared onto the dance floor. With a sigh, I slip off the stool.

*

I'm back in Berzelii Park where the evening began a few hours ago. The cold air stings my face. I still feel that kiss lingering on my skin. The plain-clothes policemen are still in position by Nybroplan. They keep out of the way, but write diligently in their notebooks. It has started snowing again.

The drinks have changed my timidity into longing. Recruits of all regiments are reeling about in the park, now almost completely steeped in darkness. They're doing their best to make an arse of the Swedish Armed Forces. Most have already sold some of their equipment for booze. A few of them are drinking straight from the bottle. Others have already vomited down their rough felt uniforms.

'We have fire, we have meat, we have cups and we have schnapps to cheer us up,' drawls a conscript whose moustache is encrusted with frost.

A couple of young girls who surely don't even have hair between their legs stand by the drinking fountain taking shallow puffs on their cigarettes, ready to offer themselves to the first bloke who can buy them a drink or two. Gang boys, too young to be admitted into drinking establishments, have drunk themselves into a state of foolhardiness and are walking around looking for trouble. A couple of well-dressed elderly gentlemen are hovering about, trying to establish contact with the conscripts. There's much laughter and toasting. I lock the bicycle with a chain and walk a few metres into the park.

'Look over there! A boy for Kvisten.'

He's one of the navy lads, seeming a bit lost standing there by himself, under a tree next to the waterfront. He's already mislaid his hat. Pity, I like it when I can read the name of their ship as they balance on their knees looking up at me.

Our eyes meet. I smile. He smiles back. I raise my eyebrows. He loses his footing.

Between us, under a streetlight not far from me, a horse guard accidentally topples into a sailor.

'Damn well watch yourself, you bastard!'

The Christmas peace is over. Curses sail neatly through the night. The sailor gets a shove and before long they're tumbling about on the ground. The snow flies around them in a fine powder. The glow of the lamp puts a sparkle in the snow crystals, and the fighters are enveloped in bright cloud. The sailor gets the upper hand, straddling the chest of the other and snapping his nose. There's a loud crunching sound. An elongated jet of blood gushes from the bridge of his nose, painting a perfect red line in the snow.

'Modin's in trouble again!' four or five horse guards call out, and come to his aid.

The girls start screaming with excitement. One of the guardsmen puts his boot in the sailor's face. He's out of the game before he's even hit the ground. They're on him like a pack of famished dogs going at an injured rat. Within seconds, they've formed a kicking circle around him.

The assault picks up pace. One of the guardsmen stands on the sailor's chest, then jumps on his face. I puff some life into a Meteor. The plain-clothes goons blow their shrill whistles but it's too late – the fight takes hold, grows like a tumour through the rings of spectators, and before long some fifteen boys are involved, mostly because they're drunk and simply can't be bothered to move out of the way when someone bumps into them. Swear words and bottles fly through the air. Hatred issues from their mouths like smoke, and violence is no longer pretty this night, violence is nothing more than a blessed jumble of feet and fists and sobbing. The boys claw and hiss desperately at each other, like a litter of kittens in a jute sack on their way to the river.

Suddenly I can't see my boy any more. I stand on my tiptoes, then jump up and down, in the hope that he has not been drawn in.

I find him on the other side of the bundle. He's backed away and stands there peering over the top of the chaos of bodies. The fight starts moving in his direction, like a whirling tornado of snow with a hint of navy blue, uniform grey and blood red. It'll suck him in before you know it. I flap my arms.

'Hello!' I holler and wave, cap in hand. A weeping guardsman with vomit and blood over his chin and chest comes stumbling towards me. I hold out my hand to stop him wiping himself against me, but he doesn't pause. I put on my cap and give him a left hook. The force of the impact shoots up my shoulder. Body fluids splatter around him like a pulse of lava. I step over his body and take off my cap once again.

One conscript rams his head into someone's stomach, and they both fall to the ground. For a second there's a gap offering a view of the other side. The young man sees me. He waves back, looking relieved. I point towards Bern's at the southern end of the park. He nods.

We meet outside the entrance. From Bern's comes the sound of tinkling piano music, while, in the park, there's only churning violence. The police are still blowing their whistles.

'You can be my Virgil.'

The boy has green eyes. His cheek is soft to the touch. I run my hand over his hair. He smiles, slightly insecurely. His washed-out blue collar droops over his nautical blazer.

'You'll give me a bob or two, won't you?'

'Of course you can have a bob, my lad.'

I pull the elastic off my wallet and press the seaman's fiver into his hand. On his wrist, the name *Linnea* is written in green-black

239

ink. It could be his girl, but when it comes to salty lads like these, it's just as often the name of some old sea-going crate.

'Is that it?'

'It's the going rate.'

'But I thought…'

I hold my wallet open and show him. 'It's all I've got. In my time you were lucky if you got half that.'

He nods. I take the five-kronor note out of his hand and tuck it into his breast pocket.

'Right, then.'

'I'll follow a bit behind.'

I nod and walk briskly towards the harbour on Södra Blasieholm. As I walk along, I slide off a handful of snow from a window ledge and press it against my left knuckles. If I'd had a few more kronor I could have bribed the guard at the royal stables to let me use one of the loose boxes, but now we have to stay outdoors. The Husqvarna thumps rhythmically against my ribs, but my heart beats even faster. I look around. My sailor is following five or six metres behind me. Grevsgränden opens up towards the water. It's still clear and starry. The ice knocks against the quay.

We pass the Grand Hotel and the Automobil Club. I can hear the seaman stumbling along behind me. On the other side of the water, the houses of Old Town are lined up like a colourful band of reservists with dirty, ochre-coloured uniforms. The black, yellow and red banner sways over the German Legation. I stop and wait for him to catch up.

'Behind here.' My voice is gravelly as I gesture for him to follow me into the little park behind the National Museum.

The snow hasn't been cleared, but, judging by the footprints, we are not the first to make use of the park this evening. The boy slips in the snow and starts swearing. We manage to make our way to the back, and I point across the water towards Skeppsholmen and smile at him.

'You're almost home.'

He nods. I indicate that he should go behind the hedge against the façade of the museum.

There's already a bloke with another sailor in the dark, narrow space between the bushes and the wall. The sailor leans against the façade with his trousers halfway down his thighs. He moans every time the bloke behind him thrusts into him.

'There's space here for more.' The bloke gives his sailor a quick breather before he gets to it again.

My sailor starts pacing on the spot. 'Not the stern thruster.'

'Okay.' Damn it!

I start pulling at his blazer, getting the buttons open and sliding my hands under his jumper, over his completely smooth chest. He wriggles. I press him up against the wall and lean in to kiss him. He moves his face away. I grunt. He breathes in. I unbutton his rough, tight trousers. He's already standing to attention. I'm disappointed; this one's nowhere near as well-endowed as Leonard. I grunt again. He pants.

'Shall I wank you off?'

I nod. He finds me down there, beneath my trousers and underpants. It's unbearably cold. He starts moving his hand up and down. I could just as well be with a woman. He holds it too softly. He pulls the foreskin back too hard.

'You enjoying that?' he whispers close to my face, his breath smelling slightly of vomit. I turn my face away. I think about the boy with the slicked-back hair on Kommendörsgatan earlier. I grab the sailor's hair and press his face against my neck. The bloke next to us starts groaning, but my cock is softening.

'You like this, don't you?'

'Stop!'

He carries on. The vein in my forehead is pulsating hard. I grab his blue collar.

'I said stop!'

I move his schnapps-reeking face close to my own. With a whimper he totters back against the wall.

The disappointment wells up from my stomach. I feel as if hunger is setting in after a week of fasting, although my jaw muscles are too swollen to chew. I stumble out of the bushes, pulling my trousers up.

'Damn it!'

Anger thumps in my veins. The snow crunches under my feet as I remove my tie, fold it up in my pocket, and rush past the Customs House. I come up on Hovslagaregatan and go around the corner. Squeezing the Husqvarna against my body with my arm, I run along the water's edge, back up towards Berzelii Park, passing the Strand Hotel. It's worryingly quiet, and I swear loudly again.

The park is deserted. The goons probably managed to get a gang together and break up the fight. Bits of military kit lie strewn across the area. The snow has taken on that trampled, bright yellow colour that one associates with the usual Christmas slaughter. Here and there in the snow, uniform buttons stare up at me like cat's eyes. I kick a bloodstained sailor's hat into the air.

I feel it in my whole body. To hell with Zetterberg, Sonja and the German creep! Back to Doris, Wernersson's Velocipedes and runaway farmers' daughters.

I've had enough.

From the undertaker's premises below, one can hear the heavy blows of a hammer as Lundin tacks on the lid of a coffin. It's getting dark outside. I leave the lights off and watch the sunset, just as I used to do in the olden days. In a minute I'm going down to pick up a suit from Beda. In half an hour I'm meeting Doris for a Christmas smorgasbord.

My lungs sting me when I inhale too deeply on a cigar. I haven't bought her a Christmas present. Even though I've left my two-line classified ad about 'detective assignments and other discreet services' on a rolling basis for the last few days in *Landsbygdens Folk*, *Social-Demokraten* and *Stockholms-Tidningen*, my letterbox has remained empty.

I stand in front of the mirror, the pinstripes of my brown suit hardly visible in the gloom. I scoop out a sizeable amount of pomade from the pot and pull my fingers through my hair before combing it. I shut one eye to shield myself from the smoke.

Really I should go and get a haircut at Nyström's, even though he's a terrible barber and usually has a cigarette dangling between his lips as he works, dropping ash on your head at regular intervals. I keep going there because he's just around the corner and he's also one of the few barbers in town that sells Fandango.

I slip the comb into my breast pocket and take a deep pull on the cigar. Leaving the Husqvarna in its holster on a hook in the hall, I put on my overcoat and push the door open.

Good Templar Wetterström from two floors up is standing just outside the door in the stairwell, ready to knock. He couldn't look more surprised, not even if I'd caught him red-handed with a bottle. He has a water-combed parting in his hair. His wife stands beside him, holding a brown paper bag spotted with grease stains. Both are in their Sunday best.

In the gloom behind them stands Nilsson from number 5, with his cauliflower ears, a green knitted scarf and black box calf boots. He fidgets as Wetterström clears his throat. His wife pokes him with her elbow.

'Season's greetings.'

'Oh, well thank you.' I put my cigar in my mouth and get out my wallet to see if I can find the receipt from the laundry.

'So, you probably had your Christmas lunch with Lundin this year?'

'It usually ends up that way.'

'Yes, I see. And the heating is working like it's supposed to in your flat?'

'I haven't had any problems.'

'No, Lundin is good in that way. When it comes to the heating.' Wetterström nods.

I find a box of matches and give it a shake.

'You'll have a bit of ham, won't you?' Mrs. Wetterström holds out the paper bag.

I stare at it. Her husband takes it in his hand. I strike a match, puff at the cigar, blow out a thick plume of smoke and put the spent match back in the box.

'Yes, we brought you a bit of ham. It turned out very nicely this year.' He holds out the bag.

Nilsson stares at his slippers behind them.

I put away the matchbox and take the bag. 'Much obliged.'

'And thanks to you also. We've been asked to see if you'll come to the New Year's bazaar this year.'

'New Year's bazaar?'

'You could bring Lundin along as well,' his wife interjects. 'And maybe your lady friend.' Wetterström stares at the door frame. 'If you'd like to. And if she would.'

'Right. Well, I'll ask her.'

'New Year's Eve, from lunchtime at the back building, number forty-one. If you want to contribute in some way you can let us know.'

'Thanks, I'll ask.'

'Well, we hope to see you then.'

The little congregation troops off up the stairs. I stand there for a moment with the bag of ham in my hand, taking a few puffs on my cigar. It's all Dixie's fault. Ever since I started dragging that fat little dog about, people around here are quite transformed.

I've only just locked the door when Nilsson comes sneaking back.

'I hope you can excuse them,' he says, tugging at his earlobe. 'They're going potty about that bazaar.'

'Not a problem.'

'And, I was going to ask, you were a sailor, weren't you?'

'For quite a while.'

'Did you go to Africa?'

'It wasn't unheard of.'

'Right, so I wanted to ask. Are they as beautiful as on the coffee tin? The Negro girls?'

'Even more beautiful.' I take the cigar out of my mouth.

He puts his hand across his mouth and sniggers. 'Even more beautiful!' He slaps his thigh and takes a couple of waltz steps. 'Thanks.'

He's still sniggering as he goes up the stairs. I shake my head, close the door and get out my keys.

A flimsy mist hangs like fine-carded wool over the block. The temperature has risen slightly. I dodge one of the ambulances from the Epidemic Hospital as I cross the road.

On the corner stands the uncrowned king of the yo-yo, demonstrating his tricks to a bunch of kids. He's a head taller than the others, and wearing proper long trousers. With a crooked smile at them, he sends the yo-yo into a spin. As I understand it, this year it has to be the Kalmar twist.

Slightly to one side of the kids, a tramp stands frozen to the spot, staring listlessly at the sky. He's bearded, and has crocheted together his multi-coloured rags. On one foot he wears a spat, on the other a cigar box.

Beda, in a large-patterned floral apron, comes out to meet me with the black suit hanging over her arm. She rubs her eye.

'Here's the suit.'

'Thanks. And season's greetings.'

'Thanks, and the same to you!'

'Things will get better now, you know.'

'Maybe.'

'Excuse me?'

'I had a visit from Doctor Jönsson…' Beda smiles.

'The doctor's for the death certificate.'

'They say I have cancer. Of the eye. They're removing it.'

I nod. The suit hangs heavily on my arm. The words freeze in my throat.

Beda smiles again. 'We'll see if it's spread.'

I nod again, put my cigar in my mouth and massage the bridge of my nose.

'I'm sure it'll go fine.' I offer her the bag of ham. 'Here, have some ham that's left over.'

The yo-yo king puts his apparatus into a spin, lets it roll across the cleared paving stones, then, with a jerk, snaps it back into his hand. A collective sigh passes among the kids. The tramp shuffles off in a northerly direction.

'We'll see.' Beda nods as she accepts the paper bag. 'If it wasn't for Petrus…'

'He'll make his way.'

'He can't even make a pot of gravy.'

We laugh. She puts her hand on my arm. 'I want you to promise me something, Kvisten, do you think you can?'

'I think so.'

'Can you look in on Petrus sometimes?'

'Of course I can.'

'So he doesn't end up in Konradsberg Asylum. Can you promise?'

'Yes.'

Beda reaches up and pats my cheek quite firmly a few times. 'Well that's good. Maybe things will sort themselves out.' She nods thoughtfully. 'If tomorrow comes, common sense will come too.'

'I've celebrated Christmas in every corner of the world,' I say, sitting opposite Doris at the Metropol Restaurant on the corner of Sveavägen and Odengatan about half an hour later.

Although it's the only restaurant that seems to stay open for a late afternoon lunch on Christmas Day, the dining room is not more than half full. The trio makes an abrupt change from 'Jingle Bells' to 'La Paloma'.

'Usually they slaughtered the last pig on board. The skipper gave the crew a bottle of gin to share, and the cook made blood pancakes and pork escalopes. Sometimes you got a ginger cake. The off-duty watch sang Christmas songs, accompanying himself on the violin. This isn't so bad, not so very bad at all.'

'Don't do that.'

Doris is resoundingly unimpressed by the huge crystal chandeliers under the ceiling, the live orchestra and the rippling water sculpture in the middle of the dining room that changes colour. After two mouthfuls of the Christmas food, she puts down her cutlery. I'm eating with good appetite, keeping the linen napkin under my chin and the silver fork in my right hand.

'And damn, on Långholmen. If you were lucky you got the Christmas edition of *The War Cry*.'

'I said, don't do that!'

'Do what?'

'Don't talk to me as if I were a spoilt child.' She fiddles with a cigarette to get it into the cigarette holder, and then lights it.

'Okay.'

I have a good go at my herring salad. It's delicious. Doris exhales a cloud of smoke and nods at me.

'Did you change your hairstyle?'

'I don't think so.'

'You had a side parting before, it wasn't slicked back like that.'

'I've always had it like this.'

'I preferred it before.'

'I'll change it, then.'

With darting eyes, Doris takes a gulp of her champagne. 'Sorry. I've had a couple of *miserable* days. My son slapped my face – on Christmas day, no less.' She has another mouthful. She's on her fifth glass of champagne.

248

'I'll be blowed.'

She sighs and looks around the room. 'Everyone hurts you in the end, it's just a matter of finding the ones who are worth the bother.' She takes a drag of her cigarette. 'Do you want children? You're still young, aren't you?'

'I had one. A daughter.' I put down my cutlery.

'What happened?'

'She died.'

'La Paloma' ebbs away, followed by a pause. I take another Meteor from my inside pocket. Outside, darkness is quickly gobbling up the last of the city. It's snowing; there are lots of tiny, whirling flakes. No people are out and about on the pavements except a boy dragging a jute sack along the pavement, his legs swaddled under his shorts.

A few tables behind us, a bloke raises a toast, and the crystal glasses tinkle as they're brought together. The guitarist is tuning his instrument.

'I'm sorry.' Doris crushes her cigarette in the ashtray. I light my Meteor with the restaurant matches, and then throw the box on the table. She picks a few crumbs off the table.

'It's long ago.'

'So you had someone, then? Were you married?'

'It must be almost ten years ago.'

'Did you leave her? Or did she leave you?'

'I never hit her.'

'What do you mean?'

'I never hit her. We almost always had food on the table and we weren't cold. Maybe I was drunk from time to time but I never raised my hand against her.'

Outside the window an old Ford picks up speed to make it to the top of the hill. The almost-empty number 3 tram passes in the other direction. I hold up my schnapps glass at an angle to see if there are still a few drops left in it. I look around, but the waiter's already on his way to our table. He holds a handwritten note in his hand.

'Mr Kvist?'

'Correct.'

'A caretaker by name of Petersén asked me to give you this. He's looked for you at home, and has been directed here.'

Sonja's lover from Boden Hotel. I wipe my mouth with the linen napkin and push back my chair. The waiter gives me the note and makes himself scarce.

'*She's on Regeringsgatan, number 67*', I read out loud.

There's a stabbing feeling in my stomach. Sonja. The missing prime witness.

I read the note one more time, then push the car keys over to Doris. Regeringsgatan is only about fifteen minutes away.

'Thanks for lunch. I have to look into this at once.'

'What does she have that I don't?'

'It can't be helped. This is urgent.' I stand up.

'All right, I'll wait at your place. And be a good fellow and send the waiter over on your way out, would you? I need more champagne.'

I nod and set off. I point the waiter towards our table. Doris has gone to the toilet. I won't have time to go home and pick up that blasted Husqvarna. I get my overcoat from the cloakroom and put it on. I step outside into the falling snow, and start running at once towards the crossroads.

Sonja, my little dear. Now you're mine.

As I head up the hill on Regeringsgatan, I pass the pleasure palace, Alcazar, at number 74. It's closed for Christmas. The snow is falling hard and, above my head, the local retailers have put up streamers of electric lights to force away the darkness and create a bit of Christmas cheer.

I continue past the spice huts with their blue-painted shop signs and the boutiques just above the bridge. The mannequins in the dark windows have painted-on bob hairstyles. They stare at me with their dead eyes. I walk onto the bridge that runs over Kungsgatan. I stop halfway across and gaze down towards Stureplan. It's an excellent vantage point. I've already checked countless times whether I am being followed, but it doesn't hurt to look one more time. All the shops and restaurants are closed, and the fashionable street is eerily deserted. The newly fallen snow on the pedestrian walkway is scarcely marked by any footprints.

'Maybe the German sod went home for Christmas.'

My voice is muffled by the snow. I snort. The wind whines under the bridge like a drive-belt in a workshop. The spans of the bridge have been decorated with lamps that meet in a gigantic shining Star of Bethlehem, exactly where I am standing and keeping a lookout. Kungsgatan has been carefully cleared and high snowbanks separate the traffic lanes from the wide pavements. Cinemas and shops jostle for space with restaurants. The evening is lit up by neons. The falling snowflakes seem to capture the lights and deflect them as a glow of red or blue shimmering mist.

I hunch up my shoulders. The cold drums against my limbs. I turn around, pace a bit, and read the numbers of the houses.

Further down on Regeringsgatan, a torch-lit procession comes slowly winding along like a giant glow worm. In the front rank, behind a mounted policeman, a couple of blokes are striding along with banners in their hands, but they're too far away for me to be able to identify which congregation they are from. Maybe they're on their way up to Johannes, to celebrate the Redeemer's birthday.

I check the address in my notebook. Number 67 is squeezed between a perfume shop and a tobacconist just a few doors further down the street. An elegant black Rolls is parked outside. I have an idea I've seen the car before some place but I can't remember where. I let my gaze wander up the façade. Most of the windows are lit.

I cross the bridge and head towards the torch procession.

The shop signs creak on their hinges and occasionally make a snapping sound in the wind. I peer into the dark doorway. My heart is racing. I'm close now, I can smell it.

I put a cigar between my lips and rummage in my pockets, then open the door and step inside. The light switch clicks redundantly. Slowly, my eyes accustom themselves to the darkness. A long, sober line of black-dressed men in fur hats and woollen mittens passes in the street outside. The flickering of their torches penetrates the window set into the door. I read the nameplate of the residents. Nothing. A smooth-worn stone staircase winds upwards through the building. There's an abiding smell of mulled wine.

I take the gold lighter from my pocket, shake it and, without success, try to make it work. Muttering, I turn around to face the stairs.

As I put my foot on the first step, a short, desperate scream cuts through the gloom and echoes between the stone walls. I freeze. The hair stands up on my neck and a shiver runs all the way down my spine, leaving my skin goosebumped. I stare up the staircase and listen.

The shop signs are still creaking. I can hear the gentle clattering sound of hooves further up the street. The scream must have come from the first or maybe the second floor.

I run up the stairs quickly, panting. Before I step onto the first-floor landing, I pause and listen again. Everything is silent. It must have been some Christmas drunk having a crack at his wife. I go up the two remaining steps in one leap. Immediately I wish I hadn't.

'Oh good God!'

At the far end of the stairwell, some three or four metres ahead of me, one of the wooden doors is open. I can see directly into the flat. The light of the hall lamp falls over a worn doormat and a pair of high ladies' boots someone has put there. The hall is small and narrow. Someone has obstinately squeezed a secretaire into a cramped space by the door, but the piece lacks a chair. On top of it is a two-armed brass candlestick. An overcoat and a ladies' umbrella hang from a couple of hooks in the light, floral wallpaper.

Sonja looks at me with her slanted eyes. She's lying on her stomach in the hall, her head towards me, her lipstick smudged across her chin. In her dark sleeveless dress, her arms shine palely against the floor. Tears have painted long black stripes down her cheeks. Whimpering quietly, she holds out a pearl necklace in her bleeding hands as if offering it to me as a Christmas present.

The German with the bowler hat greets me with the same smile as in Yxsmedsgränd. He's standing over Sonja, straddling her, his black overcoat buttoned all the way up, black gloves on his hands. In his right hand he holds a blood-caked stick bayonet that is near on half a metre long. The bastard nods, as if greeting me.

Sonja moans again. She manages to slide forwards a little. I take a step towards her. The blood from the bayonet is whisked all over the hall when the German lifts it up and thrusts the blade down.

The tip penetrates Sonja's neck, cuts right through her throat and strikes the hall floor with a dull thud. Her eyes widen, then their light is extinguished. Her hand thumps against the floor, and the pearls make a rattling sound.

I turn and run down the stairs.

A horse with bells pulls a creaking gig across the bridge over Kungsgatan. I throw my unlit Meteor over the railing. The freezing air claws at my nose and in my lungs like steel wool. The banks of snow on either side of the street mute the sound of the race. I know that I'm slower than the murderer. I hope I can stay ahead until we catch up with the procession.

Quickly I draw closer to the march struggling up the hill. My pursuer is keeping up with me; I can hear his thudding boots. Do I have ten metres on him? Five? I don't know, there's no time to check.

I reach the tail end of the torches and change into a higher gear. I gain a couple of metres and throw myself into the left flank of the procession. Embers are flying through the air of the dark afternoon with a smell of burning paper and rank wool. Someone raises his voice but I can't hear what he's saying. I force aside a few more lines of men while, at the same time, removing my hat. For a moment I think I've got away from the German fucker, maybe I was hoping that he might have been looking the other way when I threw myself in among hundreds of witnesses, but then I see his dead left eye sparkling in the light of a torch just a few rows behind me.

Gradually I work my way to the right. When we pass Alcazar and cross David Bagares gata, I crouch down and slip away from the procession. Half running, I slip into a side street, open the first door I find on the right-hand side and throw myself inside. I press myself against the wall of the corridor and try to catch my breath.

Even if the German only stays with the procession for a few metres before he notices I'm no longer there, I'll be safe. It'll give me time to scamper down the steps to the Royal Library and disappear into Humlegården, which I know like the inside of my pocket.

But I don't have time to take my plans any further. I've only just put my hand on the door handle when my pursuer is standing outside. He smiles as he draws the long bayonet from his coat, then opens the door and steps into the darkness. I back away. Sweat is running down my brow, stinging my eyes. Stumbling backwards, I tug at the doors on my left.

'*Sagt hallo zum tot!*' My pursuer slowly closes the space between us, holding the bayonet in front of him like a fencing foil.

Somewhere behind me a flight of steps goes up into the house, but I daren't turn my back on him.

I keep tugging at the doors until one of them opens, and I tumble into a restaurant kitchen. Someone at Alcazar has been sloppy with the routines.

It's a big kitchen with several worktops and a floor of black tiles. On the far side are four cookers under a row of windows where a bit of light comes in. Kitchen implements, pots and trays gleam in the comparative gloom. Quickly I look around for something sharp. My opponent makes an attack at once.

I dodge to the right and grip the knife-wielding arm with my left hand at the same time as I throw a hook with the other. The German flinches but the fist connects nonetheless and smashes into his left eye. There's a crunch in my hand, and shooting pains. Something's snapped.

The false eye jumps out of its socket and makes a little arc through the air before smashing against the hard floor. I put my right palm under his chin and push him back into one of the worktops with all my strength. As the edge of it crunches into his lower back, making him snort with pain, I bend down and bite the fingers of his right hand as hard as I can.

The bayonet clatters as it hits the floor. The remains of the enamelled eye crunch under my foot. The iron-rich taste of blood eggs me on, and I take him in a clinch, though I might as well have embraced a main mast: he has no soft parts, only the sharp edges of muscle and bone. He smells rank. I let the blood and bits of skin run down my chin.

Despite my right fist being broken, and even though I'm the shorter of us, I feel I have the upper hand. I have spent many hours in situations no worse than this.

My old trainer once said that boxing, at its best, makes you feel properly alive. This is wrong. Boxing is at its best when you're completely empty inside, pressing on like some kind of automatic doll. One movement is no more than a natural extension of another. The body is abandoned to the fight, pre-programmed and choreographed to answer in a certain way to a given situation, hardened through thousands of hours of training. The fight turns into a physical self-examination, a receipt for the time that's been invested. Street fighting is really no different; it just lacks a system of rules.

Accompanied by the slamming of saucepans and cooking implements hitting the floor, we spin a couple of times in our furious dance between the benches. Both of us are quietly grunting with the exertion of it. Our cheeks graze against one another. My eye is right up close to his black eye socket.

I keep on his blind side. I chomp after his ear with my bloodied mouth but he reads my movement and clashes heads with me. My neck muscles smart, and my breath is wheezing. I shift myself into a lower position so I can push my skull bone into his carotid artery.

If I can work my shoulder and upper arm round on the other side, I can put him in a lock that way. He pushes me forwards but suddenly stops and steps back. There's a stinging pain in my body when he thrusts his knee into my crotch.

While the pain is still hurtling inside my belly, he grabs hold of my back. He hangs himself on me, curls his legs around my body and locks one arm around my neck with the other.

I don't have much time. My head is thumping with oxygen depletion. I stamp the heel of my boot on his toes, then drive my elbow as hard as I can into his side, but this fails to break the hold around my neck. I throw myself backwards in the hope that he'll let go of me when we smash into the floor.

The fall winds him. Little droplets of saliva shoot up and land on my swelling, heated face. He's moaning in my left ear but still clamped onto me.

We're lying there between the worktops and I thrash with my legs, my eyes flickering and my field of vision starting to reduce. I claw for his healthy eye, but can't get hold of it.

In a last expenditure of energy I fumble over the floor and find a sharp object. Without ever having held one, I know right away what it is. Everything I can hear seems to be heading into a great darkness. I close my hand around the fat handle and drive the meat thermometer into him.

The world around me is shaking and vibrating. I make another stab at him.

All the light is retracting into a black sun. Dusk falls quickly. I stab again.

I wake on the murderer's arm. It's still dark outside. I'm cold. We're both lying on our backs. I turn my head and look at him, staring at me now with his empty eye socket. That bowler hat of his has gone. He has one puncture wound through his cheek, and one on his forehead. The meat thermometer in his throat shows thirty-three degrees but I don't know how long I've been out.

I stay where I am, trying to get a sense of whether I'm hurt. My right fist pulsates with pain and my head aches, but that's all. I stand up on shaky legs, all sour with blood and coughing. I give the corpse a decent kick with the side of my foot. It jumps, rattling the fallen saucepans around it.

I kneel over the dead man. The German is smooth-shaven, with close-cropped hair like a con from Långholmen. The yellow, grinning teeth between his pale lips are undamaged, but the left side of his scalp is scarred in patches, as if he was hit once by a hail of shotgun pellets. For a moment I consider closing his blue eye.

I search him. I find some sort of badge in silver and gold in the shape of a flower, a key ring with about ten keys on it, an automatic lighter, a wallet with thirty kronor in banknotes, and a photograph with a group of smiling soldiers. I do not recognise their uniforms.

I take the money and replace his wallet in the inside pocket of his overcoat, then close the coat at the front and give the corpse a little pat. I am so glad that I kept my leather gloves on through the entire fight – there's less to tidy up, and now I'm in a bit of a hurry. I check the meat thermometer. It's fallen to thirty-two degrees. I get out my comb from my inside pocket and pull it through my hair.

'Kvisten doesn't bare his head for anyone,' I mutter as I pick up the hat from the floor and press it down on my head. Time to make my way home. I have to get rid of all my clothes and I should fix myself up with a water-tight alibi; it's only a question of time before the police find both bodies. If I'm lucky, Alcazar will be closed tomorrow, but presumably the door to Sonja's flat is still open, unless they're already there. Luckily it's not far to get home to Sibirien, and the streets are almost deserted even though it's only seven o'clock.

'Doris. Kvisten's high-society alibi.'

It doesn't get much tighter than that. If I can convince her to be there for me and put her reputation on the line, I'm home and dry. Anyway she doesn't have much of a reputation to worry about. She'll do it. She has to do it.

Before I leave the place, I wash the blood off my face under one of the taps, and do up all the buttons of my coat. On my way out I accidentally step on the bowler hat of the German.

After sneaking out the same way as I came in, I find that the blustering wind that comes hounding up Birger Jarlsgatan finds its way under my coat at once, and starts tearing at my bloodied rags. I pick up a handful of snow, pressing it against my right hand, and then quietly jog past the timber yard on the left and go down the stairs towards Engelbrektsplan.

I pass the mouth of the Brunkeberg Tunnel, lying there like the snout of a huge boar in the snow, and then hurry past the tobacconist's. I'm dying for a damned smoke. The row of bare trees on Birger Jarlsgatan can already be glimpsed through the falling snow. From there it's more or less straight on all the way to Sibirien. I hardly meet a soul. The snow consumes all the sounds of the city, and everything is absolutely still.

Doris is waiting for me at home in the bed. All the lights in the flat have been left on. She's wearing a white slip that clings to her bony body. The ashtray perched on her stomach is full of cigarette butts, gooey with lipstick. She has twiddled her way to a radio station playing jazz.

'Evening.'

'Where have you been?' She looks at me with an uninterested expression. She's been at her medicine again, and now has the same, soulless eyes that one sometimes sees in resigned, impoverished folk once their anger has brewed for too long, and is now transforming itself into an acidic bile that's slowly corroding them from the inside. The only difference is that she has plenty of dough.

'Just having a look around. What are you doing?'

I go into the wardrobe and root out an old sailor's sack. I can hear Doris mumbling something as I come out and start undressing. The pain is burning in my right hand. A trumpet wails from the radio.

'Did you say something?'

'Listening to music.'

I empty the pockets of my clothes, stuff them into the sailor's sack, change into a clean shirt and trousers and jump into a pair of old clogs. I pick up a cigar and bite off the end.

'Are you finding anything good?'

She shrugs. The ashtray is in danger of overturning in the bed. 'Why don't you use the cigar cutter I gave you today?' 'Cigar cutter' is difficult for her, and she slurs as she attempts it.

'I forget that I have it.'

On the wall next to the sleeping-alcove one can see the splashes of blood from the time she whacked me on the nose. I put on my things, go up to her as she lies there with her breasts almost popping out of her shift, and pick up the box of matches that's on her stomach.

'Can you fill the big saucepan with water and put it on the boil? I'll be back in a moment.'

She nods torpidly.

With the sailor's sack, a bottle of paraffin, and a scrap of sausage for the cats in the yard, I head down the stairs and go out the back door. The night is cold and clear. A big rat from the latrine scurries across the snow and disappears behind the sheds. Someone has left the potato cellar door open. There's no sign of the cats, and the snow-covered water pump looks like a snowman made by a mentally impaired child.

I kick up an elongated hole in the snow, lay the sack in it and drench it in paraffin. While the clothes are absorbing it, I go over to the potato cellar and stick my head in. It stinks of rancid humidity and rat droppings. The smells remind me of the isolation cells at Långholmen. I shiver and close the door.

When about a minute has gone by, I strike a match and watch as my clothes go up in flames. The sharp smell of paraffin fills the courtyard. As I stand there watching the sailor's sack burning, I eat the sausage. In the window I see Lundin briefly passing, shaking his head. Pity about the new overcoat and boots, but there's nothing else for it. The goons' technicians are too smart.

By the time I come back up into the flat, the water is boiling. Doris has perked up a bit. She's sitting at the kitchen table with a glass of wine and the newspaper, and she's even put on a dark dress with a long line of big white buttons.

My clothes fall in a heap on the rag rug. I pour cold water into the bathing tub, shift it to the middle of the floor and top it up with boiling water. Doris stares at me without any reserve.

I get into the water and hang my head, an enormous fatigue emanating through my limbs. I hear her getting to her feet. She lowers a tea towel into the water, then scrubs my back with it.

'I've killed a bloke.'

I'm still hanging my head. The hand that's washing my back stops rubbing for a few moments.

'I'm sure he deserved it.'

She goes back to her scrubbing. I exhale.

'He's killed at least three people, maybe four, and he tried to finish me off as well.'

'Well, then,' she says. 'Are you in trouble?'

I nod. 'It's probably just a question of time before they're at the door.' I hesitate, then go on: 'Would you lie for me?'

Doris drops the towel into the water, stands up, goes around the bathing tub and turns her back on me. She picks up my clothes, starts folding them, and piles them on the kitchen table. When she turns the trousers upside down, the loose change and gold lighter clatter onto the floor. She picks up the lighter and fidgets with a pack of Camels from the table. The lighter clicks a few times without result.

'That's a lovely lighter.' She holds it up before her. Her mouth turns to a bloodless streak. 'Where did you get it?'

'It's broken. Doris? Would you?'

'Why are you going around with a broken lighter?'

'Don't change the subject now.' I'm cold, sitting there naked in the tub. 'Would you?'

She puts the lighter back in the trousers and pats them down. Then, in the midst of the deep silence that follows, there's a hard knock on the door. Someone tugs at the handle before knocking again. Doris looks up with a harried expression.

'For God's sake,' I whisper, rising from the bathing tub with water dripping everywhere. 'Would you?'

The goons that have come to put me in irons aren't the same as the last time. Both are in uniform. One of them is an elderly, red-nosed bloke with spectacles and large, droopy ears. The other is a severe type with a clipped moustache and a hand on the hilt of his sabre. Wearing the towel wrapped around my hips, I reverse into the gloomy hall.

'Kvist?' The older of the two men sniffs.

I nod.

'Turn to the wall!' The younger of them speaks with an irritable, shrill voice.

'Can't one even have a Christmas soak these days?'

I smile and turn around, and as I do so I notice some cobwebs in the corner between the ceiling and the wall. The pain cuts through my right hand when they handcuff me. Someone presses the base of his hand against my shoulder blades.

I can feel them tensing up when they hear the sound of Doris's heels. With a swishing sound, one of them draws his sabre halfway out of its scabbard. I look around.

She comes into the living room and sits on top of the desk. Without shaking, she puts a Camel into her cigarette holder. We watch her in silence. In the gloom, her bright buttons shine like the whites of a chimney-sweep's eyes. She fluffs up her hair.

'So? Would one of these gentlemen be kind enough to offer me a light?'

I hear at least one of the goons start patting his uniform,

263

to look for a box of matches. I nail Doris with my eyes, but she doesn't return my gaze, and then she sighs.

'Excuse us, my lady, we didn't know you were here.'

Doris finds a box of matches on the desk. The flame briefly lights up her narrow face, her brown eyes and the beauty spot high up on her cheek. She's touched up her lipstick.

'What's going on?'

The match goes out in a cloud of grey cigarette smoke.

'You'll have to excuse us, Miss, we have our orders.'

'We've been here all evening.' My voice seems nervy. 'We had Christmas luncheon at Metropol and then we came back here.'

'Shut up!' The goon shoves the palm of his hand even harder into my back. My head thumps into the wall. Doris is still refusing to look at me.

'Let's take him onto the landing and dress him there,' decides the younger one. 'You'll have to drive him to the station. I'll have a word with the lady in the meantime. Where are his clothes?'

Doris nods towards the kitchen. The younger one stamps off, while the older one takes me by the crook of my arm and tries to drag me out of the door. I resist. Doris looks at me, nods briefly and puts her hand on her heart. I smile, I can breathe again. The goon pulls me out into the stairwell.

The car is cold. I sit in the back seat, and the older constable drives at a snail's pace, hunched over the steering wheel. The powder snow whirls all about us as we move along. One of the headlights is broken. I'm shivering. We travel through a ghost city, the restaurants and shops all closed, and no sign of any trams and hardly even cars.

'You remember when they buried those Ådalen blokes?' The goon in the front gets out a handkerchief and blows his nose loudly, with one hand.

'Certainly I do.'

'Everything stopped. People put down their tools, there was no traffic for five minutes.'

'Until the factory whistles sounded again.'

'This is a bit like that, isn't it? Like the grave.'

In Vasaparken the ice rink lies deserted. A tramp leans against a tree like an abandoned snowman. I have the idea he could be dead. As we pass, a stray dog cocks its hind leg against a tobacco kiosk by St Eriksplan. We turn off towards Gloomholmen.

I wonder what the goon is talking to Doris about. There's really not so very much he could ask the director's wife. The subject is too delicate. I'm in her hands. There's not a lot to be done about it. My head hurts, and my right hand is pulsating with pain.

DCI Alvar Berglund is properly dressed in a jacket, waistcoat and a white shirt, also a tiepin with a swastika. He smiles welcomingly as I walk into the little interrogation room, then he puts down his spectacles, which he is in the process of polishing, and stands up to shake hands. I've been let out of the handcuffs, probably on Berglund's order. We shake hands, his grip cutting into my fist like a punch at an already broken rib. I break into a sweat but force myself to smile.

'Kvist! How nice! How's your Christmas been?'

'I've had worse.'

We make ourselves comfortable opposite one another.

'Have you solved the Christmas crossword yet?'

'Haven't had time.'

'You've been busy?' Berglund smiles again, twists the tip of his grey moustache, and taps his pen at the table as if to mark out the time that passes between each reply.

'You know how it is.'

'Yes.' Berglund nods. 'We've had our hands quite full here as well. Never seen a Christmas day quite like it.' He stops drumming for a few seconds before he goes back to it.

'I thought I'd be seeing Olsson.' I regret the words as soon as they have flown out of my mouth.

'The head of the Criminal Division? Why on earth would you think that?'

'I thought it was about Zetterberg?'

'Olsson is on Gotland for Christmas but you'll see him. In good time.'

'So why am I here?'

Berglund smiles again, broader than ever, and stops his tapping before offering a surprise: 'There's a witness on Kungsgatan, a widow who sits in the window all day.'

'I'll be damned!' This whole charade is starting to bore me.

'Yes. And she freed you.'

I meet Berglund's eyes. Like all goons, he takes a little detour before he gets to the point. I decide to take things into my own hands, to be rid of it.

'And Sonja. I think Sonja saw the murderer leaving Zetterberg's place.'

'Yes. And as far as I've heard you've been looking for her? And I think you found her in the end, didn't you?'

'Unfortunately not. I was looking for her, half of Klara could back that up, but it was like she'd been swallowed up by the ground.'

'I thought you were a bit of a bloodhound when it comes to women who are on the game?'

'This one slipped through.'

'Well, we did find her in the end, this evening in Regeringsgatan.'

Berglund runs his finger across his moustache. 'Sadly, she was fairly quiet.'

'Oh?'

'She had holes in her. Lots of holes.'

I flinch, even though I already knew this, of course. I think of her in the rain on Kungsgatan and I think of her father in his little workshop on Bondegatan. Now he really doesn't have anyone to follow him. Now it's only him and his weeping wife.

'Well that's very bad news.'

'For her. And for you. Where were you this afternoon?'

'I spent the afternoon with a lady friend. You've probably heard of Doris Steiner?' Now it's my turn to smile.

'She said you had luncheon at the Metropol?' Berglund taps his notebook with his pen again.

'Their Christmas table. I can recommend the pig's trotters.'

'And then?'

'Then we went back to my home and spent the rest of the evening there... You know how it is.' I raise my eyebrows pointedly, man to man, so to speak.

'I didn't think you bothered with the ladies?' Berglund smiles again, but now even that feigned civility of his is missing, the one he likes to present to the outside. I feel anger rumbling inside of me like a heavy breaker at sea. I have a good mind to lean across the table and deck the bloke.

'Well,' Berglund goes on. 'We have spoken to Mrs Steiner and indeed she does confirm that you lunched at the Metropol.'

'There you are, then!'

'And then, according to her version of events, you disappeared for several hours before coming back and burning your clothes down in the yard.'

They keep me rotting in the cell for a few days, to soften me up. The only human contact I get is the latrine cleaner and the screw who brings the porridge or opens the viewing slit and tells me to shut my gob if I start whistling some Ernst Rolf. One night the prisoner in the cell next door tries to communicate with me by means of the same old knocking. That, if anything, drives me half crazy. The wall lice don't make things much better.

I pace back and forth to work up some warmth, my left hand on the waistband of my trousers to keep them from falling down, my clogs clattering with a hollow sound between the walls. The ash-grey light of dawn enters through the little barred window. I cough and spit in the galvanised shit bucket.

I've been here for four days. They can keep me locked up for three months if they want to. One of my co-prisoners during my first Långholmen stint claimed he was once detained here for sixteen days. I wipe my snot on my shirt sleeve. At least at Långholmen, if one needed to, one could tear out a page from the Bible or the catechism.

I sit down and very carefully squeeze my right hand. The worst of the swelling has gone down, but my little finger and its knuckle are somewhere between dark blue and purple, also far more crooked than usual. Something in there has broken.

'Soon when old Kvisten shakes his fist, it'll be like a rattle.'

My voice echoes hoarsely between the graffiti-strewn walls. I try to laugh but nothing comes out. I get up and start pacing again. I smell like a tramp and my body itches from the lice. How the hell do they manage to survive in this cold, in these stone walls?

I'm startled when the prisoner in the cell on the right starts howling. He does it at regular intervals. It's impossible to make out what he's yelling, he just yells.

For the hundredth time I read the graffiti on the door: names, lines in clusters of five, swastikas and insults. Somehow, what I remember best is what was written in my last cell, two weeks earlier: *What one knows, no one knows. What two know, the goons know.*

I have spent my every waking minute obsessing over Doris Steiner. Either she sold me out to protect herself, or Berglund is trying to lure me into a trap. I don't know what to think. It's best not to think anything at all; one gets a lot of silly ideas in one's head while under lock and key.

'All things in their time.'

Out in the corridor, rushing steps are heading for my neighbour's cell. The door opens. One can't hear what the screw is saying, but the thumps that follow are recognisable. Also the yells. The door closes and the steps fade once again. Hopefully the bird of ill omen will keep his mouth shut for a while.

Probably the goon doesn't have a shred of evidence against me. At least there's nothing to connect me to the two addresses on Regeringsgatan: no blood, no fingerprints, and no witnesses. I make a listless left-right combination in the air.

I go and stand in the window as dusk falls rapidly and the screw resumes his wandering. I wonder whether Doris has realised I have a weak spot for blokes. Maybe she got the green-eyed monster when she found the gold lighter, and maybe that was why she shopped me?

I go on with my pacing as it's getting dark. Once it's absolutely black outside, the screw's endless patrolling outside my door comes to a stop, and the lock makes a snapping sound.

'The prison doctor is here, as you've asked.'

The door closes behind an elderly, white-robed bloke with a bulbous schnapps nose and a receding hairline. There's something pasty about his appearance. His cheeks hang like bags on the side of his skull. When he straightens up and pulls in his stomach, a double chin appears.

'So?' He puts his big doctor's briefcase of leather on the stone floor. 'I understand it's about your hand?'

I sit down on the bunk and hold up my fist.

'It needs to be dressed, preferably with a splint. I asked for medical help four days ago.'

'It is Christmas, you know.'

The doctor, standing in front of me, takes my hand. He mutters something one cannot hear, and gently squeezes the swelling around the knuckle.

'How did this happen?'

'I was kicked.'

'Your entire knuckle's been crushed. It's moved two centimetres.'

'That's an old injury.' I sniff.

'And the finger is wrongly aligned. I can feel a diagonal fracture in the middle bone.'

'Old.'

'And then there's an injury in the outer phalanx.'

'That swine has pointed the wrong way for ten years.'

'And lastly, here.' The doctor squeezes that part of the hand where the blue discolouring is most obvious. The sharpness of the pain takes me unawares.

'Ow, damn!' My voice bounces between the stone walls. I snatch my hand back, while the doctor mutters something. 'What did you say?'

'I should have been called in much earlier. Now we have to pull it right.'

I sigh. 'So pull the sod, then.'

I hold out my hand again. The doctor puts his thumb against one side of the finger, cups his fingers around the other side of it, and tugs. The pain that shoots up my hand makes me clench my jaws and close my eyes. My hand starts trembling.

'There we are. And now it has to be bandaged very hard. If you're still here in three weeks I can take a look at it then.'

'As far as I know I'm not going anywhere.'

The doctor leaves me, my hand thumping with pain. My ring finger and the little finger are joined by means of a greyish bandage that winds through the gap at the base of my thumb and around the palm of the hand. I pace about for a moment, coughing and spitting and holding my hand above my head.

In the corridor, the latrine man is slamming with his buckets. The snapping sound of opening locks gets closer and closer until finally a key is inserted into my door. I look up at a young stripling with a double row of brass buttons on his uniform jacket, which is too big for him. He has a big bunch of keys and a truncheon in his belt.

'Kvist has to go up to Berglund.'

I grunt and stand up slowly.

'Hurry up!'

I hold out my hands and the handcuffs click into place around my wrists. The stripling shifts out of the way and I walk down the partially lit corridor. There's a stink of shit. I stop.

Further down the corridor, the latrine man is carting off two galvanised buckets hanging on a pole carried across his shoulders. He's a bearded, stooping bloke in his sixties, wearing a grey overall and staring down at the floor.

'There's always someone worse off.'

'What did you say?' The stripling appears at my side.

'What?'

'You muttered something. What did you say?'

I stare at him for a second or so. 'Did I? I don't think so.'

He sighs. 'Sometimes I think Kvist has more pomade than brains up there.'

My right fist tightens with pain when I instinctively try to clench it. 'Are you calling me stupid?'

'Straight on, the door on the right.'

The stripling taps me on my shoulder, and I clatter off in my wooden clogs, my hands clutching my waistband. I feel the vein on my forehead thumping in time with my hand. Behind me, I hear a match being struck and the glow of a cigarette sizzling as the boy takes a drag. He's doing it just to be bloody-minded. I clench my jaw and move on.

When we come into Berglund's room, I realise that it's the same little interrogation chamber as the last time. I recognise a crack in the ceiling. The screw unlocks my handcuffs.

Berglund sits at the table. In front of him is a notebook, a black fountain pen and a thick brown file of documents. He's wearing a black three-piece suit, a white shirt, and a blue, hand-tied bow-tie with narrow black stripes. When he raises his hand and slides his glasses down to the tip of his nose, a cufflink with a coat of arms on it emerges from under his sleeve.

'Kvist. Please do sit.'

I do as I'm told. The chair legs scrape against the floor. Berglund pushes his glasses back up again and opens his file of documents. He caresses his ridiculous grey moustache.

'We've conducted a personal investigation into your background in preparation for trial. I would ask you to confirm what I am reading out, and fill in any omissions.'

'What do you mean?'

'Harry Kvist, residing at Roslagsgatan forty-three, born in Torshälla parish on thirty December, 1898. Is that correct?'

'It's correct.' I hold my thumping right hand in my left. My stomach churns, the pain is making me feel nauseous.

'Your mother's name was Gerda Kvist. Your father is not known. Your mother died in childbirth.'

'She got a fever. You want me to sign somewhere?'

'One moment. After that your grandmother took care of you and your twin brother John. He died at the age of four. The cause of death was whooping cough.'

'His blasted coughing kept me up through the night. We slept head to foot on the kitchen sofa.'

'And then the parish placed Kvist in the care of the workhouse committee?'

'When grandmother grew too frail.'

'You were more or less five years old. Do you remember it?'

'There was a workhouse auction to the lowest bid on the church hill. It was snowing that day and the bidding never really took off.'

'You were sent to live with a farmer in the area.'

'He made a partition in the pigsty in the barn with a couple of planks. I lived on one side and the boar on the other. Every morning I woke up when he scratched himself against the planks. Nice company.'

'How were things for you there?'

'What difference does it make? I didn't kill them, not Zetterberg and not the others either. You know I didn't kill them. You just need someone to blame.'

'Just answer the question, if you'd be so good.'

'You have nothing that connects me to Regeringsgatan, and the only witness on Kungsgatan freed me, isn't that so?'

'The only witness that's still alive, yes. Would you be kind enough to answer my questions? How long did you stay at the farm?'

I sniff, and scratch my head. Berglund checks his watch and goes back to fingering his moustache.

'A couple of years. I ran away.'

'And where did you stay after that?'

'With the other workhouse inmates, usually. In all I had two years in school.'

'They were hardly days of plenty, were they?'

'What do you think, Detective Inspector?'

'I think blood puts its stamp on a human, but there are instances where circumstance comes into play.'

'I don't know what you're talking about.'

Berglund leafs through the papers in his file of documents. Most are handwritten, yellow sheets of foolscap, full of smudged ink.

'When did you go to sea?'

'Early on.'

'And when did you permanently sign off?'

'After the war, with good references.'

'Always something. And since then you have lived in Stockholm?'

'I don't get this, what's the bloody good of it?'

'While doing various labouring jobs, such as working as a stevedore, you made a career as a boxer, I understand.'

I sigh. 'Undefeated to date.'

'In 1920 you marry Emma, born Jönsson, on the fourth of March.'

'What concern is that of yours?'

'And not quite nine months later, on the twenty-fourth of

October, she gives birth to a daughter at Södra maternity hospital. She's baptised Ida.'

'A Monday. It was a Monday.' My nausea gets more intense. I feel as if I've been running up a hill without water. I want to vomit. I lean back, stare at the crack in the ceiling and let my stomach settle.

'So she got knocked up, did she?'

'That wasn't the reason.'

'What do you mean?'

'She did, but that wasn't why we got married. Not only that.'

I scratch my scalp again. I hear the second hand of Berglund's wristwatch ticking away. I meet his gaze.

'A few years later, in August 1923, your wife and daughter emigrate to America. They embark from Gothenburg. You do not go with them?'

'That's right.'

'Why not?'

'The Swedish Championships were a few months later. Just a formality, they said. It would look better if I had that on the pro contract.'

I look up again. Berglund's pen scrapes the paper as he makes a few notes.

'America?'

'Where else?'

Berglund makes a few more notes.

'Are they alive?'

'As far as I know.'

'Where do they live?'

'The last I heard from them they were living somewhere near Grand Forks in a place called North Dakota. But that's almost ten years ago now.'

'Do you want them to be informed about your current situation?'

'No.'

'Do you have any others, relatives or such like, whom we should contact?'

'None.' I sniff. Gradually, the nausea dissipates.

Berglund nods thoughtfully and looks through his documents. 'The following year you made your debut in our protocols. Paragraph eighteen, indecent behaviour, in 1924. You were fined seventy-five kronor.'

'It was worth it.'

Berglund doesn't see the joke.

'Then you were sentenced for grievous bodily harm and spent most of 1926 at Långholmen.'

'Innocent as God's little lamb.'

'Really? And yet you signed the declaration of satisfaction. Then you were only out for a year before you had to go back in again. The same crime. You seem to like it at Långholmen, don't you, Kvist?'

'Like hell I do, it takes an age to get your hair back in order when you're released.'

'Further to that you've faced charges for assault on three occasions between 1924 and now without a conviction. I assume you're involved in some sort of extortion activity…'

'I'm mainly involved with private investigations.'

'Things should be known by their proper names. It's called extortion, mark my words.'

'If you prefer.'

Berglund puts down his pen and leans back in his chair. He puts his hands together over his stomach. I splutter and cough, and Berglund watches me calmly.

'Let's go back for a moment to your wife and daughter.'

My body tenses up, as if in preparation for a punch. I lean across the table. 'What for?'

'Your daughter must be twelve or thirteen now. It's a pity she has to grow up without a father.'

'What the hell do you mean?'

'What happened?'

'What do you think happened?'

'I'm asking you.'

'You have all the damned pieces in front of you. Now you only have to lay the puzzle.' As I hiss out those words, I feel tiny droplets of saliva flying from my lips, and I stare at him with fury.

The signal from Berglund's bell under the table makes me jump. The stripling screw comes in at once. His handcuffs rattle, I hold out my hands, and there are two clicks around my wrists. I grab hold of the edge of the table to stand up. The pain is burning in my right hand.

'Sit down!'

I stop myself in the middle of the movement. Berglund nods at the screw. I feel a heavy hand on my shoulder, and I sink back down.

'Could the duty constable stay a little longer?'

'Yes, chief!'

Berglund smiles and puts his hand in his inside pocket.

'Honouring one's word,' says Berglund, as he gets out a pack of Carat and shakes out a cigarette. 'It's one of the characteristics of the Swedish spirit to honour one's word.'

I feel a curious sense of calm emanating throughout my body. Handcuffs or not, I can deck them both if I want to. A phosphorus stick makes a rasping sound and Berglund lights his cigarette. The matchstick ends up in the ashtray on the table.

'So what is it that makes certain people break their promises and be faithless about their loyalties? A weakness, naturally, a defect. Deceit is in the very nature of some people. Why did this once so proud nation topple into the dirt? Well, because the Jew has a certain weakness. He belongs to a race that is greedy by nature, with a lack of loyalty, fealty, and patriotism. Who are the people getting rich now because of Ivar Kreuger's death? Answer that question and you'll find his assassins.'

Berglund inhales and sends a thin streak of smoke up towards the ceiling. I allow myself a chuckle. I wedge my foot under the chair and put both hands on the table top.

'If this country is going to rise again we have to cut out the defective elements from the body of society. So you see, Kvist, it really makes no difference to me if you're innocent or not. It'll be a true pleasure for me to lock you up in either case.'

'Whether I killed them or not?'

'You see, your perversion is your defect. It makes you unseemly and faithless.'

There's a crackling sound when the glow of Berglund's cigarette consumes a little section of the paper. He blows smoke from a corner of his mouth, and his eyes meet mine with a smile. I smile back at him.

'As in the case of your wife and daughter.'

I take a deep breath before pushing the table into his chest with all my strength. My right hand screams out with pain. There's a thump when Berglund is pinned between the wall and the table. His spectacles end up hanging lopsidedly, his eyes open wide. All the air is forced out of his lungs, and his cigarette rolls across the floor.

I stand up with my thighs against the side of the table, and lean over him. The screw yells something at me. I force the little chain of my handcuffs under Berglund's chin and tighten it until my hands meet behind his neck.

The first baton blow hits me on my right upper arm. I hardly feel it. Berglund makes a hissing sound, saliva gleaming on his dry lower lip. I spit in his face. The gob hits a lens of his spectacles and trails across his cheek. He pulls and strains at my lower arms but I latch onto him. My head explodes in a burst of darkness and light as a baton blow comes in at my temple.

Nothingness courses like a flash through my body.

A couple of hours later I vomit in the bucket for the third time. They refuse to empty it, though it's practically full. Afterwards I squat on one knee with my arm over my mouth. The thumping headache seems to be intent on blowing up my head from within, and nausea makes cold sweat break out like hoar frost over my body. For a short while I experience double vision. I'm sobbing.

'Get up and walk, there's nothing else to do.'

The trainer's words issue from my mouth. I grip the edge of the bunk. Its wood is cold and smooth in my hand. I stand up with a wobble.

Running my hand across my chin, I realise that my beard stubble has almost had time to go soft. I spit on the floor and start pacing. It's all about working through the body's limitations. To get the bastard to do as it's told.

'Nothing else to be done. Hold on to the ropes if you have to.'

My head spins and I totter off course. I reach out with my left hand and support myself against the wall. Outside in the corridor I can hear steps. There's more than just one person out there. They stop in front of my door. I have my back to them. Someone rattles the keys.

'He's in here, sir.'

I still have my hand against the wall. The door closes again, the lock rings out sharply. I hear an agitated voice: 'Harry? How the heck are things with you?'

Hessler. Of all the damned people. Slowly I turn round and change hands, so that I am now leaning against the other. Hessler hurries up to me. He puts his arm around my shoulders and tries to buoy me up. He smells of Aqua Vera and pilsner.

The senior constable helps me across the cell and lets me sink down on the bunk. I hang my head and support it in both hands. Hessler is wearing black, highly polished boots with his uniform. He sways slightly, but quickly regains his balance.

'What the hell are you doing here?'

'It's your birthday tomorrow, isn't it, Harry! You'll be thirty-four? I remembered.' Hessler slurs his words.

I stare at him while I scratch at my throat. He shifts his weight from one leg to the other.

'That doesn't explain anything.'

'As you know I don't touch schnapps any more.'

'What are you talking about?'

'It's been years since the last time.'

'Okay?'

Hessler looks at the latrine bucket with distaste and puts his hand over his mouth. The nausea takes hold of me again, but I manage to control it. There's a rustling of crumpled silk paper when Hessler pulls out a red and white cracker from his uniform. A podgy bookmark angel has been glued to the middle of it. He holds it out towards me.

'The children have been busy.'

'And where the hell should I hang that up, do you think?'

The senior constable looks around the cell. 'Maybe I can get you a nail for the door.'

'God damn it, Hessler.'

The ears of the senior constable turn bright red. He gently puts the cracker next to me on the bunk. Quickly he caresses my hair. There's a blaze inside my skull, and I turn away.

'I was thinking, maybe you'd like someone to take care of you for a while, Harry. Like I used to do.'

'You're all boozed up.'

'But we may never see each other again!'

'Go home to your wife and children. They probably need you a lot more than I do.'

'You're the only one for me, Harry. There's only ever been you!'

Hurriedly I get up. The tremulous nausea works its way through my body. Impotently I wave my forefinger in front of me.

'Go home! It's Christmas, for God's sake!'

'What if I never get to see you again?'

Hessler grabs my arm, and cups his other hand over my crotch. His breath really does reek of pilsner. He tries to press himself against me, but I manage to impose my left fist between us and push him away. With firm steps I walk over to the cell door, and start banging on it.

'Have a cup of coffee with the duty sergeant and sober yourself up.'

'You smiled at me once, Harry.' He purses his lip acidly like a lass who's been denied a cone of sweets.

'What the hell are you on about?'

'It was years ago but I still remember. Just the once.'

The door opens. Hessler gives me a last, surly look before it closes behind him. I hear him and the screw mumbling something to each other as their steps slowly fade away.

My neighbour gives off a long, desolate yell. I feel nauseous again and go over to the barred window at the far end of the cell, where I stand on my tiptoes. The window is not airtight and one can get the odd breath of fresh air that way.

The cold calms my stomach. In the evening gloom, I can see the metre-long icicles glittering like predatory fangs along the drainpipe of the tall house opposite. I ruminate on whether they could have some evidence against me, which they've not yet revealed. A sort of ace in the pack.

'Maybe someone from that damned torch-lit procession.'

That's as far as I get in my musings. With a sigh, I gently move my head back and forth, as if this might rattle my thoughts into place.

Outside the cell door, steps are coming again. Someone hollers excitedly, another laughs pointedly. The viewing hatch slides open with a metallic scrape.

I peer out. In the corridor, the stripling has lined up two other screws in uniform. The old latrine man is on the right flank. All four of them are holding sheets of paper in their hands.

'One, two, three,' the stripling counts, and then, ringing out between the corridor walls, comes the opening verse of a schottische that I know much too well:

> Harry Kvist was a hell of a bloke
> Every uppercut he hit, he went for broke
> He never took a count for a while
> At every opponent he would smile
> 'Cos Harry Kvist was a hell of a bloke

'Stop that!' I roar through the hatch. 'Stop it, for Christ's sake!'

I smash my right fist into the door. The searing pain almost makes my legs give way beneath me. The screws snigger and carry on even more loudly.

In Stockholm town in the summer of twenty-two
Kvisten thought he'd see how well he could do
He won the match without any elbow grease
And the whole thing was a right wheeze
'Cos Harry Kvist was a hell of a bloke

The queasiness forces me down on my knees. I try to get up, but my body doesn't do what I tell it to. I crawl over to the bucket and throw up sour bile, while my body is racked with convulsions. The yellow stomach fluids trail into the bucket, while the last verse of the schottische resounds through the cell:

While Kvisten got ready for his best draw
He hadn't figured on Swedish law
'Cos he ended up going astray
With his sparring partner he had it away
'Cos Harry Kvist was a hell of a bloke

I crawl off and sit in the corner with my knees drawn up to my chin. The hatch in the door closes, and the chortling of the screws slowly dies away. Wiping my mouth on my arm, I rock from side to side.

Then, fumbling with my hand along the wall and standing on unsteady legs, I put my nose as close to the window as possible. A thin, cold draught of air makes its way into the cell. I come to life. A large flock of crows takes off without warning from the top of the roof on the other side. Their ominous croaking reminds me of the whooping cough that took my twin brother, and left me all alone in the world.

When I press my cheek to the wall and gaze up through the barred window, I can see a little strip of sky, tinged with pink and purple. If I've counted the days correctly I may be able to see the New Year fireworks spreading their eruptions of light across the sky tonight. I'm hungry, but it must be hours until dinner time.

I'm no longer vomiting and the headache is not as intense, but sometimes I still lose my balance as I walk back and forth across the cell floor. My thoughts float slowly through my skull, as viscous and thick as Långholmen porridge. My cell neighbour gives off a lone, prolonged roar. He stops abruptly – maybe he's learned his lesson.

I hear keys rattling outside the cell. The door opens, and a young, blond goon stands there with a pair of handcuffs. His large peaked cap only seems to stay in place thanks to his protruding ears. Did he get the New Year's shift because of his youth?

I nod and he comes into the cell. I hold my hands out to him, and he snaps on the handcuffs. Only when he offers me a cigarette does it occur to me that I have not been wanting a smoke all day. A matchstick scrapes, and the first drag makes me shiver with wellbeing. He takes me by the elbow and leads me out.

Smoking, we move through the deserted corridors and silent stairwells of the police station, which is almost completely steeped in darkness. Our steps echo between the walls as we work our way higher and higher up into the building. I feel as if I'm smoking my last cigarette before the gallows. We cross a big hall between rows of desks, and reach a door with a pane of frosted glass. The goon takes my hands and unlocks the handcuffs.

'You have to wait in here.'

I massage my wrists and look at him. He shrugs.

'That's all I know.'

The door swings open without a sound. He shows me in with a gesture of his hand, then closes it behind me.

The spacious office, which is fragrant with pipe tobacco, is dominated by a large desk of oak facing the door. In front of it, two chairs have been positioned so that visitors can see Kungsholmen's sky through a large picture window. The desk holds piles of paper, folders, a desk pad and, under a table lamp with a green glass lampshade, a pipe rack. The window rattles slightly in the wind. Next to it is a little telephone table and a globe mounted on lion paws.

I remain there for a few moments, scratching my lice bites. When no one turns up I take a tour of the office. There's a bookshelf running the entire length of the long wall, filled with books on police work and criminal psychology in Swedish, English and German, but also literary works, including the leather-bound collected writings of Strindberg.

By the other wall is a long, low filing cabinet. I stand there looking at the framed photographs and newspaper clippings above them. The photographs are of Oskar Olsson and the new, Social Democrat prime minister; then Olsson again, kneeling by a felled brown bear. He's resting his rifle butt against his thigh and staring into the camera without smiling. The newspaper clippings describe some of the most spectacular murder cases in the last twenty years.

I am just reading about the car bomb on Pipersgatan, a mere stone's-throw away, when the door opens. I turn around.

Olsson is wearing a dinner jacket. His trousers are five centimetres too short. His cheeks are flushed with schnapps, and over his arm he carries a jacket and a belt. The latter are mine, as is the hat in his hand.

'Mr Kvist.' He nods first at me, and then at the visitors' chairs, before draping my clothes across one of them.

We make ourselves comfortable. Olsson, whose shirt piece seems a size too small, calmly stuffs a straight-stemmed pipe, lights it with a match and blows a plume of smoke at the ceiling. Leaning back in his armchair, he takes another few leisurely puffs, and I note that my desire to smoke is coming back. Olsson clears his throat.

'That photograph of myself with Per-Albin is not only intended for the gallery.' He sounds hoarse, possibly also tired and slightly inebriated. 'I vote for the Social Democrats. Does that surprise you?'

'Very few things surprise me nowadays.'

'Do you vote yourself, if I may ask?'

'I might if I get out of here, against all expectations.'

Olsson nods. He takes the pipe from his mouth and stands up. His desk screeches when he opens a drawer and takes a bottle of aquavit, from which he pours himself a decent tot into a square glass, then moves to the window, where he stands partially with his back towards me, and says, with a sigh: 'Would I be wrong, then, if I said that, in spite of all, you might be inclined to feel a certain amount of social responsibility?'

'Yes, you would be wrong.'

Olsson chuckles. He knocks back half his schnapps and takes a quick puff on the pipe. 'But maybe you feel, hmm, that the nation needs a new start, so to speak?'

'I don't know what you mean, Commissioner.'

I scratch my head. Olsson stays by the window, hanging his head for a few moments, before answering at last, finishing his aquavit before he does so.

'In a few hours, 1932 will be history. A new year is coming, and, hmm, I suppose we're all hoping it will be a better one than the last? Tomorrow a new state police force will start operating, a specialised division with myself as the departmental head; also we have a new ministry and a new prime minister. What we need now is a bit of peace and quiet to get on with our work, so to speak.'

Olsson slurs his words slightly. He runs his hand over his short hair.

'This was the year when there was something rotten in the nation. First we had the von Sydow murders, when the head of the Employers' Association was murdered by his own son. A few weeks later, Kreuger and Toll went to the dogs. Tens of thousands of workers lost their positions, tens of thousands of small savers lost their capital. And as if that wasn't enough, the prime minister stepped down with allegations of corruption hanging over him. Despite emergency assistance, one in four men are unemployed.'

'Thanks, I take a newspaper and I also have a radio.'

'The country is trying to recover from Kreuger.' Olsson continues his speech as if he hasn't heard me. I'm starting to think that he's properly pissed. 'Bloody Kreuger,' I hear him mutter before he once again raises his voice: 'Even though the Wallenbergs avoided doing business with the Match King and now seem to be earning themselves, hmm, a decent profit, there are also other heavy players in the financial market who are close to collapse.'

Olsson turns round and fixes his lustrous eyes on me. His cheeks are flaming red.

'One of the groups that bought Kreuger stocks last winter is the one that's controlled now by the almost ruined Steiner family.'

Silently I draw breath. He spins his armchair round and sits. He seems to give it some thought before turning on the desk lamp. He puts his pipe in the ashtray and starts rifling among his papers.

'I'm not quite clear about how it all hangs together here, but I think you could help me.'

'I doubt it.'

'Don't say that. Let me tell you what I know. Kvist, I think this is as interesting to you as it is to me.' When he opens a file, I lean forwards slightly. 'On Christmas Eve, an Austrian war veteran by name of Karl Herberger was found murdered in a restaurant on Regeringsgatan. Next to the body lay a bayonet bearing the finger-prints of the murdered man. This bayonet matched the wounds of a prostitute, Alice Ljungström, found dead just a few blocks away.'

So it was Alice. Not Sonja. Beautiful Alice. Bowlegged Alice.

'Furthermore, we found hair on the lapels of the dead man's coat, which, when examined under a microscope, matched Miss Ljungström's. This Alice is assumed to have been a witness at a murder scene on Kungsgatan, one you are very familiar with, namely the one relating to Zetterberg.'

He raises his eyes. I hardly dare breathe. Olsson takes the pipe out of the ashtray, strikes another match and gets his pipe going. I nod at him to go on.

'Zetterberg used to be the driver of the Steiner family, who were also, in fact, Herberger's employers.'

My heart is bolting; my hands start trembling. I try to keep my expression impassive, while Olsson takes a long pause and goes through his papers. The swine is letting the poison get to work. The window behind him rattles again.

'And even if we don't have any tangible evidence, I am assum-ing that Zetterberg was murdered by his replacement. I have a photograph of Herberger, somewhere.'

He hands over a photograph. I put my fingers on it but Olsson doesn't let go. My fingers tremble against the photograph, and an eternity seems to pass before I snatch it out of his hand. He smiles.

'The question is, how the hell can I make any sense of the lady in the photograph visiting your one-room flat in Sibirien?'

The photograph is a few years out of date. In the background one can see a blurred-looking Herberger, next to a white Packard. The Steiner family is standing on a neatly raked gravel drive in front of the car. Steiner himself smiles directly into the camera. He's a slightly corpulent, middle-aged bloke, wearing a light summer suit and a white hat. He's also a touch shorter than his wife, who is standing further away, wearing sunglasses, almost as if screened off from the others, and looking away from the photographer.

And then finally there's Leonard, a few years younger but much the same, wearing short trousers and a knitted sports top. He leans slightly towards Steiner, his hand on his shoulder.

I start to shake even more violently. All at once I understand what Zetterberg also understood. Everything falls into shape. I've heard of so many homosexuals in marriages of convenience that I should have worked it out earlier. Doris lied. The lady lied about everything, except possibly what she said about the separate bedrooms in their imposing house. I should have seen through it, but she played her part well and I let myself be blinded by her wealth. Her skinny body was not one of a woman who had undergone a pregnancy.

The vein in my brow starts ticking. The question is how old Leonard was when he became a part of the family. Probably too young. This was the information that was worth five thousand kronor a month, and it was also the information that had cost Zetterberg his life. The Steiner family set a trap using Leonard as bait. While I went up to Bellevue with the boy they sent Herberger after Zetterberg and put the blame on me. Why me?

'I saw you.'

'Sorry?' I look up.

Olsson leans back and clasps his hands over his capacious belly. 'I saw you. In the ring. I'm very interested in boxing. I saw the match with that fighter from Västra Götaland, the one you put in a coma, and I saw you against "The Mallet" Sundström. And I staked money on you for the championship the following year but you never showed up.'

'Right.'

'And not for one moment in all those rounds did Kvisten ever look quite as miserable as he does now.'

'What do you mean?'

Olsson sighs. 'If I had a watertight case against you, maybe I'd put you up for prosecution, but all I have is Mrs Steiner, and she seems, how can I put it, hmm, a bit of a case of bad nerves. Anyway I do actually believe you're innocent, except in relation to Herberger. And to even out the score, I'd say he got what he deserved.'

I sit up. 'So can I go?'

'You had some of the qualities that make for a brilliant boxer, Kvist. You didn't go charging in like an idiot. You were primarily a strategist and a technician. I hope you still have some of those attributes, and I hope you have enough teeth left to bite the sour apple if you have to.'

'You didn't answer my question.'

'The last thing our country needs is a scandal of this magnitude.'

'So can I go?'

'Kvist has to understand two things: one, this conversation stays in this room. Two, if you in any way harass the Steiners you'll end up in Långholmen. I'll track you down and I'll book you for anything, whether it's smuggling, breaking the speed limit, or paragraph eighteen.'

'So? I can go, then?'

'Wasn't it your birthday the other day?'

'That's right.'

'Look at it as a late birthday present.'

Olsson stands up and puts his pipe in his mouth. He offers me his hand, but I stare at it, then at him. He lowers his hand.

'And may I say,' he adds, 'you look more like forty-four.'

'The poor man grows up quickly, the rich one not at all.'

I stand up, and Olsson nods at my clothes on the chair. I put them on, and find a Meteor in my jacket pocket, then walk out of the room without looking back. The goon who escorted me is sitting outside. When the door opens he jumps up, ready to salute.

'I hope you know how to get out of the building.' I put the cigar in my mouth and button up my jacket. 'And I hope for your own sake that you have a match going spare.'

The stripling goes pale under his oversized hat. Far away a church bell strikes three desolate chimes, one after the other, like the gong at the start of the final round.

Outside, little neat snowflakes are whirling about in the dark afternoon. It's blowing less than I thought. Cigar in hand, I am left standing for a few moments on the front steps of the police station. The tobacco is dry and doesn't taste as good as I was expecting. I pull my jacket tighter around me and turn up the collar. A numbing tiredness streams through my muscles. I rub my beard stubble and look around.

'Kvisten needs a drink.'

I steer my steps up towards Fleminggatan and turn into the courtyard of number 23, where it still stinks of latrine. It's only been two weeks since I came here to repossess a Monark, but it feels like considerably more. For a moment I think about that old bloke with the bicycle in his miserable attic room. I wonder how he is doing in the cold. I should change jobs.

I go over to the shack in the corner. The crack between the frame and the door has been filled with jute sacking. I pull it open and push the heavy sheet of swine leather out of the way.

The drinking den hardly has space enough for its three tables. The walls are insulated with newspaper. On the tables are a couple of lit candle-ends in tin mugs of cracked white enamel. I sigh. It may not be the Cecil, Metropol or Continental, but at least it has a proper wood floor.

Along the short wall at the other end runs a bar made of lacquered planks. On it sits a tiger-striped cat with scarred ears, lapping milk from a saucer. At the other end of the bar is a bowl with a couple of eggs, daubed with dirty fingerprints. The bartender is a tall bloke wearing a thick, homespun coat. His beard stubble is almost as long as my own His eyes are cold and blue and his face is chapped by the cold. Behind him on the wall hang two paraffin lamps. He nods at me.

The only other guest is sitting at a table to the left of me, an elderly woman with black rings under her eyes; she's wearing a grey hat, the greasy brim of which glitters in the candlelight when she also nods at me. The buttons of her black coat are in many shapes and colours. She pulls her skirt up to her knees and, underneath, her legs are bare and her varicose veins gleam blue against her hairy white calves.

'Had a good New Year?'

I shake my head and walk up to the bar, taking the extinguished cigar from my lips.

'Give me a decent-sized glass. I've got a long way to go.'

The proprietor nods and puts a schnapps glass in front of me. He opens an unmarked bottle and pours out some oily soup. I fling my head back and toss down the contents. Freedom smells of fusel oil. I make an ugly face.

I reach out towards the cat, still at the milk with a faint lapping sound. I quickly drum my fingers against the counter. Blue-black scratch marks run across it, like scars on the hands of an old coal delivery man. For a moment the cat stops its lapping, and fixes its eyes on my fingers, before going on.

I put my half-smoked Meteor back in my mouth and rummage around in my pockets until I feel the familiar outline of the gold lighter. I take it out and, for the last time, read the name engraved on it. Looking round, I whistle at the old woman in the corner. She looks up, I toss her the lighter, and she catches it.

'Happy New Year to you as well.'

I turn to the bartender again. He's already got the bottle ready and a box of matches. The woman behind me mumbles something. I nod at the schnapps glass and he refills it as I'm lighting my cigar.

'Egg?' The bartender points at the bowl at the far end of the counter.

'Hard-boiled?'

He nods and I nod back and he brings me an egg between his thumb and forefinger. I take it and put it next to my glass.

'You never even came close, Kvisten.'

If the bartender hears me muttering he's not concerned about it. I pour down the shot, and, in spite of all, find that it tastes better than the last one. I think I'll have another before I clatter down the long streets back to Sibirien. I make eye contact with the bartender, and nod once more at my glass.

The door rattles and a cold breath of wind seeks its way into the shack. I hear the candles fluttering behind me. I take a pull at the cigar that makes my lungs sting, and then I tap the egg against the counter. There's a gentle sound as the glass in front of me is filled to the brim.

I raise it.

'I'll take one more after this,' I say, adding, 'I'm in no hurry to get anywhere.'

An hour or so later, I stop for a few moments on the junction between Roslagsgatan and Ingemarsgatan, even though I'm so cold that I'm shaking. To my left are the steep stairs leading up to the water tower at the top of the hill in Vanadisparken. The bare trees around the stairs reach for each other like sailors in a sea of foaming waves. The snow has not been properly cleared.

Something seems different about my district, but I can't put my finger on what it is. I let my eyes wander from Lundin's creaking sign to the Roslag laundry on the other side of the street. I have lost feeling in my feet and fingers, and my ears and cheeks are smarting.

Old man Ljung appears, leading Balder and Faust, Lundin's black draught horses, along the street. He nods at me and I nod back. Wallin comes stumbling along, his hands thrust deep into his coat pockets, on his head a hat with a worn brim and earmuffs. A piece of flotsam on a winter-stormy sea. Most likely he's already knocked back a full bottle, the New Year's ration. He doesn't usually hang about.

Lundin's doorbell tinkles as I hunch my head to go inside, seeking to avoid a conversation with Wallin for the sake of politeness. He often has the nerve for one of those once he's been drinking.

Not least since I got myself a dog. He used to have one just like it, a few years ago, while his daughter was still alive.

The undertaker is sitting at his desk, a bottle of Kron next to him. There's a faint smell of formalin and new-baked bread. The potted palm on the floor is wilting. Lundin takes his top hat from the table and puts it on his head.

'New supplies in the store. I saved this for you, brother.' He taps the bottle with his pen and guzzles down his snuff juice.

I nod, with a sniff. 'I was banged up.'

'They kept you in longer this time.'

'You know how it is.' I scrape at my neck.

'Ernst Rolf's died.'

'What do you mean? Why?'

'He tried to drown himself. Then he changed his mind. Then he got a pneumonia and died.'

'Is it really true?'

'They're saying he swallowed a lot of Veronal too.'

We fall into silence for a few seconds. Lundin hands over the bottle and I take possession of it, while he gets out his accounts book and makes a note. My headache comes back whenever I cough.

'Have you ever been knocked unconscious?'

Lundin looks up for a moment before going back to his figures.

'We're getting close to payment date.'

'The lights just go out, it's as simple as that,' I go on. 'You no longer feel your body. Everything goes empty. Did anyone call?'

'Only Wernersson. About a bicycle.'

'So no one else?'

'No. There's a party in the back building of number forty-one. A bazaar.'

'Have you been to take a look?'

295

'No. How about twelve o'clock?'

'Hopefully I'll be sleeping by then.'

Lundin nods. 'Happy New Year, then.'

'Same to you.'

I reach out with my left hand. Lundin stares at it for a few moments before he shakes it, and then I go back outside into the New Year's freeze.

My door is unlocked. I step into the hall and hang up my hat. It smells of dog piss. I go into the kitchen where, on the draining board, dirty glasses have been lined up. The frying pan on the cooker is full of congealed fat. The briny water in the bathing tub is cold.

I empty it into the sink, then put a bit of wood in the fireplace and get it going. On the floor around the kitchen table lies some of Doris's dirty underwear, also her silk stockings. I feed the fire with them, then slowly straighten my back, moving as if in a trance.

The paper bag with Christmas decorations lies overturned in a corner, spilling out red glitter balls and straw angels.

Slowly I cross the room and light the ceramic stove. The Christmas tree is leaning up against the wall, undecorated and dropping its needles. A couple of dresses lie on the floor. The contents of my top desk drawer have been emptied out over the desk. My testimonial letter from the navy, Ida's green cloth, a couple of old clippings from *Boxing Monthly!* and some faded letters from America are lying on the floor. Someone has taken them out of their envelopes and read them. My stomach turns. I used to take that green cloth, soak it in sugar-water and give it to Ida to suck on when I couldn't afford toffee or a couple of cocoa balls on Saturdays.

The splashes of blood on the wall next to the sleeping alcove are still there from the time Doris smacked me on the nose. The ashtray lies upside down among the sheets. I pull the blanket off the bed, and a rain of cigarette ash scatters over the flat. Doris's medicinal bottle bounces along the floor.

Her syringe is lying by the pillows. There's no sign of the little case. I pick up the bottle, on the bottom of which there's still a smidgeon of the brown liquid.

I go back into the kitchen. The fire is crackling nicely. I rinse the syringe in Kron and then have a pull straight from the bottle. I get out of my strange clothes. Outside, in the courtyard, someone bursts out laughing.

Using the syringe, I mop up the remaining fluid in the bottle and walk naked out of the kitchen. I leave the bottle on the desk and go over to the wardrobe. The Husqvarna is in its usual place. I put on a pair of clean underpants and bring out the pistol and a black tie with red stripes.

I get the photograph from my wallet and put it on the table in front of me. I sit in the armchair and wrap the tie around my right arm. The silk ends taste dry in my mouth. I clench my hand at the same time as I hear Lundin start hammering at another semi-finished coffin in his workshop.

The pain of the pricking needle wakes me out of my stupor, brings me back to life. I pull back a little blood with my left hand before I slowly inject the contents into myself, then withdraw the needle and open my hand.

Leaning back in the armchair, I keep my forearms on the armrests.

It doesn't take long. A curious warmth spreads through my body. My muscles open like flowers. When I breathe in, my lungs don't hurt as they usually do.

The syringe hits the floor like a drop into a barrel of rainwater. With infinite slowness, my forehead lowers itself towards the edge of the table. I breathe out once my head is resting against the table top. Then, entirely without any warning, I vomit warm lava over my feet.

I don't know how much time has passed. The table is cold and hard against my forehead. It feels good. My eyelids are leaden, the blood ripples through my veins, and my whole body is itching, but I can't bring myself to move.

I'm no longer here. I'm the one I used to be. Memories course through me, framed in pink or golden yellow. I hear myself murmuring along to one of them; my voice is dark and drawling, just like Doris's. I find I'm back in the room we rented on Tavastgatan, with Emma and Ida.

'Just think if she…?'

'Don't say it!' I interrupt.

'But what if!'

'No, she's strong.'

'Shouldn't we call for another doctor?'

'You know as well as I do that we can't do that, and he'll only say the same thing as the last one.'

'Hilda's infant died of whooping cough.'

'Hilda's child, yes, and my brother, but not our little one, she's strong.'

'But what if she doesn't recover by the time we have to travel?'

'She will, she's strong.'

'You'll come as soon as you can, won't you?'

'It's only a couple of matches to improve our prospects. No one has got the better of me yet.'

'What can we do?'

'Nothing, all we have to do is sit here.'

'But what can we do?'

'Just sit here.'

'Are you sure you don't want to pray with me?'

'It won't do any good, so stop nagging!'

'For my sake?'

'You say it and I'll listen.'

'Can you at least kneel here next to me?'

'Fair enough, but you have to do it for the both of us.'

'And clasp your hands together!'

'Don't spy on me, say what you want to say!'

'Have you clasped your hands together?'

'Yes. Let's get this out of the way.'

'Hey? You're not angry with me, are you?'

'No, I'm here, aren't I! Are you angry with me?'

'Never!'

'Right then, so let's pray.'

I struggle to catch my breath. I'm back in Roslagsgatan, smiling, while the tears run down my face, dripping from my stubble onto the rug. I open my mouth and let it all back in.

My memories darken, grow light, and then darken again. The black sun quickly rises. I am very close now.

The newly pointed wall around the imposing house on Nobelgatan feels rough against my gloves. I've walked all the way from Sibirien in my clogs, taking a detour through the deep snow around the barracks by Gärdet to avoid bumping into anyone. I can't feel my feet any more. My stomach is aching with its own emptiness and my head is filled with thunderous pains. I am overwhelmed by my own smell: old sweat and vomit. I'm still alive, though.

I check my watch again – half past eleven – then I put it back in my waistcoat. I'm wearing my best suit, tailored by Herzog.

I look around, and find a snow-covered zinc bucket that's full of old cement. I turn it upside down by the wall. For a moment I think of the murder weapon, the mason's axe. I stand on the bucket and grab the top of the wall.

I drop down heavily on the other side as an early New Year's rocket wails across the sky. A green light illuminates the undulating winter-white garden. Low, severely pruned fruit trees cast momentary shadows. The white waves of frozen snow reflect the light in the backyard. A flock of crows lifts from one of the trees and takes off.

I squat down by the wall. Somewhere in the distance, I hear music and laughter. The top floor of the house is entirely dark. I rub my hands together, draw the Husqvarna from my shoulder holster, flick the safety catch and feed a bullet into the chamber. I hold the pistol in my left hand. It doesn't matter if they are out.

'Kvisten can wait.'

Another rocket sends a broom of light over the sky. I run some twenty metres over the frozen crust of the snow, and thump my back into the façade of the house, which is still utterly silent. I wonder if Doris was speaking the truth when she mentioned how their entire service staff had been dismissed. I glance into the kitchen, which looks large and empty. A couple of decorative lamps with white shades throw a faint sheen across the floor.

I go round the corner and, squatting down, follow the wall to the corner on the other side. The crust of the snow cuts my shins as I move forwards. I lift my clog out once more. A need to cough tickles my lungs, but I keep it in check. I'm squeezing the Husqvarna so hard that I can feel the grooved surface of the hilt through my glove. I haven't had time to test fire it, as planned. Not with my right hand, even less so with my left.

I look into a window again, still at that empty kitchen. I take a few calm breaths to assuage my cough. My breath comes out of my mouth like steam. I remove my hat and mop the sweat off my brow with my sleeve. Then I peer around the corner.

The drive is empty of cars. A pale light emanates from the ground-floor windows. Faint jazz tones are punctured by high-pitched laughter. Still crouching, I make my way up the front steps to the door.

My heart starts thumping hard. I put the Husqvarna in my jacket pocket, find a Meteor and start fumbling with some matches. On my third attempt a spark illuminates the nameplate on the door and I light the cigar. I take a couple of deep drags and put my hand on the handle as I check my watch. I won't have to remove my tie. Not tonight.

At twenty to midnight a rocket howls nearby. I press down on the handle while the explosion is still reverberating. My heart leaps when I find it is open. As long as Dixie doesn't give me away.

'Damn it, Kvisten. It's on.'

I slip inside and carefully close the door behind me. There's a welcoming smell of Arrack Punch and expensive cigars. Mumbling men's voices can be heard through the jazz music. A couple of billiard balls are clicking. I'm early. At worst, I'll have to delay it. At least there's no sign of Dixie; she's afraid of fireworks, poor thing. I get the pistol out of my pocket.

I take a couple of muffled steps over the Persian rug and walk into the half-lit hall. Someone has brought in gravel and dirt. To my right, a monumental staircase flows down, supported on Greek columns. So this is where Doris makes her dramatic entrances. I can see it all now.

Immediately in front of me stands a life-size bronze statue of a young man, naked, with a broken arrow in his hand. A dining room opens up beside the statue, decorated in a deep blue colour. A gigantic crystal chandelier hovers like a jellyfish over a large oak table.

Alongside me stands a potted plant as tall as a man, with narrow, pointed leaves. It's been a long while since it was watered, and the leaves are dusty. Under the stairs, a closed door presumably leads into the kitchen. The sounds are coming from the open door to my left. Above it, a large, rectangular mark can be seen on the wall, as if there was recently a painting hanging there.

I should wait until the Skansen fireworks on the Djurgården side really get going. I steal forwards and press myself to the wall. I take the cigar out of my mouth and push my hat back with my forefinger. The billiard balls cannon together again.

'I don't understand how you can dislike the music, Father?'

Father? I chuckle. I remember that lisping man's voice all too well. There's a sudden crackling noise. Someone stops the music in the middle of a saxophone solo. I hear the radio humming to life and warming up almost immediately. I go around the corner with the pistol at the ready.

I sweep the sights of the Husqvarna across the room. The bead passes over the large billiard table and soon finds its way to old man Steiner, sitting in a dinner jacket in a leather sofa placed centrally in the room. For a few moments I'm confused, and I point the gun at the marble statue of yet another naked young man, positioned beside a crackling fireplace. Then I move it back to Steiner.

He's wearing gold-rimmed spectacles and his hair has thinned a bit since Olsson's photograph was taken. In front of him is a low table with an ashtray and a punch carafe and a few cups, and, underneath, another Persian rug. The table is flanked by two ox-blood-coloured leather armchairs. By the window to the left gleams a black grand piano, grinning at me with its row of gap teeth.

Leonard, holding a vinyl record in his hands, is standing in the background by a gramophone table. On the wall behind him hang two crossed halberds. Just like Steiner, he's wearing a white dinner jacket.

There's no sign of Doris, and not Dixie either. Presumably they're out painting the town red.

'Kvist?'

Steiner's voice is low, but tinged with an irritating shrillness. He struggles out of the sofa to perch on the edge of it. His uniform line of white teeth gleams against his pale pink lower lip. I nod.

'We heard you'd been released; we were wondering whether you'd do us the honour.'

I take a few steps into the room until I am only a few metres from Steiner. Leonard doesn't move.

'Can we offer you some punch? Or maybe a Havana?' Steiner lifts the lid of a cigar case in wine-red leather, and offers it to me. I shake my head and take a puff on my Meteor. He takes one himself and puts the case on the arm of the sofa.

'Leo and I were just discussing what music to play. Are you also fond of Negro music?'

'What do you think?'

'You're a man of judgement, Kvist! I understand we have similar tastes in more respect than one.' He chuckles.

I move quickly across the floor, lean across the table, and crack the handle of the pistol against his scalp so that his double chins wobble. It's not a particularly hard blow and it only opens a small wound, but Steiner yells like a castrated boar. He touches his forehead and makes a right carry-on.

Leonard comes charging, and I go back to my original position to regain full control of the situation. A small stream of blood runs down Steiner's forehead and drips onto his white dinner jacket. He takes off his spectacles and tries to stand up.

'Sit!' I roar. 'You as well!'

I point the Husqvarna at Leonard. He throws himself into the sofa, his silk handkerchief gleaming when he takes it out of his breast pocket and presses it to Steiner's forehead. Increasing numbers of fireworks are going off.

'That's him all over!' yells Leonard. 'He had a pop at me as well!'

Then he titters, and a broad grin fixes itself on his face, the same grin that annoyed the hell out of me in the park. I can feel my trigger finger twitching, but I manage to control myself. I realise that something's not adding up. No one laughs into the barrel of a gun.

'Kid, I think you're not quite right in the head, are you?'

Steiner puts his arm around Leonard's shoulders. 'There's nothing wrong with Leonard.'

The boy's grin widens further, his tittering gets hysterical.

'Did you hear what your father said, you hooligan!'

'Shut up!'

I take another step back. The floor gives off reflections from the bursting rockets. I point my Husqvarna at Steiner. The blood is slowly running down his forehead, changing course by his eyebrow, disappearing behind the sideburns and dripping down over his shoulder. He hides his fear well; he has more hair on his chest than I would have thought. I smile at him and cock my gun. At this range I should even be able to send the swine to the other side with my left hand.

Suddenly a round, cold piece of metal is pressed against my right ear. A barrel. Steiner smiles with satisfaction and Leonard shrieks delightedly and slaps his hands together a few times. I deliberate, make a quick decision, and lower my Husqvarna.

'Drop it!' Steiner's voice is even deeper now.

My pistol hits the parquet floor.

'You see, this is a question of primary evolution. The world belongs to those who are strong, Kvist. Someone's going to die here tonight but it's not likely to be me.' He chuckles and shakes his head.

The barrel is removed from my skull bone and Doris appears. She's wearing a deep green evening dress with a little train. In one hand she's holding her high-heeled shoes, while in the other she grips a large-calibre revolver with a short barrel. She gives the Husqvarna a kick, but it stops by the edge of the rug a metre or so in front of me. A silver snake bracelet coils itself around her pistol-wielding arm. Her face looks entirely dead. The pupils of her chestnut brown eyes have almost completely disappeared. She seems to be staring at my chest. The radio plays string music to the rhythm of a waltz. My head aches and nausea courses through my body like a cold wind.

Her make-up is well done. Her collarbones protrude from under her shoulder straps. A string of big pearls dangles across her bare back from the clasp of the necklace around her neck, like an extension of her knotty vertebrae. She isn't wearing a brassiere. As she backs away to join the others, she turns away from me for a moment. I debate to myself whether I have time to tackle her, but, as if reading my mind, she quickly turns round and moves into a protected spot behind the sofa. She puts on her shoes, then fluffs her hair before straightening up. A rocket goes off right above our heads, rattling the windows.

'I thought we'd have to telephone you,' Steiner says to his wife with a chuckle. I don't understand what he's driving at.

'Can I hold the pistol, Mother?' Leonard jumps up and down in the sofa.

Steiner smiles. 'It's probably best to let your mother take care of that detail. She's the better shot.' He lights his Havana, gives another smile.

'Oh, Father!'

It's my turn to chuckle. I throw the cigar end on the floor and step on it. Steiner flinches.

'You can drop the New Year's farce. I've already worked out you're not the kid's father.'

Leonard sucks in his lower lip. Doris looks away. She's holding the revolver level with her hips. Steiner removes the handkerchief from his forehead and laughs.

'Oh, so you've worked that out, have you, Kvist.' He puts his hand on Leonard's thigh. On his ring-finger gleams a large signet ring with some sort of coat of arms and red stones. 'But without a doubt I'm like a father to him.'

Doris looks at the floor. A drop of sweat runs down my back. I'm cold. Steiner turns his eyes to Leonard.

'Isn't that so, my boy?'

'It is, Father,' Leonard says obediently, with a nod.

I stare at Doris. She closes her eyes for a moment. Her jaw muscles grind away under her skin every bit as intensely as when I took her on the floor in the flat on Roslagsgatan. I inch forwards. Steiner pats Leonard's thigh a few times and gets up slightly laboriously, losing his footing at one point and supporting himself on Leonard's shoulder.

'You understand this,' says Steiner, as he goes over to the statue by the crackling fireplace. From outside comes the distant sound of a car going past. 'Both you and I share a fascination for young men's bodies.' He caresses the stomach of the statue.

'Don't try to involve me in your dirty story.'

'What's the difference? The Greeks had a word for the love of boys. Are you an art lover, Kvist? This is Apollo.' Steiner takes his hand off the statue.

'I hardly think the Greeks went to bed with their own sons.'

'I never said I was his father, I said I was like a father to him. Strictly speaking he's my brother-in-law. But let's talk about something more amusing. Look at this work of art. Although we've had to sell off most of the collection, I'd like to think of myself as a bit of a connoisseur.' He puffs at his Havana.

'And there I was thinking you were nothing but scum.'

'Silence!' Little droplets of saliva spurt from Steiner's shiny lips as he cries out.

I take another step towards the pistol.

'You're in my house, when I speak, you listen!'

Steiner wipes his handkerchief across his forehead. The blood is smearing over his skin. He closes his eyes, breathing heavily. He calms himself.

'As I said, I'm a bit of an art connoisseur. Do you know the story of Apollo the lizard slayer?'

'Let me guess: did he kill a lizard?'

A mournful smile flickers over Doris's mouth. Her pistol hand is swaying slightly. She closes her eyes again.

'Tell him, Father!' Leonard cries in a high-pitched voice, and Steiner nods placidly.

'Apollo, Zeus's son, was a lover of both boys and girls. In spite of his slenderness, he was the one who managed to slay Python, the giant snake. Dynamism has always been a virtue I admire.'

'Was that why you sent Herberger to do your dirty work?'

'No!' The sofa creaks when Leonard almost starts jumping on it. 'I did it myself! I did it all myself! Just like Apollo, father!'

Steiner chuckles and nods. Doris's eyes open wide. In seconds, she has put her full repertoire of thespian emotions on display. Her eyes fill with tears.

'How did that happen?'

I fix Doris with my eyes. The armchair to my right groans under Steiner's weight when he pinches his front creases and sits down.

'Possibly Leo acted slightly too rashly. The family wasn't in quite so much trouble. He's always been a passionate lad.' Steiner laughs.

Leonard grins in that way of his and looks right at me. He has the same brown eyes as his sister. Then he lisps: 'At first my father was going to hire some rough brute to do it. That was how your name came up. But one has to be able to stand up for oneself. I wanted to show Father. But I'm not stupid, I realised someone else would have to take the blame for it.'

'And that was me, then.'

Leonard titters. He doesn't take his eyes off me. Doris puts her hand over her mouth.

'I forged that letter, and the same night you got it I drove around until I saw you standing about outside Zetterberg's house. I knew you wouldn't say no, there was so much money on offer. It wasn't exactly difficult getting you to come for a drive either. And you said I'm retarded, but I'm not, am I, Father?'

Leonard smiles, showing the gap between his front teeth. Doris struggles for breath and meets my eyes for the first time that night, so that, for an instant, it's as if we're staring into the very depths of each other.

I don't know how many times I've stared down my opponents. It's a part of the game, and I don't yield an inch. If you as much as glance in another direction you're already defeated, and you may as well throw in the towel right away. I don't look away this time either – I have nothing to lose. I notice that I've been holding my breath, then straining for air. Doris cocks her pistol, her hand trembling violently.

Leonard leans back in the sofa and lays his arm across the back, briefly inspecting the state of his nails on his other hand; his trousers make a swishing sound as he crosses his legs.

'Why did you hit me up there in the park?'

'Because you're a rich nutcase,' I answer truthfully.

'That's what you think.' Leonard shakes his head slightly. 'When I woke up, I went and beat him to death. It wasn't difficult. I did it myself, Mum! It wasn't Herberger who did it, it was me!'

'Yes, you'll have to forgive us, my treasure,' Steiner interjects. 'I thought it would be for the best to keep quiet about Leo's doings and put the blame on Herberger. I suspected that it would prove too much for your nerves, and that you might not be able to fully play your own part, if you knew what your little brother had done.'

'You sent her to me so I'd lead you to Sonja?'

Doris's mouth is like a straight line. Steiner smiles, then sucks on his Havana.

Leonard looks at Doris as if expecting praise. She puts her right hand on his shoulder. Inhaling deeply, her modest-sized bust stretches the green velvet of her dress. The boy refocuses straight ahead. The crackling of the wood fire is subsumed into the explosions of the New Year rockets, their red and yellow bursts reflecting in the window-glass at the back of the room. On the radio, someone mumbles that midnight is only ten minutes away. Steiner nods and hums, while the blood continues dripping onto his shoulder.

'As I said, someone's going to die here tonight, but it won't be me,' he goes on, briefly removing his spectacles to mop his forehead. 'The world is not made that way. It's for the strong, for the dynamic. It eats those who are weak.'

'And who's doing the dirty work this time? Does the director have what it takes, or will he let his bum-boy do it again?'

Steiner looks startled, and for a moment he lets his gaze wander around the room, before perching on the edge of his seat.

'I want to do it!' Leonard raises his hand like an urchin in a school bench. 'He hit me! I want to do it!'

For a few moments the room is absolutely silent, apart from the crackling fire and the radio's mumbling. A pair of tears paint streaks of black mascara down Doris's cheeks. Her larynx moves as she tries to swallow her pain. As if wanting the smell of her brother one last time, she leans over him, closes her eyes and inhales through her nose.

Then, without the slightest trembling of her hand, she puts the muzzle of the revolver against his neck and shoots him, as if putting down a dangerous dog.

The crack of the gun deadens the ears. A gush of blood slaps out of the boy's mouth over the table. He topples forwards very hard, hits the table and falls back into the sofa. Microscopic droplets fill the vacancy where he sat like a fine, reddish mist. A stench of burnt hair fills the room. I lower my guard. A pair of teeth gleam like white opals in the gunk on the table.

Steiner shakes his head, and the fat around his throat starts trembling. His eyes dart between us, while croaking sounds rise from the back of his throat. Slowly, Doris lowers her revolver and straightens her back. She bites her lower lip, and her mascara leaves another sooty smudge when she mops her tears with the back of her right hand.

I have backed away a half-metre. A thin line of smoke coils up from behind the table and rejoins the cloud of gunpowder smoke hovering above the sofa. Leonard's foot makes a few jerking motions. Steiner holds out his hands, his cigar pointing down between his fingers, cupping his palms as if he's carrying water in them.

'Doris?' He keeps shaking his head. 'Doris?' he whispers.

His wife goes round the sofa and table and stands opposite him. Steiner puts his hands on the ends of the armrests. Doris lifts the revolver and cocks it, making the well-oiled drum spin by one sixth of a turn with a soft click. The blood from Leonard's head is running along the edge of the rug. Doris takes aim at her husband from the hip, but she seems to be looking right through him.

'Doris,' says Steiner in a firmer tone. 'You'd better think bloody good and hard now! When I picked you up you weren't much more than a drug addict, remember that!'

The armchair creaks as he leans back, splaying his legs wide. One hand is still leaning on the armrest, while the other leaves sticky red marks as he fumbles over the pockets of his dinner jacket.

'Have I not been a good husband to you? Did I ever deny you anything? Irrespective of the price tag?' He grunts and glares at her, beads of sweat glistening over his face. The edge of the rug guides Leonard's blood under his armchair, from where it emerges between his legs on the other side. Steiner's breathing becomes laboured, and he raises his voice.

'Wasn't I lenient about your little habits and vices? Didn't I look the other way when you ran all over town with all sorts of riff-raff and behaved like a damned whore?'

Now Doris opens her mouth for the first time. She still doesn't seem to be looking at anything, and the dark words issue slowly from her mouth: 'You only married me because of my poor little brother.'

For a moment, everything is utterly silent apart from the mumbling of the radio. Steiner lunges to get onto his feet, and I throw myself forwards to stop him, but another shot cuts the silence to pieces. The muzzle spits its tongue of fire across the room.

I back away. Steiner's eyes distend and he slowly sinks back into the armchair, while fumbling with his spectacles, which have slipped off his nose. A patch of blood on his stomach grows across his white shirt, so dark that it's difficult to make out against his black silk sash. He nods drowsily and drops his cigar, which goes out with a fizzle when it falls into the blood on the floor. His chin sinks down over his chest. My ears are ringing.

'I meant nothing to you,' Doris whispers in a low voice, scarcely audible through the high-pitched whining in my ears. The snake bracelet around her wrist slips down when she lowers her revolver. Though her voice is wavering, she stands firm and straight-backed, with her heels dug into the rug. 'Creep!'

Steiner tries to lift his head. His eyelids tremble with exertion but at long last he manages it, and man and wife look each other in the eye.

'You ruined me. And you ruined him.' Steiner coughs blood. 'You treated him as if he were a trophy, just another of your toys. You made him sick.' Doris takes a step towards him. 'You made him mad.' An intense cannonade of New Year rockets ring out, with hardly a pause between the explosions.

I hold my breath. She grabs his pulpy chin and forces his face up. His spectacles are smashed when she hammers the butt of the pistol twice against his forehead. The blood is spattering around them. Steiner screams piercingly and closes his eyes. When he opens them again, she pushes the pistol into his stomach and squeezes the trigger.

She's pressing the revolver so hard into her husband that the report of the weapon is dampened. I hunch up behind my arms.

When I look up again, Steiner is dead. He lies slumped in the armchair with his chin against his chest. There's a regular mess from his stomach down. Doris's eyes are shaded with smudged mascara, and the lower part of her dress is speckled red. The hand holding the revolver is smeared with blood. She pulls her husband's hand off the armrest and leans over it, supporting herself on her right arm. Her breathing is tremulous and strained, and a few little muscles around her mouth are moving spasmodically.

Anders de Wahl's languorous voice sings 'New Year's Bells' from the radio. I have almost made my way over to her when she straightens up and lifts her revolver. The muzzle is hot against my forehead. When she cocks it, the sound is louder than the bursts of fireworks in the sky. For a few seconds we stand in silence, staring into one another's eyes. Two has-beens.

A drop of blood falls from her hand, hitting the floor with a splashing sound.

'Take your pistol with you. And your cigar butt.'

I step back. She doesn't put down her revolver. She doesn't even seem to see me. I bend down and put the butt in my trouser pocket. I make the Husqvarna safe and put it in my home-made holster, before turning round and walking out of the door. On my way, I hit the light switch and the hall lights up.

Just as I'm heaving open the heavy door, the Skansen fireworks on the Djurgården side are setting fire to the whole sky, with plumes of red, green, yellow and blue arcing over the dark expanse. The detonations come rolling across the ice like thunder.

I reach the big gate and push it open, then lift my hat to wipe the sweat from my brow with my sleeve. Behind me I hear an engine starting, and I turn around. To my right, Leonard's sports car shoots out of an underground garage, skidding onto Nobelgatan in a cloud of exhaust and snow crystals, and coming to a stop in front of me. Doris winds down the window. She has wiped her face clean of mascara and had time to apply some fresh lipstick. On the passenger seat, the revolver reflects the lights of the fireworks.

'You won't get away,' I say. 'They'll keep hunting you until you're dead.'

She picks up an object from her lap and tosses it to me. I catch it. Steiner's wine-red cigar case.

'Happy New Year, Harry.'

I lift my hat, nod, and put it back. Doris smiles forlornly, releases the clutch and, before I know it, the car has disappeared around the corner.

I extract one of Steiner's Havana cigars from the case and bite off the end. The strong taste fills my mouth and I blow a heavy cloud of smoke into the night.

Just as I'm about to step into the street, someone whimpers behind me. I turn around. Dixie is standing there, pacing about in the snow halfway between the main door and the gate. The lights in the hall form a half-circle around her. Shivering with fear, she retreats a few steps, and then stops again. I get out the Husqvarna and, with a soft click, cock it and then squat down to wait for her to come running across the gravelled drive.

When Dixie is a metre away, I lift the weapon. She skids to a halt in a little cloud of powder snow, slides towards me and collides with my leg. I point the Husqvarna at her and she rolls onto her back, legs in the air and even remembers to droop her tongue from her mouth. Little flakes of snow have got caught in her long eyebrows. I put the gun against her chest. I have a sense of her pathetic heartbeats passing through the gun's metal. I squeeze the hilt hard.

'Anyway, it would be bloody stupid leaving a bullet behind.'

Dixie, reacting to the sound of my voice, looks at me with eyes as black as Durham coal. I make the Husqvarna safe, put it back in my holster, scratch the dog's stomach with my undamaged hand and try to quieten her down. She spins round and rears up on shaking legs; I scoop up the little thing and put her under my jacket, with a little scratch behind her ear.

'I don't have a lot to offer you. No silk cushions for your dumb little head, and no paté for breakfast, just the odd bit of sausage at most. And there'll be a hell of a lot of running about after bicycles.'

I stick the Havana into my mouth and button up my jacket so that only her head sticks out, next to my collar. Her warm body vibrates against mine.

'But if we keep working hard and if we manage to stay out of the way of a touchy bloke called Olsson, old Kvisten should be able to make sure we have a decent time of it.'

I walk onto Nobelgatan. There are no people around. The New Year fireworks on the other side of the ice are starting to die down. My body feels as if I just went fifteen rounds. It's going to be a long walk back to Sibirien.

I'm cold already.

—

NEXT IN THE HARRY KVIST TRILOGY

DOWN FOR THE COUNT

AVAILABLE AND COMING SOON
FROM PUSHKIN VERTIGO

Jonathan Ames

You Were Never Really Here

Augusto De Angelis

The Murdered Banker
The Mystery of the Three Orchids
The Hotel of the Three Roses

María Angélica Bosco

Death Going Down

Piero Chiara

The Disappearance of Signora Giulia

Frédéric Dard

Bird in a Cage
Crush
The Wicked Go to Hell

Martin Holmén

Clinch

Alexander Lernet-Holenia

I Was Jack Mortimer

Boileau-Narcejac

Vertigo
She Who Was No More

Leo Perutz

Master of the Day of Judgment
Little Apple
St Peter's Snow

Soji Shimada

The Tokyo Zodiac Murders

Seishi Yokomizo

The Inugami Clan